When Rita's mother died, there was a sense of relief...even if she had lived, she would have needed so much reconstructive work on her face, she would have had no life but suffering. At the funeral they kept the casket closed...thanks be to God...once the autopsy was complete Mercy General didn't do much reconstruction. Being next of kin, they told Rita about the standard charges, and checked off the boxes.

Makeup, hair color, perm? Shipping container, prepaid invoicing, return receipt? Rita settled on having a picture of her mother on top of the burnished copper casket. The picture was from years ago, so fuzzy it could have been almost anyone. The lips were painted in blood red...her mother hadn't worn lipstick for years. Maybe they were not burying her mother, but just one of the many incarnations that she had gone through. Maybe her mother was a Mom that just kept giving, whether needed or not... whether wanted or not, whether deserved or not. Without end... Rita, now in her last year of prep school, looked back nostalgically, trying to make sense of her present.

The whole damn thing had happened so fast. She was in her third year at the St. Theresa's of the Mound School, when Sister Mary Magiore came to get her out of radiology class. She was sixteen, and when she looked in the mirror, she could see plainly that she was getting the body her mother had always wanted. The radiology class had several novitiate apprentice nuns that wore special habits, but could pass for service in any Christian center. Some of her classmates, from the novitiate, seemed friendly, others more involved inside, "Gawd" knows it is uncharted territory...still, she had been able to get through the math and science of radiology and was close to the top of her class, when she was unceremoniously called to Mother Agnes' office. She didn't know what was in store for her.

Coming in she asked, "Have I done something wrong?"

Mother Agnes assured her, "No, nothing is wrong, but we do have a tuition problem. The lawyers for your father's trust have won their damage suit against your mother's trust. Their case file shows that you refused to take sides, and that was interpreted to be a breech of implied contract between generations. So neither your father's estate nor your mother was found to be liable for your maintenance until you come of age."

Rita didn't understand, "Mother established a special fund...it came from proceeds from Dad's patent on the closed cell work he did for Dupont. It was something to do with negativity."

Mother Agnes cleared her throat, "Rita, as we understand it, you're going to come into some big money in a couple of years, but for now...you don't qualify for our financial aid. Unless you have some resources that you can liquidate, we are not in a position to continue your residence here at St. Theresa's."

Rita looked down at her shoes, "Does that mean I'll have to leave?"

"No," said Mother Agnes..."unless you can't round up your tuition, and room and board. It is, let's see,"...she did some figuring, "with the McCormack stipend that you have from last year's merit scholarship competition, you still have to come up with a little under eight thousand dollars, before our next semester begins. Your parents' trust officers cannot agree which trust should be held liable during the period of your advancement between your minority and your majority. In simple language, there are charges amounting to considerable figures for your contingent responsibilities of "reguloram parentis declormae." Both trusts agree that one or the other of them should be primary, but until the court makes a finding, all trust funds must necessarily be frozen."

Mother Superior Agnes shook her head wearily and came around to put a heavy hand on Rita's shoulder, "You know Rita Marie, we were hoping you would accept the call. You are just so advanced for a girl of your age. St. Theresa's can stand some new blood. But until the rent's paid, there's no free ride, not even for us! It's such a pity. See what you can do. We'll call Mr. Nims and tell him you will need at least a week to settle up here. OK?" Perhaps you could call a relative to help you out."

"My Mom was the last of the Dougherty line. She had no brothers or sisters. And my father had only one younger sister that no one got along with. I barely remember Auntie Sarah. I think she was at Grampa Dougherty's funeral. I might be able to get her number from information. Last I knew she was at Murray Bay, Quebec. I think it was near the St. Lawrence." Rita had been in a few tight spots before. She went to her dorm room on the second floor of Warren cottage. She called Mr. Foley at Ernst & Young. He would need a release before he could disburse any more funds. She was able to get the unlisted number of her mother's broker at Paine Weber. But when she dialed the number all she got was the screech of a fax machine. Frustrated, she remembered Aunt Sarah. It had been three years since she had talked with her, and then it had been a bizarre conversation. She found the number and dialed.

"Auntie Sarah? This is Rita, Rita...you know Ben's girl... Yeah...we missed you at Mom's funeral, right..."

"I've never needed anybody's help before."

"Yeah, That's me...well...I'm in kind of a tight spot...I need money for next semester's tuition...you know...room and board and all that stuff."

Rita explained, "Dad's trust officers are not releasing any more money until Mom's trust officers agree. So I am out in left field pending their settlement, or I don't know. It's all a mess. Can you help me? Should you call the trust officers? I can give you the numbers."

Aunt Sarah's voice sounded like someone very far away. And there was a clicking sound of an air compressor or something. It was hard to hear exactly what she was saying. Something about paddling your own canoe. Rita was puzzled, there had to be a way. "I'll call you again when I know what the trust people say."

St. Theresa's had been home for Rita ever since seventh grade, when her father died in the car crash. He had visited the Jones and Laughlin machine tool plant at Springfield, Vermont when he veered of the road right on the bridge over the Connecticut river. While her mother survived, she gave up homemaking.

After that Rita stayed on campus pretty much year round with ten other girls, and three boys. It was kind of strange, but they all got along. The nuns ran several hospitals in the Midwest that were always in need of medical technicians, hence the involvement in the teaching institution of St. Therese's.

So! There she was. Six months away from graduating. And not only did she not have a pot, or a window to throw it out of, she didn't even have an address.

Rita learned that under New York law, custody reverts to the last know residence of the natural father of the child, unless, but not limited to, cases involving trusts of a perpetual nature, as therein defined. As far as she was concerned, she apparently was dead meat until her twenty-first birthday. Sister Magiore and Mother Agnes sat down with Rita, who was trembling.

"I have to stay here," mumbled Rita..."I don't know where to try to go. The only money I have is in my student activity card, maybe seventy five dollars."

Mother Agnes cleared her throat, "We've got a revolving fund that has residue from our NHI proceeds! She giggled a little bit. Mother Agnes knew the fund should be for circumstances just like what was going on.

"We can use the revolving fund to get you a ticket to Michigan or where ever Mr. Nims directs. Your registration papers list a Sarah Jane Chamberlin as your next of kin. We have her address here as Route 1, Clairvoix, Qc."

"Dad's sister? I called her already...I barely remember her." I remember only vague faces, nothing concrete. Once there were a few gray haired ladies that I remember at a wedding or a funeral.

"I was real little then. I remember being with Heide, the downstairs maid. Lots of black dresses rustling around, getting stepped on, the accolade pulling the rope, hearing the marvelous church bell...but no feeling that was warm. Heide was let go after the first estate sale." That night after lights out Rita and her roommate Emma snuck up the back stairs to the dormitory attic with their flash lights. Emma needed help with her chemistry work sheet and Rita needed some consolation. Rita had never felt worse. She tried to remember her mother, tried to visualize her face, her hair, her smell, the texture of her cheek, but she couldn't...everything was just out of reach...just like so much of her life frozen, not ugly, just on hold.

In organic chem class, Emma was having a hard time with peptids and circular proteins. It came easily to Rita. On one problem, Rita showed her that she had forgotten to indicate that the experiment needed water so that the spectrum analysis would score correctly on the hematomin graph. Otherwise you would get a left-handed protein, not a good substance!

Once Emma finished the answer sheet, she turned off her flashlight. It was a moonlit night, and they snuggled a little closer, looking out the attic window over the campus. The attic was crowded and dusty. For years families with too many girls would send them to St. Theresa's to serve the Lord. Mother Agnes had come with her steamer trunk from Nebraska. Generations of steamer trunks filled St. Theresa's attics. Serving the Lord was a one-way trip, no round trip ticket required. Almost all of the trunks still had stuff in them from years ago. Some of them were locked. Emma could pick the locks of most of them.

Emma was sharp in her own way, and loved to make various animal noises. She loved telling the story of the farmer that bought the horse that couldn't stop farting. She liked the story because it gave her a chance to show off her favorite rendition of a fart, the Justin Morgan class A fart. The farmer brought the horse back for a tune up, and hooked it up to a tidy little menthane ten watt generator. She could make a neat whirling noise for the generator.

Emma whispered, "you know Rita, you're the lucky one...you can open up and be somebody when you leave here. I can love the

Lord, but I'll just be another penguin shuffling along the edge of the path, with nobody caring a hoot."

"Emma!" Rita sputtered. "You are better than that! Drop that shit! Why don't you drop out and come with me?

"Oh I can't...my parents would never let me. My older brother John is a priest, and my father wants me to take vows. He's got an empty picture frame on the mantle at home, waiting for a picture of me in a habit."

As they looked out the attic window, time seemed to be standing still. It started to snow big wet flakes slowly drifting down. Rita didn't want to leave St. Theresa's. It was all she had.

Rita pulled the blanket closer, as the girls watched the snowflakes drift slowly down. She turned off her flashlight also. She was startled after a while, to hear Emma snore, "Come on, Emma, let's go to bed, get your flash light. Don't forget tomorrow. Hydrate your samples before you run the spectrometer." They got back to their room without anyone seeing them.

Next morning there was a note on the dorm bulletin board for Rita to see Sister Agnes.

Emma was kind of bitter because she felt people were making fun of her, when really they were laughing with her. Like when she was disciplined for her craft project. Gretchen Weinecke, a buxom blond from Oklahoma, was making a motto needlepoint, very ornate, that said "What is home without a Father," Emma thought Gretchen was after Fr. Fritchwell. She embroidered an even better looking motto board, with Japanese style gradients of colors, roses, daisies spilling off the wall or so it seemed. Trouble was, Emma had so many leaves on her panel that some of the letters had to go, so she ended up with "What is a Home without a Fart." She thought that it really was a beauty of a piece of dainty pettie point work. She was proud.

But when Emma was disciplined, she complained out loud, "Hey, it's a craft project, what should count is my perfect handiwork. Look at my background stitching. Can you see the slight halo around the letters? If you stare at it long enough, the letters will pop forward. Like magic. I did that by surrounding the green letters with the complimentary pink color, a little tint of alizarin. Besides, it's not the message I should be graded on, but rather the medium!"

But Emma wasn't appreciated in her homeland. Fr. Fritchwell confiscated it. Fortunately Emma's parents were never told.

Tony Bardwell had been in their class since 8th grade. He tried out for the football team but didn't make it because he didn't weigh enough. Coach suggested he could still go with the team if he'd help out the cheerleaders.

He thought at least he could get off campus for a while. St. Theresa's seemed to him a bit like a prison. He joined the cheerleaders and after a while got some really funny routines going with the biggest pom-poms in the league. The St. Theresa team, the Saints, still only came in next to last, 2-7.

Tony found Rita after chapel on the way to night study hall. "Rita, Father Fritch told me you're leaving!"

She told him about her parent's trusts not agreeing, and that she might have to go to Murray Bay or Michigan. They talked for a long time. He had found some close out CD's at Walmart. Classic blues, and stuff.

"Yeah Tony, maybe I'll learn how to wail like Howlin' Wolf in Murray Bay. Or maybe it will be too cold there to sing the blues. Or maybe their blues will be tightly stiff, real high pitched like an Afghan funeral lament."

"No" he said, "Ole and Lena won't be known for their hubris. They won't be on the Road Less Traveled. They'll probably not sing at all. You'll be OK, don't worry. At least you'll have your auntie. And maybe you can find your dreamboat Mr. Testosterone! Some crotch yearning to breathe free!" They laughed nervously, knowing the future wasn't now. It could wait.

There were questions that didn't need to be asked, nor answered. Tony, Emma, and Rita didn't seem to fit in anywhere. They did not want to be on the student council. That would seem to be giving into the dull gray world of convention. No joy there!

Might as well join the country club and vote republican. Ho Hum. In time they would invent their raison d'tre. But for now, all they had were hunches. Rita had her hunch, a premonition, after confession. She had confessed to having less than pure thoughts, and worried that she'd loose Jesus, and get taken up in worldly ways. She could not forget her mother. She once explained to Tony, "My mother never gave religion much thought. Her job was to look good for Dad. She wasn't interested much outside of her relationship with him. When he was away on business for the Lab, she would work on her scrapbooks late at night. The early scrapbooks were neatly pasted and labeled, but the last ones were crudely cut flowers from seed catalogs, and a few fashion plates from Vogue, Harpers Bazaar, and Town and Country. If the Douhertys or Chamberlin families were mentioned in the Social Spectator, she clipped the photos."

When her father remodeled the house up on the island, all her mother asked for was a good room for putting on her make up. She got it. The original Chamberlin house and grounds had been designed by the sons of Frederick Law Olmstead back in the 1890's. Other friends, including the Taft's from Cincinnati, built "cottages" nearby. The main house had eight bedrooms on the second floor, most with views of the river. On the third floor there was an exercise room for the gentlemen, and three small bedrooms for staff.

Adjoining the Master Bedroom was a dark chamber with overhead lights that focused on the vanity table with drawers of brushes, cremes, powders, eye-brow pencils. Soft camel hair brushes for accenting the hollows of her cheeks. Tweezers to pull an occasional upstart hair that might dare invade her lip. Several kinds of mirrors were lighted from the ceiling. Even the wastebasket was chosen with care; it matched the gold filigree tissue holder. Big flower prints on the wall showed varieties of red Tulips. She matched the colors to the pillows tastefully arranged on the little carved rococo settee that occupied the niche.

The room was a world away from the lake outside. There

were no windows. It was really not on an island in upstate New York, in the 21st century. It was on an unknown island in the Aegean Sea, near Chronos. And it wasn't 2015, but 323 BC, and Alexander the Great was overdue for dinner. Light the candles!

Her decorating spirit was gifted. The room even had the pungent odor of eucalyptus. With all her makeup on, she could have sat in for the Delphic Oracle! At her side was a small dimmer control panel for her lights. The chandelier was on a separate dimmer with a pink gel.

Rita remembered that some of the walls were smooth, almost like polished marble and darkly mirrored.

Her mother taught her the basics of makeup, but she wasn't much interested. St. Theresa's didn't allow makeup anyway. No gum, No smoking, No loafing. Doing God's work was a narrow road, a one-way road.

"He ain't heavy, He's my lord!"

"Becoming a sister couldn't be all that bad," thought Rita. "Sharing in all the tasks. The garden work, the laundry, helping the aged nuns, early morning hymns, the tolling of the chapel bells, the Easter services with incense. The processionals, the peace and quiet, the security of knowing tomorrow will be like today. That tomorrow won't have to be the beginning of the rest of my life. Tomorrow can be more of today...ad infinitum...eternity seized in the moment. Timeless."

"Yeah! Girl, Let's hear it for Eternity" she said out loud.

It was arranged that Mr. Nims, her mother's lawyer, would facilitate placement of Rita. He said his hands were tied. He could not release any more funds for her.

"My only obligation to you, under the terms of the trust, is to give you an accounting of trust's financial operations, its gains and losses. Once you turn twenty-one, you will receive twenty per cent of the capitalized value, each year for five years.

"But what can I do now? Rita asked.

"Your custody was not addressed in your mother's will. I am sorry for that one. Breaks of the game," he laughed!

Rita thought a moment, "maybe I could find a job at MacDonald's."

Mr. Nims' cell phone chimed. "Yes, yes, I am on my way. Tell Martin's group that I have taken care of her. She is going to be placed out of state. Don't tell them anything else. Is that plain enough for you, Marsha?"

Mr. Nims turned back to Rita "The nuns have told me that they will send your things to you in a couple of weeks. Your trunk is still there, isn't it?

"Yes," she said. "It is in the dorm attic."

"But you haven't told me where you're placing me. Is that the right word? Am I about to be placed? Just because a girl has a certain last name, does that mean I have to go into hiding? I feel like I am being abandoned. The trust should have covered me for such ambiguities. Besides I never signed the full and general release. Mom told me not to sign."

Mr. Nims looked at her stonily, intensely. His cold blue eyes said nothing, and a little shiver went down her spine.

"Now don't fret," he smiled, "You'll only have to be out of circulation until the trust is vacated. Take your dad's violin with you. It's the last of the trust's inventory.

"This is a receipt for the violin. I can notarize your signature myself."

Sister Angelica and Rita signed three copies of the full and general receipt, and Mr. Nims said he would put Rita's copy in her folder for safekeeping.

"Lets Roll! Turn your page."

Cervantes, The school's head custodian, drove Sister C., Mr. Nims, and Rita down to the Albany airport where Mr. Nims' Tri-star was waiting.

Mr. Nims got two more calls on his cell phone. It didn't make much sense to her at the time. She had pretty much given up anyway. Cé la vie.

As they approached the Tri-star Mr. Nims got a call, "Yes, she is...no not yet. Tell them everything will work out in the end."

"Rita, would you mind...this is important, you can get a

breath of fresh air before boarding. Tell my pilot Billy to stow your things. I'll be with you in a jiffy."

"Jiffy? Yeah, sure...whatever" muttered Rita.

Billy helped her get her stuff stowed. He was nervously shaking his water bottle, waiting for Mr. Nims. He asked Rita "Boss man like me very much. Do you like to have fun too?" He looked at her Saints sweatshirt with interest.

She knew better than to put on. "No, I owe my life to St. Bartolomeo and to Mr. Nims both." She coughed a couple of times, cleared her throat and whispered to him, "Now if they can just find a cure for my infections."

Billy looked away, shook his water a little, and suggested they board. He showed her the magazine bin and snack bar. She looked out at dreary, gray blue Albany sky. It was starting to drizzle. She called Emma's cell.

"Emma! I'm at the Airport, waiting to see where they're taking me. I have a hunch...yeah...no...un huh."

Emma had passed her test on circular proteins. And Tony was helping her design new outfits for the Saints cheerleaders. Emma said she already had a letter to mail. Tony had gotten the complete Fats Waller CD collection from Fr. Fritch as a birthday gift. Rita promised to send her address when she got settled.

Rita looked over the magazine bin for something interesting to read. Not much. Chemical Industry, Plastics, two technical journals, and a rolled up Playboy magazine in Spanish, and a Golf Equipment catalog.

She settled down with the Playboy. It would help her fluency. Besides, what's wrong with looking at beautiful women.

The centerfold featured Antonia, con las grandes tetas, an airbrushed beauty who looked ready and able to dominate the waves, nailed up as a bowsprit on a schooner. Her ponderous bosom could have taken on any North Sea tempest. Otherwise her eyes seemed blank or unfocused. Rita wondered if she had been drugged to take off her clothes like that. The article reported that in real life Antonia con las grandes tetas was taking acting lessons while running her own catering service. "Hmmm...Rita turned to the Playboy Advisor. She tossed the magazine back into the bin when she saw Mr. Nims approaching.

"Billy, check the weather at Murray Bay, and file for clearance at Windsor if it's OK. Just put Chicago in your log, Use a vital organ transfer code for Brainard's office."

"OK Boss." The steps came up, Billy locked the door, and disappeared forward.

"Fasten your belt Rita; we'll be off in a few minutes. If all goes well, you'll be at your aunt's place in two hours or so." Fortunately there's an airstrip close to her house. We can use our Telex system to activate their runway lights when we get there. So, relax, did Billy show you around?"

"Yes, but I'd like a drink."

"We've got Coke, Sprite, Heinekins, Coors, and Mountain Dew."

"No, water would be just fine. It's stuffy in here, and I might get sick." She wasn't kidding this time.

She reached for the Johlapor Journal of Applied Chemistry in the magazine bin. The formulae were Greek to her, mostly reduction techniques, crackling temperatures. What's new in sludge recovery. New Rutgers study on high temperature vacuum systems. New Directors report from the Palm Springs convention.

She could understand why some of the catalysts would drive some of the reactions, but mostly it didn't make sense.

She looked up and saw that Mr. Nims had a map out.

"Mr. Nims, what is the difference between open and closed cell polymer striation, I don't get it."

"Rita, I don't think that is something you should get into. If you ever have to, just look into the Dow patents. If you're smart, you should be able to put two and two together."

"The bottom line is this," said Nims, holding his fingers onto an imaginary string.

"Your dad's prior patent art was not complete. When he filed our patent application he left out a critical step in the process. Without that step, the reactions are very, very, unstable. We've lost several staff trying to figure it out. Dr. Martin and Dr. Halliday were good chemists, with excellent credentials. But, somehow, we don't know how, the hormone project went horribly awry. After the funerals, we just padlocked the lab.

Nims continued, "Besides the genome map shows we were in the wrong spot anyway. Our computer experiments with dogs now confirm the precise location in the brain. It's frontal lobes, balanced behind both olfactory senses and the tactile panoply of the whisker seats of sensitivity. It's very clear now. "

"The Harvey brothers agree that the tissue of the amyglia brain devoted to this sense is largely unmapped. Early success didn't pan out. Through gene splicing we found we could create many mutant types, but the Board decided not to tamper in designing new dogs. We now only are working with the calf uteri hormone receptors. This is a great short cut, and would not have been possible even two years ago.

"I don't get it. Isn't the genome operative? I thought once the code was broken all the answers were there."

"They are and they aren't. It depends upon the direction of the energy. If the stimulus moves to the left, it means one thing. If it is being read in the opposite direction it always means something different, and not always the opposite, as you might expect. It is all grays, simultaneously moving, never static. Every cell demands its own stasis, to intimately know its neighbor. Every cell, you might say, has its own comfort zone." Nims took out his cell phone and soon was giving Billy instructions.

He continued, "We've been able to clone for Iowa Beef Producers some of the biggest and sweetest bulls in existence. They're well marbled and quite docile due to the substitutions we made to the Pk245 chain. We've applied for a patent on the process, and it is purposely written to include sexual as well as asexual recombinations. Even with fast tracking, it is going to be another year before we hear from the commissioner. Our Washington office is in close contact with the Republican floor leader and the Obama people."

"There's a good chance, that if the calf uteri studies can be replicated asexually, we can promise a skin creme that will have the added benefit of keeping cranial exegesis progressive. It's as if all the unused cells of the olfactory sense have been taught new functions. The area of the brain was there all along, but not addressed, at least not directly. In fact, there isn't any way found yet, to determine the flow of the genetic map. In one individual, the gene is in full control, in another it is inoperative, recessive."

Rita thought a moment, "What controls the turning on process for the chain?"

"That's the sixty four dollar question" Nims said, pausing to freshen his Old Overholt on the rocks. "As they say, initial studies are promising. Tissue studies showed no allergenic problems for any group. Brain function was not only increased, but became more focused."

Rita mused, "Sounds like a wonder drug. How to get looking better, and have a better mind." How much does it cost, and where can I get it?" laughed Rita. Where's the catch, what are the side effects? Surely there's a down side?"

"Yes, prolonged use does cause drowsiness and loss of appetite. And there was only one study at Rutgers that noted an increase in vegetarianism. The increased neural activity uses up endorphins, producing an automatic reaction to defeat the drug. In that way it seems to be addictive, almost like a ping-pong game that never ends."

"We had one, well maybe more than one, disappointment. We just didn't know what to expect. Many of our experimental animals developed allele deviations that made no sense to us. Why would an otherwise healthy bull get horrid skin eruptions that looked like tomato blight? While dusting helped some, the malady seemed to spread among the whole herd."

The plane suddenly dropped and Mr. Nims dropped his glass. "Damn that Billy!"

Then Billy came over the speaker, "It's time we have to turn off cabin lights, boss. We're about fifty kilometers from Windsor."

Rita looked down as they bumped along through the clouds. Little cross hatched villages popping into view, then gone. Tiny veins and arteries carrying corpuscles of Ford vans were coming from nowhere, going somewhere unknown.

The plane drifted lower as they crossed the Canada border silently. She could see that they were far from the burbs. No more avenues of sodium vapor lights, with their golden ambiance, just a few mercury vapor barn lights. Then all was black below. They were over dark waters. The thought occurred to Rita, "I wonder where the flotation devices are stored?"

Billy banked north and they climbed above the clouds again. Lights came on and the air jets cooled her face. But she still felt trapped. "Mr. Nims, how much longer?"

Mr. Nims looked at his Rolex, "about an hour."

They talked about her SAT's and getting into college. She remembered her Dad talking about crew races on the Charles River. Mr. Nims thought she should go to New Haven, then head for Cambridge. She tended to agree. She had a year to decide anyway.

"I don't know for sure if I really wanted to be a doctor, even in research. To get that close to people. Been there."

Rita looked up at Mr. Nims. He was looking out the window.

She shut her eyes and imagined being somewhere else. She imagined floating along inside her own bloodstream. Thump. Quiet. Thump. Quiet. She suddenly could see clearly with her eyes almost closed. Her mind›s eye blinked open.

She was in a tubular hallway with strangely colored walls. There was a totally weird pattern of shapes, colors and textures on the curving walls. She floated along the hall mesmerized by the sequences of the patterns as they passed her. She didn't pass them.

She closed her eyes and tightened her eyelids, straining to bring into focus some meaning. She felt the plane's cool air pushing at her face. Like waves washing a lakeshore. Here she was, going somewhere she knew not, yet comfortable seeing patterns with unknown content. She looked at the walls again.

It seemed a giant duct she was caught in. She could see oily splashes of drifting greens. Even though the smell was bitter, she wasn't bothered.

She felt herself slipping away, lulled by the vibrations of the plane. But then, inexplicably, she caught herself luckily, and held the dream under her power, not its power. She kept herself focused on those weird floating patterns. There was definitely a linearity that gave direction to it. Here and there it looked like a plowed field, there were parallel furrows here and there.

There was a timeless, soundless moment that was strangely palpable. Her ears longed for a meal, she squeezed her eyelids just a little more, but nothing came, and whether she wanted to or not, she returned to the airplane.

"Mr. Nims, is there any music in your system?"

"Nothing special. No."

"Que Lastima..."

"What?"

"I was just thinking how nice it would be to hear the largo from the new world right now...it›s how I'm feeling. How about Celine Dion."

"No, not that either, you'd better buckle up."

Billy cut the engines as they descended to the little Murray Bay airstrip. He dialed the airport access code, and the runway lights came on. The airstrip was deserted, for it was nearly midnight. They taxied up to the only light in sight, next to the airport snack shop and office. There were several rows of small hangers skirting the strip, all surrounded by a three-meter fence to keep out the deer. There was a phone booth and a directory. Mr. Nims got Aunt Sarah on the line, and handed his cell to Rita, "Hello Aunt Sarah?"

Rita could hear breathing and an odd clicking in the background. "Hi, it›s Rita, I'm here at the airport. Yes, the Murray Bay airport. Can you come get me? OK, I can wait. Yes, No, we just got here. I'm next to a phone booth. Mom's lawyer said he told you we were coming. He's here with me now. OK, I›m at the phone booth here."

Rita handed the phone back to Mr. Nims, "she didn't get your message!"

"Well I hope she gets her rear in gear and gets over here!" Barked Nims. "I've got a two thirty in Chicago!"

They waited for what seemed an hour. Billy stacked Rita's bags and boxes by the phone booth. Finally Mr. Nims said that they would have to be going. He gave Rita a cold ceremonial hug, touching his heart automatically.

Rita turned away, "boy I wish this gas would go away. I get this way every month."

"Well you stay right here till your aunt comes. Can I trust you? We really have to be going now. Rita, we would like to stay and meet your aunt, but we can't. Tell her from us, that we regret, ah...we profoundly regret, any inconvenience this may cause her. Tell her, the law's the law." Billy followed Mr. Nims up the steps, and they were gone in no time.

Left alone Rita took out her cell and pushed memory one, it rang once and got intercepted. She heard a recording. No longer active account. Bummer! She sat down on the steps of the dark airport snack shop, waiting for Aunt Sarah. She had only a few vague memories of this aunt, memories of her referred to as wrong turn Sally. Her dad's family never could figure out where Aunt Sarah had gone wrong. They didn't invite her to many parties, and she in turn stayed out of their way. Rita remembered hearing that Aunt Sarah had moved to Oklahoma City, then to a boat moored near Houston.

Out of the distant fog came a flickering light and a puttering engine. It was an orange farm tractor pulling a manure spreader. In the spreader were bright blue plastic barrels, some trashcans, and a white wringer washing machine.

The drier wore an oversize parka with furlined hood. It was Sarah Jane Chamberlin, her aunt. "So you're Ben's girl!" She got down from the tractor. "Let's have a look at you. Yeah...I can see your dad's chin, and you've got the O'Neal ears for sure."

"So you're Ben's girl, all growed up."

"Yes, ma›am, I'm Ben's girl," Rita looked mournfully at her feet, "not quite all growed up."

"They weren't sure what to do with me, Aunt Sarah! Mr. Nims, he represented my Mother's trust, he told me to tell you that he, that he...ah, that he profoundly regretted having to leave me here. He said the law is the law, whatever that means. Is it going to be all right?"

"Well, Ben's girl, I guess it's going to have to be all right. It's just that I could have used some warning. I'm not really set up for guests, right now. Let's get your stuff in the honey wagon, that›s what we call a spreader around here."

"So come ahead, climb aboard the good ship lollypop. I'll hoist 'yer duffels to yee, and ya can stow 'em mid ship. I might as well do my pickup now that I'm here" She led the way around to the back of the Snack Bar building to empty the snack shop›s trash cans. "Put the garbage in the rear, Ben's girl. Recycles next, and any good stuff up front." Aunt Sarah explained that she provided trash services in return for using the airport water hydrant. Her home at Lost Grove Motors had a shallow well, but it wasn't fit to drink, or even to use for laundry. Too much acid, and too much iron.

Aunt Sarah's tractor was almost an antique, an Alles Chalmers 5600 made in the fifties. Had an oversize seat with padded armrests, radio aerials and lights. "This here," Aunt Sarah patted the tractor fender, "is Alice. They said her block was cracked and she'd never get better. But they were wrong. I didn't even have to re-bore the block. Just coated the sides of the cylinder with high temperature proto-form."

Sarah showed Rita where to sit on the orange fender, opposite the toolbox and radio. The night was quiet and crisp. Rita asked, "I expected you to come earlier, and maybe in a car. What's the deal? As they rolled along, Sarah explained, "Sheriff Hermanson took my license away ten years ago for driving left of center. They actually threw me in jail for a few hours. Man alive, that was a transforming event for me. I experienced first hand the caste system organized in the name of justice. It seemed that all the jail personnel saw themselves anointed with control. I had been at the county fair for most of the day, having a good time at the veteran's tent. I was on my way home and there was no traffic ahead. So I probably drifted to the center. Suddenly there he was with the red lights beaming everywhere. He took out his breathalizer and zeroed it out, and tested me. I was point 0.9, point 0.8 is legal. Took me to jail, finger printed me, had me take off my sandals and put on their orange shower clogs. Then they put me in a cold holding cell. Everything was hard cold metal, everything bolted down. I learned a lot in just a few hours. Here was a palpable caste system. I sensed being judged and found lacking. I felt a new station for my life. Sub-standard. I was no longer in control of my life. He had it in for me, ever since I beat him in open court on his first OMVI charge. He told me he was going to get me, and he did.

So, there›s no law against operating a farm vehicle like Alice. I know I could reapply for a commercial drivers license, but I›ve gotten used to taking back roads at my own pace. I'll go back to jail if he catches me operating a car on the highway. This way he can't get me. You don't need a license to drive a farm tractor."

Two

A half hour later they pulled up to Lost Grove motors. The only sign of life was Buck, a yellow lab-cross tied to a doghouse made from bales of straw. There were piles of rust on soil laced with glass and strips of chrome automobile trim, leftovers from cars and trucks come and gone. An old camping trailer was near a school bus that had no tires. Under maples and scrub oaks, there were the rusting remains of Valiants, Chargers, Cougars, Rams and two bread trucks. Every car, every truck, every hippy van out of the sixties, all were stuffed full. Full of cast-off small appliances, cake pans, car parts, magazines and books, window parts, roll ends of wire, weird electrical coils, tools, and beer bottles. On the ground crumpled beer cans were blending into a mat of leaves, twigs, plastic wire. Not all native flora could compete in this caustic environment. But here and there some wild flowers seemed strangely invigorated by the toxic soils. Ragweed, poison ivy, wild cucumber vine, nightshade, mullen, and several varieties of Canada thistles flourished.

"Well let's get you set up," said Sarah somewhat hopelessly. "I'll give you a choice. You can have a Bus or the Dodge bread truck. This is all I have. You might say I'm living in the open. Either way, we'll have to, ah, rearrange things in the morning to make room for you. For the rest of tonight, why don't you rest on the couch in the office? We are still using the outhouse out back, some people call it the back house."

Rita brought her bags into the tiny office that was already full. The day's events had numbed her mind and Morphias demanded attention. Rita dropped off to sleep quickly and did not notice Sarah placing a greasy down comforter over her.

Next morning Rita was nudged awake by strange sounds nearby. She opened her eyes to a new world. She closed her eyes not sure where she was. She found herself annoyed and realized she was inhaling noxious odors from the comforter next to her chin. “Ugh! What in blazes is this?” She got up and out of habit stretched her arms in the air. The sound of the motor stopped.

The office was in name only. Once there had been a service counter, now buried under manuals, parts, and empty shipping boxes. In the one remaining window looking south, was a barrel of geraniums that hadn’t been pruned in years. Vines covered the window. Rita noticed the window sill and a carpet of dead flies that had accumulated for decades. With all the fly specs, spider webs, dust and condensation on the glass, the reality outside became clouded, filtered. An air compressor started up again in the next room. Rita felt uncomfortable and oily. She stepped outside into the cool morning air.

Everything looked different in the morning sunlight. Even the carpet of trash that seemed impenetrable in the night, now seemed to have a few paths through it. While there was no cause for celebration, no sense of homecoming, there was still a reality with clear cut edges. Junk was junk, kitch was kitch, no order was the order of the day. In such disarray, any pretence to beauty or status was relegated to the back burner. “Well any port in a storm they say. I’m just going to have to make the best of it. Stiff upper lip my girl!”

Aunt Rita had the coffee pot on in the back room of the service garage. Years ago, the room had been used for parts and for some car repairs. As Rita was getting her doughnut, she heard a rustling behind the shelf and looked up in time to see two little black mice disappear. “Go on,” Rita sputtered, “git...out of here! Ugh. Mice, spiders, roaches, centipedes, millipedes, Ugh!”

When Aunt Sarah came in from her trailer, Rita asked, “Aunt Sarah, would you mind if I pruned that geranium, and maybe do a once over on the glass. It would make a big difference. I don’t know what to do. You got any mouse traps?”

“Well I don’t care what you do on your free time, but don’t expect me to pay you nothing. You have to be here for how long?”

“Eighteen months.”

“Eighteen months?

"Mr. Nims wants me to be out of circulation until the trusts of my folks estates get liquidated. I wanted to stay at school all year long, but I couldn't."

"Well lets get this straight right now, Ben's girl, you can stay here, such as it is, for eighteen months, and I won't charge you anything for rent, provided you make yourself useful around here. If you make me some money, you can have half the profit. That's the best deal you're going to get. You're young and inexperienced. If you cost me money, on the other hand, you are going to have to pay me back at full interest. Do you understand, Ben's girl?"

Rita was feeling more and more unwanted. She had wanted a little safe harbor at Murray Bay, with her kin. Instead she was about to get charged interest on her family account. Rita chose a wet lipped downcast pose, "you mean I owe you? How much? And what's full interest?"

"I'll give you seven per cent after thirty days," answered Sarah, "but I'd rather not get over extended. Cash is good. Understand?"

Aunt Sarah opened the door, "Let's see what's available in our back yard, there's a couple of campers and one large chicken coop. Put on your coat. As you can see, this building used to be a service station when the road outside was highway sixty-eight. When route sixty-eight was moved to Gottschaulk, that took most of the traffic away from here. But even before that the Pottertons, Glen and Gladys, they bought it in the 1940's, they were having problems with their health. The place had been closed up for eleven years when I bought it from the estate. There had been a lot of mining all over this area, in fact there are several open shafts down near my lower forty. So you be careful Ben's girl, those shafts are deep, if you ever fell in, no one would know where you were. You'd die for sure."

Touring the yard outside, Aunt Sarah pointed out a bread truck, on whose side was painted a giant cheeky little blond girl's face, with giant lettering, Mrs. Karl's. Rita decided against the bread truck because it didn't have any windows. The bright yellow school bus would have to do.

Most of the seats had been taken out of the bus. The remaining seats were hidden under mounds of plywood scraps, plastic tarpaulins, beer coolers, fence posts, and a saddle. Sarah and Rita soon found another place to stack the computers and video equipment. They ended up improvising tarps over some lawn chairs. Rita suggested to Aunt Sarah that they put the computers in one stack and the video stuff in a separate pile. Sarah explained she wanted the different systems to be together.

It didn't make much sense to Rita, but "Oh well, I'm not going to be here for that long anyway." They put most of the Windows machines in the blue house trailer and the MacIntoshes in the bread truck, tying the doors together with connecting cables. "You can't be too careful," observed Aunt Sarah, "people have been stealing from me for years. Even my nephew Phillip."

"Who is he" Rita asked.

"That would be Rose's son. Phillip. He only looks bright. Lights are on, but nobody home, if you know what I mean!"

Rita thought a moment, "Who is Rose, Aunt Sarah?

"Rose was your uncle Fred's second wife. Phillip, or Phillipe as he wanted it to be pronounced, he was her son, not Fred's. So, he really isn't a nephew of mine, nor a cousin to you, except by marriage. He would be your cousin once removed, Rose and Fred have been gone for years, but their no good son, Phillp, still runs the ranch. He could buy anything he could want, but no. He gets his kicks stealing. He once got caught shoplifting underwear at Stude's Mens Wear, and Stude insisted on taking him to court. When he used to drop by, I would always end up missing a tool, or a magazine, or something."

"So why did you name this place Lost Grove Motors," asked Rita.

"It was named that before I bought it. Lost Grove was named after a surveyor's notation on the first survey of the province. When the surveyor was making his map of the area, he remembered having his lunch in a grove of aspen somewhere in this general area, but he couldn't remember exactly where, so on his map he inked in Lost Grove near a cliff, with a stream below. Later mapmakers copied the words Lost Grove as if they meant something. A town road became Lost Grove Road. The lost grove limestone schoolhouse was built in 1856. There were plenty of children from the Italian miners working at the Tripoli mines."

Rita looked puzzled, "Tripoli, Africa?

"No, the mines were all around here, I don't know why they were called that. In our back woods there are some of the open shafts, so be careful.

Lost Grove Motors had no welcome sign. There was only an oversize yellow mailbox with large block letters, LOST GROVE MOTORS. Behind the cement block garage building was a woods packed with a rusting field of abandoned vehicles and trash of all kinds. Bushes of wild honeysuckle blended with deadly nightshade to obscure the exact nature of many deposits.

By lunchtime Rita and Aunt Sarah had opened up a cozy space in the school bus. Rita found some blue moving company blankets that she draped over two lawn chairs. They moved some of the school lockers in a row across the middle of the bus. This gave Rita a front room with the bus driver's seat and dashboard, and a back room with the emergency door. She found two table lamps in the weeds, and chose two bright chrome floor lamps. She used a maple leaf flag and some curtains to cover most of the windows. She made her bed on a mat next to the rear door so that she could face the rising sun. The door had windows that allowed her to have a good view of the yard while lying in bed.

Her first night in the school bus was an education. Some of the windows still worked, so she got a cross draft going. That helped clear the air a little. That first night Rita left both the light and radio on. She could lie on her side on the air mattress and look over the junkyard and garage light. She breathed heavily upon the glass next to her and watched the glass cloud over with condensation. The garage light expanded to a glow and Rita was tempted to write on the glass, but didn't.

It had been a long day. She had a bad case of poison ivy, and a few scratches from the berry bushes. She closed her eyes, feeling very alone. She thought of Emma and Tony, and the sisters of St. Theresa's. The sounds of raindrops on the bus roof increased her melancholy. She missed the slumber parties with the other girls, and listening to music with Tony.

During the night the winds picked up, stripping yellow leaves from the aspens. Morning found both Rita and Aunt Sarah in convivial moods. After a breakfast of applesauce and cottage cheese, coffee and toast, Aunt Sarah outlined the day before them.

"Normally I go to the airport snack shop on Friday to pick up their trash, and from there, to the town dump. If I need water, I fill up behind the snack shop. Then I usually head for the township dump. But since we did the pickup last night, I don't have to go to the airport. So, I'll show you where to crush the cans."

Behind the small garage building Aunt Sarah had a barrel of waste oil, and a mound of bags of beer cans, waiting to be flattened. Rita noticed a large pile of cement blocks painted mostly in a dull Prussian blue color, with a large folded beach umbrella.

"What are you going to do with the umbrella Aunt Sarah?"

"If I can straighten the pole, I think I can make it work just fine."

"But where are you going to use it? I mean, where's the beach?"

Aunt Sarah looked away, somewhat puzzled, "The umbrella isn't that old, the fringe is pretty good, the plastic is good. It might be just the thing for somebody. I got it from the dump," she said. "I always say you can get anything you want from the dump. It came with some other stuff. If worse comes to worse, I can open it up and put it over something. It doesn't cost me a damn thing to just leave it there."

"So," aunt Sarah continued, "you can crush cans any time you want. Aluminum is up to sixty cents a pound. Number two copper hit ninety cents."

"Lunch is catch as catch can around here. And sometimes you'll be on your own for supper too." Sarah showed Rita the big deep freezer on the back porch of the cabin. The woodpile was in the middle of the yard running right up to the freezer. "I don't run the freezer in the winter, don't have to" said Sarah.

"But for now, you'll probably want to organize your things. Later I got to go pick some wild grapes. I'll show you how to drive Miss Alice to the dump. OK?

"Sure! I've got nothing better to do. It's going to be a very long eighteen months."

Aunt Sarah was about to agree, but thought better, and let it pass.

Three

Aunt Sarah gave Rita the Operators manual for the tractor. "It still has most of its pages. Read this and after lunch we can go down to the lower forty. I'm thinking we can attach the mower and get the thistles before they bloom. Once you get the hang of it, you can go back to Mrs. Staber's for the dump run by yourself." Rita scratched her head, "Don't I have to have a license?" Aunt Sarah took a long pause, looking directly into Rita's eyes, "I told you when you first came here. You don't have to have a license to operate a tractor."

The next morning Rita took the operators manual out to the tractor and sat in the orange operators seat. Aunt Sarah came out to help her learn how to downshift, and use the brakes. Together they made the weekly trash pickup at the airport snack shop. Mrs. Staber and Rita went through the trash routines including emptying the restroom bags. Once a month she was instructed to wax the floors. Rita had learned well at St. Theresha's how to shine faucets.

It was a bright sunshiny afternoon in September, after getting water at the airport, Rita was rolling along when she noticed a strange oversized tricycle ahead. What a sight. As she passed she saw it was a young man with long blond hair, wearing a bright safety orange vest with bright yellow tape. A tall aerial was flopping to and fro with an orange flag. On both handle bars there were rear view mirrors and coon tails.

The man waved at her and smiled. Impulsively Rita pulled Alice off to the side of the road.

"Hi there" he said, almost too cheerfully.

"Hi" she replied not quite as cheerfully. "Where ya goin' to?"

The man looked up at Rita, "What's it look like?" Can't you tell? I'm goin' to the promised land! I gotta get to Murray Bay on Sunday. Praise the Lord."

"Yeah, Praise the Lord, Brother." She noticed how white his

teeth appeared, the beginning of a blond moustache on a very tanned face. His dark hazel eyes had the longest eyelashes she had ever seen. Rita felt he might be somewhere around thirty.

"And where are you goin?" he asked.

"Oh nowhere in particular. I just got some water and I'm heading back to my aunt's place. It's a couple of miles down the road."

Rita noticed the man was wearing a leather vest under his orange windbreaker. The vest had strange looking hairy objects swinging from it.

"What in God's name are those things," asked Rita pointing to his chest.

"These are my collection, I call 'em my twilights. Most are paws are from dried kitties I find along the road. This one here with the long nails is from a badger. He's the bravest on them all! He doesn't even know how to back up! That's courage, don't you think?"

"Yeah, I'm sure, already."

My real name is Albert, but my friends call me Pokey. What's your name?"

"I'm Anastasia, daughter of the lost Dauphin...and you're Jim, and we're going to have to float by Cairo at nighttime. No, I'm just kidding, my name is Violet Rita, and my friends call me Rita. But I gotta go, it looks like rain. See ya!"

Rita put Alice into low gear and eased back on to the road. In a few minutes she was back at the garage where she found Aunt Sarah deep into the carburetor of an S-10. Flicking the float valve, the engine would race, then back fire.

"See that," she said, "look here. See how the engine shakes at about here" She revved up the engine part way, and yes, Rita could see the whole engine was vibrating. "Not good, timing is way off, engine over heats too, with all that friction. I'm surprised it hasn't thrown a rod. Oh, and the muffler isn't the right one for this model. The right one will allow us to boost the backpressure so that our timing has a chance to have an effect. This old girl can still be a good worker for someone."

The yellow lab Buck growled and wagged his tail. Sarah squinted, "Now what is that coming?" The bike with three big wheels with an orange flag was turning into her gate. Behind the driver were two grocery carts wired together with a cooler and a rolled up sleeping bag. Beneath in the back was a dog kennel between the rear wheels.

"Aunt Sarah, that's the guy I met down the road. He said his name was Albert, but people call him Pokey. He's maybe a little off." The sky was getting darker and a cool wind started to blow through the treetops.

"Ya mind if we pull into that shed, Ma'am? Looks like rain." Aunt Sarah already had one un-invited guest. "Well I ain't runnin' a camp ground for no freaky lookin' Jesus freaks." She paused and looked directly into the stranger's eye. The whites of his eyes contrasted with the deeply tanned face. "But, go ahead. I guess you got nowhere else...Rita, you can show him around behind the air compressor, next to the woodpile. If it's just for the night. Show him the green room...that's what we call our outhouse."

"I thank you kindly Ma'am." He pulled his trike around the corner into the lean-to shed. Rita kept an eye on him, like Aunt Sarah said. "Better safe than sorry." The man opened the dog kennel between the rear wheels. That's when she saw Mr. Pee for the first time.

He was short and his deep blue gray eyes looked right into her eyes, with a calm, instant recognition. "Weird, Man!" mumbled Rita to herself. Soft pink skin without a hint of a tan.

Pokeyman introduced them. "Mr. Pee, this is a nice young lady named..I guess I don't remember your name"

"Rita" she said "Nice to meet you too."

Pokey explained that Mr. Pee was a miniature Chinese pot-bellied pig that wasn't going to grow any larger.

"I won him in a card game! That was when I was working with Tri-State Shows." He whispered something in the pig's ear and it grunted softly. Pokey needed to exercise his friend so off they went trotting as it started to rain. Aunt Sarah and Rita closed up the garage shop and went to the back room kitchen.

The next morning Rita almost ran into Pokeyman coming of the outhouse. "Morning Ma'am!" Pokey was feeding Mr. Pee next to the trike. "Breakfast for Mr. Pee is whatever comes along," Pokey told Rita, "Wednesdays are good to check the dumpsters at the Walmart. That's when they get their midweek veggies, and when they toss out the out-of-date deli stuff. Saturdays are sometimes good too, except you gotta get there early, before the Mexicans."

This morning it looked like breakfast for the pig was threebean salad, with a side of barbecued something. Pokey kept up a running conversation with his colleague, "Now you gotta eat, Mr. Pee. Your not getting any younger, and you'll never be so pretty again. Oh, Yes, Sir, Yeah...sure, yep, indeedy, you are the fairest one of all. Anyone can tell, just look at those pretty hairs on your chiny chin chin. You are my baby, my only baby...you make me happy when skies are gray" he sang.

Rita took her turn at the "greenroom" and locked the door. "His voice doesn't seem too bad" she thought.

She started to think, "if this guy starts to talk baby talk to his pig, well, I'm outa here." But as she turned to go, she heard the pig giggle and squeal with laughter.

"Well, I'd best be going, if'n I'm to get to church on time," said Pokey. "I should say adieu to your auntie."

They found Aunt Sarah busy under the S-10, "Rita, get me a 40 millimeter socket out of the drawer...the top drawer."

"Which top drawer, I can't find it." Pokey came over and reached behind her, grabbed a wrench and handed it down to Sarah. Pokey asked, "Why metric Ma'am, I thought S10's were American." They are," Aunt Sarah explained, "but the last time someone did a brake job on this, they put the calipers back on with the wrong bolts."

As Sarah rolled out from under the truck, her face was a mess. Grease in her gray hair, a black streak under one eye that made her look like a partial linebacker. "Aunt Sarah, you've got grease under your eye," Rita observed.

"And you don't! It's Tuesday and you can do the laundry. And then this afternoon, you can come to the dump with me. You might come in handy, you never know."

Pokey and Aunt Sarah worked the rest of the morning on the S10 brakes. Rita got the clothes done and spread out over some odd aluminum lawn chairs to dry. There were aluminum lawn chairs with torn webbing everywhere. The wild raspberry bushes seemed to like them, sending new shoots up through some of the webbing. Tough honeysuckle bushes had grown up among the vehicles. Damaged buckets filled with rusting carriage bolts, a length of red hose here and there, stack of white shingles, an old kitchen radio.

Aunt Sarah said, "It wouldn't take but a little time to replace the webbing on those chairs."

Rita wondered if her aunt ever benefited from her collecting, other than by giving stuff away to friends. If a friend needed a 14" rim, Aunt Sarah probably would have twenty different ones, if only she could find the right one.

Four

After lunch, Aunt Sarah had Rita and Pokey pack up the trash and garbage for the trip to the township dump which was located next to a cliff ten miles north of Murray Bay. Pokey volunteered to ride in the spreader.

Rita rode sidesaddle on Miss Alice, the tractor, as Aunt Sarah recounted the local history. They passed by the airport, and Rita thought how much she missed school. How Emma was doing in her studies. She hadn't heard from her for a week.

Aunt Sarah pointed out the rusting remains of the Helgeson Brothers egg farm. For years the farm had supplied eggs all over the province. Big low barns with long batteries of chickens, dropping eggs onto a moving mylar belt.

They stopped for a while to look at some wild grape vines growing on the fences. Looking over at the egg farm, Aunt Sarah said, "Colonel Tom, Tom Nichols, first settled over there in 1842. His father-in-law from New Hampshire bank-rolled him and his wife."

"They farmed during the summers and the men folk went mining in the winters. A small mine turned into a surprise deposit of magnesite with enough rare earths with it that the ore was very valuable. The biggest problem was to separate the rich pichblend from the iron and clay. They built the first washhouse to do that in the 1850s. Later they moved the operation to LaSalle, Illinois, then later to New Jersey."

"They had a beautiful home right by those two big pine trees behind that red shed. All that's left is the chimney and front steps. It's a shame! There were rumors that the colonel's wife was a rounder."

Rita pulled up the vines and saw small dense clumps of grapes, "what's a rounder Aunt Sarah?"

"A rounder is old time slang for, well, you know, uh...a woman of loose virtue. You know one when you see one because the gal is poor, and the heels of her shoes are rounded so much that she's a pushover for any man."

Aunt Sarah got back on Alice and turned to Rita, "Do you know what they call hens that aren't laying eggs fast enough? You know, when the eggs aren't dropping on to the belt daily? They call them spent hens."

"Years ago Helgesons would sell their spent hens for three and a half cents a pound, all plucked with the heads and feet still on. Now, I hear, they'll pay you two cents a pound, just to get rid of them." Seems like the landfills won't take them anymore."

"Think of all the starving Chinese!" said Rita.

"Yeah, it's a shame," agreed Aunt Sarah. "But, then the Chinese aren't starving anymore Rita! They got smart from what I hear. And they are gobbling up our gas faster than we ever did! There ought to be a law." Beyond the Helgeson egg farm, Aunt Sarah pointed to a yellow barn, with a big black and yellow smiley face painted on the gable. "Be careful of those folks, Rita! That's the Hare Krishna farm. You never know what kinds of nuts are camping out there. Once in a while they'll stop and ask me to help them. Or buy some incense. Once I helped a young boy, maybe about twelve, who had run away from home. I helped him find a ride back to the Gaspé. His family sent me a very nice note."

The afternoon was getting cooler when Aunt Sarah pulled into the town dump. Rita and Pokey took turns throwing their garbage bags off the edge of the bluff. Pokey picked up some pebbles and threw them at the rats while Aunt Sarah looked over the piles of rubbish carefully for anything useful. She picked up an art deco toaster that needed a new cord and plug and put it in the spreader. Pokey picked up an old vacuum cleaner, and after a moment he dropped it over the edge.

Coming home, Pokey and Rita unloaded the spreader near the path to the back house, next to a small stack of concrete blocks. Rita wondered if Aunt Sarah would ever find time to start her new path. "Well," she thought, "it's her life, and in a year I'll be out of here."

That fall brought the annual County Fair. Aunt Sarah always showed up for the demolition derby. This year she was planning to enter the Pontiac Le Mans.

Pokey removed all the glass and installed the safety gas tank. Rita spray painted Lost Grove on both sides of the car in bright day glow orange.

Aunt Sarah registered with the derby and was assigned the last heat. So with time to waste, she joined some old friends in the Legion tent. After downing all the free beer she could want, Aunt Sarah was ready for the contest.

The Le Mans started right up. Aunt Sarah buckled up and checked to see where the red Desoto was. If she was out for anyone, it was the Sheriff's son, Stevie Hermansen. Years ago the Sheriff had given Aunt Sarah a traffic ticket for driving left of center.

Aunt Sarah revved up the engine, backed off, and got some good backfires for the crowd's amusement. The grandstands hooted, and Aunt Sarah let off another round. Put put put, BANG BANG...Bang! The stands were ready. Aunt Sarah checked again...Stevie had a cigarette dangling from his too wet lips, unaware he was a target.

The starter's flag dropped and the derby was on. The track was a slippery mess, and Aunt Sarah basically played a game of avoidance. Until just the right moment, Stevie moved in right behind her, aiming for an attack on Bret Zimmerman. Aunt Sarah quickly reversed and floored the Le Mans. An unlucky swerve and Stevie's radiator crumpled. Clouds of steam mixed with the exhaust fumes. His white flag went up, leaving Aunt Sarah the last car. She revved the engine, put put, BANG BANG...BANG. The fiftydollar prize was hers.

She left the track in a cloud of smoke, triumphant. They were about to go home when she decided she needed some food. The Corn Dog stand was still open, so they sat down on the picnic bench to a meal of two corn dogs with the works.

Halfway through the first corn dog a man stepped up and ordered the same. He looked over to Aunt Sarah, and smiled an almost toothless smile.

"Well if it ain't Miss Sarah Jane Chamberlin in the flesh! I wouldn't mind a little action Miss Sarah. Last year I woke up dead broke after a night with you and Butch. How about us getting together for a friendly game? Just to make things right? I'd like you to meet a new friend of mine, Stretch."

"Stretch! You come over here, now! Stretch joined us at Frankfurt, he runs the Ferris wheel."

Aunt Sarah really didn't want to go home anyway. So Rita and Pokey bought a taco salad to take home to the little porker. Pokey didn't like to feed his pet pig hot dogs. He said it just didn't seem right.

Their toothless friend, Walter Trepling, class of '75, operated the Chamber of Horrors spook house. Many a girl was tested as the little chain driven buckets jerked couples through the maze of horrors. Some of the boys also got tested. Walt's job was to take the tickets and lock bars.

When the ride shut down, Walt was allowed to sleep among the horrors in the semitrailer rig. It wasn't much of a life. But the pay was good.

Pokey and Rita left Aunt Sarah with Walt and Stretch playing quarter ante poker.

They went through the Swine exhibit first, taking their time, for it was going to take a while for Aunt Sarah to deal with her prize money. Plus the beer was starting to sodden the picture.

Pokey knew a lot about pigs, and antibiotics. They walked through all the aisles of Dorsets, Hampshires, Red Wattles, Kunekunes of New Zealand, Meisen from China. and even a rare bearded variety.

It was around midnight and most of the swine were either bored or exhausted from the ordeals of the show ring. Most lay on their sides, breathing heavy hot moist air, dreaming about food, sex, and society. Some of the farm boys and girls spent the night with their livestock and had similar dreams. The air was warm and nurturing. Pokey and Rita were getting good at killing time together, wordlessly.

Rita started thinking, "I wonder how degrading an experience it could be for a pig, to have to parade around the ring, with everyone looking at your nose, your ears, your belly, your anus. No loin cloth, no bikini, no make up, no accessories. She pondered how Marie Antoinette must have felt, dressing for her last cart ride. The morning of the Crucifixion, did Christ get to choose his loincloth? Was he able to give his executioners a few shekels to do a good job?"

Rita and Pokey stopped to talk with some girls from the Tre-Pol-Pen Farm. They were members of the Town of Brigham 4H club, spending the night in the barn with their pigs with the radio tuned to Porter Waggoner. The girls were tanned with fat cheeks. Pokey stooped down to look their boar right in the eye. The pig started to breathe deeply, and Pokey nodded, mumbling something Rita didn't quite get. Pokey felt behind the boar's ears, as if looking for something.

"Ah here it is...Oh! And here's another!" Pokey showed the fat dog ticks to the Trejenick girls, "There not much you can do about 'em, there's ticks probably every where around here."

The air around the swine barn smelled full-bodied, earthy alfalfa marsh hay. The girls said they were worried about Donna, their younger sister. Donna had gotten the big purple ribbon, best of show for her Dorset sow, Penny.

"She was celebrating with a guy from the Pulaski club that she had met at the state sectionals. They went for a Pepsi hours ago."

As they left the horse barn later, Pokey saw a big purple ribbon for Best of Show, pinned to the back pocket of a cheeky girl with a guy coming out of the poultry exhibit. Looked like grass stains on the ribbon.

Rita imagined that the ribbon would be added to all the other red, yellow, and white ones displayed next to their dad's gun case. Years later Donna would look at the grass stains on that ribbon, and smile. Fecundity being its own reward.

The song changed to "your cheatin' heart" and they moved on.

The guys from the horse barn were cleaning up the racetrack, as Rita and Pokey walked around the track three times, talking about everything and nothing. Killing time until Sarah was ready to leave.

After a long pause, Pokey said "My Dad died when I was six, and my brother and sisters made it pretty hard on my Mom. My brother Mark and my sister Julie were caught dealing meth and ecstasy. They were both sent to Windsor. Because my other sister, Kathleen and I were so much younger, Social Service put us in a foster home. That was the best place! We had our own room, with curtains on the windows! Mrs. Thornton helped me with math and her husband Dan helped me understand cars. We were there for almost a year, until the Thorntons were transferred. It was the Thorntons that gave me my dictionary."

"Then we went to the Ridlers. Mrs. Ridler wanted to adopt Kathleen, but not me. Because the county didn't have any openings I became a state at large case. So basically I've been on my own since seventeen."

"Oh how awful!" Rita volunteered. "Why didn't you go back to your mother?"

"I did, for a while. But mom's new boyfriend, Stan, and I don't get along. He tried pushing me around, blaming me for drinking his beer. Said I was the dumbest son of a bitch he'd ever seen. Mom got mad, and kicked him. He took a swing at her, but slipped on the linoleum. He passed out, right there on the floor. He pissed in his pants, and never even knew it! That's how bad he was, or is, I should say. I told Mom I couldn't take it anymore. She said she understood, told me Stan really did care, that inside he was a very tender soul that people didn't know. She said he treated her better than my dad had."

"I finished the sixth grade while I was at the Thortons. But after the Riddle farm, I took off on my own. My tricycle comes from the Riddles. All my earthly possessions are packed in the saddle bags, with a little trailer hitched behind for Mr. Pee."

"I didn't do well in school. But I did learn to read Popular Mechanics. Mr. Thornton had me circle every group of synonyms in the dictionary in blue pencil. I got all the way to the end of the v's."

Rita asked Pokey, "have you dated any girls, or have you wanted to settle down somewhere?" Pokey shrugged his shoulders, "Nah, not much. Mama told me I was different. Special. That I'd get into lots of trouble if I took off my pants. She told me I should keep quiet and stay off the main roads. So that's what I do. And I haven't gotten into any trouble since the Riddles."

Rita told Pokey about her own mother and father, and how much she missed them. And Emma, and how much she missed her. Pokey wanted to know what she wanted to be after school. She thought a minute, "maybe a nun or social worker."

"I'll bet you would do real good either way, because you understand being alone and friendless. But you're smart too! Maybe you could be a doctor of something. They make a lot of money. But many of them are publicers."

They jogged around the track, one more time. Off went the grandstand lights and the midway lights. Most of the carneys were in their trailers with air-conditioning. Three were still playing cards in the spook house.

Rita knocked on the tin door of the trailer and they went in. Stretch was dealing, "Let's play dime store! Fives and tens wild, aces or better to open."

Walt summed up the evening, "Well, Miss Chamberlin, it's good for us that we weren't playing strip poker!" Aunt Sarah squealed, "you'll need more than a card game to get me interested in your goods."

She did volunteer that if they wanted to follow her home, they could sober up and bathe down at the creek at Lost Grove.

Driving home to Lost Grove, Sarah was on a toot. Dolly Parton she was not, but that didn't stop her from wailing out hillbilly verse, "Way back in the hills, as a girl I did wonder, what's more precious than gold, more something than..." Words began to fail. Sarah's bacchanal had crested, she wiped the sweat off her forehead with her shop rag and looked in the rear view mirror.

"There's Stretch's van, Rita. Right on time!"

"Yep! Those guys might be thinkin' that they're going to get a piece of ass out here in the woods. Rita, you follow us down to the creek. I'll swing out on the rock, and after they get out of their clothes, you quick get all their stuff. That'll teach them we're no easy pickings."

Rita didn't know who polluted the creek worse, Sarah, Stretch or Walt. Sarah took a running leap holding onto the dead grape vine. "Here I come, whee!!! She swung out over the creek and landed on the opposite side. It was pretty dark, but Stretch and Walt could still see Sarah's trim body. She knelt down at the water's edge with her Dove soap and began to "make her toilet." The lightning bugs were still dancing in the air, and Stretch was captivated. Noticeably captivated. Soon his very white bottom was to submerge in the creek. Then Walt's unshapely callused toe tested the water. He just sat down in the muddy bottom by himself, cooling off. He closed his eyes and smiled. He belched . . . twice.

Just as Stretch got near Sarah, she dove into the water, squealing with laughter. She had caught a second wind, the cool water had brought a new season to her party.

Sarah and Rita quickly grabbed all the men's clothes, and raced back up the cliff to the garage. Sarah instructed, "Put their stuff in their truck, and lock it up. Bring the key to me. I'm going in and see if there's any more beer in the fridge."

Pokey and Rita did as they were told. Pokey went to his shed to check on Mr. Pee, and Rita went to the bus. Before she turned out the light, she got out her diary to sum up the day, but couldn't think of anything worth putting down. She could hear Stretch and Walt complaining to Sarah.

"You want trouble Sarah? Is that what you want? Huh? Cause that's what you'll get." They were going to make trouble if she didn't return their clothes.

Sarah told them it wouldn't do, for them to be calling her names. "You know, Stretch, I can call the Sheriff to make a report of naked trespassers. The Sheriff can give you a ride. Rita's got you recorded on her Nikon digital camera! Now do you want your dirty nakedness, your full exposure to be plastered in the Chronicle? The full Monty...is that what yer after?"

Walt, by now, had found a bigger branch for a fig leaf. Stretch knew he was out numbered and vulnerable. Sarah still had her queen. Check mate!

Sarah continued, "Now if you want to be nice...you can be real nice! If you want your stuff, you can have it. It's in your truck, and here's the key. Stretch, all you have to do is bark like the puppy you are. And Mr. Walter Trepling, maybe you can whine pitifully. Like the pitiful muddy ass mess you are. OK gentlemen, lets hear it." Stretch looked at Walter, Walter looked at Stretch. They mournfully did their best to howl pitifully.

Back in the bus, Rita closed her diary, turned off the light, and started to think. She drifted away, to the prairie of the pioneers, away from the hustle and bustle of the 21st century, away from the internet, where unmistakably, everything is in its right place, everything in order, even the howling coyotes behind waves of grass, howling in minor thirds. Tomorrow would be the beginning of a new era.

The new era was not cheery. Sarah was very late in getting up. She smelled so bad that Rita considered suggested to her that it might be a good idea for her to return to the creek.

The Fedex guy came about ten o'clock. Pokey had ordered some bible tracts from down south. He said the voices told him to do it. He was planning on getting on the road again. Mr. Pee, he said, needed to get on the road for his health. A change of environment would surely help. Rita had to admit, Mr. Pee seemed to be slowing down.

Over lunch Rita started thinking out loud, "Imagine what it is like, being Mr. Pee. You are thinking you are an adult, you look like an adult, but people treat you like a piglet. I just look into his eyes, and see a profound longing. Longing to be tested."

Rita stooped down to give Mr. Pee some corn relish. "But maybe his fears are too great to speak of. Maybe fears are always stronger than hopes. I kinda identify with Mr. Pee." Mr. Pee just looked her in the eye, ignoring the relish. He was hardly breathing, so caught up in the moment was he.

After a bit more pondering over Mr. Pee's existential predicament, Rita observed, "Of course maybe inside you are a dumb chicken Mr. Pee. Maybe you should sit in the back of the bus...maybe you're not the smartest pig in the world, maybe not the best looking and sensitive pig. Maybe you're not the brightest bulb in the circuit, no, maybe inside you're just a dumb chicken who got the wrong suit of clothes.."

Pokey objected, "Don't be telling him that stuff, Rita. Mr. Pee can always see beyond the surface, even if you can't see it the same!"

Rita didn't say anything more, feeling the pointlessness of it all. Somewhere in her short life she had missed the train to adulthood. Here she was standing by the station, with a one-way ticket to eternity. All dressed up and no where to go. She thought she might grow crazy before her eighteen months were up.

Life at Lost Grove Motors was a world apart. From time to time visitors from the real world would stop by. Once in a while there would be a friend of Aunt Sarah, or a customer who would look twice, when she would enter the garage. Usually the bibs that Rita had on were not too fresh, and with no makeup, Rita felt she was in camouflage, safe from sexual predators. "Still, though," she thought, "most of the local yokels probably are harmless."

Or at least it seemed so that morning at Lost Grove Motors. Mr. Pee wandered slowly around the yards, making a circular tour, just like she had seen Pokey pacing in the night. Sarah wondered if he were just burnt out. Or maybe she had been too critical.

Pokey came in from his walk, got the bible tracts, and offered that he thought Mr. Pee was still highly depressed. Pokey thought Mr. Pee might even be suicidal. "I mean, how do you know?" All I go on is his body language. Seems to me every muscle is saying,

"Nem akarook huzza mene, that's Hungarian for I don't want to leave the Party. My mother taught me that," laughed Pokey.

He bent down, "Is that what's the matter, Mr. Pee. Huh guy? Do you need a fresh scene?" Mr. Pee's eyelids fluttered, his ears pitched forward to quickly capture this Kodak moment. Bright eyes met bright eyes.

A moment of calm fell over the confusion of the junkyard. A vine of trust and hope took root, tenuously, in the oily soil. Pokey and Mr. Pee looked at each other and smiled in recognition. They turned to Sarah who was beginning to get uncomfortable. She narrowed her gaze, and strode purposely to the back house, with great works ahead for the day.

Sunday, September 4th

Pokey was up early organizing his "twilights." That's what he called the cat paws that he cut from various road kills he had come across. Like ceremonial scalps or voodoo fetishes, his costume with the cat paws often elicited profound reactions from many passersby. Mostly disgust, but sometimes it was simple fascination.

Once in Walleye, Wisconsin, Pokey had been put in jail when he parked his trike right in front of the Assembly of God church. The minister told him the church showers in town were broken. Pokey was put in jail. He was let out the next morning after breakfast, after showering, just in time to get over to the church parking lot.

So Pokey was there to greet God's workers after church as they came to their cars, "Jesus Christ wants to Love you, if you'll just open your hearts and accept Him. He's waiting right now. Here's a free valuable tract called, "Riches in your own back Yard." Can you spare a buck to help me on my way? God loves you as I do. Yes sir, just spreading the Lord's Word!"

"Could you help me find a shower? I need to be on my way." The children of God in their Sunday best did not like the idea of Pokey with his "twilights" coming home to use their baths. Pokey knew also that county seats usually had Departments of Social

Service that would automatically give him food vouchers and traveling money, just to get him to the next county down the line.

It wasn't much of a living, but he was on his own, and he could travel. No one could tell him what to do. Pokeyman was not a dreamer of better worlds, and never, never complained. So what if all the church showers were frozen up. Spring was coming, and the streams would be clean, though pretty cold. Life in the open was not depressing, particularly with a friend like Mr. Pee.

Monday Sept. 5. Cloudy all day Picked apples.

Tuesday Sept. 6. Pokey came back from the dump with two televisions and parts for an aquarium. Aunt Sarah was disappointed. She told Pokeyman to leave the televisions in the spreader, to take back. But the Aquarium parts caught her interest.

"Pokey, that is not an aquarium. That's a bell jar. It's used to draw a vacuum on the inside of the bell. They use these things in labs, I wonder where it came from."

Aunt Sarah took the apparatus into the workshop. She plugged it in, turned the switch, set a dial to one side. Nothing happened. She found a red restart button. Nothing happened. "Must be a limiter setting somewhere. Either that or the motor is shot." They set it near the pile of motors that needed work. Aunt Sarah planned some day to cut the copper wire out of the coils for salvage. Number two copper is over a dollar a pound.

About mid afternoon the sun came out for the first time in several days. The red sumac and yellow birches lighted up the junkyard, heralding the oncoming winter. Aunt Sarah busied about, putting tools away. She showed Pokey how to sharpen her Stilh chain saw with her Dremel tool. It took him about an hour to get it really sharp.

Sarah decided to wait until morning to get in some dead elm from her lower forty, a scrubby wasteland that had been mined over years ago. The soil there was full of rust and sulfur, with an occasional bent piece of iron, sinking into the crust. Along one of the fence lines there were good stands of dead elm. Some massive concrete foundations were all that remained of the Tripoli Mining Company. That and two open shafts in the woods a short distance away.

Sarah had always meant to cover over those shafts, so that people or livestock couldn't fall into them. Once she got so far as to bring home some used barbed wire from the dump, but it never got in place. The shaft was about twelve to fifteen feet square. No one knew for sure how deep it was, perhaps a hundred feet. Throwing in a stone made a splashing noise after a few seconds.

The next morning they had a good breakfast, Aunt Jemima buttermilk pancakes, soaked in butter and homemade maple syrup. Aunt Sarah's maple syrup had a true north woods flavor of pine smoke. Her evaporator was just a fifty gallon barrel inside another barrel. The smoke leaked in everywhere. But the taste came out wonderfully.

They hitched up Alice to the spreader. Pokey got the saw, gas and bar oil, and they were off to the lower forty. In about an hour the spreader was loaded down with choice dead elm, all cut to twenty inch lengths. Give or take an inch.

They unloaded the elm next to Aunt Sarah's trailer house. Rita was careful to line up the front edge of each log so that there appeared an even straight edge to the whole pile. The new logs all had bright clean-cut ends, contrasting with last year's remainder. It took a little more time, but Rita thought it was worth it. The winter's supply of dry wood was self evident and comforting with its sense of order.

Aunt Sarah's collection of vehicles had been growing year by year. She would acquire a van or trailer, set up camp in it, and then start stuffing it with her finds. Soon it would be full, and it would be time to get another trailer. She had three abandoned trailer homes filled with treasures from the dump. Most of the piles had not been disturbed for many years. A box elder sapling had grown up in front of one of the doors.

Her present nest was approaching its fullness, affording little space to turn around. Thoreau's cabin, in contrast, would be spacious. Sarah had converted a Construction company's tool trailer into her little home. It had but one Lazyboy, next to a microwave and a small television. Piles of books, boxes of books, all stacked with papers and old food cartons. A bouquet of dried yellowish flowers stood in the window overlooking a yard full of depreciation. In the corner was a Remington 22.

Sarah had gotten a good deal on some Dow styrofoam sheet ends that she had nailed over the outside of the tool wagon. Inside, she put down a floor of two layers of styrofoam with plywood on top. At an auction she was able to pick up some shag carpet samples that she stapled down in a crazy quilt fashion that would make a Sufi proud.

While Rita was stacking her wood, Pokey and Sarah were busy mouse proofing her cabin. The previous winter Sarah had had a major problem with fleas coming in on the backs of little three toed moles. Sarah bought extra traps and kept score on the wall. One hundred and eighty-eight moles caught. It was only the end of September, and they were already coming indoors.

Things were out of hand, clearly. Pokey crawled under the trailer to look for holes in the sub floor. When he would find one, he'd give a victory yell and squirt in Great Stuff®, an aerosol foaming sealant. Pokey took the Great Stuff to the woodshed to see if Mr. Pee's box could be insulated better. Rita could hear him puttering about the shed, even in the dead of night. She made a mental note to ask Pokey what in the dickens he was doing up so late.

Saturday morning dawned peacefully. Pokey left early for town to see what he could find in the Walmart dumpsters. Rita heard Pokey leave, and decided to stay in her sleeping bag drifting in and out of daydreams. Far from nightmares, she wandered in her dreams from oasis to oasis. In the back of the school bus she dreamed of a Victorian A. J. Downing Gothic revival masterpiece. It was strange . . . a small dwelling that had a huge two story baronial hall, dark leather walls embossed and gilded. She knew it was a special place, a place where everything was organized, filed, and sorted. She found her way to the kitchen, passing through a modern day butler's pantry. She noted a bottle of rye whiskey on the counter. Suddenly she awoke to the sound of Pokey nailing his fox paws to the side of the shed.

She crawled out of her sack, stretched, and sat back down, wondering what was worth doing on this her free day. Aunt Sarah was still working in the garage machine shop, turning out a brake drum that she hoped to convert to a hydraulic piston. Her first three all failed when they got heated up. So Aunt Sarah was using a different brass alloy to make rings that would not burn up in service.

Rita told Aunt Sarah that she was going down to the creek to bathe, and "maybe catch a few rays." She took along a book on "Physical Properties of High Temperature System Analysis", by Ludwig Von Bertalance. Something to read while sun bathing.

She took her time getting into the stream, checking it out for any signs of snakes. Seeing none, she folded her kimono neatly in thirds and set it precisely on the middle of a rock at the bank's edge, and tested the stream with her toe. She grabbed her toothbrush and in she went, walking to her favorite spot, a rocky island in the middle of the stream. Laying herself down in the sun, she began applying sun block to her whole body, slowly and thoroughly, even into her scalp. Skin cancer was not going to be her fate if she could help it. She looked down at her calves and saw that she was going to have to begin shaving her legs. "Oh well", she thought, "who's going to notice anyway. I haven't put on a dress since I came here."

She turned on her stomach and opened her book to chapter six, Catalytic conversion theory. She scanned the text, not really understanding the jargon, but every once in a while something would make sense, and she would mutter, "Yeah, OK, got it." Still, the sun was hot on her back, and she was getting bored. So she closed the book, not bothering to put in a bookmark.

She closed her eyes and drifted away, listening to the sounds of the wild life. Somewhere in the distance she could hear a tractor. Maybe it was Alice, maybe Aunt Sarah was taking a trip to the dump. Should she go back on top to see? No, it was Saturday, and if Sarah needed help, she could ask Pokey.

She closed her eyes and was just about to go back to the Gothic Mansion, when she was startled by the sound of cow shit hitting the ground. A small herd of Brown Swiss had noiselessly appeared on the opposite bank. The cows were all in a row, all gazing at her nakedness. Rita looked at them, wondering what thoughts they were having, if any. What concerns did they have? Were they fulfilled? Was the nice ABS man kind to them? Or did he abuse them? Did they enjoy the abuse? Did they ask for it?

The cows didn't volunteer any answers and Rita drifted back to sleep, thinking it was their fault because they were a brown Swiss study. A cloud came across the sun giving temporary relief, relief that invited her to slip back into the stream that now seem a lot colder than before. She sat motionless with her chin just below the water. Birds flew down for a drink and a bath. A large blue heron flew by looking for trout. She had bathed both her body and her mind down at the creek. She dunked her head down under, and came up spitting water and laughing to herself. She decided to go back to the bus and see if Sarah needed any help. She was bored.

Sarah didn't need any help. She had sent Pokey on Alice to the dump. Rita looked at the vacuum bell jar and asked Sarah, "That bell jar, did you ever figure out what its trouble is?" Sarah grunted, "I'll get to it one of these days."

Rita looked at the base unit and the glass dome, "This glass is gross! She sprayed Lestoil cleaner on the spots of grease and gray talc. She could see that under it all, the apparatus looked like stainless steel with some painted parts. There were dials and three gauges on the side panel, all in German. It took almost a full roll of paper towels to get the dome to sparkle.

"Why don't you let me see if I can fix it, Aunt Sarah? You already have plenty to do." Rita picked up the dome and put it on the counter next to the testing bench. "Aunt Sarah, can you help me move this box of stuff, whatever it is?"

"Rita, that stuff is a good set of plumbers tools for working with pipe. See this one? It's the cutter. It's adjustable so you can cut up to two and a half inch pipe. This here is one of the threading dies and this is the reamer. Some day I'll show you how they work."

Sarah and Rita looked for an empty spot for the plumbing tools. Rita suggested that they be put under the pipe stand. Sarah went along with it all, and they lifted the base deck of the bell jar up onto the test counter.

Rita turned the unit on its side to get at the bolts holding the foot pads to the base. It was a clever way to attach the shroud and protect the motor. Soon Rita needed better light. She got a stepladder and hung a double shop light right over her bench.

Sarah closed the hood on the Chevy Malibu and sauntered over to look at the apparatus. Together they tried to analyze how it worked. Sarah was impressed with Rita's diagnostic skills, "Did you study this at St. Theresa's?"

"No, except in junior year Physics we had some simple experiments, but mostly they taught us the formulae they expected us to have down pat for the ACT's. The stuff wasn't very practical or interesting. But as a kid, I remember my Dad in his workshop. I remember it smelling really bad. He should have had it vented better," continued Rita. "He would bring home some of the failures from the Dow labs, and experiment with them. He worked with so many different projects, from Styrofoam to Gel breast implants. When he died he was working on two top secret projects for the Homeland Security Department."

"I knew he was into something big when the FBI woman paid a visit here ten years ago," said Sarah. "He never had much contact with me over the years. I guess he was too busy to smell the flowers. Too wrapped up in his work. Or maybe he didn't want your mother to see how I live."

"Do you suppose it runs in the family? I mean, look at you. You are always ready to take on another project, to puzzle over the next piece of junk you find at the dump. When is your next vacation? Hmm?"

Sarah looked at her stonily and said quietly, "When you're older you'll know better. Besides, machines don't lie. They don't fake anything. They are what they are. They don't take your credit card, and they don't get drunk every Saturday night and then expect some hot action. No, No. Machines are a girl's best friend! Remember that," laughed Sarah.

Sarah and Rita huddled over the circuit board, looking for shorts. Everything checked out, but it still blew the circuit breaker every time they switched it on. Sarah stuck her forefinger and thumb in her mouth to moisten them, and set the tester probes aside. She touched both the green ground wire and the black, then the white. "Hey, that's not right. The ground is hot."

"Someone has re-wired this switch, and gotten the wires crossed, this white wire should be colored green." Rita, now project manager, went to the bus and got a green magic marker to color the wire green. With only a little difficulty she corrected the power cord connection to the circuit board.

As she went to plug it in she said, "Now with a little luck, this should work if the transformer isn't shot." She flicked on the switch and the panel lit up. "Looks good! Should work. Maybe it's an Ebay item. Something like this may have antique value. What do you think? Antique German Vacuum apparatus, 1930s, still works. $300 or best offer?

"Nah," said Sarah. "People will think you use it for cleaning your rugs. Like a Kirby or Electrolux. Say, instead, Nazi era SS lab equipment, Rare. And start it at $1000.00 But you better make sure it works. Otherwise it will come back to haunt you."

Rita thought a moment, "How about War Department Torture device. Useful and handsome. Helps keep neighbors away."

"Nah, the Nazi is the best."

"Well, I'm going to keep it for a while, if you don't mind, Ma'am. I'll go to Google and search under games and toys, plus vacuum."

"Yeah, go ahead, but first it's your turn to do something about supper."

Rita turned off the work light, "So what would taste good to you?
Sarah opened another beer, tossing the cap toward the junk barrel. "I don't care, surprise me."

Rita went to the lean to and opened the freezer and looked over the options. Lots of sweet corn. Side Pork. Beans, tomato relish, frozen morels. She thought for a while, "What can I do different with sweet corn? I know, I'll make corn cakes, or corn crepes and layer them with tomato and cheese, like a pizza!"

An hour later Pokey showed up with a bright orange lily for the center of the table. Rita served up the fried side pork with the corn cakes and maple syrup. The cheese and tomato topping had browned nicely.

Sarah wiped her face with a clean shop cloth and sat down at the makeshift table. "So what do you call this? Is it a cake? Soufflé? Fritter? Or maybe a pie?" Rita thought a moment, "Garbage au graten, con carne."

Pokey got up, "I gotta be going. Pork kind of turns me off, if you know what I mean. Need to check on Mr. Pee. He's been alone all day." The door slammed shut.

Aunt Sarah spoke up, "Rita don't you know nuttin'? Pokey would have eaten with us except you insisted on putting pork on your pizza, or what ever you call it."

"I'm sorry, I didn't think...I'll make it up to him somehow."

"Yeah, you didn't think. Trouble is, you know not, that you know not! And how can you know anything about real people. You only can see out of your eyes, eyes that are afraid to be real, eyes that should see beyond the surface. I don't know, Rita, but the way you're going, all your troubles stack up to be other people's fault! What you are going to get will be what you deserve."

"But, but...Dad's death was an accident waiting to happen. And mom's death was an accident that could have been prevented. Dad had been drinking. It wasn't God's fault, was it? And it's not my fault that I'm alone." Rita was breathing heavily and her eyes began to burn. "How would you know anyway, Aunt

Sarah. Seems to me that you've never really given of yourself to anyone, never risked anything." Rita's nose was soon running.

Sarah watched silently, then tossed a shop rag at Rita, "Rita, I've just about done everything twice in my life, and I'm not over with it yet. I don't wear my heart on my sleeve, and I don't collect merit badges. Get it? I don't need. This time the cap made it into the trash can perfectly. "I need to get some air." The door slammed.

Rita wiped her eyes and blew her nose. She folded the shop rag into thirds, then into a triangle, and tossed it into the laundry basket. She made a mental note to remember Monday was laundry day.

After wiping out the dishes, Rita left the porch, slamming the door, just in case anyone was near by.

Pokey was spending some quality time with Mr. Pee. He heard the doors slamming, and wondered if something were wrong. He felt a little sorry for Mr. Pee. Because all there was for supper was some corn bread mix from the Walmart dumpster. Pokey vowed to get some fresh fruit for Mr. Pee, the next time he got to town.

Sarah hiked toward the twin bridges, then turned off on the old railroad right of way. The moon rose full in the east just as the crickets started to chirp. A few moments later, the lightning bugs lazily began their dance. Sarah sat down on the old railroad trestle, thinking about Rita. Thinking about her own past loves, past mistakes, past successes. Looking down at the swirling stream she could see little footprints in the mud and sand bar. She straightened up and took a deep breath, "At least she hasn't stolen anything from me yet. And neither has the Jesus freak."

Looking downstream the waters disappeared around the bend. A fallen tree in the water had gathered a pile of brush, a mish mash of flotsam. Mostly dead branches, laced with Styrofoam packing beads, bits of charred wood and an upturned Pepsi can. Clues to the end of an era. Or was it the beginning, Sarah decided not to leave her beer can for future paleontologists to discover.

Instead, coming home Sarah scouted the other side of Twin Bridge Road, picking up about a dozen cans. It was a worthwhile hike.

On coming into the cabin yard, Sarah met Pokey with Mr. Pee, "Did you get something to eat Pokey?"

"No Ma'am, and that's OK. Tomorrow I'll get some corn from the field next door for Mr. Pee and me. I checked it last week and it was almost ready. Mr. Pee is waiting for me, I gotta go. We've decided we need a good bath in the creek. So if you see Rita, tell her not to bother us, OK?"

As the gate shut, Sarah instructed Pokey to smash the cans in the barrels in the morning.

Pokey turned into the path that led down the side of the cliff to the stream, Mr. Pee ran ahead full speed. The moon was full and overhead, casting dark shadows under the pine trees. Mr. Pee waded out into the middle of the stream and ducked under the water, blowing bubbles, snorting, and giggling. Coming up on the island, Mr. Pee could smell where Rita had been sun bathing a few hours earlier. He shook the water out of his ears, and sat down to watch Pokey lather up at the creek's edge.

Pokey took his time shaving there in the moonlight, feeling for rough spots on his neck. He remembered his mother saying, "Pokey, we may be dumb and poor, but we don't have to be clean." Pokey laughed at the memory of his mother's joking around. Satisfied with his smooth face, he waded in and sat in the chilly water, splashing his face. Still naked, he sat down next to Mr. Pee on the island rock.

"Tomorrow I'll get us some real good corn, some of that butter and eggs kind. Remember how good it was last year?"

Mr. Pee nodded and sighed, "Yeah..." Mr. Pee was a connoisseur of corn. He agreed with the deer in the area, that the best tasting corn came from the Amish fields, because they generally didn't use chemical sprays.

Monday dawned right on time. There was almost a chill in

the air, with fog down in the valley. Rita was the first up and the first to speak. "Sorry about my stupid mistake, Pokey, I forgot you didn't like pork."

"Its OK, I just can't do it. I can't bear the taste of most meats, it makes me want to throw up. And besides, how do you think I can look in Mr. Pee.'s face. You might as well ask me to eat your cat or dog, I don't see any difference."

"Well, my corn cakes were pretty good, if'n I say so mah self...You can try them without the side pork. The maple syrup is great on 'em."

"I gassed up Alice for the trip to the hangers. Is boss lady up yet? I haven't seen her." Pokey checked the toolbox in the spreader to be sure there were enough trash bags.

Rita walked over to Sarah's trailer door and knocked. She knocked again, louder. "Aunt Sarah?" She banged her fist against the aluminum door, and there were sounds of movement. "Hurry up, we're ready to go."

Sarah was far from bushy tailed, "You go on, Pokey can take Alice OK. Don't forget the baskets at the Pepsi machines. Me, I'm not feeling so hot, check with me later."

Rita and Pokey were soon on their way. First stop, the cornfield where they "harvested" three or four dozen ears of butter 'n eggs. It was still early and no one was up as they went by Helgeson's egg farm. First stop, the airport.

Pokey pulled up to the dumpster behind the field office and began packing the trash into the spreader, keeping the aluminum and glass separate. Meanwhile Rita was filling the washing machine with water from the airport hydrant. All the hangers were closed but the World's End Corporate Hanger, where several executives were boarding their shuttle.

One of the World's End buyers came over to the Pepsi machine by the field office, the same place where Rita had first met Aunt Sarah. Rita was just finishing up putting a new bag into the trashcan, when the man gave her a bag of trash from the Tri-star. "Hi, ya got room for some more," handing Rita his garbage bag, neatly tied. Rita noticed that he had no wedding ring.

She had not planned on talking to anyone, and didn't feel like explaining why a nice girl like her was here in the precise middle of nowhere, so she merely grunted a general "Yahsah...right here sir." Rita was imagining she was a servant at Tara, bending her will to the master's whip. She looked up to see if the act was crossing the footlights, but the man was already turning back to the shuttle.

She finished up, throwing the Gulfstream trash and the pop cans into the spreader, thinking about the buyer and what kind a life he would be living. What he did at night in Hong Kong, Milan, Paris? Not married? Was there a reason?

While Pokey was sorting and bagging the snack shop trash, Rita looked into the neatly tied trash from the plane. She remembered Aunt Sarah talking about getting everything you need from the dump. She looked more at the bag, and it seemed to say "open me, I'm pregnant." But then she thought, it's rude to read other peoples mail.

Somehow she missed the old days, when she was only a student, rather than a fully enfranchised adult. She began to mourn a little over not having a graduation ceremony. Maybe she would never feel right about being all growed up.

Soon Pokey fired up Alice, "Yah Ready? Let's roll!" Rita hopped up on Alice's fender and they were off. They missed Aunt Sarah's tour guiding. Both heard the familiar humming of the engine, Pokey started to whistle a third above the tonic, and Rita added the fifth. She grabbed a screwdriver to tap out a little rhythm on the fender. She kept an eye on the neatly tied bag of trash, now seeming more translucent.

By the time they reached the town dump, both were giggling. Pokey pulled up to the edge of the cliff and turned Alice off. Together they unloaded the spreader in record time. Rita checked the dumpsters for Ebay items. She paused by a case of unopened paint. "Pokey, come here a minute, what do you think about this paint?"

Pokey looked it over, "I don't know, chrome oxide green...it looks pretty old. What would you use it for?"

Rita thought a moment, "well it's got to be worth something. Maybe we should paint the outhouse!"

"You're elected to head the committee," laughed Pokey.

They were just about to leave when a shiny black Dodge pickup pulled in with a lot of boxes. Rita and Pokey busied themselves until the pickup pulled away. Every box was looked into. It was good stuff, "Wow look at this," Pokey held up a Geisha girl kimono. "This'll bring thousands!"

"Nah it won't. Maybe $50.00 if you're lucky. But it is worth taking, and it looks clean."

One of the boxes had videotapes, and dirty magazines. Pokey soon was adding them to the haul. "What do you want with them," asked Rita.

"They'll bring plenty on Ebay. You wait and see. The Lord giveth and the Lord taketh. Where there's shame and guilt, there's money!" Rita started thinking how to describe the lot.

"I've never seen dirty movies. I remember some of the girls at school talked about them. My friend Emma told me she had a lesbian tape that was real different. She never showed it to me though. And I guess, maybe, for me I'm not that curious about life on the other side of the fence. When it's the right time, I'll be more than ready. I've got four years or more of college facing me, if I ever get out of here! Time to channel myself. Time to not get burdened down with dependency issues."

"You know Pokey, you and I have a lot in common...we've both been kind of abandoned. And if you are like me, when you are on the bottom, in the pits as it were, when there is no hope of a way out, or a way home, when you're totally lost, when your bread crumbs run out, when it's dark and cold... when the telephone call doesn't come in from the Warden, then miraculously, we can get reborn. And we can go on...learn by doing as they say."

"Its your choice whether you give up and accept defeat. Me?

I'm not ready for the betrayal game, not yet. It's OK to be naive when you're young. A bit of innocence is a sometime thing. Why not enjoy it? I'll be a spent hen soon enough, so, as far as I'm concerned, you can call me...Constant Hope, the purest ingenue... chaste...with purity untarnished."

Pokey didn't follow Rita's meandering logic, but volunteered nonetheless, "Well. Rita, hopefully if you're going to act virginal, you'll get what you deserve. I'd suggest you just keep to the side of the road like me."

Rita agreed. It was smart to be safe in the slow lane. The future could jolly well stay put. For now, the sun went under the clouds and a chilly wind nudged them on. They left the township dump with only a little more than they came with.

For Rita and Pokey scavenging was becoming a weekly habit, a team sport, thrilling and always novel and entertaining. It was a game with no ante and lots of wild cards. Soon Alice was purring along the ridge road on the way home.

Aunt Sarah was gone when they returned. But she had remembered that it was her turn to cook and had left a pot of sloppy joes made with ketchup, onion, beans, tapioca, and a lot of spices. Once the dishes were wiped out, Rita and Pokey took the remains to Pokey's shed for Mr. Pee.

Pokey invited Rita into his little space. It had taken him only a month to convert the milk house into his bunkhouse. He had used some salvage brick to layer the floor. In one corner was a box of clean clothes, and a box of dirty clothes. His sleeping bag was next to Mr. Pee's dog kennel. There were piles of magazines, but everything else was nice and tidy. Rita looked at the heavy curtain over the lone window, "How come you don't let in more light, its dingy and dark in here." Pokey looked down at Mr. Pee. Mr. Pee looked down at the brick. There was a moment of silence, and the words echoed in Pokey's mind. "Dingy and dark. Not right, missing some unknown factors."

He remembered his mother lecturing him, "Pokey, you're special, and better than anyone else at doing what you can do.

Don't ever forget to let others be as good or bad as they want to be. Except for the publickers, never trust the publickers."

"Aren't you going to ask me to sit down," asked Rita.

"Yeah, sure,...I'm sorry, here's a pillow, you can sit here." Pokey put a tasseled, relatively clean pillow on a plastic milk crate. He was feeling awkward with his first visitor.

Rita looked around, noting everything about this alien world. Above Mr. Pee's bed was a collection of dog collars, and in a box nearby were different costumes for fair time. Rita noticed a photo of Pokey's pig tacked up on the wall. Mr. Pee was wearing a little green beret. "That's a neat picture of Mr. Pee. Where was it taken," asked Rita.

"That was two years ago at the Edmonton swine races. Mr. Pee came in second. That's pretty good for a two year old. Pokey reached down and scratched Mr. Pee's back. Mr. Pee closed his eyes for a moment and took a deep breath. "Yes, Mr. Pee...you did good."

Rita noticed music CD's neatly stacked on the concrete ledge of the milk house. Next to the little boom box Pokey had a collection of music CD's that was very different. Mostly country and Western, most had come from the dumpsters at Walmart. "Here, you pick out one," said Pokey handing a Rita a stack. Rita recognized some of the names, and then stopped, "What's this? Dvorak's New World? I'm surprised!"

"Yeah, Mr. Pee likes the largo, it puts him right to sleep. Sometimes it puts us both to sleep."

Soon the boom box was charging forth with the first movement, and Pokey reached over to turn it down, but Rita said, "No, turn it back up Pokey, I need to hear this part nice and loud. Makes me feel good, like we are on a path to somewhere good. Like we'll never run out of sweet corn. That's what Dvorak means to me. Like its bucolic, like around here."

"What's bucolic," asked Pokey.

"It means to do with cows, I think," said Rita.

"Well then, why should Mr. Pee like it so much?"

"I don't know, maybe his DNA is screwed up. Maybe he's really a cow that got handed the wrong suit getting off Noah's ark. What should he be like? What's on the Porker Hit Parade," laughed Rita. "Maybe Carnival of the Animals? The Trout quintet? Hmm, Peter and the Wolf? Surely one of Beethoven's string quartets has something to say to pigs, maybe Opus. 130 in C flat!" Pokey didn't know what to say.

"Pokey, I just know something good is going to happen. It just has to. It's not right that everything has to be so tough. Winter's coming, and it's going to be cold again. Are you ready for it?"

"I don't think I can stand another winter if its going to be as bad as last year. We're going to have to pull in some more wood." Rita agreed that soon they should replenish the woodpile.

The largo movement came, and all three music lovers nearly went to sleep, being awakened by the kettle drums and trumpets of the final movement. Rita got up, "I've gotta go, I'm going on line, and check our auctions, see you in the morning dude."

Rita visited the green room before crawling into the sack. Before she turned out the light, she summed up her day for the diary, "Did dump duty today with Pokey. Listened to the New World. Saw Mr. Executive at the airport, six months left to my sentence."

Next day Rita and Pokey pulled in some more wood. Rita made sure that Pokey cut it all at twenty inches long, so that the pile would look tidy.

"Why do you want it exactly twenty inches," asked Pokey. "Aunt Sarah takes any size and just piles it outside her door."

"Pokey, I just like to see the pile perfectly stacked, perfectly in line. You know, anything worth doing, is worth doing perfectly. It makes me feel secure when everything is in its place. Order is its own reward. I like the pattern looking at the ends of the logs. You can see a difference between last year's gray ends and this year's bright creamy colored ends."

"So do you agree that anything worth doing is worth doing perfectly," asked Rita.

Pokey thought a minute, "How about music and sex, and maybe poetry?" Maybe with high expectations you're always going to be disappointed. Mama always said, good things never last. She said life's a shit sandwich, and every day you gotta take a bite. It's not so bad, once you get used to it."

"When Mr. Pee and I wake up in the morning, first thing we do is our morning prayers. I ask for forgiveness of all my sins. Mr. Pee always asks that God forgive the publickers. And we give thanks for all the trouble God gives us. They make us stronger."

Rita thought a few moments, "I don't know...can you love God perfectly? What would that mean? That you give up your loneliness, your estrangement? Is anything a perfect answer? What's left? A bunch a gray slop, no blacks no whites, no creamy ends."

Mr. Pee muttered something semi-obscene, "what's wrong with a bit of slop!"

"What's strange meat," asked Pokey.

"Estrangement, means to leave the pack, to be the stranger in a strange land."

"Oh...like Paul before Felix! Or Jesus in the desert."

"No, I think it's more like a castaway who doesn't even know the direction. No map, totally lost. But always there's a longing for coming home. But like they say, you can't come home again."

"Mama always said I was perfectly me no matter what I did."

"I guess that's where we're different. My mother told me the opposite, that I walked like a horse, that I'd never make it in the real world. That no man would want me unless I shaped up. She didn't like my clothes, my music, or my friends."

"My dad was never around," continued Rita, "but at least he liked my music. He was the one that put me at St. Theresa's."

"I gotta remember this," said Pokey taking out his notebook. "It's an idea for my puppet show." Pokey wrote slowly all in capital letters, LOVING GOD IS THE BEGINNING - NOT THE END.

Rita needed to get up and stretch, and get some fresh air. The milk house still faintly smelled of sour milk, now mixed with new and different odors. She was feeling a little claustrophobic. "Come on Pokey, forget about God for a while. Remember after the ecstasy, there's the laundry! I need to wrap the Ebay stuff, you can help."

"Okay, Rita, you can help me too. I need to get rid of the dirty tapes from the dump." Would you list them for me?"

"Well, I suppose I could. Did you look at them?"

"No, not really...well just enough to see if there was anything wrong with them. I mean the tapes, not the girls! Them girls... nothing wrong with them, Whew! Who wouldn't want to walk barefoot over some of them?"

"What in the world does that mean? Come on, I'll list them for you, but don't tell Aunt Sarah. She might not understand."

It took longer than they expected to pack up the Ebay stuff. Pokey enjoyed finding just the right size box for every item. Together they found ways to make their job easier. Odd shaped items were first put in a plastic bag, then Great Stuff expanding foam was squirted into the corners of the packing box. While the foam was setting up, they would gently set the item in place. After the bottom had cured, they did the same for the top packing. It was a perfect job. Rita was pleased.

After supper Rita and Pokey went on line, listing more video recorders, pressed glass, and the VHS tapes. "How many tapes are there Pokey," asked Rita.

"I've got thirty-eight. Mostly cheap ones. Mostly for young guys, mostly hetero. One was so awful I dropped it in the green room. Saved me the bother of burning it. To think they would do that to a pig. Its inhumane!"

"Well, what do you want to say? Erotic masterwork collection? Or just dirty tapes," asked Rita.

"How about five tapes banned in Sodom, banned in Gemorah?" suggested Pokey.

"Monica's top Favorites, Congressional Two Party Fun XXX?"

"T & A, can we swing with you? Year round spasms galore."

Rita started giggling, "Sin now, before you loose it...naw, I think Monica's top five favorites will do nicely."

"How about Martha Stewart's perfect jailhouse combo?"

"Or Bad moves for Good Girls. Or Miss Goody two shoes, gets fitted?" Pokey gave up, laughing, "OK, you post them, I'll box them up. Then I think I'll take Mr. Pee down to the creek for a swim. Remember, Mr. Pee doesn't like peeping Tom's! OK?

Rita was amused at Pokey's modesty. It wasn't a bad thing she thought. "After all", she thought, "I'm no Madonna either."

She finished up the listings and was about to add the vacuum bell jar apparatus from Germany. She thought she should at least try it out to see if it worked. She plugged it in and the motor began its steady pulsing, drawing the air out of the glass jar. The gauges were starting to top out when the pulsing stopped. "Hmm, I wonder if this thing really is working." She made a mental note to ask Aunt Sarah for advice.

Down at the river Mr.. Pee was happy as a pig in mud. The recent dry spell lowered the water level exposing the muddy banks. Here and there water had been left in shallow pools, now warm in the late afternoon sun. Mr. Pee found a deep pool in the shade, and wallowed as only a pig can. He closed his eyes to better enjoy the mud bath. Even his tail rejoiced and twitched ecstatically.

Pokey sat in the sun on the little island. The slow moving water was clear enough that he could watch the trout in their hole next to the rocky ledge of the island. He absent-mindedly dropped bits of bark to watch the trout rise up and return into the shadows. The sun warmed his body and he rolled on his back and almost fell asleep. The breeze caressed his body. He caressed his body. The sun warmed his heart.

Looking at the creek bank Pokey noticed little hand prints in the mud. Lots of them. "Hey Pee, looks like there's been a little partying going on here. Mr. and Miss Coon have been out courting it looks like. Maybe they're going steady. Who knows? I'll bet in the moonlight Miss Coon can look pretty good, if you're lookin' for a hot smelly romp. Maybe after eating worms and a dead frog or two, Yum Yum," laughed Pokey, "why, what kind of guy wouldn't get turned on?"

Mr. Pee found a low branch to scratch his back. The caked mud came off in bits and pieces, and soon he was back in the creek, cleaning up. Pokey waded back to his little pile of clean clothes. "Come on Mr. Pee, supper should be ready."

Rita and Pokey waited for Aunt Sarah who had gone to town to get parts. When she hadn't returned by eight o'clock they went ahead and ate leftover pizza, some pickles, applesauce, and cottage cheese. It was normal for Aunt Sarah to be on her own schedule.

Pokey retired to write down his great thoughts in his journal, while Rita was back in her bus listening to late night BBC radio. The constant murmuring about suicide bombers helped put her to sleep.

Five

By noon the next day Rita and Pokey had their packages ready to ship. Rita used her cell phone to call for UPS pick up. It seemed like too much bother to take Alice and the spreader all the way into the Murray Bay post office, just to save a few pennies.

Sarah finished up timing the S-10, which was now ready for the road, except for a missing tail light assembly.

By four o'clock Rita and Pokey were getting tired of waiting. Even Mr. Pee had a very bored demeanor, just meandering around the yard, occasionally sniffing wet spots. Pokey observed, "You know Rita, if one of us got a driver's license, we could save time, and maybe some shipping charges by going into town."

"Yes, I know, I thought of that too. Why don't you have a license? You drive Alice just fine."

"Yeah, I know. When I was with the Riddles, I learned to drive pretty good out in their fields. But they never let me go on the roads cause they couldn't get insurance for me, because I was a state at large case. And after they moved me from the Riddles, to the Norris Foundation no one trusted me. But I can show you what I know, Rita!"

"Oh, I don't know...I've never needed to drive, being in the city, we always had the bus, or Dad would send a company driver to pick me up. But it doesn't look too complicated."

Sarah wasn't sure, but she thought she had a driver's manual, if she could just find it. Together the three started to go through the piles of magazines in the garage office. Once in a while they set aside issues of the Post if they were in good condition. Rita tied bundles of magazines, parts books, catalogs, invoices, and cancelled checks from years ago. She found the account book for Lost Grove Motors on the bottom of the last pile. She paged through the numbered pages to the last entry, Jan. 10, 1931,

Received. On A. Harry Hutchinson $12.00,

Sarah was sure the manual was somewhere, but it wasn't

coming up. She instructed Rita, "First you gotta take the written test, Rita, then the driver's road test. The next time we're in town, stop at Sheriff Hermanson's house. That's where they give the test, right in his kitchen. That's the benefit of small town life. Things are easier to get done. I imagine Stevie has cooled off by now!"

Aunt Sarah found the Driver's Manual along with some unopened mail from years ago. One letter from Oklahoma City immediately got her attention. "Now there's a voice from the past." She opened it and Rita noticed Sarah's lip quivering. She wasn't sure, but thought she had a tear in her eye. "What is it Aunt Sarah," asked Rita.

"It's a letter from a doctor I did a lot of work for. We were developing pediatric x-ray programs. It required special equipment that I had to jury rig. Our techniques were written up in the Journals. The doctor used my films and took all the credit. Then she transferred me to proctology. In this letter she asks me if I'd come back to her department. I might have gone back to her, but I doubt it." Aunt Sarah got up to blow her nose.

Rita imagined what she might look like behind the wheel. "Well I'm off to study the rules of the road. See you in the morning."

Pokey and Aunt Sarah talked about the Malibou that was the present project. Pokey agreed to fill the dents with bondex. Aunt Sarah would order the lacquer.

On Friday, a week later, Aunt Sarah and Pokey dropped Rita at Sheriff Hermanson's garage. The Sheriff took Rita into his kitchen and gave her the test booklet. "The test is all multiple choice. Read the first example: when two cars approach an intersection at the same time, which vehicle has the right of way? Is it, A, the left one, or B, the Right one?"

"B," answered Rita.

"That's right, so put a mark on the answer sheet on the right answer, B. Make your marks good and black. Fill in the box completely"

"I'll be out in the garage. Come get me when you're finished."

Rita had little trouble figuring out the right answers. Ten

minutes later she took her answer sheet out to the Sheriff who was watching his son wax the squad car. "Steve, this girl thinks she needs to drive a car. Go check her answer sheet. Then get yourself back here and finish the inside of the glass."

Stevie led the way back to the kitchen table. Rita noticed he had a plug of tobacco under his lip. "Let me see how you did', Stevie looked over Rita's answer sheet, "better check number six. If you hit a parked vehicle, A is not the right answer; you should not wait around for the owner to return. Law says you must leave a note with your identity. The computer only allows five mistakes. If you get more than that wrong, you'll have to wait one month before taking the test again."

Rita had only one more wrong answer. Sheriff Hermanson explained her error. On a divided highway a school bus with blinking lights does not require traffic to stop, either way.

"So, sheriff, how soon can I take my road test?" asked Rita. My Aunt can lend me one of her cars."

"Well you have to practice drive with a registered driver. You must come here with a registered driver when you take your test. As you probably know your Aunt does not have a license anymore. You'll have to find someone else to bring you."

Rita gave Stevie her twenty dollars and got a temporary learner's permit good for six months. She considered asking for a receipt, but thought better of it. She noticed Stevie pocket her money.

Next day, Saturday, began with chilly clouds, and brisk winds right out of the north. Rita found herself bored.

"Pokey let's take the afternoon off and hike back to the springs past the lower forty" suggested Rita. "Aunt Sarah told me a story of an early trading post that burned down long ago. She said only the Hudson's Bay Company could trade with the Indians. The Indians were used to getting water from the spring that flowed year round in a grove of oaks. So Hudson's Bay built their trading post close by. They called the place Council Hill because all the tribes in the area came together there to make treaties with the whites."

After about an hour of hiking along rock branch creek, they found the site. Clear water came out of a crevice in the rock bluff. They sat on the old foundation wall, looking down into the old basement. There had been a root cellar that was still there. Rita and Pokey stepped gingerly over the fallen joists and roofing and went down into the vaulted rock chamber. It was dark and humid.

"Look here," Pokey said, pointing to rusted metal framework. "It's a kerosene cook stove, a three burner." As he touched it the rusted frame and the metal crumbled to the floor. On the vaulted ceiling were heavy iron hooks with points filed sharp. Also on the ceiling were fragile stalactites of lime.

There was a shallow niche on the backside of the root cellar where more junk had been left. Two large gallon jugs and some flower pots caught Rita's eye. "Hey Pokey, those pots might bring something on Ebay...what do you think?"

Pokey reached down to pick one up and stepped back quickly, "snakes!" he warned.

Rita was first out of the root cellar, "I hate snakes!"

"Yeah, even these little guys have venom just like their mom and dad. They are born live, so the mom can't be far away."

"Well Pokey, let's not wait to see, we've got work to do. Let's get movin' on."

Pokey wasn't through with snakes. "I see a lot of snakes dead on the roads I travel. You get to know them pretty well. Generally they want to get a way to safety, just like us. But they also like a regular meal."

Pokey went on at length talking about a house that belonged to the Erbach family, Mrs. Riddle's mother's people. The house was known to have a snake problem. But no one could figure why. A part of the house had been built of squared logs. When the house was enlarged, the pioneers sided over the log portion. Over the years the siding rotted next to the ground, allowing mice and gophers to crawl into the walls.

"So what happened was that the attic crawl space became

home to a very large colony of bats. It was a safe, warm space for the bats to raise their young. Once at dusk Mrs. Erbach counted the number of bats emerging from just one hole in the siding near the chimney. Twenty-eight per minute! Adding in the streams of bats coming out of two other gaps and hollows, they estimated, that during the day, that one attic hosted over a thousand bats."

"Sounds like it was hanging room only!" quipped Rita. "Well, at least they probably didn't have a problem with mosquitoes!"

"But wait, there's more!" Pokey continued "Somehow over the years some snakes followed the gophers into the space between the logs and the siding and from there up into the attic where they had no trouble getting to the bats. For years and years the Erbachs kept killing the snakes when they found them in the yard, but more kept coming back to feast on the bats.

"That's mother nature for you!" observed Rita.

The two spent the rest of the afternoon picking watercress from the springs. Pokey pointed out all the different paw and hoof prints along the bank. They sat in the sun for a while, not saying anything, looking across the valley at some deer approaching an old apple tree. They watched the deer, not moving, hardly breathing.

Pokey whispered, "look how they seem...unsteady...like they're drugged. You know, those deer are drunk. Drunk from eating those half spoiled apples on the ground."

As they followed the fence line, a few large cow pies tipped off Pokey that there was some bigger game to be had.

Aunt Sarah had learned over the years that cows occasionally turned up in the woods behind the airport, She found that the Hare Krishnas owned the old cranberry farm where they milked about a dozen Holsteins to supply their mission temple in Montreal. Feeding the poor was one of their most important missions.

The Hare Krishna's farm also operated as a drug recovery facility. Being pure of heart, the devotees couldn't bear killing their cattle, or even selling them for slaughter. There evolved thus a clever moral strategy. The Hare Krishna's decided to not repair the fence at the end of the woods. That way it wouldn't be their fault if an occasional cow, on her own initiative, wandered off. Therefore Pokey and Rita were not surprised when walking home along twin bridge creek, they found a Holstein down on her side, still breathing. Rita knelt down, and stroked the cow's forehead.

"In pace, requiescat" soothed Rita.

"What? What's pa say?

"That's what the priest says when he gives you your last rites. It's God's way of making it easier for us to enter his kingdom. Mozart wrote it into his Requiem.

The cow's gaze was dim, and Pokey seemed to get a far away look in his eye also. He looked down again at Rita and noticed a small tear running down her cheek.

He knelt down next to her and put his arm over her shoulder saying, "There, she's gone. Her work is over."

"What should we do with her Pokey...who wants a dead cow?" asked Rita.

"Well it's not our cow. You did your part, you gave her your blessing, and the Hare Krishna's may have done the same. Have faith! God will make room for her spirit, just the same as He will for us."

"But what will happen to her body?"

Pokey pointed upward. "Look up. Have you ever seen turkey vultures?" There were two large black birds lazily circling above. "Nature will provide. Look, the flies are already laying their little maggots in her eyes."

"Pokey, we gotta get going. It'll be dark by the time we get home. And Aunt Sarah will be wondering where we are."

Pokey picked up the watercress and they followed the fence line, broken as it was, until they reached twin bridge road. An hour later they arrived back at Lost Grove motors.

As they approached the garage, Aunt Sarah was just saying good-bye to some women with a Ford Bronco. They wanted to know how much it would cost to fix their air conditioning. They seemed satisfied with Sarah's advice, to leave it alone. As they were going, Aunt Sarah called Rita over and explained to the women that Rita needed some help with taking her driver's road test.

Rita explained that it would take an hour or less if Sheriff Hermanson was in a good mood. They agreed to return on Friday. Rita was thankful, and gave them some watercress to take with them. Aunt Sarah appreciated the gesture as much or more than the Bronco ladies. She thought to herself that this young charge might amount to something after all.

It was Pokey's turn to cook supper. He gathered some eggs from the henhouse and fashioned a unique peanut butter, egg drop soup, with cress. Sarah thought it needed some white wine. Rita wondered if cranberries might help. There was no agreement, but all had second helpings, and there was still enough for Mr. Pee.

During supper they watched the news on Sarah's old black and white Sony. "Why don't you hook up one of your colored sets?" asked Rita. Sarah just sighed, "I've got more important things to do Rita. Besides all the news is bad anyway. Why make it any worse than it is?"

Rita argued. "If you could see it better, it wouldn't be so frightening. "Doesn't fear come from the unknown?"

Pokey had to get into the discussion, "No! I don't think either of you has it right. It's just about change. Yes change is scary, but life without change is scarier! I think the trick is to not loose your grip on the thread that ties it all together. You know Rita, it's like you were saying about music this afternoon down by the old tavern. You said not to push the river. You were right, God is everywhere. You can't escape. Even if you wanted to."

"OK Pokey, then if God is everywhere, why isn't he doing something to stop wars and killing?"

Pokey looked to see that no one was around, and whispered to Rita and Sarah. "The "answer" is just as my mom said, it's the publickers and all the lawyers. My mom also knew the real story behind the Internal Revenue Service. She knew they were all in cahoots."

Aunt Sarah was about to offer another side, but decided that the debate wasn't going anywhere worth her time. She got up and opened a can of Fosters.

Six

Next day Rita and Pokey took Aunt Sarah's Camry down to the lower forty to practice parallel parking. They set up sawhorses along the fence line, so that Rita could pull up and back into the space. After an hour, Rita felt she had it down.

Coming back to the garage Pokey excused himself to go to the shed to work on his puppet project. He was eager to finish sculpting the puppet head out of the Great Stuff®. Today he was detaching the lower jaw so that the lips could open up. Inside the head, his fingers could animate the whole mouth. As he worked with the lips he devised a plan to connect a small hose to the puppet's mouth.

Rita meanwhile went on line to list pioneer jugs, an Amana Radar Range, and two Video players. Aunt Sarah was off to look at a used sawmill she had heard about. Old Billy D somehow still had his license, and if Sarah didn't mind giving him a shot of Corby's he'd go along for the ride.

Rita cleaned up the test bench, and entered the Ebay items to be shipped on her laptop. Since Pokey had troubles with numbers, and Aunt Sarah was too busy with her own work, Rita had no choice. At least they were doing good on most of the items. The World War I uniforms with the medals brought over $300.00. But two of the repaired video recorders didn't get any bids at all. Rita set them under the bench with the other unsold items. Each package had a number, and was stacked neatly with the front panels all lined up in perfect order.

With that done, she turned on the CBC for the news. On the end of the test bench sat the vacuum jar apparatus. She plugged it in again and turned it on. As it drew the air out of the glass bell, she watch the gauges register -1, -2, -9, -25, then the belt began to smoke. Rita concluded that there might be a leak in the gasket seat. She pressed the little red re-set button and polished the hard rubber plate. She used pumice and then jeweler's rouge until the surface was mirror perfect.

She repeated the process, this time wiping the glass bell jar's seat with White Rose petroleum jelly. She watched the gauges, -1, -2, -4, -25, -36, -49, -64. That was better! But the belt still started to smoke, and she had to shut it off, for it was time to start supper.

She started with eggs, added pancake flour, and fresh tomatoes. She looked at the mixing bowl, it looked vaguely unappealing. Dried parsley helped. She added sliced Colby cheese. Decided against onions, opted for celery.

Last question, should the mixture be baked in a loaf pan, or fried in a skillet? Rita decided on frying the "crepes au jour" in Aunt Sarah's No. 10 cast iron skillet.

When Aunt Sarah hadn't returned by seven, Rita went to get Pokey from his puppet project. "Supper Time!" called Rita. She peered into the woodshed to see that Pokey was in the middle of adding skin to the puppet's face. He was using a spray plastic material.

"What's that stuff, Pokey?" asked Rita.

"It's tool dip. It was invented for dipping tool handles into. Comes in seven colors plus clear. This here is the clear aerosol. I'm going to see if I can paint it later." It should be pretty neat! Lifelike."

"Well, we'll see. It's time for supper. I'm ready to eat." Pokey told Mr. Pee to be patient, that he'd bring his dinner back in just a bit. Mr. Pee appeared to pout.

Rita had just gotten started with frying her crepes du jour, when Aunt Sarah and Billy D. returned. Rita had plenty of batter, so a place was set for Billy D.

Billy smelled like a distillery. In addition there was a strong smell of kerosene. He smelled old. Rita kept on cooking while trying not to breathe when near him.

Billy and Sarah were still talking about the auction and the sawmill rig. They had bought the rig for next to nothing. Now Sarah had big plans to cut down some of the trees in the lower forty. Then if all went well, she could saw her own boards. They reasoned that it couldn't be that difficult. They made plans to take Alice and pick up the sawmill that was mounted on wheels.

Once before Sarah had started to fix an older saw mill but ran into trouble with a bent blade that couldn't be fixed, at least not for a reasonable price. That mill was rusting in the woods behind Rita's school bus. The new rig used a large Stilh chain saw instead of a rotary blade.

Billy D. and Aunt Sarah decided to have one more nip of the old barley and disappeared to the garage. Rita and Pokey cleaned up the table. All was neat and tidy, at least around the table. It still bothered Rita that there were so many mice scurrying about. She scoured the cast iron skillet with an SOS pad, until most of the hard shiny grease was gone.

Pokey took the table scraps to the shed for Mr. Pee. The routine was the same every feeding time. Pokey would sum up the days events for Mr. Pee, who seldom argued with his master and friend. Usually Mr. Pee just listened, but once in a while he'd look puzzled. Pokey was nothing short of a perpetual enigma for Mr. Pee.

But for now it was time to put a final coat of tool dip on the puppet. As Pokey painted the puppet heads he imagined children laughing in the park. He could see, that to have that happen, he'd have to have a little help.

"What do publickers look like?" asked Rita one night. Pokey thought a moment, "What does the devil look like? Pubs," he whispered, "are very, very hard to spot. Sometimes all they leave is a distinctive odor, a musky, thick smell of rottenness. Kind of like ammonia, only sweeter. Once you've smelled a publican, you'll never forget it. Sometimes they're called publickers."

"Yeah but what do they look like?" persisted Rita.

"Well, it's more in how they act. They usually try to look like everybody else. They are like chameleons! And frequently, I believe, they work very hard covering up their weakness. They can be wise in the ways of the world, or they can be dumb. Maybe, because of a natural profound lack of faith in God, they are left to search for substitutes to fill that void. Can't you see it? "

"If they could accept the void, they might not have to prove themselves so much in war," observed Rita.

"War is the antidote for peace!" said Pokey!

Rita chuckled, and asked again, "So do they have big heads? Little eyes? I mean in general?"

"Well, most of the Pubs are well dressed, though their clothes smell of back home if you get close to them. Their wives smell about the same, except they cover up more."

"A lot of times it takes a while for the pubs to get out of puberty. That sounds funny, doesn't it? Most of the time they find fault everywhere, and blame others for the world problems. They thrive on a victim mentality. They know that everybody else is taking profit at their expense!"

"Do they have pointed heads, or big eyes?" asked Rita. "Well, most of them have little eyes that are a little too close. That makes their noses seem too big in comparison to you and me. And there are lots of lines around their eyes from squinting at the little type at the bottom of the pages."

Warming to the topic, Pokey continued, "they are low down, like snakes in the grass, and they start every sentence with "clearly." They see it as their job to fight simplicity" to make loving your neighbor impossible. How can they discover the pleasure of giving of themselves, when deep down they are ashamed of themselves? They are in the process of denial! Ask any of them who they really are, and they'll look away! Try it some time. The eye contact tells almost all. That and the tone of their voices. If you just listen with your intuitive heart, you can hear everything. I hear it all the time. ALL THE TIME. That's a good reason not to get into other people's lives, it can be a sticky wicket for sure."

"Well how are you going to fight your Pubs, Pokey? Why fight them, why not help them? Or, at the least, lean toward ignoring them."

"The only way, is to get the little pubs before they wrestle with puberty, and to do it in front of the pubs auxiliary. Show the children that the danger is in the warrior class. Instead of throwing the baby off the stage, I gotta throw the hammer-head general with the bomb. Maybe I can make a hammer puppet. And we can decapitate it."

"Or maybe we can start a fellowship, like the boy scouts."

"Or get them where they are. Have the Brownie Scouts sell condoms for chastity," suggested Rita.

"No, there's gotta be a better Miss Land Mine Pageant, Or a TV quiz show, or a high school Chapter of the Guillotine way. That's the only constant I can see. That and that there is always a bottom to the barrel."

"Take this guy here," Pokey put his hand into a dark haired puppet, "see my eyes, I can open wide or clam up, just watching stuff." Pokey was practicing his animation looking into a mirror.

Rita addressed the puppet, "What's your name, Sir?"

In a deeper voice Pokey said, "Muh name is Bolt, Ma'am, Bolt Uptight. I come from a long line of Uptights, in fact there was a Nathan Uptight who came over with William the Conqueror."

Pokey brought out another puppet that was made from a white fox pelt, glued onto parts of a yellow glove, "Well howdy doodle miz foxy lady," said Pokey in a high sweet voice. "Can I plunk your magic twanger, hmmm? Just for a little while? Aw come on! You know you want it, don't you."

Switching voices Pokey replied, "How dare you! I am so ashamed, so very, very very ashamed!" Back and forth the puppets argued. Rita helped Pokey paint bright red lips on one puppet with fingernail polish.

Time flew by unnoticed. It was midnight when Rita yawned, "Pokey, I gotta go, time for bed. Tomorrow is my driving test, and I gotta pass. See you in the morning." Rita retired to the school bus, made a brief entry in her diary, and climbed into her sleeping bag. The whirring of the little quartz heater lulled her to sleep after a few moments.

Over breakfast, Pokey quizzed Rita on the rules of the road.

Aunt Sarah surfaced long enough to get some coffee, when the telephone rang. There had been an accident and the women with the Ford Bronco were not going to be able to take Rita for her driving test. "Aunt Sarah, isn't there someone else that can take me into Sheriff Hermanson's? My appointment is at two."

Aunt Sarah's mind was somewhat discombobulated after her night of revelry. If she felt like focusing her mind on anything, it would be finding a parts book for the Stihl chain saw mill. Instead, she found herself on the phone. There was just an answering machine at Billy D.'s, and other possibilities ran out. Pokey and Aunt Sarah weren't legal.

But just when it was the darkest, the cross bearer, Ed Harris, stopped in looking for an alternator for a mustang. Aunt Sarah had a '73 mustang in the weeds behind the shop. But it would take her at least an hour to cannibalize it.

"Well as long as you got nothing to do for a while, it would be just dandy if you could take my niece here, Rita Marie, into Murray Bay for her driver's test." Ed really needed that alternator, so he was more than happy to oblige.

Ed and Rita got into the S-10 with Rita at the wheel. In the back of the truck was Ed's portable cross to bear. Twenty minutes later they arrived at Sheriff Hermanson's home office right on time.

Rita knocked on the side door. No one came to answer. She could hear the sounds of sports radio coming from inside. She rapped louder with her fist, and soon the Sheriff's son, Stevie appeared, "Yeah, 'whaddaya' want? Oh, if it isn't old Sarah's Chamberlin's little girl! What would she like? Hmmm? You think you can be trusted on the highway?"

Stevie opened the screen door, flicking his cigarette into the weeds behind Rita. The smell of boiled cabbage drifted out, "Do come in my dear."

"Is the Sheriff here? I need to take my driving test at two," said Rita, not entering.

Stevie let the screen door swing shut. "Paw's not home yet, he had to file reports with the insurance company about the accident over at Slades Corners. He said I could give you the test, if you wanted, and he'd sign for it."

Rita could smell liquor on Stevie's breath. It was against her better judgement to get in a vehicle with this thick headed lout. But she was in a tight spot, so she volunteered, in her most demure voice, that "if you don't mind, I'd sure appreciate it, suh."

To be safe Rita also volunteered, "We have to be done by four o'clock so I can see the doctor about my infections." Stevie looked away for a moment, not sure if he had time. "Where's your car Miss Rita?

"I don't have a car. I've got a small truck I'm borrowing from a friend of my aunt. Stevie looked out at the S-10, "Isn't that Eddie's truck?

"Yes, do you know Mr. Harris?"

"Bout as well as I know anybody. I know he's a bubble off, and full of it to boot."

Ed Harris got out and unloaded the cross. "I might as well canvas this side of town. How's Mr. Little Sheriff today? Of should we address you as Chief Inspector Hermanson?"

Stevie took his clipboard and told Rita to get in.

Rita put on her seat belt, and asked Stevie to do the same. "Don't you have to buckle up too?"

"Why? Do you think I need to? Are you going to run into a tree or something?"

"No," said Rita. "I just thought it was the law."

"Miss Rita, the sooner you realize it the better! We pretty much make the law around here. We're helping you. We're going out of our way to help you. We want you to not cause us any trouble. Do you understand? We stand ready to help you, like now with your driving test. And in the future we expect you to not make us a problem. Cause then you have to pay. If that happens, it's up to you as to how you want to pay for making so much, too much, trouble. If you can't pay the fines, you won't have a license for very long. Understand? Comprendes?"

The smell of liquor kept Rita from delving into the practice of law and what constitutes justice. She was bright enough to avoid jousting with this windmill. "Oh Mr. Hermanson, Ahh sure enough don't know what's gotten into your mind. I promise, cross mah heart, never to cause you the slightest bit of trouble. No No! Not the slightest."

As they left, Stevie patted Rita's knee, "I know it's going to be a good time, because you're doing so well, already, let's take the Bay avenue west."

Ed Harris had been carrying the cross through the south side of Murray Bay, past the Golf Club, down to the river landing where he soon had several curious teenagers wondering where this man of cloth was going. Ed placed the cross against a tree next to the water's edge. He opened the hidden compartment in the cross to get his pamphlets. He gave each child a different tract. "Now you boys and girls have the biggest answer right in your own hands. Now I don't want to see any of you leaving these behind when you go home tonight. Be sure to take these wonderful truths to your moms and dads. Tell them it's never too late to repent, never too late to accept the Lord Jesus Christ as their personal savior. If the Lord will accept me, with all my sins, he's bound to accept you. Step into the light, and behold the Savior is within you."

Ed was reaching full throttle in his testimony when Rita and Stevie returned, "When I was just a little boy, just about your ages, I had a friend named Bobby. I used to stay over night at Bobby's house. One night Bobby's older brother, Scott, had a bottle of Hudson's Bay whiskey, well...Satan was alive and well. Did we all sin that night! Things happened so fast; so many ugly and different thoughts went through my mind. Bobby threw up all over me. Scott called me a chicken, and I tried to show him I wasn't a girly boy."

"But I missed hitting him, and he got me good. See my nose boys and girls? He smashed it! That was forty-five years ago. Then I had to lie to my mother, telling her I fell out of a tree. She believed my lies, but inside I was tormented. Torment right from Satan in all his majesty."

"So boys and girls, you gotta know that your Personal Savior stands ready to keep you pure, until the open grave welcomes you. All you have to do, is just ask for forgiveness. It is as simple as this: say with me now, I'm dark and dirty, I'm worthless and despicable, but Jesus can wash away my sins. Come Jesus, now! Breathe the joy into my heart that can only come from the holy ghost."

"Boys and girls! I can feel the Lord's presence with us right now! Listen! Listen here in this wilderness for the faint echo of God calling you...there!...hear that? Oh blessed Jesus!"

Ed dropped to his knees and looked upward, breathing heavily, clutching his throat, "Thank you Lord Jesus, Oh thank you."

The children gave blank faces, not at all sure about their need to repent. After a few moments Ed was able to recover from the visitation enough to shoulder the rugged cross and be on his way back to get his truck at the sheriff's house.

Rita performed her driving test perfectly until she had to parallel park. She had trouble finding reverse, and then ended up with the truck three feet from the curb. She tried it again and again. Stevie told her that to pass the test, the truck had to be within one foot of the curb. She could take the test again in six weeks. Rita brought the truck to rest at Sheriff Hermanson's house.

"Isn't there anyway you can tell your father that I did OK on the test? I did get it right eventually!" Rita moved in closer, even though she had to endure Stevie's odor. "You know, if you wanted something for your trouble, we might arrange a party or something."

"Yeah, something like your swimming party! Not on your life. Sorry Babe. Six weeks. The decent folks around here want safe roads."

Rita saw Ed Harris coming up behind them with his cross. He stowed the cross back in his truck, tying it down so that the winds wouldn't take it. On the way back to Lost Grove Motors, Ed and Rita practiced parallel parking. They reported back to

Aunt Sarah that Rita had failed and that it would be six weeks before Rita could repeat the test.

"I'll practice, and I will make it, I swear!" said Rita.

Ed Harris asked Aunt Sarah if she could help him find a wider steel rod for the wheels on his cross. The present axle needed to be wider because semi trucks nearly blew the cross into the ditch sometimes. Ed thought he could control the cross better if the wheelbase were wider. Rita found some extra three quarter inch threaded bolt stock that they used to spread the wheels further apart.

Aunt Sarah wouldn't take anything for the new axle. She was happy that Ed was on his way,

Rita thought she was dreaming, when she awoke in the dead of the night, hearing Pokey crying out "Wanda...Wanda." She looked out from her bed on the floor at the rear of the school bus and saw him walking in circles. He looked like he was staggering, out of balance, like Aunt Sarah. Rita was puzzled and was about to see if he needed help, when Pokey went back into his shed.

Next morning it was Pokey's turn to cook. He usually took pains to be overly positive in greeting the day. But this day, he seemed preoccupied. The morning news was blaring out. There was a woman on Ebay who was auctioning off a bumper sticker, "To Hell with Housework!" Pokey's face showed no emotion, his eyes were motionless.

"I saw you last night Pokey. It must have been four o'clock in the morning. Who is Wanda?" asked Rita.

"I don't know. I think I'm loosing my mind, It must have happened some time ago, but I can't tell you when or where, but what I can remember is so vivid that God must have been telling me something important, but it was in a language I don't understand.

"There was this farmhouse on the side of a hill, with a driveway and lots of big oaks around it. That's where I met Wanda."

"You see, I had been taking the long way home and I stopped by a woodsy bluff area, and somehow I found myself walking down through dense brush into a passageway with no ceiling. I could see blue sky above. The walls became perfectly flat and smooth. As if in a rat maze I went to the end of the hall and took a left, and then a right, and it ended. Just a woods at the end of it. So I retraced my way back to the road.

Mr. Pee was no help at all. But that's when I saw Wanda's house. I figured that whoever lived in that house probably would know about that hallway in the rock. So I approached the house. There were several cars and pickups in the yard. I could hear people in the house. It almost looked like a country auction was going on. There were two hay wagons with crocks and jars, and some produce.

I asked the man who answered my knock if any one knew anything about the strange rock formation down the road. He told me he was just visiting, and took me to the corner room where he introduced me to Wanda. I didn't catch her last name.

I spent what seemed like hours with Wanda, talking about everything! She would finish my sentences for me, using words I hardly knew...and some I had never heard before. But the house started to fill up, and it looked like I had better be going. On the way out, Wanda introduced me to an oily dude in a black suit, he owned the house and let Wanda and her husband live there rent free, just to have the house lived in. Otherwise vandals, he said, would soon destroy it."

"I wanted to stay longer but I couldn't. And I didn't get her last name or her telephone number. She was old enough to be my mother, and I felt so good just being in her presence. Every once in a while, now I feel she is here, just around the corner. And if I could only yell her name the right way, she would come to me. I don't know why I am drawn to her. I think she is drawn to me too, even if she is married."

"Anyway when I got outside, the neighbors were all exchanging produce from their gardens. I took some stuff for Mr. Pcc. When we left, Wanda told me that we would meet again. Last night I thought I heard her calling to me. I was so happy!

But she had gone away by the time I got my pants on and got outside. Didn't you hear her calling me?"

"No, Pokey, I was asleep until you woke me up."

"I'm sorry Rita, I can't understand why she didn't wait for me. She could have come during the day! That would make sense. If I had her number I could call her. She is Wanda the midnight wanderer! I still don't see what she sees in me. All I know is when I looked into her eyes, I sensed a connection of soul to soul, so strong that I couldn't look away. It's both a comfort of the highest order, and a pain in the ass!"

Rita laughed, "Maybe that's Wanda's message for you. That everything has two sides. Even God! Maybe Satan is just the dark side of God. Have you ever heard of a one sided coin?"

"Yeah, that kind of makes sense, but it's still a pain in the ass. I mean, like if God or Allah, or the Buddha is created in Man's image, I mean, does God get really pissed, or is he or she, above it all? Or maybe he is just chuckling about how dense a material man turned out to be. How can we tell?"

"Next question?" joked Rita.

"Well, does anything make a difference to God? Like how do we know that he cares at all?"

Rita picked up the dishes, "well if it really means that much to you, maybe you should talk to a minister, or go to Sunday school."

The next morning Pokey seemed in a better mood. "It sure enough was cold last night, it makes me wonder if'n I should head south, get away from this cold."

"Yeah," said Rita, " I would if I could, but I can't, so I won't. Come next September, I'm out of here, anyway."

"I don't know, but at night I hear Mr. Pee kind of wheezing, like he's got the flu bug. And his nose is kind of dripping."

Aunt Sarah thought it over a moment and volunteered that, if it were up to her, she'd go south, maybe back to Houston or Galveston where she learned how to drive dune buggies. Except she had too much work left to do at Lost Grove Motors.

"Pokey, if you don't have anywhere else to go why don't you

move into Mrs. Karl's bread truck, It would be a lot easier to heat, that thing is almost air tight."

"But what can we do with all the video and computer stuff that's in Mrs. Karl's?" asked Rita

Sarah suggested, "Most of it can go in the old milk house."

By ten o'clock Rita and Pokey had exchanged all the inventory, and Pokey was setting up his few things in the bread truck. He had wired up speakers in every corner.

The next day he spotted a small basement window unit in the weeds behind the garage. It took longer than it should have, but by noon Pokey had installed the small crank out window in the side of the bread truck box. So he had a little natural light.

That afternoon Rita and Pokey made the trip to the airport snack shop to get the trash and were back to Lost Grove by nightfall. They stopped at the town dump but found nothing to bring home.

It was Rita's turn to make supper. In the refrigerator she found leftover bean casserole and lime jello salad surprise. With grilled cheese sandwiches it would have to do. For Aunt Sarah and herself, she added ham to the Colby cheese.

Aunt Sarah asked how the Mrs. Karl's was for Pokey. "I like it better. It's going to be a lot easier to heat. The milk house was really drafty.

After supper Rita went on line checking the Ebay auctions. There was a problem updating credit card expiration dates. While she was engrossed in figuring out if it were a scam, Pokey was carving away at his puppet heads. After several minutes Pokey stopped carving, "I don't know if this is stupid or not, but I was just thinking about the Gospels again. Gospels say that God created Adam before he created Eve. My question is, do you suppose God looked at Adam and was disappointed? I mean, why didn't he just leave it well enough alone?

"Why in God's name did he take Adam's rib to make Eve? Was he bored with men? Weren't men praising him enough? Or if God is a woman, maybe she likes a good fight! Maybe she pretends to care for mankind, just because it's more fun for her to see mankind stumble on the road to insight."

Rita turned away from the Ebay screen, "Well, Pokey, you're not the first to question. Mother Teresa had grave doubts too! You can take your puppets and teach your audience about insight. But only so much can be taught, the rest has to evolve, doesn't it? I mean, do you love God for his perfection or for his imperfection?"

Pokey was silent..."I don't know. The feeling I get from being around Wanda, my midnight wanderer, is that there is a lot more to experience in life than we can ever know. I've tasted His divine presence in other people, in my twilights and their spirits, they are all telling me I'm on the right track. I feel it. I can't escape them. But lots of time I'm not sure. I can't focus. I'm lost without a clue. But I know one thing, I'm not going to turn to hard drugs or booze."

Putting down the shopping news, Rita announced, "here it says there's going to be a costume Halloween party at the Murray Bay golf club. That sounds like it could be fun!

Pokey turned away, sweeping up the crumbs and shavings from his puppet work. "Those people aren't my kind, Rita. Count me out."

"Pokey...don't be a stick in the mud. Some of them have to be OK. We saw some of them at the County Fair. They didn't look so bad. And wouldn't it be fun to dress up, to do something different. I'm tired of just forever cleaning things up. Just once, I'd like to go somewhere and listen to a band. I don't care if it's not live, I want to dance...dance my fool head off! With a costume on, nobody will know it's me. And no one will know it's you either! We can play real second life!

Pokey still had reservations. "If it is inside, it's going to smell bad if there are many Publickers. I might have to leave early, I gotta tell you now. My asthma."

"Does that mean you'll go?

"OK, but don't complain later that I didn't warn you. We're safe now, hardly anyone knows who you are, and nobody knows who I am. And I want to keep it that way."

"Great!" Rita impulsively hugged Pokey. "It'll be loads of fun. Now...where can I find a costume? What should I be?

The next two weeks flew by. Rita decided she wanted to be the wicked witch of the West and Pokey gave into being the cowardly lion. Both started taking extra vitamin supplements to get their immune systems cranked up for the party.

On Saturday Rita and Pokey started to work on their costumes. Rita experimented with makeup to make her face ugly. "Pokey, what do you think? Am I repulsive?"

Pokey looked at the bags under her eyes, "Yeah, Rita, you look almost dead. But if it were me, I'd want to look even worse."

"What! What more can I do?"

"Well, I'd mix a little more green into your foundation, and then push the color into your hairline. And don't forget your neck, it stands out to much."

"Yeah, I know, I'm planning to wear a black turtle neck. Green Huh?"

"I've got some chrome oxide pigment you can have. Pokey's eyes went blank as he stared at Rita. "I've got an idea. Why not add some running sores, with just a little pus. Not to over do it, you know what I mean?"

"Yeah...would you help me, that sounds really tasteless. Right on dude. I'm depending on you."

Friday came and Rita took the trip to the airport and dump. Pokey stayed at home to work on his puppets. Gluttony was the name of his new monster puppet. It was a new style, an experiment with an old hot water bottle and two Ziplock bags filled with marbles. Gluttony's face had jowls that rolled on their own as he talked. Pokey spoke to his creation, man to man:

"Morning Mr. Gluttony, or can I call you Mr. Gee?"

"Good Morning Mr. Pokeyman"

"What's up Dude, How's the old appetite. Ya gitten enough?"

"Yeah, the Lord do provide a corno, yep, a cornucopia of satisfaction. Except my stomach can't take much more, and my knees and ankles are giving out."

"Well, what are you going to do about it?"

Pokey held up Mr. Gee, with jowls sloshing, "I've had too much, ahh...too much at last. Finally I've had my fill. I've had enough. I'm packed full of candy, full of corn, full of apple pie a la mode, full of orange glazed duck, but, but," Pokey coughed and made a long gurgling noise. "Ahhhh, I'm throwing up...Ahhh."

Pokey concentrated on making Mr. Gee really repulsive. He decided to add some running sores to the hot water bottle.

His initial sores were made with Elmer's Glue and dry wood putty, but the sores tended to be too brittle. Rubber cement wouldn't harden up, and modeling clay wouldn't stay put on the puppet. Finally, Pokey found a system that would work. He took a sheet of paper and covered it with Saran wrap. On this base he squirted pimples and scars from his caulking gun. Once the caulk set up, he painted on flesh color, adding a few extra hairs and dots of black heads.

"Can I squeeze your black heads Mr. Gee?"

"Yeah, when I'm done with dessert, that would be just fine. Just Fine. Oh no! Oh No! Just when I'm almost full, Oh No! Aaaaahg, I'm going to throw up."

The gurgling sound with the rolling marble cheeks and jowls worked well. But more could be done. Pokey was still working on Mr. Gee when suppertime came. He showed Rita his new invention: Instant blemishes with pus.

Rita was delighted. Pokey showed her how to take the sheet of sores and warts and cut them apart. All that was necessary to apply one was to lick the back of the plastic film and press it where ever necessary.

Aunt Sarah was amused and was tempted to look for a costume for herself. But she decided that it would be enough just to take Rita and Pokey to the back edge of the Golf Course where no one would see the tractor and spreader. She could visit the Fin 'n Feather lounge and pick up the pair on her way back home to Lost Grove Motors.

After supper Pokey hooked up a short hose to the inside of Mr. Gee's head. On the other end of the hose he connected a two liter plastic Coke bottle. In a couple of hours Pokey had a puppet that could throw up on demand. Pokey stomped on the plastic Coke bottle and a vomit stream came out of Mr. Gee's mouth.

Rita went on line the next morning. "I've got an idea Pokey. Can you make some more sheets of those running sores? I like the ones with pus!"

"Sure can, how many do you want?"

"I'm thinking, if a girl had a supply of these running sores in her purse, well, anytime a girl might walk into trouble, where she was afraid of getting raped, well she could pull out one of these sores and glue it to her face or neck. The uglier, the better."

"Great!" Pokey put ten sheets of computer paper down on a board, side by side. Over these he rolled out ten feet of Saran Wrap® then the caulking, and lastly the painting. Rita was painting a few herself when she had a brainstorm. She first applied cold cream to her face and then a large piece of Saran over her nose and cheeks.

"Pokey, I want you to make my nose bigger, and uglier."

Pokey had a sure and steady hand on his caulking gun, squeezing out beautiful warts, veins, and scar tissue. It took surprisingly little to transform Rita's nose into a hagly witch.

"Boil, cauldron, boil," she moaned, looking into the mirror. "With a little dark blue eye shadow, this will be perfectly ugly."

Pokey advised that she should probably leave the caulking on her face for at least an hour, so it would set up right.

Rita went back on line, listing the fake blemishes as Universal Rape Preventers. The sheet of sores didn't scan too well, but she used it anyway. By bedtime Rita's new nose had set up perfectly. It came off easily and held its shape. She trimmed away the excess Saran, and set it on top of her monitor, ready for the Halloween party.

Seven

Pokey was the first to get his costume on when Halloween night rolled around. He found a Bozo the Clown mask at Walmart for only $3.97. He painted the red nose black and glued on tufts from an old wig. He used the same wig material to make his paws and feet from gloves and sneakers. Rita helped glue on more hair on the back of his jacket. He practiced his growl and walking on all fours.

Rita made a witches broom from willow branches. Her hat came from a small lampshade with black paper added. At the last minute she plugged in her glue gun and added black sequins to the hat and her skirt.

"I haven't had a skirt on since I left school. At least I don't have to act so prim and proper. In this outfit I can try anything!"

Aunt Sarah had been in the Murray Bay Golf Clubhouse years before, but had never returned. Chasing a little white ball around a field made no sense to her. Plus she had nothing to say to the matrons. Men in business suits held little fascination for her either.

Rita and Pokey were riding in the spreader as Aunt Sarah approached the golf club. BMW's and Volvos cruised by on their way to the party. Aunt Sarah turned Alice toward the service entrance behind a row of pines that led to the club kitchen. She left Rita and Pokey in the dark bushes, saying she would return at midnight. She planned to look for Ed Harris at the Fin 'n Feather club in town.

Pokey led the way, following the row of pine trees, keeping in the shadows. They came upon the swimming pool that was now empty, ready for winter. They noticed some of the partygoers having a smoke at the outdoor service bar. They heard the music blasting from the bar inside.

"I can smell 'em right now Rita!" said Pokey.

"You'll get over it...come on, loosen up. They don't know who we are. It's time to see if they'll serve us. Try breathing through your mouth."

They needn't have worried; the party was in full swing, with trays of punch and plastic cups of wine being passed around.

After the second round, Rita was beginning to catch her stride, whooping it up. It had been too long since her last party, and she was making up for it. Hours of practicing John Travolta moves came back to her.

As she steamed up she began to sweat, one of her sores came off, but the nose stayed on. Pokey tried to imitate Rita's moves. He was doing a turn with his arms flailing when he bumped into Rita, causing her hat to fall off.

Quickly she retrieved it, and continued dancing. More and more partygoers came in from the dining room. There was another witch with almost the same garb. This witch was a lot taller, and a pretty good dancer also. She had a matching broom.

The witch was dancing with another girl dressed as Little Bo Peep. The girl had beautiful blond curls that looked real. Pokey and Rita started dancing, and drifted over next to the other witch. It was evident that the other witch wasn't a girl. She had a mustache.

Rita asked Pokey to go cut in, so she could dance with the other witch. The music got louder when they put on Annie Lennox. The crowd was all on its feet, dancing in a frenzy. The two witches improvised with their brooms, and soon they were the center of attention. The crowd cheered and laughed at their antics. Rita got on her broom and circled around; the other witch followed close by.

Rita stopped by the punch bowl and found Pokey sitting with Miss Bo Peep, who appeared to be quite flushed. "Pokey, what are you doing? Come have a dance with me...I can't dance alone."

"Naw, Rita, I told Megan here that I'd stay with her until her friend Charles comes back in."

Rita headed out onto the deck area. She found the witch

now known as Charles at the outdoor bar. He had taken off his pointed hat and was sipping a Hinekins. Rita ambled over, "Beggin' your pardon Ma'am, can I borrow ye a cup of toads eyes?"

Charles laughed, "Sorry, I'm out...but I got a pail of private parts just waiting for the right witch to come along. You're quite the artistic dancer! I sure like your broom work! Where do you get your inspiration?"

Rita fluttered her big lashes and picked at her nose, "I guess it just comes naturally, my Daddy used to do a lot of flying around. Besides, you're no slouch yourself. I'm going back in, come on along." They went back in and soon were singing along with Erasure while outdoing each other in turn.

Pokey cut in and whispered in Rita's ear, "It's eleven thirty, and Miss Peep is asleep, or passed out. They looked over to see Charles and one of the waiters helping Miss Peep. They got another girl to help her into the little girls room. Charles returned to Rita and Pokey.

"My name is Charles, I don't believe we've been introduced. We haven't seen you around here before."

Rita looked into his eyes. She immediately liked what she saw. She knew he could dance, and dance well. That might mean that he was still in touch with his body. As they talked she sensed an easy flow of words.

"Oh, I thought I introduced myself, I'm Veronica, witch of the West. And this here is Leon, the cowardly lion."

Pokey looked at his watch, "Come on Rita, time to go."

Charles saw Miss Bo Peep coming toward him, "Ahh, so it's Rita is it?" Aren't you going to wait and see who gets the prize for best costume?" Rita scowled at Pokey, "Yeah, maybe I'll see you again."

In a few minutes Rita and Pokey retraced their steps behind the row of pines. They stayed in the shadows, waiting for Aunt Sarah to come. Rita peeled off her nose and looked at Pokey who still had all of his lion face. They stood there waiting, until nearly all the Volvo's and Lincoln SUV's had nearly left the club parking lot when the familiar put-put sound of Alice came around the bend.

Rita and Pokey quickly got on board. They kept their heads down, and snuggled together in the honey wagon, unseen by Charles and Miss Bo Peep who sped on by in their shiny black Chevy Tahoe. It was late and in a few minutes Rita drifted away. Pokey felt her cheek drop onto his furry chest. He smiled, suspecting Rita had fallen asleep. The purring of the tractor nearly put him to sleep also. In a half hour they were back to Lost Grove.

The crew first visited the green room, and then assembled around the kitchen table. Aunt Sarah wanted the details, "well, dear ones, how was the party?"

Pokey volunteered first, "It was just like I thought it would be. There was that humid smell I warned you about. But if you breathed through your mouth, it was OK. Rita showed me how to dance like Michael Jackson."

"Pokey, you already knew a lot. Anyway, Aunt Sarah, we had a good time. There was another witch there that was kind of fun. It was a guy dressed almost the same as me. He wanted my name, but I didn't give it away."

"He told me that he was a pilot."

"I don't know about his taste in women," explained Pokey. "His date was a humdinger, quite on her way to be a real rounder, or at least that's the way I took her. Awfully pretty, long bleached hair, lips outlined in brown, pancaked and rouged...yeah, I know, she was Miss Bo Peep, but I think she really was pretty simple, so her get up wasn't much of a transformation at all."

"Well I'm too pooped to give a shit," said Rita. Maybe I am a witch at heart, just ready to form a coven. I'm not going to analyze that one. Good Night all."

Pokey reported back to Mr. Pee that the night had been not too bad. That booze seemed to make the publickers more peaceful. While it was fresh in his mind, he opened his folder of great ideas. And found himself, in a far away place, writing notes in the margins of his previous great thoughts.

- for a fact to emerge from the chaos, it first has to be noticed. Then analyzed.
- it is easier for the fact to emerge if it is surrounded by similar facts. Alone, the fact is less potent.
- change is dynamic. It always is double acting, pulling and pushing. From the known to the unknown. and vice versa
- fear is nourished not by unknown, but by the known. Figure-ground gestalt.

QED expect your neighbor to sing off key.

Pokey grabbed his Webster's Collegiate to look up fear.

Eight

Rita and Pokey stopped in the airport snack shop after they loaded the World's End trash. It was at the end of the day, and they were the only customers. Mrs. Staber was complaining about the federal regulation, all the traffic reports and EPA regulations.

On the bulletin board Pokey noticed a help wanted notice. "Wanted housekeeping person to clean Corporate Jet, flexible off peak schedule. References required. Inquire within."

Rita remembered the tall executive who had given her bags of trash before. She asked Mrs. Staber, "How much are they willing to pay? What do they want done?"

"Well, off the record, they don't care what it costs, just so every Monday it's ready for take off at six. I have the hanger keys, and there is a closet of supplies. You have to empty the two toilet tanks, and check the snacks. That's about all. If you are interested, I'll give them your name."

"OK, give them Pokey's name, Albert," said Rita.

On the way home, Pokey noticed a large dead bird at the side of the road, and had to stop. He got down and picked up the bird tenderly. He spoke to it softly, "there, there, you're in a better place now. Yeah, I know, it didn't work out like you thought it would. Sure...yeah...I know, you meant well."

Pokey put the red tail hawk in the spreader.

"Now what are you going to do with that?" asked Rita.

"I'm going add her claws to my twilights. And, the skull I'll add to my collection of animal heads. I've found lots of skulls along the road. Let's see, I've got a chicken, cat, dog, fox, deer, possum, coon, mouse, a couple of cows, and Oh yes, I've got a whole mink skeleton."

"Oh ick! How are you going to clean it? asked Rita.

"Don't have to clean it, mother nature does it for me. I'll just put it in a safe place so a fox won't eat it. Then the flies will come and their maggots will clean up all the bones."

"Oh, sorry I asked," said Rita.

It was nine o'clock next morning before Pokey came out of Mrs. Karls bread truck. Aunt Sarah was busy fixing a vacuum sealer on the test bench. Rita was cleaning up the breakfast dishes when Pokey came bouncing in.

"What's up, Pokey...you look like you just struck it rich."

"Yeah! In a way I have. Funny how things work out. Last night I went to bed wondering about how we fear so many things, and make so many bad choices."

"This morning I was shaving and I looked at myself in the mirror, and a strange thing happened. I kind of hypnotized myself. I realized that my reflection was more real than I was. Wow! I said to myself. I still say it. WOW!

Rita looked at him skeptically, "Are you sure you're not on something?"

"Yeah, Rita, I'm on to something alright. What I mean, is this...look! You're trying to find yourself, I'm trying to find myself too. Who isn't? We look inside to try to understand ourselves, to discover and use our talents. But when we look inside, we discover things that aren't so pretty. And we start to feel bad about the world. I think we start to die in a way. We start pretending everything is OK. But it's not OK. Ugh! When I started to believe in my reflection in the mirror, I bridged the gap. I was scared at first, you know, to depart from the normal reality, to approach the fear of the next step. But I did it, Rita. I did it! When I got to the other side, I could look back and see my old self clearly, more clearly than ever before. I could look back and, as if in a dream, I could see myself more clearly than ever...I was able to see, hear, and feel my soul in the relationships I have had with all the people I've ever been with."

"Now, some of spirits I've dealt with don't shine with glowing radiance, some people aren't awake. The numinous is not in focus, so to speak. Rudolf Otto understood that!"

"Who's Rudolf Otto? asked Rita.

"He one of those German philosophers who tried to

weigh the weightless. Very poetic, probably on drugs. When I lived at the Riddle foster home Mr. Riddle was always quoting good old Rudolf."

"Anyway, I say wow because all the time I was looking for myself in the wrong place. Looking inside is what a fool does. No surprises there! No! To find yourself, you gotta look outside your self. Focus on the faint light that comes from yourself reflected in the eyes of your friends, and even in the eyes of your enemies. Maybe even more so with your enemies!"

"It made me think that all we really are is the sum total of all the relationships we have with each other. QED, its our choice to be alive or not. Being so alive, means we vanquish death, in a way. Not being alive means we kind of just missed roll call."

Pokey continued, "You can comfort your self all you want with compensatory pastimes. Take care of your cat. Weed the garden. When you're alone, you're alone. Might just as well be in a casket, four feet down. No. To find your real self, that self is only in relationships, its outside, not inside!"

Rita thought a minute, "Pokey, did you read that somewhere, or what? Does that mean you are nothing inside?"

"No, Rita, I've been having these strange dreams that don't seem to fit together, yet they do have some sort of thread. Like segments of a whole, or links in a chain. It started when I looked into my own eyes in that mirror, and I saw that the mirror needed cleaning. You know, the through the glass darkly routine. I realized that the haze over the mirror, the dust, the grime, the flyspecks, all of that stuff was helping me see my real self, that, that...the stuff was necessary. Can you understand? To remove the shit from the mirror would not be a step forward! My mind needs the confusion, the noise, to see into the reality beyond the mirror."

Pokey laughed in spurts, he was so happy with himself.

Rita laughed too, "You know Pokey, I have changed my mind. I don't think going to church, or going to see a shrink is going to help you. I think maybe I had better go myself. But listen, we've got work to do. Why don't you tune into the stove...it needs its essence warmed up."

"OK", Pokey stepped outside to the woodpile and brought in an armload of red elm. He closed the draft vents so that the fire would last almost to dawn. "There."

Soon the fire was crackling merrily, and the flames flickered through the isinglass "I'm thinking," he continued, "this connection of soul, to the divine, to the primal energy, what ever you call it, is still a two way street. It can be a benign infection. Like, don't wash your hands?"

"I don't understand," Rita interrupted, "are you talking about the holy ghost? Or are you talking about you in the here and now, accepting the here and now for what it is, and nothing more?

Pokey's rhythm was broken. It took a few moments for him to calculate if he was here now, in reality or just here in theory. He continued, "What I think I'm saying, is, you should go to church to sing. Go to church not to pray, but to bridge the gap. That kind of prayer isn't about communication. It's just wishful thinking. Nothing wrong in it, it's just not synergistic."

Rita picked up her coat, "So what kinds of prayer are there out there. Do some work and some not? Is it possible for a prayer to back fire? Who was it that said, "be careful what you pray for, because you might get it?"

It was a relief to spend the rest of the morning wrapping the Ebay orders. UPS came right on time. Four o'clock came and Rita told Aunt Sarah that she was going for a walk.

She returned to the path down to the lower forty to the small stream that flowed through large boulders. She sat on one near the edge, with her legs dangling over the water. Her mind drifted as the sun warmed her face. She tried not to push the river. She tried real hard. She closed her eyes and listened to all the sounds of the birds, calling and answering. She heard angry crows in the distance, a male cardinal protesting an intruder. She whistled a reply, and the cardinal was quiet. She was comforted by the harmony she felt. Even the rock under her seemed to infuse special warmth to her state. Her hands tingled as she slowly caressed the warm rock. She pulled her legs up and struck the lotus position. With her eyes shut she practiced her Sufi breathing, cleaning her mental house.

She smiled as she felt vague wisdom accumulating with each intake, with each deep breath. As she exhaled she imagined toxins being cast away. She opened her eyes and saw that sunset would be soon. She jogged most of the way home.

Pokey was up before dawn the next day. He had looked into his dusty mirror again, and, fortunately, he was still there! He knew there must be a reason for his being right there, right now. It was becoming clearer, that he was on line to something a whole lot bigger than he had ever dreamed of. Bigger in so many ways.

He asked Aunt Sarah if he could take Alice into Murray Bay to the lumberyard. He needed to get some half-inch plywood. It was time to build a bigger and better stage for the puppet show.

"How was your night?" asked Rita over breakfast.

"I woke up like always," he replied, and said my morning mantras. I looked into my gateway mirror and noticed that the image in the mirror was out of step with me. I couldn't tell if it was going faster or just a little slower. First I thought I was gaining on it, then, oops, I'd get a little out of balance, and have to slow down. Then I'd seem to be following the lead of the guy in the mirror.

"I took a sudden deep breath, and the man in the mirror told me, Albert, take care of your body. Rita, the man in the mirror isn't me anymore. If I close my eyes, I get lost in an amber sea, where there are no solid things to hold on to, where all there is...is echoes of the big bang. Getting fainter everyday. Where does the guy in the mirror want me to go?"

"Sometimes the man in the mirror won't talk to me. Sometimes he almost looks like he is from a different race and I'm afraid he isn't at all what he looks like. If I wanted to, I could see a woman, and a pretty one at that. And they all share one thing in common: They feel justified and want me to agree with them. I sense that each one of them wants me to unlock them from the mirror. It's getting so, that I don't want to look in the mirror."

Rita could only nod, "Yeah, Pokey...that might be a step forward...for now though, there's the laundry to do."

Nine

"How can I teach you about anything. Can't you ever understand?" Pokey was talking with a whole new puppet. As he put on the final hairs and eyelashes, he breathed spirit into his creation. Suddenly, he realized a small shock. Somehow the old man that was being born, looked too much like one of the visages he caught looking at him in the mirror. But there was more. As Pokey sculpted the old man's jowls, the puppet also took on a decidedly swine aspect, as if Mr. Pee had something to say.

Pokey switched voices, now being Mr. Fat Oldman, "Its not my fault you know. The voices made me do it".

Pokey slammed the puppet on the desk, "Ouch! Ouch! Oh, that feels good. Ouch! Good! Ouch, OOOoooh, he swooned.

Pokey heard the faint put-put of Alice approaching. He put on his jacket and went out to see if there were any dump proceeds. Indeed there were. Rita was returning from the dump with boxes of books. There were two heavy boxes of 78 rpm records, and some classical LPs. Rita suspected that someone had cleaned out a basement and just didn't care about the value. It was a good haul that included a box of letters from the 1800's. There was a large black board with strange sculpted letters screwed onto it. They spelled A*S*T*R*O*N*O*M*I*C*A*L L*E*C*T*U*R*E C*O* As soon as Pokey saw the sign board, he said "WOW! Is that neat or what! Bitchin!"

"Oiu, Tres boss" agreed Rita.

Aunt Sarah came into the shed and saw the signboard and records. Looking among the old letters she saw the name Pollard several times. "Listen to this," she said, reading from a yellowed page, "Dear Miss Pollard, When Ernie came in today and told me what you said about me, I couldn't believe you would stoop so low in telling lies about me. There's a law against such lies and you could go to jail. I am going to let the proper authorities know about you. And that butternut cake you brought was awful. Signed,

Millydred Eckstein. PS You tell Levi to stay away. If you know what's good for you."

Rita and Pokey laughed, "That's a good one. You wonder who they really were. What was Millydred doing with Levi?"

Aunt Sarah put her glasses away, "I remember stories about Levi Pollard and his sister. Years and years ago there was this hotelkeeper whose father was also his grandfather. In other words he was a product of incest. But the strange thing was Levi ended up marrying a neighbor girl who was also a product of incest. I remember that they got along pretty well, had four boys. The two youngest were in special ed. Keith was the oldest. He was in my class in high school. He died of carbon monoxide poisoning when he was out drinking. Something about a faulty muffler."

Aunt Sarah looked at the signboard with the letters ASTRONOMICAL LECTURE CO. "This must have been from Levi's grandfather, or father. Whichever. Levi was a humorist who traveled the mid west in a horse drawn buckboard. See these iron brackets. They would have fit into the sides of his wagon."

The sign was a little wider than a buggy seat and had raised Egyptian style metal lettering on a black curved board.

"Wow!" was all that Pokey could say. "Is that beautiful or what? I gotta have it. Maybe it will fit over my puppet stage. Let me take it and see."

Pokey took the old sign to his trike that was in the woodshed. "It fits! It's an omen! Gosh, if that just don't beat all. I swear!"

"It does fit pretty well" Rita agreed.

"Anyway Pokey," continued Aunt Sarah, "I need you to bring in some wood, and I need you to help me weld some rods that I'm adding to a Cutlass frame."

Rita Volunteered, "I can help you, if you like. Pokey and I have our room and board money from our Ebay sales. The video tapes have all been sold, and most of the books are gone. Orders for our Universal Rape Protector kits are now becoming kind of a bother to have to make."

Ten

It was Sunday Morning and Aunt Sarah had left for church, all wrapped up with a fur hat, driving Miss Alice. Rita was listening to talk radio while looking out the back door of her school bus home. She watched Pokey walking around in circles out side the bus. Mr. Pee was just sitting by the green room enjoying the sunshine.

Pokey was talking to himself. "I know there's more for me to learn, I can feel it. Somewhere there's an answer, I can feel it in my bones."

He straightened up and took a deep, deep breath. Suddenly something dawned on him, and he bounced up and down, in a kind of jig, and rushed to get his big thoughts book. He wrote:

If you want to know where you are going, look not forward, but backward. Go back in your memories, remember and focus on early learning experience. Remember how it felt when your awareness increased, when you finally got it. Your dénouement, if there were betrayal involved, so much the better. The insight gained is the measure of tested adaptability. This kind of learning may be habit forming, like an addiction.

There's a strange reflex that happens when you focus on that kind of epiphany, suddenly you can look into the mirror and watch your reflection come back into focus.

But then there's the existential trap of mind-no-mind. At that point the best thing to do, and the only thing to do is to breathe, but breathe right. The Buddhists and Muslims had it right...but the Christians missed the boat.

Pokey closed his book of big thoughts and stepped back outside to the most glorious of fall days. He breathed again deeply and closed his eyes, then held his breath while listening more deeply. Suddenly the birds were a lot closer, and a lot friendlier...he felt radiant.

Aunt Sarah meanwhile parked the tractor and spreader

on the far side of St. Mary's cemetery and walked through it, passing the Chamberlin plots, the Huxtables and Harris's, Trevarros, and Trelawnys.

Inside the candles were lit, and Hestor Dupré was stumbling through a Faure voluntary on the organ. It was the early bird service and only a few were in attendance. Aunt Sarah chose a warm spot where the sun cast colored lights from the stained glass windows.

She knelt to pray, "Hear my prayer Oh Lord."

She closed her eyes and let the words dribble out of her mind, as she coaxed her mind into submission. With eyes shut, she drifted, until Father Fitzgerald broke the bread and invited the flock to come forward.

Father Fitzgerald blessed each of the faithful as they left the church, "May God be with you, remember the Pilgrim Fellowship youth discovery program is tonight at seven thirty."

Rita remained in bed watching the world from the back exit door of the bus. Pokey had been going in circles, and then had disappeared. As she lay there listening to the birds, her cell phone rang suddenly.

She picked it up to hear a voice from the past, Emma Bovary from St. Theresa's: "Rita! This is Emmy! I've been trying to get a hold of you for months. How have you been? Where are you? Oh! I miss you so."

"Emma! I miss you too. The lawyers tell me that I have to stay here until the end of their fiscal year. They told me after my birthday I can be free to come and go as I please."

"Oh Rita, you sound great. When's your birthday? I don't remember...how's life? Can we see each other?"

"I'm doing OK I guess. My Aunt Sarah sometimes is pretty tough on me. But other times I hardly know she's around. She runs a fix it shop, you know, fixing cars and trucks, lawn mowers, chain saws. I help her out."

"Do you have an Email address? Asked Emma.

"Yeah, but I'm not supposed to give it out. I had to get one to sell stuff on Ebay. If you promise me that you won't tell anybody, I'm Butch at Gonads dot com."

There was silence on the other end, then a chuckle, "No way, you've got to be kidding. That doesn't sound like the sweet innocent ingenue I used to know."

"Times are changing, Emmy. How about you?"

Emma reported that her father had died unexpectedly and that she and her brother had come into some money. Her brother wanted to buy a large old mansion near Tanglewood, to make a musical bed and breakfast. Emma wasn't sure. "Rita, when you come of age, you can come and stay with us. Bring your violin."

"Oh Emmy, if only it were so simple. The funny thing is, that, I had to leave St. Theresa's because I couldn't afford the tuition and room and board. Now because they cast me out, and because the lawyers put me here, I am making pretty good money. There's a guy here, named Albert, we call him Pokey, who helps me. He finds a lot of the stuff along the roadside as he wanders around, in fact, you know Schubert's wanderer fantasy? It's his favorite piece. He didn't get far in school, but he reads a lot. Come Spring he says he is going to move on too. Right now, I can see him out my window. You won't believe this, I'm living in a school bus. I haven't played the violin or piano since I got here."

Emma agreed to not call anymore for safety's sake. Instead she would use Pokey's email address.

Rita threw on the yellow negligee that had come from the dump and went into the sunshine. Pokey was still circling. "Morning Doodley" Rita sang out, greeting the morning.

Pokey turned and smiled, took a deep breath and sang out, "We're all in our places, with sun shiny faces, Good Morning to you too, Missey Chamberlin. Wads up?

"I just had a call from a girlfriend back at school. She seemed so far away, and I guess she is. I've forgotten what it feels like to be in a classroom. Trying to learn what they say I should learn. Being ready to fail, not getting it."

She continued, "School was good to me, but there were bad

times too. I remember in PE, the coach would take two of the outstanding girls and tell them to pick sides for a game they called Pom Pom Pull away. Of all the girls there, I was next to last in being chosen. Only Wanda Wolfer was last, and she weighed 300 pounds. Not to be chosen first, but rather last. To be tested and retested, I worried a lot."

"Yeah I know what you mean, Rita. Believe me, I gave up pretty early, never could spell worth a darn, and my handwriting was always bad. It didn't matter which hand I used, it was always the same, big awkward letters, Teachers never thought I could do anything well. And my clothes were different from the others."

"Well Pokey, I'm off to the creek, I need a once over before I can face the world."

The fall leaves of the aspen glowed a bright yellow, quaking gently, as Rita threaded her way back down the path to the stream. The water was crystal clear and chilly. Rita debated whether the water was too cold, and decided to risk it. It took her breath away but she got used to it.

She climbed onto her favorite rock and dried off in the warm sun. Out of habit she twisted her towel and rubbed her back with it. She sat down on the towel enjoying the smell of the morning, the call of the meadow larks, the distant bellowing of the Krishna cows.

At the sound of a jet plane over head, Rita looked up wondering, "I wonder what I look like from up there. Maybe I should put on my clothes."

Charles Comer had been in Hong Kong doing a photo shoot for the Spring Big Book Catalog. He was exhausted and somewhat hung over. The night before leaving he had gone out with the stylist to a going away party at Thunder Bay. Then he had taken the hydroplane over to Macao for a couple of hours at the casinos, after which he had boarded his Singapore jet to San Francisco, thence to Ottawa, and now the Shuttle to Murray Bay. He vowed the next time he had to go to Hong Kong he would go through Gatwick on Air India.

Approaching Murray Bay, he looked out the window of the Gulfstream, watching the landscape below. The crazy quilt patterns of yellow and brown fields. The cornfields being picked, other fields being plowed getting ready for next year's crops.

"The next year"...he thought. "Will next year be more of the same...or will it get better...or worse. Why give a damn, anyway. What difference will it make?"

The patchwork of yellow and green fields gave way to wild prairie and forested hills, with streams twisting their way to the St. Lawrence.

"That's planet Earth down there, Look at her veins flowing with waters, almost black, they look like the veins on my hand!"

As the Gulfstream approached the Murray Bay landing strip he was somewhat in a daze watching the streams below when he thought he saw a woman sunbathing in the nude by a creek. He smiled and wished he could be so free.

Pokey was beginning to annoy Rita. More and more he was pacing to and fro. She would wake up in the morning and there he would be, pacing. One morning on the way to the greenroom, she asked, "Is something wrong Pokey? How long have you been out here?"

Pokey admitted "I don't know what else to do. I can't sleep like I used to. I used to just love sleeping, it was a way to get away from everything. Solace, that's the word, sleep gave me solace, a chance to get away from all the crap in the world. But nowadays, come nine o'clock, I can't stay awake. My eyes get dry, and I can't even breathe right."

"I can't resist, I just can't. But boy do I drop off to sleep, BAM. I don't know where I go, but I find a world of beauty. Of involvement, a world of light. A world of stories that are deep with meaning, stronger than the reality that you and I are having right here. I want to go back, but I can't. I used to trick myself into bridging the gap, but I can't anymore. I tried more melatonin, that didn't work. I don't want to take Xanex either, or Prosac."

"Maybe you should exercise more, run down to the twin

bridges creek," suggested Rita.

"In last night's dream, I was in a lumberyard and this Cape Brenton type guy came up to me, kind of looked both ways and asked me if I were interested in buying some philosophy books. I said Oh yes. But then he left, saying they were in his attic and he would have to go get them. Then the scene shifted into act two. I can't remember what happened in act two. But the last part I can remember, ooh! Boy do I remember. The first guy never came back!

Suddenly I was in a dark warm place, like a butler's pantry. It was a cramped space and I was in there with two big black waiters who were serving a table of three or four persons. I could see into the dining room, it was very dark and there was a table with light emanating up from its center. The faces of the men, I think they were men, the faces shown in a warm light as if there were a candle or something in the middle of the table."

"The same scene was in a book of paintings by Rembrandt. I knew I had seen that view, with the warm light of the table surrounded by darkness so deep you could cut it with a knife."

"It was even darker in the closet with the black waiters. One of them goes out to the table, and returns, he comes back to this dark space. And I over hear him, telling his friend...he says, and get this: "Its fantastic in there, Christ is alive, in the relationship of those people." I know the guy didn't use the word people, and he didn't use the word diners, or customers either. I don't even know if I heard the last word. The message my brain concocted was, invited or not, the essential spirit of Christ is more than a figment of imagination, or dreams. Christ actually can be summoned into our lives, but only really alive in relationships in the moment. I can feel it now, here with you."

"Boy am I glad I don't have your problems," said Rita. "I still think you should get some help, it's not right to be so wound up in this God trip. There's got to be something better to do with yourself. I mean really! If you are made in the image of God, then what do you do with your animal nature? Does God have a sex drive?"

"Maybe next time you drop off, how about aiming for Mary Magdalen's bed chamber. Whoopee. She could help you I'm sure! Or if you can't make that trip, go back to your black waiter friends, and ask them for directions to Whoopi Goldberg's house."

"Rita, don't make fun of me," said Pokey with tears in his eyes, "its not my fault!"

He continued, "As time goes on, I keep going to the other side of the mirror. When I look back, everything makes sense. I can see why people do the things that they do. And when I'm on the other side of the mirror, there's no surprises. Everything is predictable and in a natural flow. It would be boring if it were not so incredibly enjoyable. That's a good word, joy. I'm going to look it up some day."

Rita had enough, and needed to get on with the day. "Pokey, I think you should look up the word sex, or animal. Why don't you go into Googel and do a search under images for lust. Maybe you could put quotes around "lust non-spiritual" or maybe look under groups for "non-spiritual lust." That's the beauty of those non-selective search engines. You get new connections, comparisons that lead you into today's reality. Wow, I can't believe I said that!"

"Yeah Rita, I hear ya. When you take off the blinders, it is all out there. All reality is in front of us all the time, just waiting to be decoded. Google helps to decode, to define new relationships. Google is a mirror too!"

"So bright one, what is different about your joy, versus plain old empathy? Sure would be nice if there were no surprises in life, but that ain't going to happen."

"If you ask me, life is a dance. Not a communion. There's a difference. Communion seeks a plateau, an ecstatic unity of resolution into a locked down fusion. Dance, on the other hand, is a process characterized by movement and reaction to things. A dancer never is completed, never requited. The dancer never understands concepts as we do, yet has infinite energy to bounce from one flight into another, from one pace to another, being swept up into the frenzy of the moment."

"Pokey thought a moment, "Maybe a communion and a dance both can be spiritual, in the sense that the spirit can enter into any pastime. The only requirement is that it be summoned, like in a seance. You could ask for divine participation in any situation. We pray all the time, but maybe we don't ask the right questions. We ask for support from above, rather than asking for insight into what's here below. Instead we should look downward into the soul of man, who generally doesn't have a clue about himself. And talk about false gods! The publickers tell you to pray for peace, while they wage their wars. Fits for them, not for me. Nope."

Rita was getting bored. "Pokey, you're too cerebral, you're wrong if you think you've got your quarry cornered. Your next problem, if you're lucky, is already in the mail."

"Come on we need to get to work. Aunt Sarah should be home soon." After a late lunch Aunt Sarah started taking the bottom plate off a vacuum food sealer. "What's that?" asked Rita.

"Its a food sealer. When it was new it cost more than one hundred and fifty dollars. It still has some of the pouches on a roll, see? Here's the little motor, here's the crank, and the diaphragm pump. And here is the pressure limit switch. See? It looks like it is stuck in the off position"

Rita watched Aunt Sarah put a drop of 3-in-1 oil on the switch. "Now, see, it's humming beautifully."

"You know, Aunt Sarah, you amaze me. You can fix anything," said Rita. "But one thing puzzles me. Forgive me for asking, but, how come you never got married?"

"Well it wasn't because I wasn't asked! replied Aunt Sarah. "I could see what was going to be expected of me down the road. To take a back seat in the bus, to be ready to satisfy on demand, it was kind of, degrading. The game wasn't worth the candle as they used to say. Besides, this way I don't hurt anybody."

Aunt Sarah was bored with this introspection, and pulled out the Vacuum bell jar that had been gathering dust. "What's the story on this?"

"I almost listed it on Ebay, I think the limit switch isn't working. It will work pretty good, except when the vacuum limit approaches zero, the motor should turn off. But it doesn't, it just keeps going, getting hotter and hotter. I opened it up, so you can look at it."

Aunt Sarah turned the base over to expose the wiring. "Looks like a short over here" said Aunt Sarah pointing to some discolored varnish on one of the resisters."

Aunt Sarah showed Rita how to trace circuits, with the test probe. "See this resistor, the one that has the two yellow and one green band. It would be my guess that it's failing. It's sending too much through. And there's another problem I can see. You've got a ground fault. See here, someone has replaced the power supply with a two conductor wire. It needs, I'd wager, to have a three conductor, well grounded cord. These things won't work well without a good ground. Its like they are computers, built before the computer age. Its what you'd expect from Germans in 1940."

The wind suddenly blew open the door sending leaves across the garage floor. Rita shut the door, "I'll see if I can find that part in the online Radio Shack catalog."

In the Mrs. Karl's bread truck, Pokey was deep into modeling another puppet head around a set of eyes that he had cut from an old doll he had found at the dump. The new puppet now could blink its eyes naturally. Pokey talked to the emerging character..."Sometimes I get so depressed, I feel like a prisoner of the moment. I see everything, but I don't know where it's going. Do you know where we are going? And by the way, what's your name?"

The puppet was mute, for the time being, but not Mr. Pee. He had over heard Pokey and had ideas of his own. He grunted and came over to Pokey to have his ears scratched. "Yeah, I know," said Pokey looking into Mr. Pee's dark eyes. "I think too much...I gotta work on that."

Rita knocked lightly on her way to calling it a day. "Are you

OK? Everything alright?" She came in and knelt down to see the new puppet. "Hey, Pokey, this guy is really shaping up. What is his name?"

"Maybe...Gwendolyn or Constance. Something pretty. Maybe Grace or Eunice."

"Well until you get some hair on her, she looks like Bruce to me. Maybe Eric. Maybe he's a friend of Bolt's. Maybe he's Bolt's partner. Call him Nuts!" Rita laughed, "You know, nuts and bolts, they go together. Gives a whole new meaning to screw you, buddy!"

Pokey laughed too, and Mr. Pee grinned.

The winds blew through the trees in a minor mode, casting a pall of oncoming winter over the mood. "Pokey I gotta go, it's been a long day." Impulsively Rita gave Pokey a kiss on his forehead. "You know I really like your mind. It's twisted, but good twisted."

"I'm going to exit left...see you in the morning. It's your turn to cook. OK?'

Rita climbed into her sleeping bag, turned on her BBC, and was soon asleep.

Eleven

Rita was the first up. It was Monday. She listened to the morning radio news while brushing her hair. The Americans were thinking of revaluing the dollar. The New Dollar was going to equal one hundred old dollars. A Mormon missionary had been kidnapped, flu vaccines were late this year.

A dull rain was running down the bus windows, making the outside world seem to vibrate. She turned off the radio, mesmerized by the sound of waves of rain rolling across the roof of the bus. She felt adrift in a sea. Pulling on a poncho she headed to the greenroom, then into the garage office expecting to see Pokey. But no one was up.

She started a new fire in the cook stove, got out the juice glasses, cereal box and milk. Soon the coffee was ready. She watered the geranium and sat down with the Radio Shack catalog looking for the right resister.

Aunt Sarah was next, wearing a strange combination of clothes. A red and black plaid wind-breaker over a pink hooded sweatshirt, with dark green sweatpants. Rita noticed that her socks didn't match, but didn't say anything. When Pokey hadn't shown up by eight o'clock, Rita went to check up on him. As she was about to knock, she could hear the sounds of muffled sobbing coming from the bread truck.

"Pokey? Are you alright?"

Pokey came to the back door, "Yeah I'm better than OK! Wanda came to me last night, and she brought some of that yellowish light, all around her. I felt like she plugged me into the circuit. She came so close. She was so warm! I'm not used to that. She came onto me! I swear, I swear I'm not making this up. We made love for hours it seemed, taking breaks and talking about God. She uses a different word for God, I don't remember it too well, sounded a little like mahatma or mahari. She told me to start thinking about nothing. And to think real hard, harder than ever before."

"At first I was so happy to be back with her that I didn't really want to listen to anything about her philosophy. I just wanted to be with her, feeling her warmth. I felt I could tell her anything and she would understand. And I did. I told her about my mother, about the Riddles, about being a state at large case for the welfare department. She rocked me, she massaged my back. And we made love again. Or maybe we didn't. Where does the river begin anyway?"

"Just before dawn she was stroking my forehead, she told me she had to go, but she would be back. She repeated that my answers were in nothing. And you know, I have faith, I feel that yellow light, and I know Wanda's right."

His tears of happiness brought tears to Rita's cheeks also. "Pokey, maybe your ship has come in, and you didn't even notice. I'm happy for you! I really am. You have a little of that glow right now. It's kind of a yellow light all around you, and it's a moving, vibrating light. Pokey! You is touched!

Pokey was silent...his face dropped into a gray zone, "Tell me, Rita, what is nothing? Is it the sound of one hand clapping? Cause I know that sound...it's like the tree falling in the woods with no one there. Going beyond the known, is that where it's at? You know I was looking in the wrong spots for so many years, now I know, to live life you must love life. As Edgar Lee Masters said, to put meaning in one's life may end up in madness, but life without meaning is the torture of restlessness and vague desire. It is a boat longing for the sea and yet afraid."

Rita nodded, "Well Mahatma, after the ecstasy, there's the laundry. You forgot it was your turn to make breakfast. You owe me one buddy,"

Pokey agreed, "I'm sorry, I lost all track of time and place. How about me doing the dump run today? And I can help Sarah doing some repair work." Two snow blowers were dropped off, a toaster oven, and a half-inch drill that needed new brushes and a good oiling.

Rita packed up the Ebay orders and ordered a new supply of express mail envelopes for the Universal Rape Protectors. When the mail came she was happy to find not one, but three Paypal checks from Ebay. The total came to almost $450. After Aunt Sarah's cut, she would split $300 with Pokey.

She was oiling up the vacuum bell jar pumps when she heard the familiar put-put of Alice coming back from the dump. She put on her windbreaker and went out to inspect any proceeds. Aunt Sarah got there first. "Looks like you got some good stuff, Pokey" said Aunt Sarah picking up an electric griddle out of the manure spreader.

"Yeah, and I got the cover for it too, and the cord. It looks like it's never been used." We got some more video tapes...the story of the Bible, Yoga Exercise, Julia Child's the art of French cooking. And I got some plywood scraps that I can use for making my puppet stage. Aunt Sarah, there are more books too. There are a couple old Mark Twains, and the complete works of Bulwer Lytton. All seven volumes. They're in real good condition, except for a little rain damage, I think they'll dry out."

After a supper of vegetable soup and day old bread, Rita and Pokey cleaned up the dishes, setting the table for breakfast. Pokey put some oak in the stove and set the damper down. He looked over at the test bench and saw the bell jar apparatus all polished up. He asked Rita "Did you get that thing to work?"

"Almost...I ordered a resister that Aunt Sarah thinks is shorted out. If it works, I'll bet we get three hundred bucks or more."

Suddenly Pokey had a thought, "What if you didn't turn off the pump. What would happen if all the air were pumped out of the bell. What would be left? Nothing! Right"

"Wanda told me to study nothing, that nothing was the answer for me. Now all I gotta do is figure out how nothing is going to help me. If I can just get a handle on it, like I got a handle on the yellow light, energy, and mass...then I'll be home free and ready for Wanda to come live with me. Maybe she can help me with my puppet show. Oh if she only would, we could bring light into all the world. Think of it! Me! Dumb old Albert the Pokeyman, now instead, a beacon of light for all the world. Me! Me who couldn't read until he was ten. Me who never had lessons on how to act proper. Indeed, the Lord works in mysterious ways."

"Pokey, I don't think it is possible to get out all the air. I think there always is going to be a little left in the jar. Isn't it just space after all! I mean, yeah, you got your inner space and you got your outer space. You tell me where the border crossing is. And maybe you gotta work at finding the key to the lock."

"What would happen if you put some my Great Stuff in the vacuum bell? Could you somehow trap a vacuum in the soft foam before it sets up? Before you send it out on Ebay, let me experiment...I have a hunch that I might be on the track of the nothing, or the almost nothing, that is going to help me make sense from the something. It may be like you can't have a one sided coin. It's the ying-yang of the totality. It's time for me to explore my dark side, however vague and troubled, however tortured is my desire. If the universe is expanding, I gotta at least try to catch up."

Rita looked at Pokey, "I'm not sure I follow you. What would happen if your desire were satisfied? Wouldn't that be sinful in some way? Is torture a two sided coin too?"

Pokey reached for his book of great thoughts, "Yeah, Rita, somehow everything is a two sided coin. Name me anything that isn't in relationship. Night and day, God and Mankind, the hunter and the hunted...you and me, and Aunt Sarah and her projects?

Twelve

On the following Tuesday, UPS delivered the parts order for the resister. Aunt Sarah watched over Rita as she repaired the circuit board. "Rita, be sure you can trace the green ground wire all the way through the fused line. There's your protection, its absolutely required."

Pokey was back in a few minutes with a can of Great Stuff. Rita finished the repair and replaced the metal base to the apparatus. Pokey could see all kinds of potentials opening up, and was acting like a child at Christmas. "Rita, here's what I want to try. I'm going to squirt some of the Great Stuff into this balloon, and then I want to quick put the balloon into your vacuum bell. You turn it on, and we'll see what happens."

The experiment proceeded. The balloon was inflated with the sticky yellow foam, and put under the glass bell. Rita turned on the pump. As the pump pulled the air out of the jar, the balloon got larger and larger. "Great! Look at that," said Pokey. "Better turn off the motor before it overheats. I want to leave the balloon in there until the stuff sets up. Then we can take it out."

An hour later Pokey figured that the Great Stuff was fully set up. Rita opened the relief valve to let air back into the bell, and watched with amazement as the balloon slowly rose up in the glass bell jar. "Wow! It works," said Pokey. "The great stuff now has a negative weight. Can you beat that?"

Rita was speechless, staring at the balloon. "Better get a string Pokey. We don't want to loose your invention."

Aunt Sarah returned from town with Ed Harris and came into the garage shop. Rita and Pokey were all smiles, holding their balloon on a string. "Look Aunt Sarah, Pokey has an invention!"

Aunt Sarah wasn't impressed. "So what's the deal...balloons are balloons." She opened a couple of beers.

Pokey handed the string to Aunt Sarah. "Take a feel of the balloon...it is not filled with hot air. And it's not filled with helium, or hydrogen. Its solid. Its the first lighter than air solid, and Rita and I made it right here!"

Ed Harris set his beer down and came over to the vacuum apparatus. "That's some machine. What's gonna happen if you let go of the balloon?"

"Well, I suppose, it will act like a helium balloon," said Pokey. It will float higher and higher in the atmosphere, until it finds its equilibrium spot. Maybe a mile up? I don't know."

"That shouldn't be too hard to calculate," offered Rita. "Start with you normal atmospheric pressure, say 29.80 inches of mercury, cut it in half, and you get an equal opposite weight factor pulling against the gravity. Thus, the thing floats both in water and air. It's not rocket science."

Rita was studying the balloon. "Pokey, what would happen if you took the balloon off of the great stuff?"

"I guess nothing would happen," answered Pokey, "Lets try."

Pokey took out his penknife and stuck it into the balloon. The balloon split off and dropped to the floor. No bang, no noise whatever. And the globe of great stuff seemed to rise up a bit higher. "What would happen if we left the vacuum pump on longer?"

During the next three weeks Walmart had to order extra cases of Great Stuff sealer. Rita and Pokey found that too much of a vacuum produced a bad result, a form that held its negative pressure for only a day or two. They found the right point where the cellular formation remained closed. The vacuum had to be contained perfectly. They also found that they could restore the negative weight by putting the form back in the chamber for a few hours. But it was only a temporary fix.

"Well, it's a law. Nature abhors a vacuum," said Rita. "But still I think it's a great invention. You should be proud."

Pokey nodded, "I can't take credit. Wanda told me that my search would end in nothing. And this is as close as I can get to nothing. Somehow I am getting to be a human version of your vacuum pump. I draw all the meaning out of reality, and I am left with nothing. I've turned over all the stones to find the hidden messages. I can accept reality for face value. My head is not in the clouds. I think I've got my feet on the ground. But who knows. How do we ever know if our lives have been in vain?"

Rita thought a moment, "Don't they say that you have to be either are a leader or a follower? Either follow or get out of the way. When the open grave beckons, how much of our agendas will be left undone? Now that's where you really need to focus your attention! Funny I didn't see that before."

Rita's eyes were ablaze, "Think of it Pokey, how sad most people are when death comes. Our passion should be in realizing from our disappointment that life isn't better than it is. Look at Aunt Sarah. She is a whole lot better than either one of us at accepting life. She doesn't have to strain, burdened with injustice."

"Forget about not pushing the river, Pokey, you'll never get anywhere swimming against the current. Some might say that you are in denial, Pokey. What's it going to take for you to come to your senses? Talk about through a glass darkly! You can't see beauty except far away, in vague outline. You gotta recognize the beauty in the imperfections seen right up close. Perpetual high standards are a cop out for everyone who can't accept their shadow sides. All this spiritual work makes Jack a dull boy. But don't let me confuse you with reality, you've got a lot on your agenda."

Pokey didn't know what to say. Basically he felt he was on the right track, but he couldn't see ahead to the next station. That night he talked with Mr. Pee until they fell asleep at dawn. Mr. Pee asked Pokey how many vacuum balloons it would take for him to get air born. Pokey said he'd work on it. It might be quite a draw for the puppet show. Maybe he could call his show THE FLYING PIG ASTRONOMICAL LECTURE COMPANY. Besides it might help Mr. Pee get out of his depression.

Thirteen

Thursday night Aunt Sarah decided to attend the Pilgrim Fellowship fall dinner benefit at St. John's in Murray Bay. She went every year, and she went late every year. She had learned that there was always too much food. Food that often was offered for free, if only someone would take it. She brought home a gallon of beef vegetable soup, and six slices of chocolate cake.

Along about noon the next day, Father Fitzgerald stopped in to have Aunt Sarah look at his hedge trimmer. Aunt Sarah introduced him to Rita and Pokey, "This here is my niece Rita Marie, and our side kick, Albert. Albert is just passing through."

Pokey looked down at the priest's shiny black shoes, and mumbled, "My friends call me Pokey. And these are my twilights." Pokey waved a cat's paw at the priest. "I travel around a lot" continued Pokey, "and I take care of our little friends that get killed on the highway, get killed for no reason! Lot of times our little friends get killed at twilight time. I keep these little paws to remind me of their sacrifice. Somebody's gotta do it."

Father Fitzgerald paused, "Yes, I'm sure Albert, Some day if you like, we can talk about it...but for now, I need to have this trimmer back before the weekend. We've got a wedding on Saturday. Is that possible?"

Aunt Sarah said it would take at least four hours, and even then, if she had to order parts, it might not get done in time. "But," she said, "I might have a different trimmer you could borrow. I can drop it off Friday Morning, would that be soon enough?

Father Fitzgerald seemed reassured, and offered to pay in advance. Aunt Sarah declined, saying she couldn't tell how much time it was going to take. On the way out, Father Fitzgerald said, "You know I drove right by your place and I didn't see your sign. Luckily I saw your yellow mailbox.

Later that afternoon Aunt Sarah soon had the trimmer running smoothly when Rita asked, "Aunt Sarah, you know

Father was right, you could use a sign. Pokey and I could make one up, I'm sure."

Sarah thought a moment, "Yeah,...I remember reading in a book about remarkable men by Gurdjieff, he talked about opening a fix it shop in Turkistan. The man put up a sign, We fix anything. And the work just flowed in. But I don't know if I need more trouble. I'm pretty busy as I am without asking for more grief."

Rita countered, "But we're here almost all the time anyway. And Pokey and I could help, if you could tell us what to do. Is it a deal?"

By suppertime Pokey and Rita had primed several pieces of plywood for a sign. Over supper they discussed what to paint on the signs. For years Lost Grove Motors had been the name of the Texaco gas station.

Sarah wanted to keep the name Lost Grove, Pokey liked Fixall, and Rita thought Shoppe added a nice flair. So it was the next day that they lettered:

Lost Grove
Fixall
Shoppe

They convinced Aunt Sarah to pay for a larger mailbox that they brought home from Walmart. They painted it a bright yellow, just like the older box. Next to it they installed their largest sign on the cement island that once had held the gas pumps for the station.

Rita seemed to be taking a new lease on life. Organizing and discarding took place every morning, Monday through Friday. Pokey went along with her in this new clean up drive. Now when the crew set off for the dump they sometimes had a full load going both ways. Gradually a new look was coming to Lost Grove.

Pokey checked on the red tail hawk that he had put out for the maggots to clean up. He seemed pleased with the specimen that now was a dried mesh of feathers and bone. The beak and scull were bone white, the tattered skin mostly tan.

Pokey admired the banding on the tail feathers and set them aside for his collection. He looked intensely at the cracked wing bone that had been broken. He got out his magnifying glass and studied the inside structure of the bone. "Jesus! Is that beautiful! The form perfectly follows its function. I'll bet if it were solid it wouldn't work as well," he said to himself.

He took a wire cutter and snipped off the bird's reptilian feet with their talons still sharp. He felt lucky to have found such a nice addition to his twilights.

Less than a week later Aunt Sarah was home alone when Sheriff Hermanson pulled up in the county squad car. He left his hazard lights blinking while he went into the garage building.

"Oh! I didn't hear you come in, Inspector. What can I do for you?" asked Sarah.

"What's going on here? You're taking a lot of stuff to the dump. People are talking. We've had one complaint that you don't have a permit for that new yellow sign that someone put up. I'm afraid I'm going to have to give you a citation, for erecting a sign without a permit."

Sheriff Hermanson handed Aunt Sarah the complaint and summons. "Court is always Monday morning, but then you know that don't you?"

"You've got to be kidding Inspector! We've had a sign there for as long as anyone can remember."

"Yes, but not as big as what you have out there now. It may be too close to the road. You can get an application at the Courthouse. You should have checked for current rules before you put up the sign."

When Rita and Pokey returned Aunt Sarah caught them at the door, "Guess what? Your new sign has cost me a fine! A fine of $50.00" plus Court Costs."

Pokey volunteered to get the application for a sign from the County Planning office. The next day Rita filled out the application that called for a sketch of the proposed sign. She asked Pokey if he could do a sketch of the sign, and he asked

"Why not just take a digital shot and Email it to him?"

"No, I gotta have something to enclose with the application." Pokey went out on the road with his Sony DC-9 and did a photo print of the front of the garage with the yellow sign. Rita put the application together and neatly folded it. Next day she gave it to the mailman with explicit instructions to deliver it to the Court.

A week later Sheriff Hermanson returned, leaving his hazard lights on again. "Sarah Jane, there's a problem with your application. The Court cannot accept your application for remedial variance."

"Well, confound it, what is wrong now! Damn it all! We paid the Court the $50 fine, and we sent in the $35 for the Sign permit, just like they said." She dropped a ball peen hammer onto the workbench. Her cheeks were taking on a rosy glow.

Sheriff Hermanson, chuckled, "The law says you are supposed to attach a sketch of the proposed sign. The Court says a photo is not a sketch. If it makes an exception for you, then who knows what would be next? So you will have to reapply with a sketch of the proposed sign. You can use the same application papers, just staple the sketch and a new check onto them."

After the Sheriff left, Rita traced a sketch on some tissue paper and showed it to Aunt Sarah. "Do you think I should put in color? I've got a yellow pencil that matches."

"No," said Aunt Sarah, "there might be a law that says the sketch must not be in color. The Court might say that if they wanted a finished drawing, they would have asked for a finished drawing. You can't go wrong if you follow the letter of the law. Of course, with Sheriff Hermanson, the law might change, you never know."

Fourteen

After supper in the old office, Aunt Sarah usually retired to the tool shed that served as her bedroom. She had set a goal for herself to read all of Michener's work.

Rita and Pokey cleaned up the dishes, swept the floor, while listening to the BBC news. Sometimes they would work on projects in the garage. This particular evening found them in Mrs. Karl's Bread Truck where Pokey was working on another puppet. Rita asked Pokey to put on the New World symphony.

Mr. Pee rustled around his bed and came out to lay down next to Pokey, who stroked his pet's ear with the puppet head. The largo movement came and Pokey nodded in time, transfixed, out of control, at his gateway again. He felt both liberation from the music, and dread of the onrushing flow that held his soul at bay. The void beckoned.

"I'm not sure, Rita, but I'm getting more and more afraid of this void. It's dreadful, and inescapable. Just when I think I understand it, poof! It's out of reach. Like now, listening to Dvorak, I feel like I'm flying, cresting with the music, looking down at the fields, following the setting sun. I feel like a bird skipping from cloud to cloud."

"Then boom! I'm back here in nowhere land"

Rita picked up the puppet in process, "I don't think that is odd at all. I'd just call it instinct. It's a natural function, just as every beggar dreams of being Emperor."

Pokey put on his George Washington puppet and changed his voice..."I suppose every Emperor dreams of being a pauper too! For me, I'm not afraid of being poor like a lot of people I know. I've been there. Mr. Pee and I always seem to find a way."

Rita and Pokey finished the New World and then put on Vivaldi's Seasons. From time to time they would hear the fans come on, blowing out warm air. Rita noticed a glaze come over Pokey's eyes as he stared at the fan blades going around and around in the heater. He was no longer listening to the music.

"Rita, that fan blade going around and around, it's like a helicopter on its side. What would happen if you pointed it straight down? How fast would it have to go to beat the forces of gravity? I was just imagining making a huge fan blade out of our vacuum foam.

Pokey grabbed some cardboard and sketched out a large saucer shape, complete with a stick figure hanging from a bicycle with pedals. "If you had a big enough volume of the vacuum foam, and spun it fast enough, you could go anywhere! Talk about not polluting! Rita...you're brainy, how fast would it have to go?"

"Pokey, why don't you put the fan on a scale, and point it up or down, and then measure the difference of its weights. That might give you an idea. I imagine, like anything else, the lift you would get would be non-linear, a bell curve of some sort. At some point, a faster speed isn't going to do much for you. At that point all you can do it increase your radius." Rita penciled into Pokey's sketch a section of an airfoil. When it came to the edge where the tips would intercept air, she put a question mark. "Here's the spot that I imagine would be critical. Here's the springboard to lift."

Rita left Pokey working on the drawing and went to bed. Mr. Pee went out for his constitutional and also retired.

Pokey went on line to Google and studied drawings by Leonardo Da Vince. By morning he had two drawings done of his theoretical flying machine. One featured a unicycle hanging from wide opposing blades, propelled by pedals. The other just had an engine compartment in the center. The actual structure resembled the inside bracing of the leg bones from his red tail hawk. When Pokey and Rita showed the plans to Aunt Sarah she sat down, and at length said. "Boys and Girls, the plans are beautiful. What's the next step?"

Pokey wanted to build a full size prototype, but they settled on a scaled down version to be mounted on a platform scale. It would give them the answers they needed. The next few weeks were spent on fabricating the individual spokes, and the pie shaped segments of rigid vacuum foam. Aunt Sarah brought in her Stilh two cycle chain saw. This in turn was mounted inside a simple washtub. By bolting the opposing foil to the air intake of the chain saw motor, they achieved double the lift, while countering the gyroscopic drag. Together Aunt Sarah and Rita cruised the internet, Googleing "vacuum Plastic," "helio motion," Motion wave theory." Every once in a while they would have to stop and think, whether their idea made any sense.

The controls for the gas engine came down through a spline joint directly into the center of the experimental craft. Aunt Sarah and Pokey started another design with two chain saw engines in the wash tub. They debated whether to put the engines in series or parallel. Rita preferred putting them in line, so that the additional engine could work as an afterburner. Since both engines were attached separately to the crank, it was easy to wire them together.

Once the engines were secure in the tub, Pokey and Rita started building the fans. Cases of Great Stuff® were consumed. The bell jar pump seemed to be going all day long making vacuum segments. Finally they had a half size model bolted to the platform scale.

Rita went to the cooler and brought out three cans of beer. "This is a special time. Think of Orville and Wilbur. Think of Amelia Ehrhart. Think of Alan Shepard, Gus Grissolm. People have been seeing flying saucers for years, and here we are. It's not rocket science after all!"

Rita raised her beer in a toast, "Ladies and Gentlemen, start your engines."

There was no built-in starter, but Pokey easily took hold of the upper fan and spun it in a clockwise direction. Put put, put, put. He backed off the choke, and the machine started blowing dust and papers all around the room. "Hey, easy! Pokey!" They looked at the scale and determined they had a stationary lift of eighty-five pounds. If Rita's calculations were right, a full size version would give them 385 pounds of lift at fifty rpms.

Aunt Sarah finished her beer and got out a bottle of Old Mr. Boston rum. As the hour passed they could hardly take their eyes off their machine. The rum put Aunt Sarah on a crash course. She squealed, ranted, and raved. Rita knew where this kind of talk was going. It's us against them.

The County tax assessor had been by and had decided that the property should be classed as a business instead of a woodlot. Taxes would have to go up, unless she could get it back to pasture class, she could save seven hundred dollars in property taxes.

"They told me I could run one cow on the property and it could be reclassified as pasture. But I'd have to fence it all in. Don't they know that these trees are what gives us the oxygen we breathe? Soon her mind got ahead of her speech, and then she lost her train of thought. She mumbled something about Sheriff Hermanson. When Aunt Sarah fell asleep in the overstuffed chair, Rita and Pokey decided to call it a night. Pokey covered Aunt Sarah with a crazy quilt.

Pokey was first up the next morning. Sitting in the outhouse, he left the door open. As the sun rose the trees and bushes began to sparkle with frost. One spot on one bush seemed to outshine all the others. Pokey stared at it. It was unnaturally bright, a beacon of sorts.

"There's the burning bush," Pokey said to himself softly. "We've been here before...wherefore art Thou now...make of me an understander."

Pokey watched spellbound as the crystals melted to form dew that fell like drops of rain. He watched the drops form on the bare branches; he watched them grow into tiny globes of light, only to drop away.

Pokey wiped himself, "Maybe God is not eternal, but only found in the moment. Maybe God leaves her tracks everywhere, but most cannot see them. But maybe not."

After morning prayers, Pokey told Mr. Pee that the saucer was going to help build a real good puppet show. But for now they were going to have to find a bigger barn to build the new craft.

Over breakfast Rita asked Pokey, "Got any ideas for a name for our new bird. Eagle, albatross, hawk, have all been used."

"How about Turkey," laughed Rita. "The turkey has landed! Or, I have it, call it the Dervish because of the whirling blades."

"Yeah I like that, we'll call it the Dervish One."

This morning Aunt Sarah made her rounds alone as she had been doing for the last twenty years. It was easier in the early years when she had her driver's license. Now astride Alice it took at least twice as long to get to the airport snack shop and landfill.

On the way she passed the familiar sights, Helgeson's Egg Farm, the Hare Krishnas, the twin bridges.

She loaded the snack shop trash and stopped in to talk with Mrs. Staber and to have a Fosters Lite.

Mrs. Staber was closing up, "Tell Albert that he got the job of housekeeping on the World's End Gulfstream. It will be once a week usually on Friday night or anytime on Saturday or Sunday. Tell him to stop by and I'll give him the keys and detail sheets."

"Now that's a job I wouldn't want. Pokey can have it," said Aunt Sarah.

Mrs. Staber agreed, "They pay well though."

Pokey and Rita called the snack shop the next day and arranged to meet Mrs. Staber Friday afternoon. Pokey got his identification card and the job detail list. Mrs. Staber had only two customers at the counter who were old flying buddies that were just killing time. They watched the shop while she took Pokey and Rita over to the World's End Hanger. It was the largest hanger of several near the fuel pumps. Most of the hangers were for single engine planes, and a couple of the hangers was used for storage. The World's End hanger had three large bays, one for the Gulfstream, one used for storage, and one extra that was not used.

First step was to log in on the system with the ID card, then to turn off the alarm system. Next was to enter the code 069 or 096 for rear access to the Gulfstream G400. Once the stair was down, the cleaning routine consisted of vacuuming, and wiping down walls. The toilet exhaust fans did a good job getting rid of the bleach odor. The cockpit door was to remain locked.

The detail list provided for checking inventory of snacks and beverages. Mrs. Staber helped Rita and Pokey fill out the forms. She also showed them how to set the coffee maker to start the brew cycle for Monday morning. The trash bins were emptied, water system flushed and filled, waste drained.

In all it took about an hour to clean the plane. It was still light when Pokey and Rita pulled into the town landfill. They pitched their recycles into the dumpster, and the rest over the edge of the cliff. Pokey looked over the piles of material and harvested a few books. Rita was about to throw the Gulfstream trash into the dumpster when something made her stop and look into the bag. She inspected the contents with the zeal of a TV crime scene investigator. Mostly plastic cups, magazines, tissues. She picked up a large manila envelope labeled "interoffice-only/ initial and pass on". Since there was stuff in the envelope, Rita put it in the spreader for later reading. It might be interesting to figure out what the lives of these World's End people were like.

After supper Rita took the interoffice material to Mrs. Karls bread truck where she found Pokey working out his puppet routines in the mirror when Rita knocked. In a high pitched shrill voice he answered, "Who's there?"

"Tis I, grandmother, Goldilocks" said Rita.

"Oh do come in my dear. My sweet delectable earthly delight! Oh do come in little dearie."

Rita knelt down next to the puppet stage. "So are you really my grandmother? I don't know...you smell better than my grandmother."

Pokey laughed, "So do you!"

"Guess what Rita. I've been thinking again."

"Oh no, not again!" said Rita.

"You know I was just thinking, most people live under the weight of a massive inferiority complex. They have to lie to themselves and to everyone else, pretending to be whole and worthy. Most children are born with pure grace and beauty, or at least I'd like to think so."

"Then life teaches them in one way or another, how little they know. The trick, is not to accept defeat, and to know your song is all yours, to fashion it any way you please. It is your right and duty to follow your passion, wherever it leads. Remember old George Gray. Life without meaning is a torture of restlessness and vague desire. Measure for measure, you get as much out of life as you put in. How can you arrive if you never depart? That's what my puppets have to do. They urge the little people to find and follow that inner possible grace. Once they loose sight of their souls, it all becomes a game."

Pokey continued, "Everybody gets along, so long as no one blurts out the real truth, that the emperor has no clothes. But you know, I'll bet people in that kingdom, not so far away...I'll bet the guy who sold that last suit of clothes to the Emperor is still doing a thriving business. He's probably got a web site. Probably designing new campaign buttons for the army brass."

"My puppets have to be like the little boy who noticed that the emperor's penis was smaller than he expected!" laughed Pokey.

Rita smiled, "Speaking of penises, how's your animal nature? I thought you had decided you were a little unbalanced, that you needed to let your little hamster out of his cage."

Pokey turned off the radio, "I'm doing Tai Chi now. Remember that Video Instruction Tape? I'm up to exercise twelve, The Jade Mountain. It's doing me a lot of good. My back ache is gone, and I can breathe much better."

Pokey continued, "I'm trying to give myself a break. I say to myself every night, "Albert, tomorrow don't be so hard on yourself. Mediocre doesn't have to be a bad thing. You know what I mean? I can be a perfect storm of mediocrity. Kind of takes your existential breath away, doesn't it! "

Pokey's puppet took center stage. "Only by accepting your own mediocrity, can you triumph, to self-actualization. Along the way we instinctively court disaster, without thinking. We're only human as they say."

"Some get it, and some don't," said Rita.

"Yeah some get it, but don't know what to do with it. Some can't integrate it and many don't finish the installation. It's like they organize, and dust, and polish the parlour. But that rotting carcass of an elephant is still in the next room. That's grounds for schizoid partitions."

"Yeah, Pokey, Someone once said that you are rich in what doesn't bother you. I wonder if you can accept death without accepting life. Or vice versa."

"I know one thing," continued Pokey, "I have to stay away from mirrors, they must have been invented by the publickers. They just aren't helpful anymore. Once those people in the mirror seemed to want to help me. But now there's one guy that even smells bad. He's got bad breath, one of his front teeth is gone, and he rides around in a Dodge truck with another guy. Long dark gray hair and a gray mustache."

Pokey picked up his buxom lady puppet, "Puppets are like my twilights. Each one has a lot to learn. Take Miss Antonia Tetas here, she's a sadder and wiser girl after being abandoned by guy after guy. She thought she had one hooked, and oops! He got away. She wonders if liposuction would help. Everybody needs help. Where's the wizard when you need him? Hmmm? How much does a new nose cost?"

Rita replied "Didn't you preach to me about not trying to be perfect? I seem to remember you were dreaming about going to get philosophy books. Remember?"

Pokey stopped breathing for a minute, "Yeah, of course I do. The dream told me to value ancient wisdom, but yet, damned me as unworthy, forever uninformed."

"Well, Pokey, maybe what your dream is telling you, is that the past is the past. Leave it alone, and just focus on the now. That means you must accept as much as you can without prejudice. Do you understand? The mere act of reacting, of defining, of categorizing, limits your awareness, unless you can step out of your self for an overview."

"So, Rita, maybe we are both right. Maybe God can't decide whether Mankind is a successful invention. So maybe we're a balancing act of spirit. Maybe God is simply postponing judgement, waiting to see if we ever figure it all out."

"QED We must be perpetually undecided, unconvinced, just like God. Ready to be confronted with chaos, confusion, and all manner of deceit. From such a mess we are asked to sprout, grow, vegetate, and blossom! With no two alike, with infinite variety."

Pokey put down Antonia. "Such a messy playing field can be toxic to the tender hearted, or it can be fecund, ready to nourish. Fecundity! Isn't that a great sounding word? Sounds wet with a peculiar odor."

"Sounds dark brown with yellowish green spots," volunteered Rita. "Go back into your mirror, Pokey. But this time, don't get so involved. Don't worry just to be worrying. That obviously isn't going to help you. And most important, don't put expectations on everyone you meet. Keep some distance spiritually. Be puppet master over yourself. Pull your own strings. Leave others to their own devices."

Pokey laughed, "That's right on Rita! You know me pretty well. It seems that it's a mistake to think we have ever solved the puzzle. There will always be a piece that doesn't fit, or is missing altogether."

"All the world is a stage caught in a moment never to be repeated. Yet there is a cycle, isn't there? Don't things come into focus then disappear. Every discontent has its season."

"Yeah, Pokey, I think you have to do more than pull your own strings. You've got to author your script, and be your own lighting director, and prop master too."

"Would you help me Rita? Help me raise the curtain, so to speak. I want to put my show on the road. I need to find out what works."

Rita put her fingers around Pokey's puppet, "I'd love to help, but you know, come next September I'm out of here." Rita's thumb and forefinger gently took hold of the puppets chin, "You can do it, I know you can. I know you can, I know you can."

"Maybe you should scout out the church school in Murray Bay. You gotta start somewhere. Aunt Sarah and I could help you set up the stage, and you can give your astronomical lecture with all your puppets."

Pokey brightened, and Miss Antonia's voice with her southern drawl, came forth, "Oh! We get to go to church! What can I wear? Should I get a veil? Oh! I swear to God I'm going to swoon, such is my passion! "

"Rita, I want to have some music of some kind behind me. Can you help with that?"

"Well I suppose, if you're good to me, I mean real good, maybe I could get out my dad's violin, or I could play one of the Roland keyboards."

Pokey's puppet leaned forward close to Rita's lips, "Give me a kiss to seal the bargain." Rita tenderly kissed Miss Antonia.

With his other hand, Pokey brought out Vito, the burly Italian with a thick neck. In a deep gravelly voice, "Is that the best you can do, Babe? I got this hamster looking for a good home, and you know you want to be helpful, don't you?"

Rita took hold of Vito, and silently looked into Pokey's eyes, sensing a familiar warm yellow light. She looked at Pokey's delicate mustache, and his shiny, moist lips. She patted his hamster cage, saying. "All in good time, Vito. You know Miss Antonia is a good looker too! Decisions, decisions!"

Pokey smiled as Vito kissed Antonia. In his deep gravelly voice, "OK dream boat, I can wait. Like they say on the tele, when the moment comes, I'll be ready, if you know what I mean."

Pokey looked at Rita's hair and the way it flowed over her ears, down around her jawbone, splaying onto her Packers sweatshirt. Her lips looked sad and withdrawn. He thought to himself "Rita doesn't know my hamster as I do."

He leaned over more than half way, and said "When the time comes I'll be gentle. After all, doesn't animal husbandry start at home."

Their lips met halfway. Rita pulled back for a moment, "Can I trust what is happening? Is this real?"

Vito caressed the back of Rita's neck, "As real as anything can be." The next kiss had no end. As their tongues wrestled and embraced, their spirits came to blossom. For each, doors opened with freshness unexpected. So captivated were they that their minds left their bodies to fend for themselves. Rita swooned, falling back, "Even if it isn't real, it'll do nicely until something better comes along."

Pokey laughed, "God loves us. And maybe this is all that there is. If it isn't enough, we'll have to suffer anyway. So get used to it. I'm thinking there's always a dark side, even to the most sublime moment. The reptilian brain must have its own needs!"

"So that's what you call it! A reptile? I thought it was a hampster. I suppose you're going to coil around me like a boa constrictor and put me out of my misery!" Rita smiled, "I'm calling it a night."

❧ Fifteen

Next morning, Rita had a special glow about her. She got up early and put on her pink and orange flowered blouse under her khaki bibs. She found her makeup purse that she hadn't opened for months. A few dabs of cologne reminded her of St. Theresa's and the other girls. She remembered being with Pokey the night before. She hadn't planned on him hitting on her, and she hadn't planned on swooning.

She smiled remembering her audacity. Would Pokey treat her differently? She looked in her own mirror at her pretty blouse, at the purple hibiscus flowers that always reminded her of a Georgia O'Keffe watercolor. But she decided to change back to her regular denim men's shirt with the pocket protector that had belonged to her father. Today she was an engineer before she was a woman. That could come later.

After visiting the green room, Rita went to the office to see if Pokey or Aunt Sarah were up. On the table she found a fifty-dollar bill and a short note from Pokey,

> "Wanda and I are going on a vision quest. Here's some money for Mr. Pee. Let him out when you get this. Tell him I won't be gone forever. I don't want him following me out and down the road. I may be back tomorrow or at the latest forty days from now. Wish me luck!
>
> Yr. Friend, Albert."

Aunt Sarah came in for coffee and was not happy to read Pokey's note. "Doggone it all! He was going to help me fix the yard light. What's this vision quest crap? I've got better things to do. You'll have to do the dump trip by yourself. I think you can handle the job pretty well."

"Yes, Aunt Sarah, I've been carrying good sized loads both ways. I thought today I'd bag up some of the trash in the henhouse. There are only six hens left, including Henrietta. None of them is laying. You'll have to help me, if you will. I know there's some stuff you may want to keep."

"Some of the Great Stuff® scraps have floated up into the rafters. I can bag it with the vacuum cleaner, but then I have to add some ballast to the bags before I can drop them at the dump. I almost let one bag get away last time."

"That, and I thought I'd round up some of the aluminum chairs, rotting wood, clothes, you know, stuff that we can't sell on Ebay. Is there any market for aluminum?

A week went by with no news of Pokey. Rita tried to cheer up Mr. Pee, without much success. The routine every day involved taking in a few jobs at the service counter, helping Aunt Sarah with parts ordering, and taking the trash to the dump on Miss Alice. When she was done filling orders for the rape protection kits, she continued to work on the vacuum foam production.

But somehow Rita was getting bored, even though the end was in sight with the oncoming first flight of the Dervish. Pokey had been at the center of the Dervish project. Without him, somehow, the passion was gone.

But Aunt Sarah wasn't giving up yet. She was nearly finished with testing the Dervish's bicameral power system. She had built in pure redundancy. Either of the two small turbines could be depended upon to keep the Dervish airborne. In addition, unexpectedly, when both engines were perfectly tuned there was a system wide cancellation of noise. A small but powerful vacuum was drawn uniformly from each segment at the hub.

Aunt Sarah and Rita together found two ways to keep the Dervish parts from getting away from them. In the center of each segment there was the vacuum void that they filled with water as ballast. Once the craft was assembled, they planned to drain away some of the water to achieve the amount of static lift required to become airborne. They learned to crush unwanted foam scraps so they would no longer float up to the ceiling.

A second week went by with still no word from Pokey. Rita

took Mr. Pee down to the creek but it was too cold for swimming. She sat on her favorite log next to the creek, enjoying watching leaves fall from the trees onto the endless flow of water. She remembered a famous Chinese poem in her world lit course at St. Theresa's. Something about, "When the breeze comes from the shadow of the North, there begins the poem." Rita mused out loud, sitting with Mr. Pee at her side. "Where begins my poem...?"

A wind blew the yellow leaves across the lazy creek, as Fall was ending. Rita sensed a new kind of loneliness. She missed Pokey and his campaigns. She missed their long talks with Aunt Sarah. And she missed listening to all the different kinds of music with Pokey.

She smiled thinking of that first and last kiss she had with Pokey. She closed her eyes and tried to reconstruct just how it happened in every way. She felt his warm hand in hers, while slowly she felt Pokey's prickly chin against her neck. She remembered playfully nibbling his lower lip, and his response.

While thus enamored she was shocked to have her cell phone chime. No one was supposed to know her number. She hesitated, Mr. Pee was looking at her, also wondering who it could be. Thinking it might be Pokey, Rita answered, "Hello?"

"Hello Rita? This is Emma!"

"Oh Emma! I've been wanting to hear from you. I tried calling you a while back but got no where."

Emma explained that she had a different number now. Rita entered the number in her memory. They talked as Rita and Mr. Pee threaded their way back up the path to the top of the bluff. Rita brought Emma up to date, telling her about the Rape protection kits, and the Dervish project. Emma didn't understand the Dervish, but thought she could use some Rape protection, just in case. Rita agreed to send her the standard packet of bruises, cuts, and infections.

Emma reported that SAT's were being given again this year in the gym. She didn't know if she would take them again, since her junior year's test results were in the ninety-seven percentile. This got Rita thinking.

"Emma, I've got an idea. I need to take the test again myself, but I can't take it here. Can you take it for me? When you hand in your answer sheet, just put my name on it. I can give you my social security number. Who's to know? Use your bother's B and B for my address, and I'll use it on my applications too. I'm going to apply to Radcliff, Yale, and maybe Pembroke in case I get rejected."

Emma wasn't sure if it was the right thing to do, and said she'd check it out and get back to her. In other news, the Saints hadn't finished up too well in their football season, winning only one game against the District School for the Deaf. Emma was volunteering at St. Coleta's Nursing Home and had made friends with several of the patients.

"Oh, Emma, I've got another call coming in, call me again, will you?"

Sixteen

The call came from Mrs. Staber at the airport snack shop. The World's End Gulfstream was away for maintenance so Pokey and Rita wouldn't be needed for cleaning.

Rita and Mr. Pee got back to Lost Grove motors just before suppertime. They found Aunt Sarah making experimental waffles using a bag of calf food instead of flour.

She explained, "Rita, when you're poor you find ways to make do, to stretch your dollar. See this milk replacer? I got it from the Farmers Co-op store. Ten pounds of seventy per cent protein, twelve to fifteen percent fat. That's the equivalent nutrition of beefsteak at forty dollars a pound. For it to be perfect, all I have to do is cut it with some bran fiber. You can thin it with whatever you want. I've used orange juice, milk, and water...even cider or beer works. Pineapple juice doesn't work because it gets too sticky."

Sarah continued, "There are other bargains at the Farmers Co-op Store. There are medications like Tetramyicin, Aureomycin, and Tetracycline Sulfate for cattle and horses. No prescription necessary. Good antibiotics for humans also, at a fraction of the cost you'd pay at the drug store."

"But, Aunt Sarah, I thought antibiotics are overused, that the body sometimes gets weaker through their use. Don't the viruses just mutate?"

"Yeah, you're right, I think its good to switch from penicillin to sulfas, and then just go off all drugs. Trust your body to tell you if it needs help."

"But, not only does that sound weird, I mean, you must be taking a big risk, I mean, you know, you're not that poor!" Rita watched Sarah pour her concoction onto the electric waffle iron. In just a few minutes the pair sat down to eat golden brown waffles, garnished with applesauce, and homemade maple syrup.

After a while Rita forgot that she was eating cattle food. "I wonder why Pokey doesn't call. He's usually so thoughtful. It's not like him."

Aunt Sarah took a deep breath, "He left his pig, and all his stuff. He has to come back, like a bad penny he'll drift on. That's what drifters do. What I think is odd, is that he seems to be so bright. And creative, look at the dervish! It was his idea, and if it pans out, who knows where that could end."

"I have no idea," continued Rita. "He's was talking about a woman named Wanda that he met at an auction or something. He said she comes to him at nighttime. But to tell you the truth, Aunt Sarah, I'm not sure at all that she exists. Like all the trouble Pokey got into when he looked in the mirror too long. Then he leaps across to his parallel reality. Maybe it works for him, but for me, it's just too confusing. Kinda like Castaneda's Don Juan."

Aunt Sarah agreed, "We're going to have to finish the assembly ourselves. I have to fine tune the gyro on the computer, and test the prototype model. There's only a few unknowns to work out, so, with luck, I think we could get airborne in a month. We'll have to see how much payload we can support without the ballast. If my calculations are right, at maximum warp, the bell curve suggests a load 510 kilos at a land speed of 60 kilometers per hour. I found that increasing the vacuum on the system cancels out the noise, just as it did in the first little model."

"If Pokey doesn't come back, who will be the test pilot?" asked Rita.

"Lets not worry about that. He'll be back. Mr. Pee has always counted on him."

Seventeen

The familiar orange flag on the radio aerial was the first thing Rita and Aunt Sarah saw of Pokey. It was just after lunch, and the terrorist level was back down to orange. At least that's what the television was saying. Pokey's trike looked just the same. Without thinking, both Aunt Sarah and Rita joined Pokey in a tearful hug. "Come inside and we'll have a nice cup of tea!" said Aunt Sarah, awkwardly blowing her nose.

"Well I'm back" Pokey said sheepishly, looking down cast. "I've had some trouble, and didn't know where to go. Except here...I've been away in more ways than I can tell you. I've gone places with Wanda that I never dreamed existed. Some places we went, I couldn't understand what the people were saying. They seemed happy, but unconnected. I was lonely while I watched Wanda work the crowd."

"You see, it was my puppets that started it all. And we were doing pretty good for a while. Wanda said it was my fault, and maybe it was. It all happened one night after we were at a revival meeting down in a little town called South Hero, Vermont. I told her that I was going to go inside my head, so it shouldn't have been a shock to her."

"I put myself into my trance state, like I usually do, except this time I went deeper than ever before. I started in a relaxed posture, slightly bent over, so that my lungs weren't inflating fully. I slowed my breathing and shut my eyes, not too tightly. Then I listened for all the sounds around me, and I relaxed my hearing, cancelling out each sound, one by one, until all that was left was static and the extremely high frequencies that sound like computers. Then like, I always do, I waited for the inevitable pause in the sound, hoping that when it came along, I could jump into it, and hold it, and use it."

"The black hole in the sound chamber came, as I hoped it would, I jumped for it, got it, and held on to it, but only for a couple of seconds. Then back came the high pitched whirl, then the gap again, and this time I held it for perhaps a minute."

"I checked my breathing, still with my eyes shut, motionless. I let my mind wander, and I looked for tensions in my muscles and bones, and I let go of all it. Piece by piece. Again the high pitched faint screaming came and went, and I went back down away from my mind. Far from words and ideas."

"It was a far away place within. The integration was total. Muscles remembered the good and the bad. Bones knew the truth and let the blood know it. The soul looked at itself, and forgave itself of a lot of shit. I learned, right there, that forgiveness has to start at home. I looked down at myself, and smiled. Man! Did that feel great!"

"Whole chapters flew by silently, and I deftly sorted the painful from the joyful. I could watch, and comment to myself on the play within, without any prejudice. And without condemnation."

"I think the reason I got so deep was that I found I could turn off my defences, to focus on the field in front of me. I remember seeing myself, my being, as having morphed from a jellyfish, or some other primitive life form. This was elemental me, pure and alone. I could see the keys to the kingdom! I was going to fit in after all!"

"But nothing lasts forever. My normal senses came back to me, one at a time, in the order that they had left. When I signed off from that reality connection, I felt I was fully charged and aware that I had achieved the dream state that I had always wanted. So to emphasize where I was, for my waking mind, I purposely awakened in slow stages. It's like I left psychic bread crumbs to bring me home again. And here I am!"

Aunt Sarah had a glazed look, "Pokey you could have planned things a helluva lot better. I could have used some help, like I thought you had promised. The dervish needs some changes in the foils. If you don't mind me saying so, from where I sit, you seem to be getting more and more self-centered, and, in a way, kind of useless! Maybe a good thing, maybe not. I don't know if you're too tight or too relaxed! Maybe you better watch out over this self-forgiveness shit. You might be taking it too far. Like you might be throwing the baby out with the bath water!

Pokey brightened, "Hey! That would work in my puppet show...that would be fun for everybody. Let's all find new ways to punish ourselves!"

Rita agreed with Aunt Sarah, "Pokey! Here's a question for you. Can you have forgiveness without condemnation first? Can you have your redemption without first trespassing on someone or another? The guilt you feel over your regrettable past, is that not the price you pay for membership into a caring society? When you loose your innocence you take responsibility for your actions. At least that's how I make sense of it all. Who after all, is without sin? Are we not all flawed?"

Pokey stroked his wispy goatee, thinking..."yes, you're right, we have to be flawed by initial conception, it's not our fault. The Designer allowed for infinite variation, and who's to say what constitutes a flaw? No apology is necessary! To go forward, however, is necessary."

"Main thing...is Mr. Pee okay?" asked Pokey.

Rita nodded, "He's been better."

Pokey opened his saddlebag, "I stopped at the Walmart dumpsters and got Mr. Pee a few loaves of corn bread. And here are three door closers that look pretty good. How's the Ebay stuff?" asked Pokey.

"The rape protector kits are still doing well. We're producing about seven hundred units a shift, that's almost double with the same man-hours. That's pretty good efficiency. In fact there's a firm in Boston that wants to private label them, through grocery stores. And there's a man named McAdams, down in Alabama that wants to put them in women's rest rooms in taverns and rest stops along the interstates. I told them, we are already at full capacity. Doesn't that sound like we are a successful company?"

Rita's cell phone rang. It was Emma again from St. Theresa's, "Can I call you back, Emma? Yeah...no, I haven't decided. Do what you think is best."

Pokey continued, "The question in the end has to be this: For direction and growth in your life, do you look within to set your goal, to define who or what you are or want to become. Or do you look for goals outside of your vision field. Do you look for the pained in the world to offer them solace? How are we connecting, are we looking for inputs or outputs?"

"Do we worship a dead conviction, set in stone, or do we look for an alive version, juicin' it up so to speak. Do our teachers hammer us into shape from outside, or do they allow each child to flower from within. Children have only general appetites that evolve, specialized talents. Adults, similarly, have potentials."

"Wanda told me to watch out for the vain glorious. She explained it this way...insight can be very dangerous, if you don't know how to handle it! She saw it happen to her own dad. The more he preached, the less he could see. He glorified in his role following the good shepherd. His shepherd's crook was always at his side. Pride got him in spades! He felt he was channeling the Holy Ghost."

"Wanda told me her dad loved being a leader, experiencing the power of his position over his flock. The seductive pull of impersonation, that separates us apart from our authentic selves. Wanda's such a snail finder. She hasn't found a rose yet that was perfect. Man o'live, that woman tests everything she meets. You should only see what she puts her suitors through. Whew! If we had a PM like her, Canada would rule the world."

"We were in River Park, in Winnipeg, and I had set up our puppet stage. Wanda told me twice to be more direct, that other people weren't too good at decoding what I was saying."

"You see we were doing the throwing up routine with the George Washington puppet, and the kids were laughing like hell, as I spoke through the curtain, being the President, you know, as if George were alive. Well, I got kinda carried away with it all. I started, through the puppet, to complain about the weather, and a whole lot of other things. I even complained about the woman George had met the night before, as if Mr. Washington was a real rounder, if you know what I mean. Well, anyway, the more I preached about reality therapy, the more the crowd dispersed. Wanda could see by the end of the story that no one was there. They had forgotten about the vomiting that my puppet accomplished."

"So, after I cleaned up the fake vomit, where did that leave me, except with an empty stage, all lighted, ready for a fanfare or call to order."

"So, Rita, Mr. Pee and I have to talk. He's been with me most of his adult life. If he doesn't want to follow me down this uncertain road, we may have to part company."

"I know I invited him on board, but now I find that I can't be the same for him, or anyone. The future is clouded for me, and I can't promise fidelity to anything. Like the gap in the sounds of my mind, if I am going to find any reward in life, it can only come after abandoning fear, and, most importantly, accepting the frailties of imperfect souls around me. There, without the grace of God do I also go. The gap that invites our attention, our focus... that gap will always be fraught with dangers, some sensible, some foolish. The choice from moment to moment, then becomes whether to be real or false."

"So far, I can't wholly go one way or another, but I am leaning toward being transparent. And it seems to be working."

Rita looked down at Mr. Pee; "I suppose Aunt Sarah could make a place for him, along with her spent hens and other lost souls. Such a fix-it shop we have here, indeed. But I think you may have missed one point; being real may feel like a good trip, but sometimes being false can be the better choice. Like the old adage, better to be safe than sorry. Maybe the guileless naive ingénue works for a while, but it could be a dead end too.

Pokey wrote in his journal, "when an obstacle looms, it tends to depress me until I can process it, to understand it. Obstacles aren't always gateways; sometimes there are battles that must be lost for growth to happen.

Yearning to understand the world might be a task for Sisyphus, for as it has been observed, all intelligence is fugitive. Every conclusion soon gets out of date, which kind of leaves me astride a horse without reins. If you don't feel like a stranger in a strange land, you are not alive. If depression must de facto precede epiphany, should we cultivate depression as a springboard to self-discovery? Is your soul similarly fugitive? The greater the sacrifice, the greater the reward? God, like us, gave his only begotten son, that we might have life...but what kind of life? When do we set pity aside, and say enough already. There may be a time for Zorba to dance after all. To help things along, fasting brings about a chemical readiness for new ahah! experiences. Long distance running, smoking tobacco or marijuana, some exercises, all can promote inner vision. Makes perfect sense in a ying-yang polarity. In the way of opposites, there are activities that can hinder self discovery: gluttony, alcoholism, narcotics, indolence, vanity, power, position, some habits, From vague aspirations come small fruits.

Eighteen

Pokey slept late the next morning, for the night had been heavy with changes. He had tossed and turned all night and when daybreak came he fell asleep.

Aunt Sarah was already working on a fuel pump for Ed Harris. Rita was bringing her geraniums into the old bus for the winter. She had gone for a walk down to the creek where she picked wild purple asters and some bright yellow tansy. When she got back to lost grove motors, it was already about noon and time for the UPS man.

Rita knocked gently on Pokey's door..."Pokey! Time to get up...Pokey?" She eased open the door into the old Mrs. Karl's Bread truck. The sunlight beamed in upon Pokey who was still mostly under his covers. At the side of the mattress Mr. Pee had his own quilt. Both looked up at Rita.

"Oh Rita, it's you! You couldn't guess where I just was. Wow! What a night of dreams. Wanda came to me and took me far away. She let me watch her and some of her friends work over a town. I learned to see things a lot better. You know what I mean? Like I was blind! Like I can see now, how just about everybody is injured and hurt in some way. Wanda found ways to help everyone she met. She discovered needs in everybody! What they didn't do! After moving all around the town, helping people do little odd jobs, they organized a bake sale and an auction of all the junk they had accumulated."

"I don't know where they were going next. She wouldn't give me her numbers. At one point they had a picnic where Wanda ended up washing the feet of total strangers, I swear, Rita, there was an aura of that yellow light that I've seen before; do you remember at the old inn in Emmaus?"

Rita remembered, "Yes, Pokey, I remember your telling me, but that was just a dream, wasn't it? I think you were here all night. As far as I can tell."

Pokey looked down at Mr. Pee. Mr. Pee looked up at Pokey. Rita watched them both, "So what's going on here?"

"I guess you're right, it was a dream...but it was so real, I remember waking up, saying her name. You know, when you're half awake. I felt her warmth next to me, and it felt better than anything I could imagine. I didn't want to leave her warmth, her safety."

"Even if it is a dream, I'm going to hold on to it. For Wanda and her group are a lot like I imagine Jesus Christ must have been like, back with the apostles in John 13. I can't get over watching Wanda wash those feet. Dirty, grimy feet. Smelly, crusted, weird colored, worn out feet. Calluses, weird toenails, varicose veins. I watched her face, and it seemed she was in heaven, a slight smile with her eyelids half closed. Rita, it was so real to me. It makes me want to try washing your feet, or anyone's feet. Just to learn what it's like to understand someone in a different way...without words."

Rita looked into Pokey's eyes and didn't see the man who had kissed her with such passion. His eyes seemed blank, focused somewhere else. "I hear what you're saying, Pokey, I hear you working so hard to find your way out. I don't know. I do know that the idea of going around volunteering to wash people's feet, well, it's going to turn a lot of people off. It might even be illegal, like you probably need a permit for washing a non-relative's feet. I might wash Aunt Sarah's feet, 'cause I'm her niece. You'd not be legal. I'm just saying maybe."

Pokey brightened, "I know...I can have my puppets do the nasty act on stage...and it'll be almost the same as if I were washing their feet. In a funny way, I need to find ways to wash the emotional feet of my audience."

"Pokey, that might work. Kind of like tickling. Go ahead... figure it out. If you want to find yourself in someone else's foot then go ahead. Find ways to tickle your audience! Put it somewhere between burning the baby, and George Washington's throwing up. But for now, are you going to get up?"

Pokey slipped out of his sleeping bag to get dressed,

forgetting that there was a young lady present. Rita couldn't help but notice Pokey's fresh white buttocks, as he pulled on his jeans. He didn't seem to be wearing any underwear. Pokey continued, "Maybe I could make a foot fetish puppet! Then Mr. Ego and Miss Id could get together and wash it. Yeah! Or kiss it! That would work...somehow. At the least it would be a definite step in the right direction. We gotta take the audience at its face value. They have a need to be lead, the poor lost souls. Don't you think?"

"Yes, Pokey, Suck that toe! Suck all of them! Them's marching words! I'm sure you must be right again. You're always right, but for now, I have more pressing needs. I am all out of running yellow sores for the rape kits. Can you run a few batches?

"Sure Rita, if you don't mind me using Handiwrap rather than Saran. It's a lot cheaper. I'll start after I finish with your aunt's job. She's got another transmission that needs a bolt extracted."

Pokey decided to skip lunch so that he could run a few extra batches of yellow sores. He did the product molding in the old chicken house alongside the dervish forms. Like always he sprayed the master mold with Pam first. Then he unrolled several rolls of Handiwrap over the mold. Next he used a hair drier to melt the Handiwrap down into the cavities. Lastly he laminated the back onto the double adhesive paper with carrier paper printed on the Epson 1880 printer. There was a nice contrast between the scabs and pus.

But the work was boring. Even the music on the radio was boring. He turned it off and began to listen to the silence of the late afternoon. He heard a car go by on the hard road. Then another. He heard the outhouse door close...twice. A mouse rustled in the wastebasket.

As night fell, Rita approached the henhouse and looked in to see Pokey sitting on the cockpit seat of the dervish. He was gently swaying back and forth, forward and backward, in a regular rhythm. Rita could only see the back of his collar, with his blond ponytail.

She knocked on the glass and stepped into the light. Pokey

was startled, "Oh it's you...I was day dreaming again. I kind of heard the spirits moving around the room, in the shadows. Not all the time, just every once in a while. And I think I've got a mouse."

"In my dream someone seems to be telling me to reach out, to connect. It's not Wanda, this one's younger, she's just starting out. First I'm called over there. I go there and get ready to be in the moment, for enjoyment, and what do you think happens? Bingo! The moment is gone! Moment? What moment? My attention shrinks and I loose control. That's when the voices start talking about me."

"So then the spirits call me over to another spot, and you guessed it. Same thing happens. Just like a country dog chasing a car. I guess he keeps doing it because he thinks his barking and growling is working to scare away the enemy."

"Pokey, Isn't it just a dream? Why can't you just let it go? I mean, they're dreams. Just because they're on the other side of the mirror, well, that doesn't mean you have to go there. Weren't you telling me that I should live right now, in the moment? The same should hold for you. It seems to me that all your investigations leave you more miserable than ever. I'd like to think you would be getting tired of it all by now. Hmm?"

Pokey got down from the Dervish and started to roll up his last batch of scabs and pus. "Here, take this scissor, you can cut them apart. Cut on the blue lines. You don't understand. The question is always the same, but everyday there's a new answer, that is...if you are alive in the moment. The problem most people have is looking for eternity in the moment rather than the opposite. That's the paradox. It's a dead end, one among many! Me? I see no point in not aiming for the center of the target. How else can I prove who I am? Do you think God wants mindless nerds worshipping her? What, after all, can make God happy? Those pearly gates aren't going to slam in my face! Not if I can help it!"

Rita thought a moment, wondering if it was stupid to weigh these weird arguments. "Have you been drinking or smoking something?"

"No, but I wouldn't mind some schnapps. I know I should relax. Mr. Pee has been telling me that for the last year, ever since we got here. It hasn't been easy for us."

"Pokey, you were talking about making God happy...if God is unhappy with you or me, how can we tell? What makes him unhappy? Isn't it pretty hard to tell?"

Pokey rolled out more Handiwrap for the last batch, "Maybe God and the Devil are two sides of the same coin, just like my mirror has two sides. God is the word, and the devil is the non-word. They meet only here in our very imperfect present! All we can do is wipe the lens a bit. Don't ask me to make sense. I can't do it, at least not yet. I'm still sorting things out. Sometimes I have to try things just to find out if and how I can fit in. I could still go back to school if I could afford it. If I was a college graduate I might make a lot of money."

"If I were a college graduate," corrected Rita.

"If you were?

"No, you. Yeah, were. It's subjunctive. It means you're not a college graduate," clarified Rita.

"I thought that's what I said, Rita. 'Were' sounds weird."

"Pokey, we're already making pretty good money. I've been keeping track. You've got more than $24,000 in your rainy day account, and that's after all the money that went out for the cases of great stuff."

"Really? Maybe we can help the less fortunate. Maybe that's the answer. We can't take it with us. I'm thinking I should leave it there until I can figure out what kind of taxes I have to pay."

Rita picked up the three batches of sores, "I'll take these over to the shop; there's another order from the Grand Union broker. And Ralph's and Cosco want samples of everything. Pokey, when you're done here, I could use your help."

Later that evening, Aunt Sarah came home from the Bay with Ed Harris. They had been having a few after hours with the city road crew. Soon the bottle of schnapps was empty and the talk drifted to the ungodly, to transmissions and alternators. Rita yawned and left for the green room, followed by Pokey and Mr. Pee. It was the dark side of the moon, and the shadows were in triumph, with the light of day vanquished. Rita left Pokey at his nest in the Mrs. Karl's bread truck. She felt uneasy and alone, challenged and uncertain, she was loosing her grip and direction. She hoped sleep would soon comfort her.

The next morning things began to fall into place. Her period had finally come, Pokey was back finishing the rape kit orders, and Aunt Sarah had finally got the right transmission for the Mustang. Rita put the wrong one on Ebay and there was a bidder posting questions in fifteen minutes.

Rita took some sweet rolls back to Pokey for midmorning break. "Here you go...thanks for all your work. Here's your address labels."

Pokey and Rita finished the shipment and were out on the road by noon taking a brisk walk down to the creek with Mr. Pee who stopped to relieve himself. Rita made a mental note of the location on the path, not wanting to step in it on the way back.

There was solid ice except for the rapids and near the muskrat hills. They walked on the ice over to the large rock and sat on the creek bank, until the wind came up from the west. As they tramped back up the steep path Pokey asked Rita if she had seen his book of great thoughts, "It's lost and I don't know if I should start another one. I can remember a few of them. But a lot are gone forever. But maybe there's a good side. You know they say that it's an ill wind that blows no good."

"Maybe you should start a new volume! You seem to be at a dead end with this mirror problem. But yeah, I think I saw it by the cutoff saw bench. So have your great thoughts lead you to any conclusions? What's your bottom line?"

"Well, Rita, maybe nothing is clear to start with. Maybe everything depends upon getting a clear insight into the fabric of mankind, to separate fact from fiction, cause from effect...I look in the mirror now and can see many strangers. One of them is really beautiful, but very lonely. I want to help him, if I can. I don't know anymore where this is leading, and it's scary sometimes. I feel I might love him more than myself. Go figure!"

"I know," said Rita, "maybe all real gifts come to us in disguise, cloaked by fate. When mankind appears to be a divine experiment, gone horribly wrong, then, and only then, can remedy be sought. Maybe things have to get worse, before change can happen. Like a rat in a maze, how many dead ends will it take, before we can enjoy a bit of cheese. Brute force and aggression can provide a pretty ugly security. You don't pray when things are good."

"Well speak for yourself Rita, I thank my maker for everything she gives me, even all the hardships of spreading her word."

"But Pokey, don't you kind of enjoy your suffering? Otherwise you would take some of your money and get yourself a set of wheels? Maybe you could get a van so you and Mr. Pee wouldn't have to pitch a tent."

"I don't know...wouldn't that mean I'd have to get a vendor's license and everything? I don't know if I'm ready to join the real world, not as it is anyway. Like my mother advised, as long as I keep to the side of the road, I can get along. My mission is not to minister to the powerful anyway." They reached the top of the cliff and turned back onto the hard road.

Rita and Pokey were in lock step, marching briskly along breathing deeply. It was all the Mr. Pee could do to keep up. Pokey continued intermittently, "Maybe the lesson for me... is not to take notes...just wait...till the spirit...manifests. And maybe...God won't come...during our lives. Maybe mankind will have to work things out better...before we can deserve to be...acknowledged by our maker. Patience! Always we have to consider the purposes of adversity, just like the runes say. Just like Ecclesiastes three, four.

After a moment of reflection, Rita agreed. "Isn't it all about the journey through time, not necessarily in the destination!"

"Right!" said Pokey "Think on it! Does God exist outside of this moment?" I don't think she can be in both places. You agree?"

As they approached Lost Grove Motors the three all had the ruddy bloom of youth, bright eyed and bushy tailed. The air was becoming noticeably cooler.

"Can we have movement through time with no change?" Rita continued toward the door, "Which would be more tragic... if...in this life...we never meet God face to face, or if...there is no God, not even here now. What if we are alone, swirling around in a nothingness? Maybe there is no meaning, only action without meaning."

Rita took off her windbreaker, "Pokey, in the real world out there, it's all about style. Last year in world lit class we read Camus' stranger, he was just passing through too. Maybe you should check out No Exit by Sartre. Seems to me I remember there were little mirrors in that story." The outhouse door creaked shut.

Pokey couldn't wait to relieve himself, disappearing behind the hen house for a minute. Rita emerged seeing Pokey zipping up. "What's going to happen, Pokey, if you spend your whole life looking for God, or looking for your true self outside of yourself. I think that's a waste of time. Excuse me! The nuns taught us that we have to find God within our hearts."

Pokey thought a moment and shook his head, "I don't know anything any more. I found out a lot with Wanda, but now that seems years ago. She hasn't been back, and I don't know how to reach her. I'm going to have to move on down the road come spring. I'd better finish up my new puppets. I'm almost done with the baby Jesus and the baby Mohammed."

"What about a baby Buddha?" asked Rita.

"I don't think I need him, at least not now. Besides I only have two hands! I have to rebuild my stage and fix up the astronomical lecture company sign. It's going to be great! You wait! By the way I could use your help with my stage curtains. You help me with them, and I'll help you with your driving. Deal?"

"Deal."

Nineteen

Rita was up front at the counter when Ed Harris drove up in his maroon Chevy ST. His cross was out of alignment after an accident on the Linden parkway. He needed the cross arm fixed in time for the County Fair. After checking with Aunt Sarah, Rita told him to bring the cross into the back room.

Sarah came in after a few moments chuckling, "Is this going to be charge, or cash and carry?"

Ed opened his little tract compartment in the cross, and produced a pint of Corbies. "You want to help lighten my load Sarah?"

Aunt Sarah welded an angle brace onto the crossbar while Rita watched from a bar stool at the old parts counter. Pokey came in with his new baby Jesus puppet.

Soon Aunt Sarah turned the welder off, and removed her helmet. "There! Good as New! Or should I say good as old. Do you want it to look old or new? This welded joint needs some attention, should we paint it mat or gloss black? Wouldn't you expect a new model cross to be kind of glossy? And the old rugged one should maybe be dull, without luster. I mean if this is supposed to be the real thing, then how should it look, put yourself in Pontious Pilate's spot. He had to order the first cross. It was probably a Jewish jointer who took the job. There is the carpenter's workshop, a deal had to be struck. I imagine, even back then, there was a cynic in the shadows muttering you get what you pay for."

"So, here Pilot's got his job to do, to follow the court's orders. And this fast talking cross salesman comes by uninvited, saying he's got a special on used crosses! He can also give Pilot top of the line, imported in the latest styles, or, if he'll take a quantity, and keep quiet about this foolishly low price, he's got only one left in Christ's size."

"Pilot does his due diligence, as a good bureaucrat should, and figures out that if he gets a quantity discount for three or more crosses, he can save on executioner labor costs. He figures no one will notice the plastic backs. And by erecting the crosses at the same time, the men can be home from Golgatha by nightfall."

"Maybe, maybe not" observed Rita. "Is it cash and carry, or does Pilot have to wait for the tax levy to come in. With the weather uncertainty and the overhead, maybe Pilot would bunch up his underwear and say, "screw convention, I've had enough with the old rugged crosses. Not only do you get slivers in handling them, they are notoriously hard to keep clean. What we need is a whole new line of crosses, adapted to today's need, to today's lifestyles."

Pokey was manipulating his baby Jesus puppet as he spoke, "There's a problem I think. There's some product liability if some unlicensed executioner decides to put the cross to use. Or maybe the cross doesn't perform as warranted. Who pays damages? Talk about wrongful death suits! John Birch Society or ACLU won't care a hoot about style, gloss black or mat. Every means can be justified with single-mindedness and purity of soul. John Birch Society would vote for crucifix recycling, trade fairs, councils on government standards, lead paint issues. So I think Ed's cross looks perfect as it is. It looks well used as any treasure should look. Like a Sufi's jacket."

Aunt Sarah finished the last of the schnapps, "maybe Pilot didn't go out and buy crosses for the crucifixion party, maybe the crosses were always up on Golgatha just as a public spirited display, as a reminder that death is eternal. Maybe he was smart and was saving his crosses for a rainy day. I saw it rain in the movie, the robe. Oh my, didn't it rain, didn't it rain" crooned Aunt Sarah.

"Oh yeah, didn't it rain" joined in Rita.

"Oh yeah," chimed in the Baby Jesus puppet.

Ed Harris packed up his cross, "well, I like the mat finish. We'll be seeing you later at the fair. Albert, are you going to take the astronomical lecture company to the fair?"

"You bet, we're all going. I'm even taking the new baby Jesus.

I'm setting up outside the Youth Ag building, next to poultry exhibit. Rita is thinking of entering something or other."

"Albert, would you mind if I hang out with you, you know with my cross?" asked Ed.

"Well, I don't know. Could you pass our hat for us? After the show? I had planned to have Mr. Pee pass the cup, but he's resisting me. Like it's beneath him to beg! I can give you a service fee for your help. Or how about some schnapps for doing God's work?" So it was decided that when the flames came under the baby Jesus, Ed would come and save the day! Rejoice! And pass the hat.

Twenty

Clarvoix County Fair days were always the last weekend in August, opening Thursday and running through Monday.

On Wednesday morning Ed came to Lost Grove Motors to help move the bread truck puppet show to the fair. Pokey had given the sign board a fresh coat of gloss lacquer. Since neither Pokey nor Rita had a driver's license, Ed drove the bread truck, and Aunt Sarah followed in Ed's S-10. She hoped not to get caught driving without a license.

They parked the bread truck right under the lamppost at the edge of the racetrack. Pokey laughed, "Rita, remember last year... when Aunt Sarah got into it with Stevie Hermanson. You and I did ten laps right here!"

"It seems that was years ago," sighed Rita. "When Ed gets back, do you want to start?"

"No, we can wait till Friday morning. Then, you can put out the children's chairs and I'll do a final sound check. I'll cue up our opening hymn Praise the Lord! Long live the Kuklapolitans! Down with the Publickers!"

At lunch Pokey explained, "I had the neatest dream last night, a dream I'm still trying to make sense of. I watched in my dream three women riding a big old white mare. They couldn't agree on which direction to pursue. Each woman was holding one of the reins. It looked like each woman could spur the horse faster if she wanted to. The problem seemed to be that the women are all different and can't agree on where the horse should go. Thus two of the women usually pull on one side, to the left or two the right. This usually causes a circular motion. Professionally it could be termed Le Tour Circleque, a habit pattern that is reinforced by stubbornness and fear. It also leaves one of the women, the singleton, in a pissed off isolation. Thus it is evident that when stalemate has been achieved between warring impulses, outside influences of minor import can exercise surprising strength, perhaps when harmony is found within the horse. This psychological spinning in indecisions provides a melancholic ennui that many, perhaps most, interpret as "life". The horse becomes mired in a time warp, a noisy stuttering of reality, a mindless inventory of past injustice. Wow, such complaints become a trap. The pilgrim makes no progress! The old white mare passes gas only."

"So what is the lesson to learn? If dreams "R" us, how do we exit, stage left or stage right? Do we court adventure, do we plunge ahead, or complete we pull back on the reins. In my dream, the three women riders aren't all looking forward. The gal in the middle is riding side saddle, while the other two are astride, one facing forward and one backward. The woman at the rear looks at where they have been. I'm thinking she never is surprised. She lives in the twilight zone and sees a lot of horse shit. Every day is an old day. Her color is brown, and she sleeps a lot.

I'm thinking the woman at the front lives in the dawning edge of night, surprised by everything, she raptures over birthing each new insight. She devours experience not worrying about meaning. Every day is a new day. Her color is mixed yellows and greens.

The gal in the middle has little control and probably has the best sense of humor. The horse tries to understand all three.

Pokey summed up, "For me the lesson in my dream is that sure, we want to understand and make sense of our identity and position, but tragically satisfaction is elusive.

Rita thought a few moments, "don't we always come back to Edgar Lee Masters, Life without meaning is the torture of vague desire, a boat with furled sail, at rest in a harbor, longing for the sea. It is our human condition, so get used to it and don't complain. If you insist on this estrangement to control you...well, I for one, think you're being stupid and kind of boring. Music doesn't have to be understood to be enjoyed. Just like life. Can't you somehow just accept that yes, you are here. And yes, you have to prove yourself. You do have to leave the harbor! It is all an artform, sometimes coherent and sometimes not.

Twenty One

It was Friday the thirteenth of November. Rita got off to a late start on the airport run. Pokey had wanted to stay home to work on his puppets, so she set off alone. It wasn't the first time she had picked up the trash at the airport by herself. She checked the gas tank of the tractor, and put the empty water jugs in the front of the manure spreader.

The weather had been unusually warm and gray. The green hillsides were dotted with late purple asters. The yellow poplars and quaking aspens were mostly stripped of their lower leaves, leaving only their top leaves pointing upward. The tips of the poplars were strangely a blazing yellow. Rita saw pointed paintbrushes and smiled.

The routine was the same. She got to the airport snack shop by three and after checking in with Mrs. Staber, she headed over to the World's End hanger to do the cleaning. The new Douglas 737 barely fit the hanger. There were no cars in the parking lot so she pulled the spreader right up to the front office. She found the entrance locked and all the lights off inside. But Pokey's passkey worked and she soon was in the maintenance office. She logged in with Pokey's password. While cleaning the crew quarters wasn't in the cleaning contract, Rita and Pokey had decided it was worth doing. She emptied the ashtrays, collected all the red shop rags for the laundry service, then polished the mirrors and faucets in the bathroom.

Rita remembered St. Theresa's where she had to do bathrooms her freshman year. Emma taught her that if the mirrors and faucets were spotless and shiny, she would get extra points on her conduct rating. Students with good conduct ratings got special privileges.

She was startled to hear a noise in crew quarters down the hall. Coming out of the loo, Rita encountered Charles. She hadn't seen him since the Halloween costume party. He smelled just the same, Petuli and Fosters beer.

"Oh! I thought you were my wife coming to get me," said Charles. "You must be the cleaning people. Didn't I see you over at Mrs. Staber's lunch room?"

Rita realized that Charles didn't recognize her from the party, "Yes'um, I'm filling in today, suh."

Rita looked down at her shoes, trying not to smile. She remembered the costumes, the wild dance she had with this guy right in front of her. She remembered his wife, little Bo Peep, throwing up, then the chilly ride home nestled up with Pokey in the back of the spreader.

"So, you're the Pilot?" asked Rita. "That's gotta be a fun job, bet it pays real good. Suh."

"I don't mind it, most of the time." Charles tapped his Marlboro Lights on the table and lighted up. "And you? What's a nice girl like you cleaning bathrooms?"

Rita turned away and sprayed Windex on the window, "well, suh, my man's up the river right now, and I got a lot of bills. Please don't tell anyone you've seen me. No one is supposed to know I'm here. They pay me in cash. American."

"But you're not wearing a wedding ring" observed Charles.

Momentarily caught off guard, Rita was almost ready to tell Charles the truth, that her real name was Cinderella, but then thought better of it. "Maybe some day my prince will come...but for now this girl has to clean your 737. You could help Cinderella if you wanted."

As soon as the words were out of her mouth, Rita knew she could be in trouble. One damn moment of indiscretion. Charles was more than ready to help a damsel in need. He followed her up the rear steps and disappeared forward to the cockpit, bringing back a pint of Johnny Walker Black. Soon he was rambling on and on, about life in the stratosphere. Getting the big picture.

Rita felt her record was skipping, "My that's just fascinating suh, just fascinating."

Charles continued "But, as far as a lot of money, it's not there.

You see, I work for the trust fund that my father set up for me, after my marriage failed. It was a plea deal I should never have accepted. But I was young and didn't have any sense. The 737 is registered to the home office, we contract for its use on a cost plus basis, with a monthly minimum guaranteed. It was a perk Dad demanded when Phillip Morris bought out Chuck Schwab's interest in World's End. Both my sisters, my brother Tom, and I got a generation skipping special stock class that has no voting power, but instead we get 125% of any regular stock dividend."

Charles loosened his tie and got some ice and two glasses from the galley. The vacuuming and dusting were soon done. "Can I offer Cinderella a little pick her up drink?"

Rita paused and looked into Charles's eyes, "Oh, I don't know suh, they're going to miss me at home. They might get worried and call the police. And anyway, didn't you say you were expecting your wife?" asked Rita.

Charles poured a generous shot of the scotch, "here, taste this...it's ten years old. Yeah, I'm still married, but kind of in name only. We're an open marriage so to speak, and besides we are on the road a lot. We each get lonely, so we agreed not to discuss our affairs with each other. Sometimes I wonder if she's fucking my brother. Sometimes it looks to me like they can't keep their hands off each other."

Charles moved a little closer "I sometimes try to visualize the two of them. I'm not like my brother Tom...he's always been kind of a light weight toad in the sneakers, if you know what I mean." He stood up to adjust his underwear and sat down again. Rita thought she noticed a growing potential problem.

Rita observed "Oh you big boy! I think I know where this might be going. I think I see a hamster in your pocket! I'd better freshen up in the loo! I'll be right back; you stay right where you are! Okay?"

"Okay, don't be too long!" said Charles, "My hamster might get restless."

Rita forced a giggle and disappeared aft.

The toilet compartment was a lot larger on the 737 than the Gulfstream's. Rita noticed that the mirrors looked like they hadn't been cleaned for some time. And there was a general foul odor of tobacco and sweat. She tried not to breathe too deeply.

From her purse she pulled out her rape protector kit and a little tube of zinc oxide. She peeled off a number one and a number two pussy sore and carefully moistened them. The first she placed just under her collar, below her ear; the other right next to her navel.

As she came out of the toilet, she tightened the cap on the little tube of zinc oxide. Coming over to Charles, Rita slowly breathed, "There you are, you big boy! Can the big boy help poor me? I can't seem to get this cap off this tube of my ointment."

As Charles took the tube from her, Rita assessed the stage, to see where was the best light coming from. She adjusted her posture so that the light struck the left side of her face, next to her collar.

"Thanks big boy!" Rita said, squeezing a little dab of the bright white ointment carefully onto her index finger. She took pains to slowly center the dab of ointment on the pad of her fingertip. She watched Charles's eyes as she set down the tube of ointment. She had his full attention.

With one hand she pulled back her collar exposing the number one pussy sore. With her other hand she applied the zinc oxide to the fake sore. "Oh that feels better! Do you think I got it all?"

Charles didn't really want to look. "Uh, yeah. You got it all." Rita considered pulling up her blouse to expose the number two sore next to her navel. But when she looked at Charles, he seemed ready to vomit. The hamster had fled. "You don't look so good, you know you should take better care of yourself. What would your mother say?" Charles was nonplussed.

"I'm going to go now, you be good to yourself, you be real good to yourself. Okay?" Rita bent over and kissed Charles on the forehead. "Remember to wash your hands!"

Twenty Two

Rita relaxed on the way home, in more ways than one. Once the tractor reached cruising speed, she could disassociate herself from the cacophony of the purring four cylinder Allis Chalmers, and easily cruise along as Jonathan Livingston sea gull, reaching higher and higher. It was late, and there was almost no traffic for miles. The tractor was making that D flat hum again that almost was lulling her to sleep. She started humming an alto part, first a third above then a third below. Soon she was imagining music, the blaring sounds of trumpets, a fan fare for her triumphant return to Lost Grove Motors, a maiden still unspoiled! Her sojourn at Lost Grove Motors was definitely taking on quite a noble aspect. Pulling into the yard behind the garage, Rita saw no signs of life at all. She deftly backed the manure spreader over to the recycle bags and turned off Alice.

She was still thinking about leaving Charles and laughed to herself, "there's got to be something better, a tad more uplifting than gettin' dicked on demand by a drunk, even if he's rich."

Coming out of the green room Rita noticed that the lights were still on in the henhouse. She quietly stepped up to the windows and peeked in. Pokey was up, still working on his puppets again. Mr. Pee was asleep at his side. She recognized Tchaikovsky's violin concerto.

She knocked, "Hi, Albert, what are you doing up, it's after midnight." Pokey was sitting cross-legged on the floor, next to the dervish. He was stitching together some black velvet into a small hood.

"Hey Rita, yeah I know! I'm working on a new puppet... this is Mr. Reaper...Mr. G. Reaper...aka Grimmey or Grimey. What do you think? I'm making a hood over this light bulb that I sprayed matt black. I gotta make a scythe now...that shouldn't be too hard."

"But why the grim reaper? That'll really bring down the

house. Don't you think it will have a...chilling effect on your children out in the audience?"

"Yes and no. Here's how I see it. Nothing is more important than death, in the greater scheme of things. You know what I mean? Even my puppets have to know that! Duh!! Anyway, I'm feeling like I gotta get my plan together. It's starting to feel like home around here, and that's not good. I just can't get plugged in here. There's a whole lot more that is out there. I know kinda what I don't know...and it's pulling me toward the light. Sure, there are a lot of shadows, stuff that I just can't figure out. But I do have a good hold on something big. It's there, just around the corner, I want to stay here and finish our dervish.

Pokey patted the dervish mold next to him, "just to prove that the idea works. But after that, I'm headed for the long road less travelled."

"What can I say, Pokey, I get to go back to the real world myself next September. Gotta go learn college stuff, you know, philosophy, math, gym, English lit. That's going to be my plate. For now, I think I'll let eternity take care of itself. I'm for the moment. That's long enough for me."

Rita yawned, "So for now, I'm off to slumber land, I've had a weird day. Charles! You remember him? At the country club Halloween party? Well, he was in the World's End 737 when I went to do the cleaning. He had been drinking, and made a pass at me. I was all alone, you know. It might have been different if you had been there. But you weren't. So it got a little out of sorts, and I had to use one of our number ones! Was I glad it was in my purse!

"Shoot No! Charles? I never thought he'd get into rape!"

"Well it really wasn't rape," explained Rita, "but I thought I didn't want to take chances. Rita pulled up her blouse a little bit, "See, I still haven't taken the number two off! He didn't even see this one."

She peeled off the plastic sores and dropped them in the wastebasket. "Ugh, I'm going to have to put some lotion on my belly. It feels hot."

"Here Rita, this is Aveno medicated," Pokey squeezed out a generous amount and slowly massaged Rita's neck and shoulders. Rita closed her eyes "Oh, there, you hit the spot. Ooo! I didn't know that was there. I must be more uptight than I thought." Pokey spent a little extra time massaging Rita's upper trapezius and sternomastoid muscles. For a moment Pokey's blond mustache and his moist lips caught Rita's eye. As she relaxed, her gaze fell upon his crotch, for a moment she imagined what might be hidden. But then the last movement of the violin concerto came on, and part of her knew better. She found her hand on the doorknob, "Night night, big boy, see you in the morrow."

Pokey closed his eyes and followed the last movement. Lastly he got out his book of great thoughts and signed in.

Murray Bay October 10th

Observation: Everything is irregular. Instead of simplifying and generalizing, theorizing, characterizing, and concluding, an adept mind learns how to filter intent. As always, consider the purpose of adversity.

As in all sciences, there are some keys to finding the way. There are diagnostic techniques that are common across many disciplines.

Firstly, it is not rocket science! Adepts know where to find the bridges from the mind to its maker. Yes, we have to agree, for our own sakes, that God created man in His own image. How could it be otherwise! Well, does the creator of the lion look like a lion?

The only way to God is through the living mirror.

Nothing is alone, every thing is in relationship.

Noise, in this scenario can be cancelled or amplified by your choice.

This is not to say that one should ignore change. Just the opposite. Growth is change. Intelligence only flourishes in a moving context. Chaos wave theory unifies in music and structure. Thus there is activity with no movement or change?

Things are. Things come into focus. Things go out of focus. Focus happens! Attention drifts.

For the moment to be fully realized, one must shut the door to the past, as well as the door to the future. That is to say, your hopes for happiness need to be put on the back burner. Similarly, thoughts of revenge, anger of all types, prevent illumination.

In fact, to be really in the moment, you should forget everything you know. Instead focus on everything you don't know. I don't know, and I don't care. That's the gateway! It's all a balancing act. So when you leave here, forget the straight and narrow, give the moment a chance, breathe without purpose.

So I woke up this morning, thinking, Hey! We got just enough assholes in our life to make it interesting...

Perhaps Pokey gets instruction from Ed Harris regarding the trick he uses to find God...the Sufi whirling while focusing uncomfortably upward, until slight pain is found. Thus anchored one can focus in unexpected new ways that perceive reality (God) in new ways. Once the lock on the gate is picked, entrance is assured. Expectations are not always productive. Hopes similarly become generic. In this light, it is the opposite from the art of Zen archery. Ignore the center of the target. Forget about future arrivals, forget about your plan for final happiness. Fear not opposition and misunderstandings. Don't just look for truth alone, or even God alone. Study and get a feel for what is the nature of the false assumptions that impede our journey.

If you understand why some activity is fun to do, you destroy the fun through your mendation (meditation perhaps is dangerous that way?) What provokes your smile, your contentment? Whom are you letting pull your strings?

Conversely study not your tears. But let them flow unabashedly, or ignore them, because you have the right, nay obligation, to be authentic.

Being a perfectionist can be depressing. There's never a perfect bloom, never a perfect union that lasts. All is decay and rot. Every rose has its snail.

(episode at puppet show: front person gives puppet a rose. "Thank you, but it's already dead...or dieing! What's more valuable, a live dog or a dead lion? Maybe the beauty comes from the fact that it is temporary, finite."

It is a neat trick of mind, to look at something and see it as something founded in the past, and also in the future. In this perception, one is balanced like a tightrope walker on a tense cord.

Similarly, one's goals must be subject to change, and should change as life progresses. Stay the course is the last resort of the unimaginative.

It is a mistake to believe that everything has to have meaning.

I have an existential hunger for validity and worth. Who doesn't?

When I can't decide, I partake of youthful meandering that avoids achievement. Meanwhile fantasy grows poignant, Walter Mitty triumphs.

Every person seeks pride of his rank, his achievements. What is Pokey proud of? Sarah? Rita? Who has what kind of shame?

Some souls are more vulnerable than others. They become prey to various ploys. Confidence men or women are only one variety of mis-use. Of course, this is only one frame of reference. From the confidence man's point of view, is it logical that God (for want of a better word) could imagine and create something foreign to its self? Is there trash in heaven? Can I take my dog when the time comes?

The next morning there was a strange silence when Rita awoke. She looked at the window next to her and the world was gone, or at least that's how it seemed. The window had ice on the inside and frost on the outside. Over night the weather had changed from below zero, to a warmer, moist front. Ice crystals were gently falling, sparking tiny light shows everywhere, in the trees and bushes.

Rita lounged for a while thinking that this was the kind of moment that must drive poets wild with longing for just the right word. She smiled, thinking about Walt Whitman biting his lip for want of the right adjective. She imagined, Shakespeare, the bard of Avon, with head in hands, sobbing, "Wherefore art thou, now summer made glorious winter, Oh Winter! The season of small berries that drop silently. Oh wordless debate!"

Junk cars, and windows were also covered with dense hoarfrost. Inside the school bus the little electric heater took the edge off the chill, but couldn't keep up.

She stepped out into the quiet of the new day, a day unlike any before. The hoarfrost sparked new value everywhere. The meanest trash was bejeweled into diadems more precious than gold. She paused and smiled in wordless gratitude for such simple pleasures.

She saw Mr. Pee sitting at the greenroom door obviously waiting for Pokey. The door opened, "Bueno Dia, mi amiga, commen talley voodoo?" enjoindered Pokey.

Rita smiled, "Ah, mi amigo, Los Dios hablan, escucha! Mira! Isn't it beautiful this morning!

Their solitude was suddenly interrupted by Aunt Sarah bursting forth from the garage, "Albert! Rita! I need your help. Something weird is happening."

Aunt Sarah led them around to the north side of the garage where they had parked the Honda Accord the night before. "Look here. Look at it."

She pointed to the left front of the car that had dropped down to where the bumper was nearly on the ground. The tire had dropped down because the ground somehow had caved in under it, creating a black hole. Pokey started to go nearer when Aunt Sarah cautioned, "careful, who knows...we could all drop into hell! Rita, you go get a flashlight, Pokey...you hold my ankles."

Pokey held Aunt Sarah's ankles as she crawled on her belly toward the Honda and the black hole under the tire. She approached the gaping hole on her hands and knees until her forehead was next to the hubcap. Rita returned with a flashlight.

"What do you see?

"It's dark! And it smells like the spring down by the highway.

I can see water going from one side of the bottom to the other. It looks like just a lot of mud and rubble."

Rita and Pokey took turns holding each other's ankles while looking down into the darkness. Rita noticed a square rock ledge near the bottom of the chamber, "You know, Howard Carter must have smelled something like this when he knocked into King Tut's eternal living room. You know, doesn't sulfur kill life?"

"I don't know, but, we should move the Honda before the hole gets larger."

It proved to be a good move, for by the next afternoon more of the driveway had collapsed, leaving a bowl shaped crater showing layers of color. Rita was fascinated with the pockets of red clay with sparkling tetrahydral calcite crystals the size of her fist. When they looked down into the shaft, it appeared that they were looking into a passage way with water flowing along the floor. Rita observed, "You know, this reminds me of a Roman sewer and it smells like one must have." The sinkhole had become large enough to bury more than one Honda.

Twenty Three

For lunch Aunt Sarah presented a six-quart casserole full of something she called Chilli. During winter she had a practice of adding leftovers to the pot. "If you're hungry, it's there...night or day, it's our default lunch" she had instructed.

Pokey brought in some day-old bread from the dumpsters at Walmart. He turned to Aunt Sarah, "What do you want done with that hole? I think it is done collapsing for now."

Rita brightened, "I think it's a blessing from God! That's one big hole! We can git' rid of a lot of stuff. Maybe start with those piles of cement blocks. Aunt Sarah, you're never going to use them."

Aunt Sarah opened a Fosters. "Rita, how do you know exactly what is useless? Maybe you think that pile is mostly in the way, but those blocks are still usable. Just the other day, I saw a passive solar collector on the tele, made out of, guess what? Old storm doors and cement blocks.

Rita wasn't ready to give up. "What about all the aluminum lawn chairs with bad webbing? If there's one, there's a hundred. And yes, I know, they are all fixable. But they could also help stabilize our fill, like reinforcing rods in cement. There's enough room in the hole, that we could get rid of some of those chicken cages you brought home from the hatchery auction. You're never going to use them, I'm sure."

"Well, maybe, some of the cages could go." Aunt Sarah was not happy to abandon any of her treasures. The cement blocks had come from the Linden dump and hadn't cost her anything but the gas in her tractor.

Pokey had other thoughts, "before we fill up the hole, I think someone should go down in it, and take a flash light. It looks like there might be a passage or tunnel going somewhere. Maybe it's nothing. Maybe it is dangerous. But how will we know, if we don't look?"

"You're not going to get me down there, no way!" said Aunt Sarah. "How do you know the air is fit to breath, maybe it's full of methane and radon and you'll die down there. How are Rita and I going to haul your body back? Hmm? Have you thought of that?"

Rita stood up, "Can't you send a canary down? Isn't that what the old miners did?"

Pokey thought a moment, "Well we do have a chicken or two we can lower down. Would that do?"

That afternoon Pokey found a fifty foot yellow plastic cable that easily reached the bottom of the hole. Aunt Sarah improvised a chicken cage out of a milkman's basket. She chose Henrietta, her least favorite hen, to be lowered into the hole. After a wait of five minutes Pokey brought the hen back topside. Henrietta had gotten wet in the stream that flowed through the bottom of the hole. The hen was not happy, and voiced her objection strongly. But she was alive, but now covered with an orange slime. The air down in the hole was probably not toxic.

Aunt Sarah and Rita watched Pokey rappel down to the bottom. He shouted up, "There's spring water running under all this rubble. I can see it coming from the north side. And I can see some broken wooden beams. The passage is pretty low and it is blocked by the collapse. I guess we're done here. Whew! There's a yellow slime that smells putrid"

Pokey got back topside without too much difficulty, "So, Miss Chamberlin, what's next? Shall we fill her up?"

Rita added, "Aunt Sarah, maybe we could put a roof over the hole, and use it for a bomb shelter!" Aunt Sarah didn't like that idea, or Pokey's suggestion that the hole could be a basement for some sort of building. She did give in and allowed the hole to be filled with worn out tires, some of the chicken cages, and some of the aluminum garden furniture. Rita and Pokey worked their way toward the old chicken house. There came several wheelbarrow loads of bright red corncobs with a few very disturbed baby mice.

Rita soon was working up a sweat sweeping out the chicken coup. She smiled, remembering her mother being quite upset with her once when she had complained about white stains from her antiperspirant. "Ugh! I must have something wrong with me. I sweat too much," she had said.

Her mother had gently chastised, "Rita, horses sweat, men perspire, and ladies glow. You need to learn that real ladies are known by their language, their deportment and gait. You must be trained in all these womanly arts. You must not walk like a heavy mule, no, no! Learn to dip lightly and smoothly. Learn your lessons from those who fail."

By the end of the afternoon Pokey and Rita had the hole nearly filled. The old henhouse was now almost empty, the service yard cleared of a lot of the accumulated trash, and Rita again was glowing, wishing that there were a shower at Lost Grove Motors.

Earlier Aunt Sarah spotted a chrome bumper in the hole that she thought could bring something on Ebay, so it was pulled from the amalgam. One of the last items tossed in was a five hundred gallon fuel oil tank that had holes in it that couldn't be patched.

By five o'clock Pokey was done for the day in more than one way. Aunt Sarah and Rita had been bickering all afternoon. He was amused and laughed good-naturedly sometimes, but at other times Aunt Sarah pulled rank and frustrated Rita's plan to transform the junkyard. Rita became more determined and depressed at the same time. Sometimes every other sentence had a pun or double-entendre. Pokey wondered why it seemed everything would be going along so well and then tempers would flare, almost monthly.

Aunt Sarah surprised Rita and Pokey when she returned from town with two large pizzas and a case of Fosters. "Come and get it boys and girls. One's a supreme, and one's a veggie."

Pokey switched on the tele and lit a candle while Rita sliced the pizzas, "Boy, I could eat a horse!"

"Yeah, me too," said Pokey. "In fact, horse burger tastes pretty good. I once worked on a mink ranch where some of the ranch hands ground up the horse meat just like beef."

After supper Pokey wryly observed that he had helped others

getting their holes filled. He told the story of once working with a landscaper who was hired to fill in a basement after a house had been removed. When the crew arrived they saw odds and ends left in the basement. Since it all was going to be filled in anyway, they helped themselves to the detritus. He told of finding a box of old vinyl records that he got for nothing. "Old blues, Memphis Slim, Little Richard, Big Bill Brunsie and strange Gregorian chants. There wasn't a Willie Nelson, not any Beetles or Elvis. Just one Whitney Huston. It makes you wonder where those people came from! Or where they went to."

"Went," corrected Rita.

"Went?"

"Yeah! Went. You're not supposed to end a sentence with a preposition. Where they went."

"Well, OK, Went." Pokey continued, "anyway, if you were writing a detective novel, what clues would Sherlock Holmes see in that strange pile of assorted records?"

Rita got up to go, "First question would be, Dr. Watson, was it an accident or a deliberate act, with them leaving that stuff. Or a release of some subliminal genetic impulse toward a species-wide goal that now becomes our job to decipher. Is this symbolic of something? Like where is our culture, our society, going? Like what were Gregorian chants really saying? Hmmm? What was Pope Greggory doing while those castratti warbled? All those men sitting together and singing? Plainly the people that moved the house away no longer cared for centuries of accumulated wisdom. Perhaps they went beyond speaking and singing in tongues to a space age form of music, ultra-gregorian, an up-to-date switched on pre-bach! Infinitely compressed. Maybe they broke their connection to this world. Maybe they just had it with the windows friendly age. Maybe they agreed that it all was beyond irtnog."

"Irtnog?" asked Poky.

"Yeah, Irtnog. The summary of summaries. It's the answer to the final question that most people are condemned to never ask.

Look it up on google."

Aunt Sarah tried to close the debate, "Some folks wouldn't notice reality if it bit them on the hind end! Oh sure, everybody notices details here and there, but the macro function? If you ask me, the ancient prophets only talked about what they wanted us to know. They didn't write down their human traits, their wet and sticky veneries.

"What's a venery?" asked Pokey. "Sounds kind of ugly."

"Oh no!" laughed Aunt Sarah. "Just the opposite. Venery deals with Venus, the Roman goddess of the garden. After Adam and Eve got into trouble and left, she busied herself with a whole lot of sex! The Greeks called her Aphrodite, the god who tended the same garden. Venus and Aphrodite were worshiped with wine, music, and sexy story telling. Music loves wine too."

"Awesome!" Posited Pokey, "Don't Muslims and Christians both sometimes get carried away with whipping themselves? I think I saw it on public TV."

"Yeah, Pokey," Sarah continued, "I think all religions make room for suffering. Show me a saint that didn't suffer. Maybe spanking is similar, an avenue of self-discovery! How important is suffering? Maybe Everyman was the name of those strange people that took that house with them, those strangers in a strange land, maybe they were done with being victimized. Maybe they chose not to suffer. Been there done that, you know? Let Death take care of herself! Talk about black holes, maybe our Mr. and or Mrs. Everyman were that. Tiny immensely powerful, itty bitty, black holes that sucked in every bit of reality that ever existed."

Rita found her own conclusion, "Well, still...why...or how could they leave Memphis Slim behind, I mean, you said they sucked everything into their black hole?" Rita smiled and looked Pokey in the eye. She countered, "No, it's not like they're not making burning bushes like they used to, it's just that God doesn't feel like repeating himself, or herself. We should be able to heed the good advice from the good book! In a way I think the Bible is a good place to start, maybe not a good place to end!, And furthermore don't forget that Christ had a middle eastern temperament. Things would have turned out a whole lot different, if Christ had been born in southern Germany or Norway. What if Christ had to spend forty days and nights out with the rein deer in Lapland. Mein Got och mein ring unt walderhaus. Oivay! For communion we'd be having the holy lute fisk wafers with aquavit!"

Pokey thought a minute, "yeah, but strange people have been going on vision quests since day one! They come back with mixed metaphors that end up all in a paradox."

"Ah yes, the agony and the ecstasy," swooned Rita,

"So...who wants to be the last lemming on the cliff?" asked Pokey.

"What do you mean?"

"Are humans like lemmings? Are lemmings in an avoidance mode, or are they in an approach mode. You know, maybe lemmings, like mankind, have an approach avoidance conflict! On the one hand, there's a safety in numbers, and a fear of standing out, looking different. And on the other hand, there's a need to be known and recognized. If all your friends aren't worried, why should you wrestle nightly with your demons? Therefore, QED, your fears balance out your hopes. Balance. Poise. It is unthinkable that you can arrange your life in such a way as to avoid fears or hopes. They say hope springs eternal, but there are lots of other notions that also spring eternally. For me life is the answer, and we have to figure out the question...just like jeopardy on the tele!"

Rita laughed, "If I accept my fears, doesn't that somehow cancel them out as an irritant? Like the balm of Gilead? Like, if we worked at it, we could update Christ's parables into today's vernacular. We can take turns, barring our bosoms, eyes closed, pleading to the world, here I am, please use me. What did the farmer say, better to wear out than rust out. Fear is rusting out. Fear is always connected to danger. And danger implies your own salvation. For years I have used that as kind of a mantra. Look closely at your fears, for therein lies your salvation. That's what my dad used to say."

Pokey got up and looked Rita in the eye, "Yeah, this one is going to take some cogitation, some real pondering. Yep! I agree with you about the burning bush! Life is so unfair, youth, always wasted on the young! An old story. Maybe that is mankind's eternal mission, to consciously look for the burning bush."

Rita concluded, "I agree. Maybe we won't find it unless we are looking for it. Maybe the burning bush starts out very, very, tiny. A spark cast into some tinder. Like the Indians did. Kind of smoldering, hardly any fire or smoke at all. Reality can knock on our door, but we don't have to bother to answer it. Who makes our reality for us here at lost grove anyway? Do you define yourself, or do you let others do it for you? Do you spank yourself, or pay others to victimize you." Rita laughed, and with a flourish wrapped her cape around her shoulders.

Pokey thought a moment, "Yeah, that makes sense somehow. We don't automatically learn anything. Whatever conclusions we make are always flawed. We yearn for absolute truths in a sea of uncertainty. Instead of absolutes...we are given only relatives."

Rita agreed again, "And life proceeds, examined or unexamined. Ah! Sweet mystery of life! Excuse me, I gotta go to the john."

Rita had been gone only a few minutes when Sheriff Hermanson stopped by the Lost Grove Motors office. The open sign was still in the window. No one answered his knock, so he entered the workshop, and not finding anyone there either, continued out the back door. He gave a yell, "You hoo, anyone home?"

In the tool trailer Aunt Sarah was working on the soles of a pair of her boots that she was winterizing by screwing small sheet metal screws into the soles for traction on ice. She yelled "Over here!"

Sheriff Hermanson came across the newly cleaned up yard to the trailer. "I see you've been doing a lot a cleaning up, Sarah Jane."

"My niece Rita Marie, and Albert did most of the work. We had to fill in a big hole, probably a drainage shaft for the old Tripoli mine. It had water flowing through the bottom of it."

"You mean it was a stream?" asked the Sheriff.

"Well, yeah, it was that or a sewer. Depends on how you look at it. Albert said it smelled aweful, he went down at looked at it. And when he came back up his boots smelled to high heaven!"

"Miss Chamberlin?"

"Yes Sheriff Hermanson."

"I thought you'd know better! I'm sorry to have to tell you, there's a law against filling in creeks. There are severe fines. It's the clean water act of 2012. If you like, I can send you a copy. It's pretty long and involved. We can give you a copy of the law, but there's a cost. I think its twenty cents a page. Plus postage."

"But Sheriff, you've got to be kidding!" The hole in question just opened up by itself. We didn't do anything. Do we get fined just for being alive? Is there a law against cleaning up after weird occurrences, like this tunnel collapse?"

"We don't make the laws, Sarah, we just enforce them. Simple as that! I'm sorry to have to tell you all this, but that's the law. If you want to, you can contact the district attorney",

"Well Sheriff, are you going to report us? And just what are you recommending us to do?"

"Miss Chamberlin, I don't know. The law can't be expected to cover every case. Ottawa meant well, I'm sure. But for now you better pull all that shit out of the hole. You can start with getting rid of that oil tank."

"Sheriff, what are we supposed to do with all the stuff in the hole?"

"Sarah Jane, the law doesn't say. You might as well just dig a hole somewhere and bury it all. But whatever, the stream has got to flow, I know that."

Aunt Sarah wasn't ready to cause any problem. Some day she hoped to get her driver's license back again, but for now she didn't want to swim upstream. "OK, Sheriff. It's going to take a lot of work. I don't even want to think how much work it's going to take."

Twenty Four

For the next two weeks Pokey and Rita averaged three trips to the township dump every day, except Sundays. In order to carry more in the spreader they set aside the wringer washing machine and the trash containers.

Even though Rita had found some part time helpers, production of the rape protectors was suffering. Pathmark stores were threatening to drop the line if they couldn't get their orders filled on time. Pokey and Rita had plenty of time to talk about their business while doing the trash runs. Six times a day they passed the Helgeson egg farm that was still deserted. A bright red Pyramid Realty for sale sign dangled from the gate.

So it was that Rita suggested to Pokey that they approach Aunt Sarah about renting the egg farm. "Aunt Sarah, we've got quite a bit of money saved up, the orders for the rape kits are more than we can handle. We need more space. Pokey and I don't have any credit to get a loan, but you could probably get the bank to help us."

Pokey had another idea, "maybe we could use one of Helgeson's old chicken houses for assembling the dervish in full scale. I'd like to do that with you all before I hit the road. Ed Harris and I have been talking about going on the road for Jesus! Glory hallelujah!"

Aunt Sarah wondered how Rita and Pokey were planning to get back and forth, since neither had a driver's license or a vehicle. Rita had it all figured out, that when Aunt Sarah needed the tractor and spreader, for whatever reason, it was always her call. When it was free, Rita or Pokey had second call. If there was a conflict, Ed Harris could be called. Rita summed it up, "Besides, if sales keep increasing, we can hire someone to take us."

Aunt Sarah looked worried, "But, Rita, you're the one after all the money. It's all you do. And that's OK. So it should be you who calls the realtor and sets up a lease in your name, not mine.

People around here know that I don't have that kind of money. If it gets out how much you kids are making, well...I'm going to loose my credibility. People will be pestering us to contribute to all kinds of shit, like the Policeman's Fund, the Altar Society, Dare, instead of calling us when the church potluck dinner is over to come help with the garbage. I don't want to give that up, at least not now."

Rita thought a bit, "But if I use my real name, somebody might connect me to New York State, and Mr. Nims made me promise to stay out of the country, until the trust issues are settled. Maybe if I could slightly change how I spell my name on the deed. How about I just add an "h" to Rita?"

It took Mrs. Epperson from Pyramid Realty about an hour to get to Lost Grove Motors. "You can call me Lois Honey," she said enthusiastically. Rita introduced Pokey, "And this is Albert, my associate partner."

Mrs. Epperson extended her hand to Pokey and shook hands with him a little longer than protocol might have suggested. Rita narrowed her gaze.

"My friends call me Pokeyman, or sometimes just Pokey. All I ask is you call me in time for dinner" laughed Pokey. Mrs. Epperson giggled a little too loudly. Rita watched as Pokey climbed into the front seat of the shiny black, four-door, Chevy Durango for the ten minute drive to Helgeson's. During the drive, Rita watched Pokey and Mrs. Epperson in the front seat, warming to each other. Kind of like smoldering tinder. Mrs. Epperson had streaked highlights in her hair, brown lip liner, and a predatory smile. Rita immediately was on guard, just out of instinct. She couldn't put her finger on it, but this woman conjured up a Frankenstein image, complete with exaggerated canine teeth.

Rita didn't want the wolf to get too close to Pokey as they approached the egg farm office. She positioned herself between him and Mrs. Epperson as they entered the office area. As they looked around they saw a few items that probably hadn't sold at the auction. In one closet there was an old IBM card reader and a mound of Jim Beam bottles. Pokey found the men's room and a shower room.

During the tour of the warehouse and sheds Rita made sure that the broker knew who was in control. "Well, Mrs. Epperson, you can tell the Helgeson heirs when you see them, that we're ready to lease with an option to buy, starting tomorrow, if the details can be worked out. Tell the heirs that we've done our research and have some questions about problems with on-site contamination that may need to be remedied, some other code violations. We would want to be indemnified in case there are any description difficulties."

"Other than that" continued Rita, "we would assume that all brokerage costs, and title insurance are charged to the seller."

"But, Miss Rita, usually the buyer pays for that."

"Yes I know. But we're not your usual buyer. We checked up on everything last night on the Internet. You just present the offer. It's a real offer for a run down property. In fact, we may have to look real hard at your property condition report."

On the return trip Rita sat up front with Mrs. Epperson, hearing stories of the golf club, some new rich family from Albany that was connected to the World's End business. Pokey, sitting in the back seat, was dreaming of putting the dervish to its final test flight.

During lunch Rita and Pokey told Aunt Sarah all about the tour of the egg farm. It was going to be a cash deal, month by month. With Rita's new name, they agreed that Rita could leave at any time, and not be liable for the lease. Pokey was quietly doing dishes when Rita asked if something were wrong, "You seem sad Pokey, are you having second thoughts? You know you can leave anytime you want!"

"Yeah, I know. I'm kind of stuck on the dervish. One of the Helgeson's brooder sheds, the one with the big red doors, I think would be big enough for a full size Dervish. We'll have to get a hanger door set up, like at the World's End hanger.

Pokey continued. "The next stage design is critical. We are still learning. We know how strong the void is, that "none" thing that holds it together. But we can't tell for sure if we can control the "none" thing. I'm afraid of the unknown again. Maybe it'll blow up in our faces! I can understand the vacuum thing, that's purely linear, but the sympathetic dampening that cancels the exhaust noise, that just blows my mind! The outgassing might cause a problem."

Rita thought a minute, "Well, in that case, maybe we should lease it to terrorist groups, Bomb, bomb, ba bomb! Wouldn't that be copacetic! I mean, if it is that dangerous! Bottom line Albert, I think you worry too much. You need to step back from worrying about your worth, your depressions, your performance, your power. Others should not have power over you in any way. If you put yourself in God's hands, and stop comparing yourself to others, you maybe can be content with a beautiful, if somewhat narrow, concentration. Alternatively, find God everywhere outside of you. So, God can be found inside and outside, it just depends on your perspective. Maybe you can use your puppets to redefine the Lord's parables with the right accent to be believed. It is almost a con game you know. Always start with a verity that all believe to be true. Then proceed to pull in your fish. Maybe you should have named your puppet show, The Astronomical Fish Factory!"

Pokey laughed, "You're right, something is fishy here in more ways than one! Maybe all fishermen have an odor! What did St. Paul smell like? Maybe prophet feet smell a certain way. I know I smell kind of gamey myself. Why don't we do the dump run and check out the showers at the World's End Hanger."

Sarah cautioned, "That's not in your contract. Though maybe Mrs. Staber might give it an OK."

Rita thought a moment, "Aunt Sarah, why don't you come along with us. You can be our look out, and warn us if anyone is coming. Come on, we did all this for you. We got your hole filled, and the henhouse all emptied, ready for your next haul. We'll check the dump with you, and then head over to the airport, and have a decent shower."

Aunt Sarah decided that if she were going, she wanted to get the garbage from the airport snack shop first, then to the dump and home. She insisted on driving Alice, with the manure spreader. Rita joined Pokey on the chrome dinette chairs in the spreader. The empty white wringer washing machine was back between them. The trip brought back memories of the Halloween party, and Rita remembered how attracted she had been to both Pokey and Charles, the new stranger.

The wind picked up a little and a chill went over the spreader. Pokey found an old green patchwork quilt to put over their knees. "There, that's better." Pokey's hand rested ever so lightly on Rita's hand, "you're cold, you're shivering."

"I know, and I've got a sore throat. Your hand feels good, but remember to wash again. I don't want you to catch whatever I've got."

As they passed Helgeson's deserted egg farm, Pokey brightened, "it is going to be great to get at that shower room. You know, they didn't have a women's room at Helgesons. Maybe just the men worked there."

"Well don't count your chickens until they hatch. We don't know if they're going to take the deal or not." Twin bridge road passed by and the Hare Krishna Farm. Six miles further they pulled up behind the airport snack shop. Mrs. Staber's niece, Carla was at the counter when the lost grove crew entered, busy talking to a crop-duster from out west. Two couples from the Chukutieme mines were just finishing up fish and chips. They had refueled and planned to be home by midnight.

Carla came over and took their orders. Aunt Sarah ordered a Fosters and circulated, joining the crop duster. Then she moved on to the Chukutieme couples who ended up giving her their recipe for corn relish. She had a way of making friends without putting on any airs. Her tattered, greasy overalls were not pretentious. She gained an automatic veracity and simple presence in many situations. She was a strong believer in, what you see is what you get.

Rita and Pokey took the pass key for the World's End hanger and entered the dark crew quarters. Pokey stood guard in the dark entry until Rita came to trade places. "There" she said, "I'm a new girl, I needed that. This could get to be a habit." They jogged back to the snack shop and collected Aunt Sarah and four bags of trash.

At the town dump the crew pulled next to the recycle dumpster. Rita watched the smoke curling up from the edge of the cliff. In the dim light she could see rats scavenging among some boxes that someone had neatly stacked at the edge of the bluff. Aunt Sarah spotted a Stihl weed wacker that looked good enough to take home. Pokey threw a few pebbles at the rats. After dumping trash from the cafe, the crew headed home to Lost Grove.

As they passed by Helgesons Rita unexpectedly started to think out loud, "I don't know if I ever want to get pregnant...you know...breed!'

"Uh...where's that coming from?" asked Pokey.

"I mean, I was just thinking, my mother wasn't much into mothering, and maybe I'm not either. I don't know if having a child is all that it is cracked up to be."

Again Pokey wrapped the green quilt over their knees, as they continued to talk about their projects. Aunt Sarah turned on the tractor lights as they passed by Twin Bridge road. Rita got that far away look in her eye, "you know Pokey, I haven't had a dress on since I got off the plane from Albany! It's been blue jeans and bibs. I'm getting worried, that it's getting too comfortable. Maybe I don't need college, I mean, we're doing pretty good with the rape kits. What's college going to give me?"

"Pokey, you remember telling me about your dream of that horse with the three riders? It means something to me too. I can relate to your dream in my own way. One side of me fantasizes about what it would be like if I married into a famous family. I'd be a work in progress for sure. You know, Mom taught me how to broaden my "ahs." I know which 'yahd' to 'pak' m'car in.

I'm sure I could be a good, maybe great, hostess for somebody important. But I can fantasize being a nun too. You know, maybe being celibate is more than safe. Maybe old virgins know best! Or maybe there's a deeper meaning in becoming a mother of ten, married to Big Al, an abusive thug who has body odor and gray hair all over his back."

"But another side of me wants to forsake my expected role. Sometimes I want to chuck it all, get good and drunk and get laid, maybe by a stranger. Isn't that just awful Pokey?"

"Golly sakes miss Rita...Well no one ever said that being good doesn't take work, for after all, what do the words noble and ignoble mean anyway. A work in progress! What does that mean? A work in progress! Does that mean, as life goes by, you learn this or that, then add it up by addition? Until your brain is full? When does your education really begin? Were you born yesterday? You don't look like Judy Holiday."

Pokey blew his nose and continued, "That's what happens with my puppet troop. They give meaning to words, that's what quickens things, gives flavor. You know what I mean? Some say that you start to become an adult when you experience your first betrayal. Your first big disappointment. Oh! Such a surprise! Betrayal, kind of by definition, has to involve painful learning, when you reluctantly cast off your innocence, your simple notions. But then, I dunno, maybe you haven't come to that stage quite yet."

Aunt Sarah down shifted Alice as they coasted into Lost Grove Motors. Rita agreed, "Right on, life is more than the beatitudes. Maybe we just need to swim with the current. Smart fish don't make waves. Dumb fish get caught with their pants down, so to speak."

Pokey laughed and blew his nose again,"ya know, shit happens, I never asked to be born, and I haven't asked to die... at least not yet, so why should I feel guilty for being confused in my own way. Lets not confuse our memories with reality! Reality, with or without God, can only be experienced through that glass darkly. Our fevers, even now are only partially under our control that, like ambition, can be seen as good or bad. Did you know that? That ambition isn't always a good thing? It took me a long time to understand that one. My dictionary told me ambition comes from the Greek, to wander around looking for votes! In that light, ambition is kind of stupid. Like if you are ambitious, by definition you are bound to be unhappy with the status quo. So you get on the treadmill chasing after happiness, forever fugitive."

Rita saw life from a different angle, "Feeling depressed, I think, usually involves feeling victimized, and, to me, it can become a comfortable habit. Sure! You want your connection to God to be seamless! Not possible. But don't let that stop you from trying. There is nothing ignoble in your quest. You might as well teach Mr. Pee to fly."

After a pregnant pause, Pokey continued, "Every sword cuts more than one way. Maybe your thug, Big Al, with the gray hair all over his back, well...he may have a special message for you, the very answer to your desperation. Bottom line: don't be confused by the packaging. I know I am always surprised at the stuff I find everywhere. The simplest weed, the shiny trail slugs leave around the garden, half a robin's eggshell in the weeds. Maybe all that is accidental or maybe not. Maybe there's a message everywhere if we listen hard enough. And maybe, maybe I will teach Mr. Pee to fly the dervish. Mr. Pee is smarter than you might think."

Twenty Five

Pokey slept well after a full day. Rita also woke up to a sunshiny day. After using the green room she paused looking at the chickens scratching in the leaves. They seemed to be in a good mood, chuckling. It was Saturday, but still a workday. A pretty large order for the Rape Kits had come in from Winn-Dixie. Rita found that two of the dripping pus pieces were going to have to be back ordered. She noted on her Ipod a note for the broker.

Rita made pancakes for breakfast using Aunt Sarah's milk replacer from the farmer's store. Over breakfast Rita and Pokey went on line and downloaded a dedicated link to a new inventory control site, called postitplus. During lunch Mrs. Epperson returned with the signed acceptance agreement. Rita wrote the check for the first six months rent. Pokey received keys for the Helgeson gate and office building.

During the next three weeks Pokey and Rita worked with Ed Harris's two brothers, Toe Head and Peter, planning the manufacturing production of the rape kits. In line digital spray jets now produced truly ugly sores at a fraction of the cost of only a couple of months before. A new shrink wrapping machine cut the waste by half. Toxic propellents were eliminated in the process, so that EPA could certify the facility the highest level, Greenmagnet Plus.

Out of habit, Aunt Sarah kept an eye on the discard pile as the Harris's remodeled the egg farm. Rita appreciated Sarah's help setting up the packaging line. Helgeson's case sealer was put back in service with an optical scanner in line. When an order was complete the computer would instruct the machine operator to segregate a new order number.

Rita ran into Tom Openshaw, a designer for World's End at their corporate hanger. Tom suggested that the rape kit appliqués could be packaged as Halloween novelties. Rita laughed, "I should have thought of that! Because that's the way we got into the rape protectors! Pokey was helping me make my witch costume, making fake warts. It was my idea to put them on Ebay.

Rita turned to Tom, "do you think we should package the Halloween uglys under our own brand name or do you think we should private label them. It's a seasonal focus thing, isn't it?"

Tom thought a minute, "you would have to imprint different bar codes for each item for each distributor or chain. If you give them a good price point they may not require you to guarantee long term pricing. That way you can raise your price once movement heats up."

At the end of the week the staff held a planning session in the old Helgeson lunchroom. All three Harris brothers joined Rita, Pokey, Aunt Sarah, and the office manager. In new business, Rita brought up the Halloween project.

A sixpack of Fosters was soon gone, so Toe Head went out for supplies. Rita observed that some of the scab production was looking too thin, almost like tattoos. Ed Harris wondered if he could have a fake tattoo made that he could put on his own body, anywhere he chose. He thought God is Love, with the rugged cross behind it might be nice. So what if the tattoos faded away after six months...he could change his mind.

Pokey went on line and googled images of tattoos that they could copy. To his dismay he found a plenitude of ugly transfers already available. "I don't think the game is worth he candle," said Pokey. "But coming out with Halloween items might be good."

"I agree," said Rita. "We really don't have to change our molding machines, or the sprayers. We don't have to find new brokers and distributors since we can use our present network. I can't see how we can loose."

In other new business the Board authorized a last minute arrangement with Toe head to be hired full time with a company vehicle to shuttle between Helgeson's and Lost Grove. Plans were made to shuttle daily until the ninety pie shaped segments nearly filled the brooder shed.

There were two shipments of Great Stuff that didn't clear

customs at Detroit. Fortunately the new office manager had a brother who worked with the Detroit office who got the shipments expedited.

After supper, Rita took out her diary, "If I intend to be the perfect "me," what should I have to discard along the ways? ide, on my journey? Stop pretending for a start! Stop looking for new, it will take care of itself.

So, noise is both an impediment and a gateway. I remember the experiment with noise and recognition threshold. A person's awareness can be focused to perceive relationships unknown in quiet times.

So for one to find harmony in life, in looking for God, it is a mistake to seek constant bliss? Like, what did St. Theresa do with herself when she "recovered" from her ecstasy. Chop wood, carry water?

Some major thinking about the dynamics of mental gymnastics. Following the adage that all drunks, all beggars can and do dream of being emperor. The process of dreaming is an allele to religions in which our isolation from God, spurs our devotion, our supplication. For Prayer then proceeds from a want of satisfaction.

To effectively pray it may help to accent the negative, the danger of an uncertain future, prayer can be an effort to compensate, to approach equilibrium, to gain a modicum of power. Turn concern into worry, turn worry into terror. Exaggerate the threat, demonize your enemy. To accept Jesus as your personal savior...saving you from certain death, as well as forgiving you for all the shit you've pulled on others. Is the word Panacea?

Then there is conditional denial of the threat. We can agree to put our heads in the clouds or in the sand.
We have to recognize what drives our fears, and find different ways to accommodate our lives. Bloodshed maybe shouldn't be habitual for our country to feel good about itself.

Rita concluded, "Maybe God was just having a bad day when

he created Man. I'm thinking, maybe death is a great cure for boredom.

Pokey took out his own journal,

"Must life have a conclusion? Maybe life is everything but a conclusion.

Maybe a life view never comes into focus. Maybe as we age we automatically discard irrelevant content, like skinning my feelies.

The center of our target is not a place outside of us; rather it is a spot in time, inside of us. It is most common to see persons quite distracted from the moment. In a sense...You keep looking for answers, and all you find are more questions. Ask yourself what truly bugs you. What insult is pardonable? Is avoidance your best strategy?

Sure! You have energy for change. Some sort of elementary angst. But how or where can you attack, when you can't describe the enemy?"

Pokey finished the remodeling of the back end of the Mrs. Karl's bread truck. He wired small speakers into the two end doors that now opened to reveal the puppet stage, complete with working red draw drapes and a painted backdrop.

The show could go on the road as soon as Aunt Sarah could fix the brake line leak.

Twenty Seven

Pokey and Aunt Sara were having morning coffee break and the subject turned to figuring out exactly how a birds feather works. They got out the magnifying glass and looked at the surface of hawk feather, amazed at the economy of form. Pokey noted, "You know the designer of that feather figured out the mechanics of circular reciprocity in terms of exertion that is almost uniform through the cycle. Almost effortless. So too I think our passage through time is a cycle where we are always just becoming, taking our circular tour. Follow the bouncing ball. Learn all we can about our fears for there is our salvation. Our quarry should always seem just beyond reach.

Maybe the greatest pain of old age is not being able to cure the world from all its imperfection. The beacon dims, and the waves proceed.

So, you ask me, why do I listen to Mr. Pee? He has music in his heart, and it is beautiful music, with structure and color, variety and flavor...that pig knows best...a lot more than I do..."

"It was Mr. Pee that told me how wrong I was about the whales. Do you remember all the to do about the Alan Hovanes "And God created the Whales" music?

Mr. Pee could only hear crap coming from the whales. Pissed off fish. Hey! Didn't they choose to swim off into the murky blue yonder?"

"So," continued Pokey, "bottom line is even the whales have their problems. Every species has agendas and mutants."

"Before you were born, where were you? What happens when you die...where do you go? Are you timeless? Why worry? Is fear an intoxicant? Does one's pulse quicken at the graves edge? Or does fatigue eventually quiet our inquiry. Perhaps there are as many kinds of death as there are kinds of life."

"But no, Buddha knew best...contemplation of the putrefaction of the flesh, enhances our now. Somewhat like the angst of existentialism, the sting of self-flagelation. "Oh Death where in thy sting!".

" Death then is a process by which our species renews itself. Transmutation, transfiguration. Some lessons, and perhaps all lessons, have to be relearned by every individual."

"The first convenient cop out is to agree that death doesn't exist. No final retribution, no reward, no sense of return, of completion, of final harmony. No! Death is for us, an absolute. You can't be kind of dead."

"But so is life! If you want to experience it to the fullest. know that not every moment can be ecstatic. One's connection can be of any order, from the lowest vegetable caress, to the most sublime musical innuendo. From the most animal grunt of pleasure, to the most holy incantation of the Holy Spirit.

The last time you spoke to GOD, did he or she use any words that you didn't know? In other words, have we fashioned our image of god in such a positive way that he or she might have perfect communication with us. Believing in God's presence assumes we are capable of infinite sympathetic resonance with the Godhead. Such an assumption is faulty to the degree of obfuscation, or darkening. Is there any spot in the universe that is totally dark and cold?

After winnowing the chaff, we cannot avoid realizing, that our animal heritage will always confound us, directing and controlling. We never can say that we are in total control, for always, the sirens call...the burning bush intrudes, the light fades, the rose wilts, and mold grows.

The ultimate personal goal may be to love yourself. Not above any other. To know yourself is to love yourself. Sometimes it is easier for others to love us, than for us to love ourselves. That means to excuse our own smelly, odoriferous faults, to see our unique, totally individual faults, and enjoy our own vicissitudes, without prejudice. Avoiding the trap of vanity and pride.

Sometimes I reach that bingo state of mind, that sublime connection to the godhead...to blossom. Drifting in harmony, music then is a metaphor, a parallel universe involving both sides of my brain.

I see that life can be seen as a journey without a destination. Along the way we can find hidden faults in all of us. I could have been something, except that....

Look at the San Andreas fault in California. Faults happen when macros can't accept micros. All is well, except this tiny irritation. I know I should be strong, but. I have always been obsessive about my stupid obsessions.

So the words came to me, Pokey! You're not all that you think yourself to be. There are sides of me that only now are coming into focus. I can see the tip of the iceberg of myself, mostly drifting along with the current. But looking deeper, and I see a variety of imperfections, irregularities.

If you were intent on becoming the perfect "you", what would you have to leave beside yourself along the wayside, on your journey? Stop pretending for a start! Stop looking for new, it will take care of itself. Best check out the now.

Why is it so easy to feel victimized? To be paranoid is to be perpetually on guard, expecting doom.

Where would we be if we could not find room to improve our actions? Perfect chastity is impossible. Each of us acquired shame at Eden's gate. Shame, ugliness, discord, all proceed from our social contacts. Even if we can't define it, we still feel the effects of being found inadequate. In fact we develop attitudes and the habit of inviting patterns that reinforce our negative self-image. Again, consistency trumps creativity.

Life energy fluctuates between "stasis" and "extasis" which is to say, activity vs. rest, allegory, paradigm...

I can elect to feel ever so much in the moment, or, upon my whim, I can elect to see and recreate all my past, and feel being the end sum of my life, ready for a period. Also known as the full stop!

What could be lacking in such perspectives?

Our present is not much different from our past! The psyche

rides the moment, but is always separate until death.

Some of us long to return from whence we came.

Depending on your appetites, you can explore or avoid everyone. But in the end, a part of each of us longs to connect and be understood by the world around us. How can we play with puppets and point the way?

Is it a mark of grace, to accept the inevitable? Once accepted, there can be a relatively happy existence of unquestioning, called having the faith.

But to imply purpose to the process of life, might be a stretch. Are we supposed to understand our maker through his/her footprints left in our DNA? Lots of luck translating that.

Perhaps music gives us a back door entrance to defining our passage through life. Music, like life, is only a series of transitions. Music becomes a symptom of an inner life. Similarly, art is a distortion, a response to life.

It is normal not to notice God entering your life when it first happens. Inspiration, like life itself, evolves from the interplay of only a few elements. In the primordial amalgam of a few sticky proteins, life began. Similarly a few right-minded individuals can effect change in society.

The change can be modest, or even retrograde. It can be exponential and transformative.

Levels (or qualities) of consciousness exist for our pleasure and for our pain. For some, the doorways of our perception may never open to some vistas. Some of us won't be called to lead. Our appetites are varied and usually not equally satisfied. Emotional deficits, like all handicaps, can prompt unexpected compensations. With lack of direction comes infinite variety! God shakes many dice! There's a time to have no direction, no goal. Getting into the moment means to not see the target. Just breath. It's OK not to sing.

Hunt as much as you want to find God's purpose for you and you are bound to be frustrated. Remember mother Teresa's profound angst for not sensing an answer as she approached her end. For God doesn't exist outside of us. God does exist in an existential way in and of our spiritual life. Not outside, to be worshipped from afar, but inside to be felt here and now. The miracle of life can only be experienced in the moment.

Such identity doesn't allow for much time off. You are awake, alive, or dead, gone from the moment. We go to church not because we understand what life is all about...but just the opposite...we don't have a clue...god hasn't downloaded his plan for us...Oh no, we are losers before we begin. Nietche any one?

During the first week of August, the last pie segments for the Dervish were delivered to the Helgeson hanger barn. Pokey locked the last segment to both the topside and the belly entity with an asymmetric parabolic ratio. This allowed the Dervish to hover noiselessly. To descend the bivalves compressed the air volume, thus increasing the ambient weight, which in turn brought the craft to a gentle landing. A single wooden gear shifter from a Pontiac Le Mons now controlled the movement of the Dervish. Reverse the procedure and the vacuum gently lifted the craft. Pokey planned to practice elevating with out leaving the old brooder shed.

Ed Harris brought in the GPS satellite receiver from the latest Google Universe that included current mapping. The control console had ample space to install the Dell lap top screen.

Pokey and Rita had different ideas for the LED's that might be needed for nighttime flying. The Dervish was very fragile; running into a tree could destroy its protective layer, just as commonly found in nature. The lithium battery pack acted as a central ballast, strategically placed off center, somewhat balancing the passenger and fuel load.

Aunt Sarah and Ed Harris worked out a loading system that transferred fuel automatically among the three on board bladders to compensate for variations in the pattern of load weights and placement. Aunt Sarah remarked, "You know, the Dervish is a lot like the engine in a good race car. To get efficiency you have to fine tune the timing so that it's not knocking, fighting against itself."

Pokey nodded, "There's a message for me there...sometimes I feel like I'm fighting myself. The Dervish looks like it's gonna work. I should be happy, but I'm not. I'm depressed instead. Already wondering where my next disappointment is coming from. I remember last fall sometimes I confronted myself in the mirror. I remember what it felt like to be happy as a simple innocent child. Back before I started looking for meaning in my life. I remember the time I confronted my self in the mirror. Back then, I thought it was a step forward to accept myself. I did. It worked for a while, and I thought there was no problem. But then, doubt crept back in, and my newly acquired insight blurred. So I find clues and then discard them. Same old problem. No clues last very long. Big picture? Little picture? All is a haze. But as they say, I never promised you a rose garden. Saint Theresa understood it best. Talk about good sex! How do you think the Virgin Mary felt when she got impregnated? Did she notice anything when the Holy Spirit entered her? Morning sickness? Can you imagine what Joseph said to her?"

Rita laughed, "Pokey maybe there's the message for you. You've tried just about everything else. Maybe you should look into the Kama Sutra.

Pokey was first up the next morning. He fixed Mr. Pee a nice corn mush breakfast with maple syrup, and then mixed up some batter for pancakes.

During breakfast Pokey cheerfully reported that he had another epiphany. He had taken several Tylanol plus sleeping pills and still had trouble quieting his depression. But finally he succumbed and found momentary solace in a new scene. He imagined the burning bush, on stage. "I got a great idea! I'm gonna make a burning bush puppet. Somehow I need to get an old vacuum to blow air into streamers to make it look like burning flames. Yellow, orange, and white streamers. Maybe they could puff in synk with my voice."

Rita agreed "Yeah that could work, but wouldn't it be simpler to not have a noisy vacuum, but do the same thing with a fireplace bellows. You could work it with your foot, just like your gluttony puppet that throws up. You know you might use some little oak branches tied around the end of a hose. Or maybe colored yarn teased out."

"Yeah that sounds doable. Maybe we could use one of those Christmas optical sparkling trees. Somehow we could voice activate the LED's. That way the burning bush would be truly animated, kind of spell binding."

Rita added, "You know...the bush could be at the edge of the stage, not always part of the action. Just like God, watching us mortal's flounder, wondering how long it is going to take us to figure out His plan. One of your puppets can ask the bush for guidance. The bush can answer, fiber optic lights pulsating and foliage flopping in the breeze from your fireplace bellows."

"Well we've got our work cut out for us. All along we've been planning to put the stage at the rear end of the bread truck. But maybe we should think of putting it on the side. Either way we can run our sound system in stereo."

Pokey turned to Rita and Aunt Sarah, "You know, or I hope to tell you, I couldn't have done this show without you both. I still have to run some caulking around the proscenium on the back of Mrs. Karls. The salvaged ASTRONOMICAL LECTURE CO. sign will sparkle over the stage."

I wonder sometimes what would have happened if Jesus had lived a little bit longer. If the last supper wasn't the last, but the first. Can you imagine Jesus just stopping by here for a neighborly visit. What would you end up talking about? What's new Jesus? You, being the great communicator!

Rita thought a moment and laughed, "hey guy, is that your cell phone ringing in your pants or are you just happy to see me?"

"No! Seriously, what would concern Jesus in today's complex world? Some of His wisdom surely applies today as it did in His day. But the Bible doesn't have much to say about today's genome, gay rights, cruelty to animals, et cetera, et cetera."

"So, Rita and Aunt Sarah, I can use your help in making up

my dialog. I don't want to be preaching, that just turns off a lot of people. Thirty minutes should be enough time. Remember it should be a learning moment when the audience makes sense of the situation and forms its own conclusion. We should not conclude the lesson with the answer. Leave it up to the novice to participate and own his developing insight. I'm thinking of the real old time Punch and Judy puppet shows. Punch sometimes is dressed up in fool's clothes, with a diamond pattern, and sometimes with a little bell on his cap. Those are all Sufi symbols. Punch is a fool in that sense. So, it makes sense that Judy complains and leads the audience, heating up the dialog. Rita... would you be my Judy? I have to play against something. I just can't rail against life in general!"

Rita got up to leave, "Pokey...Aunt Sarah might be better than me, I mean, she's got age behind her...like witches in Shakespeare, you know, boil, cauldron boil!"

"Somewhere at the end of the show, my Everyman puppet can say something like...uh, we pray to God to help us out of our tragic mortality. Why can't God show us the way? Can we make heaven on earth? And where would God be without us? Listen for the sirens pointing the way. For God, as we define her must be hard to find. Out of chaos and confusion we have to discover ourselves. And even then all of our feelings exist only in relationships. By ourselves each of us is alone and void of meaning. Don't anybody want to argue with me?"

Twenty Six

Rita started packing up her laptop and program disk to take with her. The music files took up most of one suitcase. She debated whether she should take the backup files for the rape protection business. And in the end she would leave them for Aunt Sarah and her accountant, Peter Van Halen. With Pokey going on the road with Ed

Labour Day came on September 6th this year, so it was pretty quiet at Helgeson's. The production line girls that shrink wrapped the gonorrhea sores got together singing harmony. They ordered two kegs of Fosters, and recruited Kenny and Joey Hubert to set up a proper pig roast. They parked their smoker next to the break yard where some of the second shift girls still took cigarette breaks.

Kenny had some car problems getting started and they ran out of starter fluid for the charcoal. Gasoline was used and Joey got his eyebrows singed, but by late afternoon they were artfully slicing the boar. Kenny spread the coals and threw on some applesauce, hoping to kill the flavor of the gasoline.

Most of the staff was on hand to see Van Halen open his briefcase. His report was brief and contained no surprises. Transportation costs were now a bigger factor affecting overhead. But unexpectedly the overseas business with China had doubled with the decline of the U.S. dollar. American workers were out performing the Bangladeshis.

His advice ended with the admonition that as a Sub-S corporation it was going to be forced to issue year-end dividends. It meant double taxation on their income, first at the corporate level, then at the stockholder level.

Van Halen further recommended that a profit sharing plan would be a deductible expense for the corporation, and everyone could benefit in proportion to their gross salaries. Even the mailroom guy could be happy with some profit sharing. Van

Halen summed it up, "If we work the numbers just right the only looser is the province! It won't get a cent!"

Rita was quiet for a while, thinking. "Well, then, don't we shareholders each have pay at least capitol gains on the income?" Van Halen indicated that there was more than enough loss carry forwards to balance the gains. "It might be a bit more of a problem in doing the province depreciation schedules," he advised. "I'll run it past Tom Shroeder, the Auditor General, when we meet again, just to be sure. We're both on the Province Bar Reform committee."

Rita set about picking up all the dishes, and empty bottles, dead soldiers in Aunt Rita's jargon. Kenny and Joey volunteered to help, but Rita convinced them to get out the violin and 'cordeen. Soon all joined in "ninety nine bottles of beer on the wall"

At breakfast the next day, Pokey explained that he had a new idea for the Astronomical Lecture Company. "I've had another epiphany! I'm gonnna make a new drop for the puppet stage. It's gonna show the elephant in the parlor. But not all the elephant. I'm gonna show the rear end, with the little tail that looks so stupid. And you know what's under that flickering tail...yep! An elephant sized dripping anus!"

Rita almost knocked over the milk replacer, laughing, "I'll help you. You know, you could use the same foot pump you used for the gluttony puppet. You could make that ass hole look like a mouth, kind of. So it could talk to the audience."

"That'd be mind blowing! Yeah! And you can be out front, talking to the elephant, as if it had always been here. So what ever is bothering us, well, we can discuss it with the biggest ass hole, the most prominent normally hidden and not talked about aspect of man kind."

Pokey seemed to be drifting, in thought. "So what are the real elephants in the parlour? Lets make a list. Slavery? Hypocrisy? Graft? Pornography? Drugs? Bull fighting? Cock fighting? Dog fighting? Prize fighting?"

"No Pokey, the list can come later. We need to redecorate the stage, fancy it up like a proper palace. Maybe red velvet drapery, perhaps a little lace in a dark creme color, cafe con leeche. Kind of out of archy digest."

Aunt Sarah came in for a bowl of cereal with milk replacer. Rita and Pokey explained the new plan for the puppet stage. Aunt Sarah had her own idea, "why not make multiple puppet stages and put them out for sale on Ebay. You have extra space at the old chicken ranch."

By nightfall Pokey had finished modeling the impressive, expressive posterior of an elephant puppet. It took a while to get the right texture of the elephant hide. For a while it looked more like pimples on a gourd.

In the middle anal area it looked like Preparation H was sorely needed. Pokey showed his forms to Rita, "You gotta tell me honestly...is this too gross? When I paint the mouthparts, should I make them look healthy? Or like the rape protectors, we could paint it to look sickly, infected. Or we could keep it healthy. The fact that it can both talk and poop out of the same orifice, well, if that doesn't grab the pre-schooler in all of us. And have the elephant speak the truth!"

" I don't know. Pokey. You might be getting too far out, too foreign, Guilo, as the Chinese say. That means foreign devil. Un extranjero. By the way, what are you going to name your elephant in the parlour?"

"Well, if its a girl, how about Elly?"

"And it its a boy?

"Ah...maybe Elvis B. The "B" stands for bull!"

"Or maybe it should stand for Barnum, you know, P.T. Barnum! In fact, maybe you should look closer at what circus is all about. Well, whatever, we need to practice. First, we have to do the tape recording. Then we'll practice the action with your puppets. So it's going to be "The Greatest little show on Earth." If we plan it right, we can maybe get sponsored by churches for summer Bible school. Maybe you can play background piano for the hymns."

Rita was quiet for some time. Pokey noticed her blank face, her gaze unfocused. "You know, Pokey, I was just thinking, what do you think of the idea of doing a video blog on You Tube, based on your puppet show. If you find you have touched a nerve, maybe Nike could sponsor you."

"Well, aren't you going to be a part of it? Nike can sponsor you, our crusade, and me if you want to call it a crusade. That might be a turnoff for some. Because, don't we have a common purpose?"

Rita thought a moment, "I'm not at all sure. Sometimes we agree, but not always. Sometimes, I think Wanda spoiled you. You've got this devotion to an abstract god that admits to no fault. It seems to me that you want to be perfect, without any faults. You want to hide your human side, your carnal appetites."

Pokey stammered "I…I 'm not sure who I am, so how can I give myself to anyone when I can't predict what I will do. I might have to leave for another forty-day circular tour, like I did last fall. Sometimes I wonder what its like to be a lesbian. Did you know that some doctors can give you an operation to change your sex. But I think it costs a whole lot. Anyway, there are things I can do, just as I am. I'm happy to be a worm, a caterpillar, not quite ready to fly off into my adult stage."

"Yeah," agreed Rita. "The child part of me will always be awestruck, amazed at the perfect beauty of a drop of dew hanging from a wet raspberry leaf. You know, my mother had that kind of mindless admiration for the man of her life, my dad. It didn't make much difference to her if she understood him or not. Worship, in that sense, was purely a one-way street. It would be a big comfort if we could see God's underbelly, some sort of flaw, some defect. Something that might humanize Him!"

"So aren't we back to the beginning again. Like the circular tour takes us inside where we see the maker outside of us, in the mirror, in our reactions, in a timeless embrace. Back to St. Theresa's ecstasy tripping, or Castenada's Don Juan on his far out journey. In that sense, God's handiwork is with us everyday in His shadow. We can't escape or hide from God. Even if we wanted," observed Rita.

"Or Professor Timothy Leary taking eighty tabs of LSD. Always trying to distill reality into something tangible, looking for the center of the onion. Is that our maker's mark?

Rita got up to go, "you know, how are we to know, maybe God is schizophrenic and temporal, without beginning or end. But if that is so, heaven has to be timeless, merely a concept, which at root doesn't seem to be supported by fact."

Pokey smiled and looked Rita in the eye. "Like do they have toilet paper in the heavenly rest rooms. And I've forgotten, how many virgins do I get when I arrive? And are the virgins little blond girls or boys just getting ready to shave for the first time! If I've lead a virtuous life, can I have a little of everything?"

Rita opened the door a crack, "Pokey, that's for you to decide. I've read about sexaholics really never getting any cure. No release. So you better be careful. Some problems should be left alone, for fear that you might be getting into uncharted waters. What if you create your own little world. A world that only you can feel. Where does that leave you? Hmmm? It seems to me that there's more than one kind of vacuum. You already have your grim reaper puppet, your elephant in the parlour, foxy lady, George Washington, and Vito. Isn't that enough? asked Rita.

"Yeah, and now the burning bush. The bush could represent more than celestial wisdom. It might also be schizoid, i.e., maybe it has its own carnal desire...maybe its got something smelly in its roots, something that it is hiding. Maybe the burning bush hears voices in the sky. Voices saying, burn baby, burn! Oh suck my stamen."

"Or, Oh Baby, light my fire! That could work for our processional anthem. Anyway, I gotta go. I'm expecting a call from my old friend, Emma. She might be coming for a visit. I've got to find another sleeping bag for the bus."

It was three AM when Rita got the call on her cell phone. She had been dreaming that she couldn't find anything to wear.

Nothing would fit, and she didn't know the name of the store or if anyone was going to help her find the way home. It was a relief to wake up to Emma's voice, "Rita, We're here at your office, and the door is locked."

"Oh I thought you said you would call when you got to Murray Bay. I'll be out in a minute." Rita threw on her work clothes. It was going to be great to catch up on everything back at St. Theresa's.

She unlocked the front door of the service shop, and found Emma and Tony sitting on the hood of a dark green Chevrolet Camaro, "Oh Emma, you look great! And Tony, you too! Come on in, we'll make some coffee."

Tony explained that he had decided he wasn't getting anywhere at St. Theresa's. He was failing most of his subjects and saw no point staying after mid-term exams. So he borrowed his stepmother's garden truck and was heading west. He was planning to drive alone, sleeping in the back of the truck under a canvas.

Emma had a different tale. A friend, named Bruce, was having a hard time passing his French proficiency exam and was not going to be able to graduate. Emma knew better, but she agreed to go to the test and write F. Bruce Kern's name on the answer sheet. Bruce had taken the exam twice and failed.

Emma explained, "Most of the exam was to translate Moliere's "Le Corsicas". It was pretty good in French, and I made it better in English!"

"Problem was someone on the examining board knew F. Bruce Kern. We had to hand in our answer sheets and this professor figured out that I wasn't Bruce. I figured it would only be a question of time before they would figure out who I was. That would probably result in me not graduating and then not getting into college. So I thought it best to leave. I knew Tony was going away after midterms, and I asked if I could join him. Both Bryn Mar and Pembroke have already accepted me on the basis of my junior years advanced placement tests. In fact come next September 12th, I have a room on the fourth floor of Brokaw Hall. I think there are three other girls that share a common kitchen. I won't know who they are until I get there."

Rita stirred up a batch of pancakes made from the milk replacer from Farm and Fleet, with home made maple syrup. Pokey came in as they were finishing up. Rita introduced Emma and Tony. Mr. Pee also enjoyed the pancakes. Emma was quite impressed with Pokey and after breakfast she and Tony followed Pokey and Mr. Pee back to Mrs. Karl's bread truck to meet some of the cast of the Astronomical Lecture Company.

Pokey introduced his puppets one by one, ending up with Preacher Man whose voice was getting a southern accent, "Today's sermon, Miss Emma and Mr. Tony, can be called the sermon on the dismount. Like "git" yah off your high horse! Stop trying so hard to be the best you can. Don't worry if you occasionally come in last. Give yourself some credit whether you think you deserve it or not. Beauty is always, always, in the eye of the beholder."

"I call it my Yin-yang game, like the symbol. What am I, in the greater scope of things...a mere speck in the timeless sea of humanity. How vain it is to desire recognition from your teammates. If our vistas, our perspectives, are taken away from us, what is left?"

"Chop wood, carry crap. Accept your servitude. Isn't that what our redeemer did? In that light, it is really rude to complain. So you didn't find a rose garden...duh!"

"Bottom line, do you represent a force from the shadows or a source from the light. We are told, that there is some extra value to the forces of the light. But don't the forces of the dark balance everything? Of course!"

A balanced psyche knows a lot about both the shadow side of the intellect, and the laudable bright side. A balanced psyche should seek pure accommodation of an inquiring timeless mind."

Rita thought a bit and chuckled, "Well don't they also say that the devil is in the details? Like it is just a theory that may be flawed and unprovable, full of exceptions and false hopes. But I suppose even a flawed theory has some use. Every personage, every puppet, deserves at least a modicum of respect and tolerance and accommodation."

"What's modicum?" asked Pokey, still with his Preacher Man voice.

"Means a small share, more than a trace, less than a full share. But, you know, it's still like you were saying. Whatever...your audience has to figure out God's plan for themselves. By using their experiences, they stumble on the truth. I think your task is to provide a discovery channel."

Tony picked up Miss Foxey Lady and in a soft seductive tone inquired, "Does Preacher man ever stumble on the path?"

Pokey answered, "Oh Yes, but the Lord always forgives. After all, the forces of evil are never squelched. Hell never freezes over. You know that! Without hell, and Satan, we have no contest. No challenge, no conscience. The church can't exist in a vacuum! Divine elucidation depends on process and a devil incarnate, guilo again! The devil has countless forms, always ready to tempt us. So the pathway to the top is never straight and easy. And the path markers sometimes can be misleading, when we don't see them clearly. Sometimes you can have all the best intentions, and things can turn out badly. Just look at Jesus! If even the Son of God had to be punished, what chance do we have to escape from sin?"

Tony had his own take, "well, Miss Foxey Lady, maybe it's like you were saying, sometimes you have to really explore the dark side to see the contrast with virtue. Is your life selfish or selfless. You seem to need some peculiar focus, to animate all your characters, including yourself!"

"Right on!" agreed Emma. "They used to say, there's no prude like a reformed whore!"

Rita's cell phone jingled, it was Aunt Sarah. She was going to make a dump run with Alice and the spreader. "Aunt Sarah knows we could afford to hire a proper driver and van, but she kind of likes the open air I guess. Was it Thomas Dewey who observed that habits, are often habitual? Anyways yaw'l are welcome to ride along, if'n you don't mind riding in the spreader. My aunt Sarah calls the spreader her honey wagon, and the tractor is an Allis chambers, she calls it Alice."

Pokey preferred to stay at home, finishing painting the puppet stage and the parlour curtains.

On the way to the dump Rita asked Aunt Sarah to pull in for a trash pick up at the Helgeson Egg farm. Since the remodeling was done, there wasn't much trash to load.

Rita showed Emma and Tony the workshop and packaging line that was running the rape protectors. The second shift girls were on coffee break until the blister pack machine was fixed.

Emma noticed that the crew seemed strangely quiet in Rita's presence. Rita offered to buy coffee, but Aunt Sarah said she wanted to get on to the dump. They could get some free coffee from Mrs. Staber's airport snack shop.

Tony and Emma were full of questions for Rita as they continued their honey wagon excursion to the dump. Emma was excitedly asking all kinds of questions. "Rita, how can you deal with all the clutter? And your buddy, shall we say? Albert? Is he weird or what?"

Tony agreed, "Yeah, Rita, I'm not sure who around here is the brightest bulb on the circuit. You know the deal, lights on, but nobody home. Sometimes he seems to make sense. But then he goes places I can't understand. What's his background?"

Rita agreed, "Yeah, sometimes he gives me pause also. He's a good soul. No way is he mean spirited, I know that. But sometimes he seems afraid to lean on anybody, unless it would be Mr. Pee, his potbelly pig. They've been together for three or four years.

Emma wondered, "you seem to get along pretty well with him, so, ah...has this relationship got legs?

"What do you mean? We aren't heading to the altar any time soon. I promised my Dad that I'd graduate from college before I'd ever get hitched up. In fact, I think it is part of the trust document. Of course, it doesn't keep me from having fantasy dreams about what it would be like...you know, shackin' up and getting abused. To get reasons to turn to the bottle. When nothing makes sense, why not turn to the bottle?"

"Well," Emma observed, "you're forgetting all your faith in the Lord, aren't you. The straight and narrow can keep you safe from a lot of potential sand traps, but it can also be a different kind of trap. Being safe may be the opposite of having fun. Don't you think? Not to mention, ignoring the basic life forces that infect us with uncertainty. Perhaps the devil works for our benefit in an existential manner, tempting us with all kinds of mirrors, so to speak."

"Well Albert sometimes comes across as dim witted" said Rita, "on purpose, I think it's better to remain quiet and be thought a fool, than to open your mouth and remove all doubt? "

Aunt Sarah slowly pulled into town dump and circled around looking for treasure, stopping next to the recycle shed. Emma and Tony followed Rita along the edge of the bluff, picking up gravel to throw at the rats. Emma was attracted to a pile of clothes inside a large garment bag. "Hey guys, check this out!" Emma had uncovered some western style clothes including a black leather vest with handcuffs dangling from it. "Anybody got a key?"

Tony laughed and tried on the vest. "Its a shame, I think this is a women's size. It would take a bit of cleaning to get rid of the stains. But it shore is purdie."

"Let me see it" said Emma. "That's too swishy for you, but maybe not. I think it's a keeper, whether for you or me. Somebody took some time with the Rhinestones."

Rita agreed, "Maybe its showy enough for Captain Pokey's Astronomical Lecture Company. We've been planning to open at the county fair this August third. Pokey asked me if I would try being his stage partner, you know, his hostess out front. I'll ask him what he thinks. It's his show. His Kukla needs a Fran Allison."

"What's his Kukla?" asked Emma. "Is it what I think it is?"

"No. Kukla was a puppet on television years ago, about the

same time as Howdy Doody. Fran was the straight girl out front, in vaudeville I think they're called the interlocutor, the person on stage that speaks to the audience."

"Like Pee Wee Herman?" asked Tony.

"Or even George Burns" continued Rita. He had his foil in dimwitted Gracie. Bud Abbott had his Lou Costelo, Dean Martin had his Jerry Lewis. Jackie Gleason had his Art Carney".

"Well, don't they say that opposites attract" asked Tony. "Who's going to take over your spot when you leave for college?"

"I don't know. Sometimes the thought of college is turning me off. But if I leave, maybe our friend Ed Harris can try it out. Time will tell. And speaking of time, we should get on our way."

They found Aunt Sarah bagging up some magazines that had been left in the paper recycle bin. "These are all 1958. Life, Holiday, National Geographics. There are a couple of rare ones I think."

When the tractor pulled into Mrs. Staber's airport diner, there was hardly an empty booth. An Air Canada excursion 727 had made an emergency landing. Charter buses were expected to arrive to take the high school tour group on to Quebec City. Some of the girls were sitting on their luggage smoking cigarettes. Rita was still wearing her bibs with a pocket protector, flash memory card attached. The college group was returning from two weeks on the Riviera. Emma was soon entertaining the group doing imitations of Madonna, Celine Dion, and Elton John, all in French.

Rita was impressed and couldn't stop laughing. "Oh I wish Pokey were here. You could add a lot to his show. Sometimes you remind me Whoopie Goldberg."

Rita showed Tony and Emma where they used to take showers over in the World's End crew quarters. Tony thought he could use a shower, so the girls stood guard as Tony stripped, "We'd join you, except people might think the wrong thing if we were discovered!"

Rita held the towel for Tony, "Those are some hot chickens over at Mrs. Stabers. Yes siree!" Tony looked her in the eye,

"You're not exactly chopped liver yourself dude!"

Aunt Sarah had taken one of the 1958 Holiday magazines to show Mrs. Staber. They decided to have supper at the diner. The special was scalloped potatoes and ham. Tony helped himself to the salad bar, and got a small takeout for Pokey and Mr. Pee.

By the time the crew returned to Lost Grove most were more than ready to turn in. Tony planned to sleep in the back of his truck if it didn't rain. Rita looked forward to sharing her school bus with Emma. There still was a lot of catching up to do.

Tony wasn't quite ready to call it an evening. He cracked a Fosters from his truck and knocked on Mrs. Karls bread truck. Hearing no reply he continued till he found Pokey and Mr. Pee in the old henhouse. "Hi Dude" said Pokey, "how they hangin'?"

"Great! Rita tells me you might be needing some help when she goes back to school, that is, if she goes back."

"Well, I don't know. My friend Ed Harris is planning to help out, but he can't leave his wife for very long. There might be a spot later on. What makes you think we'd get along on the road. I know Mr. Pee and I are pretty used to having our own way. We're kind of spoiled."

"Well it wouldn't be much of a stretch to work the puppet routine. I think I'm pretty good at pretending. Do you think it would make much of a difference that I'm not the motherly type?"

"Well you could have fooled me," said Pokey. "Can you sing?"

"Yeah, I sang tenor in our school double quartette. And last year I took some voice lessons from sister Mary Majorie. She thought I was more of a baritone. Would you like to hear my Ole' Man Rivah," asked Tony.

"Maybe, another time. You should realize Tony that you would have to earn your keep somehow if you join our crusade. You'll have to get good at passing the hat. After the county fair we are planning to work the Octoberfest that Ed Harris' home church is having. Rita has been going on line and has found a couple of other possibilities. Our video feed is better than ever. Maybe you can help create some sort of a contrasting character.

Like Cowboy Ed on the Peewee Herman show."

"Yeah, I've heard about Pee Wee, but I've never seen, or I don't remember Cowboy Ed. But other than that, I've thought about working the sales convention business. I had planned on working for a while to learn the hospitality business. I've got a chance for a trainee position with John Gooding and associates at Emeryville California, that's just across the bay from San Francisco. I can learn how to adapt our process from evangelizing Jesus to selling any product or service. We pretty much know our product development flow from initial trials to final shelf placement. I'm sure I can be a big help, and it would look good on my résumé"

Twenty Seven

Tony and Emma had said early on, that they were just passing through. But their departure now seemed a while off. Tony and Pokey built a new home practice stage for the puppets. Tony and Rita set up new video cameras that were a vast improvement. Now, Tony was putting together bits of their practice sessions into marketable Youtube downloads. Tony was teaching Rita the basics of a different music composition program, called Finale.

One evening, Pokey felt a depression coming. He scratched his head, absentmindedly, "You know, we need to focus more on the shit all around us! Yes, Yes, it sure enough is. Look everywhere. Unhappy people, trapped. Yes! So sad. How pitiful! How hopeless!

Pokey stood up "But wait, there's more! The shuttle bus to the New Age will soon be coming to your town! But, please don't hold your breath! We can't be everywhere that sin and corruption rule. But do trust in the Lord! And don't forget our pledge to return God's love to you every day, rain or shine. It's for the children of tomorrow. Oh! We all feel the power of the warm glow of godly people, swooning in ecstasy. Come Lord. Hear our prayer, Hear our prayer. Amen!"

Emma laughed, "Right on! You might as well be another Elmer Gantry"

"Elmer who?" asked Pokey.

"Elmer Gantry. He was an evangelist played by Burt Lancaster in the movie. Now that man was a hunk and a half. Whew! We should order it from Netflix. You might get some ideas."

Saturday night before the fair, Pokey set up his microphone in the new studio. Together with Emma and Tony, they worked up a series of "moments musicale" with several of the puppets. Emma was happy to voice the part of Foxy Lady. She adopted a southern drawl in a sexy come and get me voice! Now!

Tony took care of the sound editing on his MacBookPro. By

the end of the evening they had settled on about twenty minutes of material.

Rita kept pretty quiet, serving snacks and cleaning up. Aunt Sarah stopped in with Father Fritch. They had run into each other at the tractor pull and decided to check in to see the developing puppet show.

Tony previewed the twenty minutes on his laptop. Father Fritch wasn't sure if it would fly. He thought everything was getting too far out. Things were becoming inaccessible to the average bloke. "I know that God works in mysterious ways, not always clear. But, somehow, the stranger in your strange land isn't getting any more coherent, just the opposite." Father Fritch asked, "How long do we have to wait for Godiva? Hmm? I don't see your plan."

"You mean Godot?" asked Tony. "Of course, you being a priest, maybe in the back of your mind, you will always be waiting for Lady Godiva!" Tony chuckled, "I see lots of questions, but not many conclusions. Are there new commandments? What comes after the first Ten Commandments? Lets have a suggestion box for new commandments. Or at least some updating might be in order. What would Christ say about Muslim veils?

Aunt Sarah invited Father Fritch to cap the evening off with a glass of snappes. Rita excused herself. "Tomorrow is going to be a long day for us. I told Pokey I'd help him with his puppet show. I'll be out front, ad-libbing with the children."

Pokey came in and the conversation continued. Pokey was gaining in his conviction that the Astronomical Lecture Company was going to make a difference. He wanted to plan the show in detail, but Rita had to opt out, "Pokey, I just can't stay up any longer. I need some quiet time, some very quiet time. Maybe with my keyboard."

The schnapps was circulated as the conversation flowed on, Pokey insisting that there had to be some audience participation. "Don't you see? When we get a child up in the spotlight, nose-to-nose with one of my puppets, it becomes a teachable moment for the parents in the audience. But wait! There's more! If we can take a digital photo of the event, puppet, child, and maybe Mom, well...we can print it on the Epson Printer, and frame it for Fifty bucks. Is that a deal? Such a keepsake would be a treasure easy to peddle. Don't you think? Wholesale plastic frames can't cost much. We could even offer the photo as an applique on a Tee shirt, or bowling sweater. I'm just not sure what, or how we can label the art, if you can call it that. I don't know."

Father Fritch was the first to suggest, "The Annunciation." Then he changed his mind, "Maybe just noesis...a Greek word nobody knows! It's a word like cognition, with a poetic Greek twist." Pokey liked noesis,"But wait, noetic might be even a better word."

Pokey took a moment and Googled noetic and saw that it indicated the exercise of intellect over the animal nature of mankind. "Now isn't that a lofty target? It's kind of coherent with our Astronomical focus. Don't cha think?"

Father Fritch warned, "you better keep it simple, there's usually someone in the back row that doesn't hear everything; when in doubt, my advice is, keep it simple."

"Well, we can't postpone it." Pokey continued, "Tomorrow is opening day of the fair. We'll set up the little people's benches in front of the stage in the morning. Tony is going to run the audio while I do the puppet handwork. I don't have to say anything until we get to the end. Then, with your help, we do the pitch. Help us Love God for the children! Do your part for a more beautiful tomorrow, free from strife and indolence. Or whatever! All we can do is run it up the pole and see if anyone salutes."

Father Fritch agreed adding, "They look but do not see. It's been my experience that looking at your own mind can be a slippery slope which can lead to unexpected vistas. Focusing attention can be additive or subtractive, or a transforming transition.

Words can point the way to the target within which is locked up in the moment. That self is one of many. That self must be put to use in contact with the environment. In the process of living, the self is uncovered and tested for validity. Society is group think, tribal.

Father Fritch was more animated then ever "Attention must not be a sometime event, to be laboriously engendered occasionally. The goal, of course, is to be turned on continuously in the now. Accepting the fluid field around us, without complaint. Render unto Caesar what is Caesar's, render unto Pan what is Pan's, yet return home. That's my advice" concluded the father.

Rita had a few words too, "When that self evolves into music, for me, it can be a transforming, self-actualizing experience. Communication hopefully may result. Music by definition is not static, lifeless. It need not be eloquent, nor understood to be appreciated.

As food fuels the body, music, for me, can fuel the soul. Music gives ground to the figure. It is insane, or at least pointless, to think otherwise."

Rita had quite sensibly hired a new plant manager to keep costs in line. She had met him at the Food Broker convention in Denver. This year she had rented a suite at the Holiday Inn for most of the company's brokers to come together to exchange information and strategies for market penetration. Fortunately there was little competition. Halloween mask production had really taken off. The Barac Obama mask was a sell out as soon as the first one was shown on CNN. The blow molding machines now incorporated programmable painting systems. Nearly every day there was a call for a private label promotion.

Rita authorized a small Internet project, offering a prototype process for new products. The new motto was: "If you can imagine it, we can build it, sculpt it and color it." Give us your UPC numbers and we can ship beginning of next week. After the initial test market, we will share with you our print outs, comparing ninety per cent the possible North American market areas.

Rita listened a lot more than she spoke. Finally she

concluded the conference by encouraging each broker to network and form alliances. One broker from Chicago, Gene Mollendorf, from Federated Foods, seemed to have brand extensions that involved many of the other metro areas. There were just so many tie-ins that Rita promised Federated an additional two and a half percent brokerage for advising all the sub-brokers. Many benefits accrued to those outlets with automatic shelf placement. Federated just simply guaranteed shelf placement. The only problem was that profit was somewhat seasonal because the Halloween masks only moved in the last quarter.

Gene Mollendorf suggested that Federated could pick up the cost of the broker's trip back to the airport, but Rita insisted on paying, "It's the least we can do for all your good work and ideas."

At the final morning session on Friday, Rita and Pokey showed the brokers a sample new item, The Puppet Factory. Included in the retail carton were all the materials for children to create hand puppets, beginning with a can of Great Stuff®. Pokey demonstrated with Miss Foxey Lady who also appeared on the packaging. Rita cautioned the group that the UPC symbols used on the catalog sheet were for position only. "We have catalog sheets with ample space for you to imprint your logos. You can use your office copiers," instructed Rita.

Rita said her good byes to the brokers and returned to Lost Grove in the company Subaru. She was uneasy and somewhat bored, almost feeling her period was imminent.

Aunt Sarah and Pokey were enjoying a few Fosters with Emma and Tony in the garage. Pokey turned on the bell jar vacuum motor. "This is where it all started. Rita and her aunt fixed the electrical problems and they were about to flog it on the Ebay."

"But, guess what? One thing led to another. We learned how to capture a vacuum, and put it to use. We ended up with our Dervish, the first and only major flight improvement utilizing negative specific gravity technology. But we have a problem: These lighter than air components still have a half-life of only six months. But we are hoping to find better coatings as time goes on. Fortunately we aren't the only ones in the field. Just google the word vacuum and any other word. Rita used the word insulation and she got connected to U. S. patents, including all the Dow chemical work."

Aunt Sarah cautioned the group, "you all must pledge that you can keep all this a secret. For now, all we are here, is a fix it shop. That's our cover, and to tell you the truth, I like to remember back when things were a little simpler."

"I agree" said Rita, brightening, "Just this afternoon on the way back home, I was feeling good about our business. The rape protection business looks bright. Mollendorf is going to really smooth things out in our distribution. You said you missed the simpler life. So do I! There's a big part of me that I feel is dormant. Hidden from my own awareness. Do you understand? I know it's there, but it involves a language I barely understand. It involves symbols that I barely understand. For me not only do I miss the simple life, I also miss my musical connection. For me, the act of improvising on a keyboard used to be wholly holistic. You know what I mean? It's like my mind is multitasking, watching my own body create its music in the moment."

"I know what you mean," agreed Pokey. "We all start out with very vague desires. Rita, do you remember that line of poetry you read to me that talked about the torture of vague desire."

"Yeah, it came out of Spoon River! Edgar Lee Masters. And it's so true. We're so lucky to have these options. These choices. For me I feel, my destination isn't that far away, because I feel it's within. I feel something like a hypnotic inner focus of a professional jockey, seamlessly guiding my inner steed. Somehow I'm learning how to focus on the trip, ignoring possible contradictions. Talk about getting high? Talk about ecstasy? Finding a way to get around your vague desire. Sometimes, I have to tell you, I don't want to leave here. I confess, I'm kind of addicted. Addicted to this quiet country life, with lots of quiet time. Around here you never, never hear the sounds of police and fire sirens. I remember hearing them all through the night when I was a child. Except when we went up to the island. There, at night, all you heard was hoot owls and ring-necked loons. You might say the silence was deafening! Some people couldn't take the silence. Me? I took to it, like a duck to water. It's a well for me, and I am learning that I can cast my bucket down into it and find music, not that far from me. Of course the music sometimes is only seen as through a glass darkly, and I have to approach it, humbly, looking for the special nuances that surprise me, that make it alive and forever new. Talk about Aha experiences! I can't think of any prospect more likely to please my inner seeker. You know I'm not dumb! I expect the voyage will have some convolutions; some stumbling, but not to worry, the desire is not vague. It's my own private Idaho."

Pokey stirred the fire again, "So when are you going to decide?"

"Now I wish I knew if I should commit to college. Right now my guess is that, for my own good, I should go on to college, only because I really don't have a good idea about what I don't know. I know not what I know not. Surely there must be surprises lurking about college life. Maybe, my insight needs tempering like a Damascus steel sword. Friction defines...and around here there ain't much confusion."

Pokey and Emma were still at the sidelines, not really on the same page, Pokey observed, "Well, for me, the thing I want to avoid is pride. Pride truly causes many to falter, to fail. So, I guess, that just makes me an enabler. But, gosh sakes, wasn't our savior an enabler? I can't see how our crusade could ever be misconstrued. But then, we gotta expect the unexpected. Some fool will be threatened with new ideas! Untested ideas. So, as I see it, my goal, my quest is right out of Don Quijote. I can dream the impossible dream too. From here on, I tramp La Mancha with my puppets, with my crone friends in the wake of Wanda. If the bell tolls for anyone, the bell tolls in her shadow. But after her, who does the bell toll for?" asked Pokey.

"Whom!" interjected Rita.

"Whom?" asked Pokey,

"Yeah, whom. Object of the preposition. For whom does the bell toll?

Pokey looked into the firebox on the stove, stirred the embers a bit and added a walnut log. "I sure like the smell of walnut. It's almost as good as cherry. Yeah, OK! For whom the bell tolls. Main thing is, when we reach the check out line in life, we should be ready to list our apology to mankind, showing that we had good intentions, but Alas! We failed. Isn't that the essence of humbleness? The opposite of pride? Doesn't pride become a symptom of the elephant in the parlor?"

Pokey continued, "Next question is, can proud people get into heaven? If not, where do they have to go? Some say they go to purgatory, to join their shameful brethren. Seems like it's such a narrow path for the righteous."

"And I wonder," interjected Emma, "did Christ and any of his apostles ever have a good laugh? I have a hard time imagining Jesus splitting his sides in laughter. I guess I have a hard time imagining any of the gods laughing."

"Well," added Tony, "for that matter, maybe it's impossible to entirely overcome the templates that come with our human minds. Don't we learn as babies to expect understanding to evolve? There's no laughter in that. The wit and wisdom come only in the perspective gained with age."

Aunt Sarah opened her laptop and started to type a search. "And besides," she concluded, "the reality I experience is not the same reality you experience. So advice for me could be dangerous for you. You might say awareness is the slow eroding of misconceptions. First you discover your nakedness, just like Adam and Eve. Then your youthful grace and agility become a memory, leaving behind a husk, a husk with few pretensions and a lot of memories. At my age my vision may lack some detail, but it is, in my humble opinion, nonetheless eloquent."

"Right on!" Pokey summed things up, "Isn't pride a bit like an elegant web spun by a dutiful spider. The web stresses precise angles and measures; the stance of pride rests on pillars of convenient convention. That's the trap of ambition, fueled by a failure to accept what is, in favor of Valhalla, the impossible dream again."

Emma looked confused, "Pokey, I guess I'll never really understand what pride is. Is it a good thing, or a trap? So what are possible dreams? Forget the impossible dreams; toss them into the dust bin. Must dreams always be complex and hard to interpret? Maybe not! Didn't Freud identify a lot of operators activating our puppets? In psych class we learned how Carl Jung added some poetry to the mix, but we are still left with only the outline of what to expect. Every day, every moment gives us a new now, the spark of life, that illuminates everybody's soul, for want of a better word."

Pokey concluded "I agree. So many people are asleep, unaware of the magnitude of the reality washing at their feet. Be aware of the deafening roar of the indecisions in front of you."

Aunt Sarah had been quiet for some time, having been engrossed in the repair manual for the S-10. But something must have resonated, for she volunteered, "Well, boys and girls, the next thing I expect you to debate is the number of angels that can stand on the head of a pin. Perhaps you can find other paradoxes, maybe your awareness can't be analyzed in any direct fashion, but only indirectly."

"Like we're back to the looking glass" Pokey observed. "I used to have an unquenchable longing for a lover that could meld with me as hand in glove. I longed to escape from the loneliness of the open road. Well what happened! I came to rest here, this never never land, this poverty row of continuing amusements. I am realizing that there is no escape. Even at the edge of my grave, I shall be somewhat bewildered. As the music of my life finds its decrescendo, I will find my full stop, the period to my statement. Nothing more."

"Most importantly," Pokey continued, "I think I have discovered that the trick is to control our imagination. Look for what ever seems appetizing. And watch for, and obey your own puppeteer. Who or what is pulling your strings! Can you imagine, can you picture, that motivator? That controller? Is there a successful destination we should be looking for, a final definition? Probably not, but we can enjoy looking out the window as we flow along,"

After listening for a while, Aunt Sarah felt hide bound to clarify the issue, "I think it is all about communication. If you can step back from your mind, do so. Your vision may be clouded at first, and you may become fearful and disoriented. This may be par for the course and should be welcomed, like another new stage of puberty. The mind has no choice but to accept its partnership with its animal host. Sometimes there's is an amicable shared goal, but not always. In fact, I would guess most people are conflicted. Most people don't practice what they preach. Sometimes I remember Pokey's drawing of the three muses on horseback. Which one has the whip?"

Rita opened her Websters Collegiate, "Charm, beauty and creativity are the three graces. It says it right here. So for me, I ask myself, how do I know which of them needs working on. Each of us is a bit out of balance, kind of eccentric. You might think that it would be a piece of cake to nurture the inner you. But no! I find it is one of the hardest battles, to over come useless habits, to advance to new levels. Some days I don't feel very charming. Some days I don't think I am that beautiful. And now I'm not so sure I am that creative."

The wind must have picked up a bit, for the damper on the stove clicked shut for a while, then opened, and shut again. Pokey reached over and patted Rita's back, "There there, Tara will never be the same Miss Scarlette. You know that you can't go home. Your next chapters await, my dear."

Emma laughed and reached over to Pokey, "You know, in a way you remind me of Mahatma Gandi, and that's not too bad. Like far out Dude!"

"Yeah I guess Gandi certainly was far out. I guess he

personified the collective conscience in some ways, but I have to say, I can only guess his flavor. Hard to imagine Gandi having sex, except the Kama Sutra was a classic sex manual. As a young inquisitive man, Gandhi might have experimented to learn the ins and outs of sex. He might have learned more while in prison."

"Yeah, we had a whole chapter on him in our world religion class" said Emma. "It's hard to imagine what it must have been like on his wedding night. Gandhi's father had set up the marriage for the fourteen year old children. If I remember right Mrs. Gandhi had three or four sons right away. I'll bet you could write a play from her viewpoint. Remember she didn't even have a chance to say no."

Rita closed her dictionary and opened another Mountain Dew, "As I see it, my focus shifts sometimes quixotically, beyond, or outside of rational definitions. Just like Cervantes' Don Quijote. My focus is unique. Just like your focus is yours. Sometimes I think in terms of poetry, like almost imaginary robots invade my stream of consciousness. When I feel the urge to examine these strangers whom we meet in this shared real estate called MIND, the moment once apprehended is doomed to rest in the past. But other steeds can come to us, already saddled and fresh. Along the way we can find infinite variety of applications. Some of these applications don't need a hard drive, and don't need mental effort. Day dreaming can be such a useful artform, with goals and techniques."

"I agree," laughed Emma,

Tony and Emma brought in a twelve pack Fosters. The general plan evolved, and the sound track was saved in iTunes. It was then that Tony suggested that the Astronomical Lecture Company was missing the boat if they didn't have some sort of parade that could draw people to the show. "Think of the greatest show on earth!" said Tony. "Somehow, there's got to be a bait for the trap, there's got to be a balm from Giliad, solace for the disinherited, rest for the weary. There are plenty of things to worry about. Let's not go there. Lets just make a joyful noise to the Lord. Let's remember not to lose our style."

"Speaking of which, don't cha all think you could stand some fresh wardrobe ideas? What should an Astronomic look like? Something certainly out of the ordinary, in more ways than one."

"I agree," said Emma. "But, let's not make them look like uniformed armed police. Maybe think of Elvis, and Elton John. Or maybe Daisey Mae, Dolly Parton, Lady Gaga."

"Yeah and Michael Jackson too," Pokey continued, "So we gotta frame the current episode as a reaction to the outside threat. You know, trouble right here in river city. We're looking at our savior, but we're not quite sure about what he is saving us from. The fires of hell? No, there's got to be another thread of insight that can tether us to reality. Take off the blinders. That's what our show has to advise. But let's just leave it open as to the exact nature of the final revelation. Like all dreamers, don't awake! They say the devil is in the details, so doesn't it make sense to keep it simple. Praise the Lord, pass the hat!"

"Right on!" agreed Emma, "Yeah, if you're not afraid, you might be lost in uncertainty. And besides, it seems to me that it will be safer and easier to entertain first, and teach second. For now, all we need do is to prepare the ground for later planting. Even a little flatulence is pardonable. Ooo we, Oi vay, pardona may wah! I remember Justin Morgan. Now that was state of the art flatulence! Pure Saul Alinski flatulence."

There seemed to be no further need to be explored. After a few moments of quiet crackling of the walnut in the stove, Pokey concluded. "Yep!...Nothing beats fun,"

The silence was broken when Aunt Sarah returned from mass aboard Alice. She pulled in and parked next to the spreader. She planned to go scavenging in the morning.

Aunt Sarah brought a jug of fresh water into the office for the coffee maker. She set the timer and set out two loaves of date bread she had picked up at church.

Twenty Eight

Since Pokey and Tony had bought their own keyboard for the Astronomical Revival, Rita now had her Yamaha electric keyboard back in the front of the school bus. This morning she was idly doing chord exercises and scales when she discovered a deep and complex relationship between D major and G minor. As she explored the harmonies she had to take a deep breath. It was as if she were drowning in confusion. The spring air was laden with decay, warm and sticky.

She ran her hands through her hair and stood up, breathing the warm morning air deeply. What relief! She remembered the Sufi breathing routines she had practiced. As she inhaled she imagined her spirit gathering up the remnants of her daily toil, feeling them rise to the top of her head, then releasing as she slowly exhaled. She noticed smoke coming from the range in the garage kitchen. Pokey must be making coffee. She was ready to meet the glory of another day here in River City. After a short stop at the outhouse she stepped into the garage. The FM radio was on and Pokey was frying some pancakes. She opened some canned applesauce, "Morning Dude"

Tony and Emma soon joined the breakfast club, "Morning everybody!" Pokey flipped the pancakes, put some butter on each, and then served them.

After a while Pokey came up with a new question. "You know, I was thinking again, the hardest thing about being human is self acceptance. Feeling really, really, at home with yourself."

"I was looking in the mirror, and I asked myself, Albert, how can I accept myself if I can't even define myself as an individual. I end up reacting to others, not focusing on my own internal needs. This quest is another side to Don Quijote. Like I want to dream the impossible dream. If someone asked you to define your own penumbra, what color do you think it would be?"

"I don't get it," said Tony. "What's a penumbra? And what

difference would it make what color it is?"

"It's just symbolic," continued Pokey. "The penumbra is the dark side of the moon. Just as there are color opposites, there are lots of other opposites. Some are complimentary like blue and orange. Mixed together they cancel each other perfectly. One is defined by the other, as man is to woman too. So, I can still ask, what does your dark side look like? And don't say you don't have a dark side. Almost everybody has a bit of shame, some dirty laundry!"

"Which reminds me, I need to wash some of my dainty gray things" laughed Tony, opening another Fosters.

"Point is," continued Pokey, "I'm thinking there will always be an uneasy acceptance of our sense of self. This unease may be, quite simply, the essence of life. And I am guessing that such angst cannot be medicated effectively."

"The unease may be coherent. If this confuses you, just go on line and Google General Systems Theory. You can see a whole lot of illustrations of various dualities that can both qualify and quantify. All life is becoming. On the one hand we are encouraged to be strong in self, not yielding to the foe. And on the other hand we are urged to grow, adjust and change the person on the other side of the mirror. Change? Who lays out our available choices? Culture and tradition evolve. It's cognition through the glass darkly. The unease, the insecurity, the tenuous grounding, can be negative and perpetual. The challenge then for each of us is to get practical and learn constantly new ways to accommodate life."

Tony turned on the evening musicale on the CBC that was playing a piano concerto. Rita perked up, "listen...that piano...I know that music, it's...that's Lang Lang, again, he's the best. A genius for sure. From time to time I lose myself in music," said Rita. "I ask myself what really is music? I'm not sure! Is it a sonic process of some sort, in which the self enjoys predictable pleasures of deepening harmonic awareness that cannot be described in words? Music, thus, may be wordless communication. And I guess not all of it is pretty."

"Or you could just say, Music! I know it when I step in it!' laughed Tony.

Rita continued "If I had to bottom line it, you know, summarize it, I'd like to really check out this spiritual greed thing. Isn't it all about intent? What about Zen meditation? Isn't there a target there? It seems to me, before you can enjoy a satisfaction you have to first visit the house of needs. There, experience your new, maybe pathetic condition, your new position and define its qualities. Approach this, avoid that."

"So...Doesn't it all revolve around appetite and fears?" asked Tony.

Rita continued, "Yeah, as I see it, there's a basic instinct to accept life as a given, to find predictability as reasonable. Motivation then becomes a learned habit. Reasoning then becomes the process of characterizing appetites, and planning their satisfaction. You know, routines, habits, relationships...they all add up to our character. Everything is in context. I'm guessing the practice of Zen meditation might help focus on higher mental states. But let's be careful on how we characterize these higher states versus lower states. These states share some functions similarly influenced by some drugs. I wonder, is there any parallel with self flagelation as practiced by some devotees."

"Well," said Emma, "think of all the bulimic girls that purge themselves for a peculiar high. Who is to say that their high is any less noble than yours or mine? Perhaps variety is the spice of life."

"Any focus is a concentration that excludes some data in favor of other data. Think of the conscious contemplation of a seeker...that's the Buddha in bliss, that's the Dalai Lama having the over view, the big picture if you will. It seems to me sometimes that there are a lot of potential teachers out there, waiting for connection."

"I don't get it," said Emma. "Connection?"

"Yeah." Rita continued, "What's a teacher without a student? Isn't that one of your one sided coins? Put another way, there are no absolutes other than death itself. The question we must answer is this: Is the grave a gateway or is it our final destination?"

"I'm sure I don't know," concluded Emma, "I'm going to put the whole thing on the back burner so to speak. I've got a little time before my appointment with the grim reaper."

Rita concluded, "Just because some reasoning is corrupt, doesn't mean that conclusions reached are necessarily invalid. I think reasoning is an art form, a living process providing each of us our own special Idaho, our unique experience."

Emma wasn't sure. "How is your special Idaho any different from mine? Like we said before, self-discovery doesn't happen by accident. Satisfaction cannot occur without cause. Check out the prophet by Kahlil Gibran. My agenda today doesn't have to be spontaneous. Serendipity, while sometimes unpredictable, nonetheless can be encouraged by setting up likely combinations of agents and environs. You know what I mean?"

Rita thought a bit, "I don't know. There's times I get so confused. When I can't be sure I see things clearly, then I don't know where to turn. Thank God I can turn back to my music, it sustains me. I am not crazy. I know it sounds weird, but as I play the piano, my soul finds expression. Its like it comes into focus. And only then! Otherwise, I feel like the stranger in a strange land. Alone, with no direction. Instinctively I know I am wrong. There has to be a real involvement. For me I can find passion with my piano a lot easier than with people. I'm thinking that most people don't know themselves, sad to say. If you're not careful, such an unexamined life can become meaningless, and can slip away through your fingers, just out of neglect. Not for me!

But now I am learning how to get along with the boredom I feel most of the time. I realize it is up to me, to find meaning. For life without meaning is that torture of vague desire. Just like Edgar Lee Masters said. We've been there, and know better.

Doesn't every dream contain its antithesis, its own Achilles' heel? Don't approaches have something in common with avoidances?" Rita concluded, "I'm thinking, to think otherwise is to deal in one sided coins. Sometimes we can't see the center of the target very clearly, but we can see it broadly in the center of our swirling cosmos. Broadly counts! Its presence may have no handles, but one can hear it on the other side of the door, however faintly. Thank our God that we can see Him broadly. We yearn to bring Him into focus; that's where every soul starts its inquiry. Fuck details. They might come to us if we set our expectations appropriately, when we need to see it more clearly."

Pokey agreed, "Where can we gain instruction for how to find our optimum connection to reality, our own methodology to unlock reality? It's life management 101. Can our Astronomical Lecture Company point the way? Without getting lost in detail? Words are only handles for things we can grasp. The problem with life is that vague desires prevent us from rejoicing because we feel no sense of achievement. Self-induced defeat, self-induced depression. Anyway, that's my conclusion right now. Tomorrow, I hope will bring change," concluded Pokey.

Twenty Nine

Over lunch the next day, Pokey summarized how the production was stacking up. "It's got to be right in a lot of ways. Characters, music, actors, I ask myself, what constitutes success? How do we judge? Maybe just do it, and move on. But how can we judge our effect? Do we see something change? A brute, somewhere, has to suffer in the process of learning compassion. How can we find our quarry? What does it look like? Are we inviting conflict? Best thing, is we should evaluate our effects after every show. Maybe make a list of what works and what doesn't."

Rita spoke up, "You know, this whole campaign, or whatever we're calling it, involves strategy, assessing the task before us. From where I sit, as I see it, it would be a mistake to focus too narrowly. Better to throw a wider net. We can evoke love between souls, let's smash out loneliness. No man is an island. We meet at the altar, humbly. Hallelujah!"

Pokey didn't miss a beat, "Here are the keys to the kingdom! All you have to do is to get off your high horse and come down to the ground. You don't have to lead! It is OK to follow! Specially when you are following our peaceful God, who goes by many names.

Fellow Christians, and also followers of Krishna, Budha, Kabala, and others. We share common aspirations. For all of you who question, listen to your own soul. Your friend, who knows you best. Listen, now, to Miss Foxey Lady." Pokey went back stage and got his puppet.

He brought Foxey Lady onto stage to sing the introit hymn Jerusalem, Jerusalem, my happy home.

Emma was enjoying playing the straight gal out front, "Gosh you sure know something about singing. What a gift you have Foxey!"

Now in the character of Foxey, Pokey started his sermon, "Honey...my message for you all today is real real simple. It is good to learn to accept yourself, as a given. Yep! Know and accept the fact that God made you. And God does not make mistakes. No doubt about it. I can see it in your eyes. You are a gift to us all.

But, or also, you gotta recognize, that, as a work in progress, you have to cultivate your defects. Take care of, and weed your garden. Even if you can't figure out exactly what's wrong. Here's our rationale, it is like the ancient Chinese fortune telling, E Ching. You take three coins and shake them up. As you cast them they are either alike or different, heads or tails. There's a lot of fortune telling routines that in the end are almost worthless. Not the E Ching. The E Ching is a gateway, opening up visions of possible new relationships. Do you understand Miss Emma?"

"Well, yes and no" answered Emma. "I guess you have to believe in something or other. Don't you have to either fear change or seek change eagerly."

"Well that's one way of putting it," said Pokey, still as Foxey lady. "It takes a while to know for sure you can trust this new groove, so to speak. But after a while it can become a good habit of mind. It provides you with a hyper reality, unexpected clarity. But even so, for a moment we are released into another reality. Then the goal becomes one of controlling and directing our poetic permutations available to the creative mind. Don't you agree?"

After a while Rita agreed, "to be both coherent and creative must be the sin qua non of genius. Next question, why should genius be so difficult to exercise? To ask why, is the human question, always inconclusive. Accept it. Life is an experience in time, with peculiar odors and flavors, always in change.

And we go on, freeze framing moments into our archives, always looking for validation. Where is home? How do we recognize home when we get to it? Home may be the summary nucleus of our whole life relationships. Elegant! Our existential home still has trash here and there. Part of a "homey" atmosphere includes trash. We may experience life as an experiment, testing reality."

It was a crisp morning when the crew came together for the

Saturday show. Pokey was still in good humor, "I had another dream last night. Wanda came and reminded me that I should be grateful that I have an exit strategy. We have not been condemned to live forever. Eternity does certainly exist and can be found in every moment, as yin fits nicely into yang. That's how she put it!"

During coffee break, Rita put on her current favorite CD, Stravinski's Petruska ballet. They snacked on some homemade corn bread with honey. As they watched the people passing in and out of the Youth building, Pokey explained. "I need to come across a little bigger than life size. Like the ringmaster at a circus. If I am all gray, nobody is going to notice. Right? But on the other hand, sometimes I like to disappear, into the shadows behind the curtain. From there, I can take my time and really study what life puts in front of me. It is a challenge for sure!"

'What amazes me is how much shit I have to discard before I get down to the essences. Everybody has layers of syntaxes, styles, constructs, that serve as foundations for their viewpoints. Do they make sense? It's a question I ask myself every day."

Pokey concluded, "But the answer is hidden in the wind! We end up with vagueness that may be palpable, but still kind of lifeless. In such an unfocused attention, we touch death, and recoil. Meaning! There has to be meaning. Life asks us to make choices, with incomplete data. Of course, surprises will result. That's just common sense!

So, my advice is...stop worrying, and prepare for timely surprise gifts. Be content with your incomplete education, your lack of perfection, your personal snails!"

"Somehow I feel like I'm paying for some mistake, I am being punished for some misdeed, that I totally don't understand. Christ on the cross, Why this? Why me, now? Did God answer Christ's supplication, Oh Father why have you forsaken me?"

"You remind me Pokey of a character right out of Kafka. One of his characters named "K" was on trial and he couldn't find out what his offence had been. Talk about existential frustration, Kafka was there. He was on the same page as Mother Teresa.

Both of them were looking for substantiation for their identities, and both were disappointed, crying in the wilderness. If only Kafka had explored music, or if Mother Teresa had explored her sexual needs. They might have felt more answered, "un affair complete." I wonder sometimes if both could have benefitted from some counseling."

"Well, Pokey, it's time to start our eleven o'clock show. Did you rewind the tape?"

"Yeah, as soon as I'm back from the john, we can start."

After supper, Rita put another log on the fire and was enjoying reminiscing with Emma about school days. "It seems so far away from today. I just wasn't comfortable around dainty lace things, but I didn't really know in what direction I should go. No one around me gave any advice that meant anything to me. Sure my mother meant well in coaching me, but somehow it didn't take. Or at least I needed to be real to myself. Not an act. Sometimes I still wonder if I should have gone to the convent."

Emma agreed, "Yeah, I know what you mean. I'm not sure if I can paint my face good enough to land a good package, if you know what I mean. I can hope, you know, that some guy with a lot of cash, might take the bait, so to speak."

"Speaking of packages, Tony seems to be carrying a load. With you two traveling together, you know, has he made a pass at you yet? Didn't you say that you slept together in the back of his truck?"

"Yeah, but we each have our own sleeping bag. Truth is, we are a little like twins, not identical twins mind you, but maybe fraternal twins. I know he's probably gay, and somehow I find that attractive, and honest. It's not confused by some hidden sexual agenda. We can still make a team of sorts. A single man or a single woman can sometimes be seen as prey. Danger lurks in the shadows. As things are, together we sure don't have to feel used or abused."

The wind picked up a bit and the windows rattled. Emma continued, "I don't mind if people think we are in a relationship, no harm that I can see. Sometimes I wish I could go with him to San Francisco, but I can't. My brother depends on me at our bed and breakfast. We are going to be busy with the Berkshire Music Festival, and then the Christmas season. It's our bread and butter. We plan to shut down for the month of February; I might be able to fly out for a couple of weeks. That is, if you ever get out there. When is your Spring break? Maybe we could both fly out together and meet up again. That could be fun"

"Yeah!" Laughed Rita, "If I do go on to college, if worse comes to worse I can always come back to Lost Grove. I don't have to sell my shares in the Rape protector business. Any profit can go toward my college tuition and room and board. I don't have to worry. It doesn't matter if the family trusts run out of money."

"Well Rita, you know you are always welcome any time at our bed and breakfast in Springfield," said Emma.

Sunday Evening Aunt Sarah unloaded the honey wagon, getting ready to make an early foraging trip. The Murray Bay Fall Sweep days were over, and there would be piles of unsold used items now placed on the curb for garbage collection. Her first destination was Country Club Estates on east river road. Over the years, she had gotten to know some of the staff at several of the large homes. At the old Taft cottage, she picked up a pair of old fancy bird cages made from bamboo, complete with the glass feeders. They were collector items for sure.

Aunt Sarah was back in time for lunch on Monday as Pokey called to order a planning session at Lost Grove. "I think it was a big mistake to think we could tour with our Astronomical Lecture, and get a free will offering for our ministry. At least not enough to cover our expenses. But if we have something to sell... that might be a different story. We have our souvenir framed photos of the children. And now we have our new scratch and sniff applicays." Pokey carefully unzipped his duffel bag and held up a plain gray envelope. "Here is a true giant leap forward in the whole field of rape prevention."

Pokey had the attention he needed, "Now I ask you, what parent would want to send their adolescent out into the real world without this last resort, rape preventer. Your child can wear our other brands, but none can compare to our latest defense against rape of children or adults. Our latest dispenser is worn as a classic broach or as part of a necklace. Its simple to operate; when the rapist begins to make his, or her, first move towards you or your child, simply twist the cross members so that the phenome spray is aimed at the assailant. I warn you we have tested this and it gets pretty foul. Sometimes it may take two or three applications if the assailant has been drinking."

"Now mind you, these are not toys, and should be used sparingly. Your first unit comes with five charges, enough phenomes to pacify ninety percent of the human genome. Unfortunately, we can't say that these are universally successful. Maybe in the future we can improve. But for now it's like we're the one eyed king in the land of the blind. I expect that you all will want to proceed so I have plugged this item into our developers program. We will still have to do some final test marketing."

"And of course, we want feed back on your experience in enjoying your safe and secure trip."

Tuesday morning, Rita and Tony had finished with the dishes when Pokey wandered in with Mr. P. "Wanda has gone off the deep end I think. She tells me that she now hears music almost all the time. She says it is becoming a real chore to quiet her mind. She says the music that plagues her is really not that bad. In fact as string choirs go, she tells me it's pretty mellow, sotto voce. But even so, she says it is distracting, and she wants to find a release, to find silence, comforting silence. I keep telling her that I have been there, done that, and that the void will always be there. Why worry when we cannot understand our limits. You know what I mean? Rude to complain again!"

Rita didn't answer right away. "I don't know Pokey. If your friend is lead by evil forces, she sure would be well advised to remain alert to the moment. I remember only too well how you used to battle with your mirror issues. I'd want to watch out if those violins and cellos start speaking to her like the sirens in the Valcouri. But wait! There could be more. Ask her if she can either write it down or hum some of the music. That might tell us something, I'm not sure what...but wouldn't that be a start?"

"Well maybe next time I get a chance, I'll see what I can get from her. I want you two to meet, but I never know when she will be back."

Rita exhaled, "Yeah...I can wait. Besides tomorrow is another day. We'll see how many protectors we can flog."

Pokey had this blank look. "What do you mean, flog?"

"Flog means to peddle, get rid of something for some sort of gain. It's a word my dad used. I think it is British or Australian slang."

Pokey continued, "So it's not too clear to me where is our target audience? So far, all I know is that we are here only temporarily. Do we leave a mark? Maybe! Push your pause button, and think it over."

Tony had been quiet for some time. "Is there something wrong in wanting to be a special guy? To stand out from the maddening crowd? Aren't there both peacocks and peahens? Maybe some of us don't mind being a peacock, we've got our jobs to do. Same thing happens with bees. There's only one queen, a few manly drones, and a lot of worker bees. Me? I'm no queen, and maybe I'm not a good worker bee either. So what's left? I'm learning to be the best drone I can be. Emma has been a breath of fresh air for me. She has helped me a lot."

Rita began with..."OK, I'll start with what is not important. Wrapping is not important. What you are wearing might mean something, but not that much. What is under the wrapping is inner content, beyond style issues. That content has to grow in relationships in order to exist. Those relationships cross-fertilize sometimes, but other times some relationships can be toxic and confusing. Nobody bats one thousand on the road toward Satori.

As far as what is important to me on the other hand, is my

health, followed by practicing piano and maybe cooking."

Pokey began with..."imagine the allure of God's only son... his disciples were his lovers. Was Judas pissed because Christ didn't show favoritism? Or did he expect to be forgiven cause he needed the money. Has anyone looked into Judas' family background? Maybe there were extenuating circumstances."

Aunt Sarah opened her laptop, "Well, lets just see. Judas... Judas Goat, Judas Iscariot, Judas," she looked up from her laptop, "As a matter of fact, the story of why Judas betrayed Jesus has many, many versions. Do your homework...just google it, and get back to me. Things might have been different if Christ had listened to women."

"Remember your ruins," continued Aunt Sarah. "Ah! What mystery of life! We can feel it moving along, without any insight into it. The application of any viewpoint has to be preferred over having no conclusion! Life goes on in spite of our attempts to understand it. Sleep then is a relief from the challenges of life."

Rita had to get her own view of life's mystery, "My view is that the most we can do is to act as if we understand life, even though we flavor our experience for the sake of variety. Only God knows where he or she came from."

"Do you suppose that mankind evolved because God was lonely and bored? Do you suppose God is happy with the way things seem to be going today?"

"What if we find that we are not experiencing a new high to a liberated, final, full blown, exulted, state, but rather only on the first step of a ladder whose top we cannot discern. In other words, how many levels of consciousness do we have to go through on the way to the top, which we presently define as God, the highest?"

Pokey had his own problem, "That's a good question. If God is the highest, what is the lowest? Is God the father without blemish? Or maybe God has to have some imperfections, otherwise he couldn't have invented us."

"I'm not sure I understand," continued Tony, "Maybe God

tired of dealing with perfection...maybe she decided, just for fun, to roll the dice and give mankind a chance to evolve so as to provide her with companionship. Can we imagine a world without echoes? Of course not! Neither could God! So, now, can we agree that probably God was fucking lonely, and bored...being all alone? It can't be a whole lot of fun being a one-sided coin."

"Yeah, I agree," said Pokey, "I remember Father Radke once was reading a book on the imitation of Christ. He said next to the bible, it was the next biggest seller. It was by Thomas A. Kempis, a catholic.

He said it can become ennobling to suffer. How many ways can we invent to suffer? Isn't the bible all about suffering? Bible says, suffer ye the children. Suffering is a process. Probably as many ways as we invent to succeed. Both are unavoidable. The future has to multifaceted, with infinite permutations of cognition. Nothing is entirely true or false. Somewhere in our process we become self-aware, perhaps uniquely so, perhaps not. Think of Mr. Pee's world. He's done his best to keep me grounded. Maybe that's the benefit of walking on all fours," laughed Pokey.

Tony reflected for a moment, "You know, I think, to many persons, a successful life is one that avoids pitfalls. A life of avoidance, rather than a life of engagement."

"I agree, kind of" said Rita. "Life's a trip! And a lot depends on how you look at it. Through your own lens, so to speak. I remember practicing the piano when I changed how I looked at the piano exercises. I found myself in a strange spot in my mind. I lost my mind in some ways and found myself in the music. Like riding a horse, all was process. What fascinated me was the slight gap between my mind and my body. In that gap, my whole mind body became one entity, if just for once. What a relief. Nothing for a moment was out of place. Talk about beauty! Talk about Buddha! For a moment there was no snail on my rose."

"But that kind of refuge lasted but for a few moments."

Pokey and Tony arrived first for the Friday morning show at

the fairgrounds. The speaker system developed some feed back that took a while to fix. One of the power cords was missing a ground causing a sixty-cycle hum. Emma and Rita were all dolled up in the style of Dolly Parton and took their places in front of the puppet stage. Tony helped children find their seats on the little benches down in front. On the stage there was a red and white clock sign, "Next show" with one arrow pointing to 11 am.

Pokey chose his Foxy lady puppet to remove the signboard from the stage, then to ring the bell for attention. Emma stepped up to begin the show, "Hi folks, thanks for coming. My name's Miss Emma. There's still a few seats down here in front. Lets have a big hand for the legend in her own time, the sweet heart of home sweet home, Miss Foxey Lady. Comen Tall lay Voo doo?", asked Emma.

Pokey used his falsetto southern drawl for Foxey, "You haven't seen my Prince around have you? I have been looking everywhere. I tell you, I'm getting tired of kissing frogs. About all I'm getting are wet chapped lips."

Emma laughed out loud, shaking her goldilocks pigtails. "Well gosh! Maybe you're not kissing the right kind of frogs, said Emma. "Unless your Prince is a hermaphrodite, he is probably of the staff side, rather than the distaff. In other words, keep your eye out for bull frogs."

"Well, Miss Emma, sometimes I don't know come here from sic'em when it comes to boys. Like from a different planet, Like Mars or Venus as they used to say."

Miss Foxy reacted "Well, you know, some of us are blessed with almost an over dose of feminine pulchritude. You know I draw boy's attention! It's not my fault. Like moths to a flame, flies to dead meat. Its all the same."

"Miss Foxy?"

"Yes Miss Emma."

"Can you help me understand myself better? Is there more to life than I see? So...is life accidental with no plan, or do we have to discover what it's all about? To find some kernel of interior truth, the real reality. Or do we have permission to create something new. Maybe that is where we advance God's plan for us." Emma turned to the audience, "Are you as confused as I am? What's the bottom line here and now?"

Foxy Lady summed things up, "Here Folks is the bottom line. Doesn't it boil down to either letting life passively happen to you, or taking control where life takes you. Call it intentional living. You go somewhere, not just to see what's happening there, but also to engage yourself in some purpose. Your purpose doesn't have to be grand. It can be mundane. But purpose has to be central. The desire cannot be left as vague, but rather focused, explored in all of its possible complexity, so that through experience we define ourselves. For our selves and for others it's the Tao, the goal of every seeker. It's the road map to glory, that we have outlined in our manual. This manual will help you find your own, very personal achievement plan."

Pokey excused Foxy Lady from the stage and went out front with God's plans for sale. "Cash or check, make your checks out to Open Road Ministry. If you want your own copy of our workbook and a year's worth of lesson plans, please add an extra $24.95."

Emma also circulated among the parents with a sample booklet while Tony replaced the clock on the puppet stage, next show 12 noon. The crew decided to have an early lunch at the veteran's burger stand where they found Aunt Sarah having a morning beer with her old friend, Stretch who was still operating the Ferris wheel. Walter Trepling joined the group, still a little under the weather.

It was the season for fresh sweet corn and the veterans were well set up. Every one had at least two ears, drenched in butter, each bite better than the last, or so it seemed. Some of Emma's bo peep make up wore off by the time they returned for the noon show. Rita and Emma found the fair office and their rest room to freshen up Emma's Goldilocks image.

There developed a cycle that seemed to repeat every hour or

so. First the idle chit chat between Emma and Foxey lady, then the message, the challenge before us, then the solution, the rape preventers and the home study course for finding God, with the CD Piano companion.

Their last show was over by five o'clock, the time the grand stand show was about to start. This year the program featured Lyle Foley and his Fogey Bottom Boys.

On the way home, Pokey shared more details about his progress, "So, anyway, yesterday, I was looking into the mirror again. And suddenly it got kind of spooky. I could not see myself, at all clearly. Maybe it was bad lighting, something out of focus. Bottom line, when I looked into the mirror, all I got was vague outlines, beauty way out of focus. Everything kind of dark, and I am not sure, whether it was foreboding, threatening, or maybe a good sign, maybe not. I absolutely could not understand. I felt vaguely threatened. So what did I do? It was kind of a dilemma, one involving dreadful options. The open grave beckons, inexorably. What a horror. I found myself enjoying the quiet relief a couple of Foster's give me."

Pokey summed things up again; "I'm glad that I sometimes can be free from that trap, always looking for extra meaning. For God's sake, let reality take care of itself. Don't be pushing that river. It's OK to enjoy the ride. Enjoying simple pleasures, those are the best, and sometimes hardest to find. I'm learning to look for a fresh start. Get a good nights rest, then accept both our dreams and our fears. There's a reason human beings feel dread, it's Okay to be paranoid, for a while. But then, if you know how, you can make a pact of sorts with the devil and move on. Call it selective vision, a positive thing."

Rita agreed, "I'm guessing that Its normal to discover interior defects, don't worry. Correction and atonement can be exercised. You can come out ahead, slightly redeemed by the Lord above. But it won't happen unless you prepare the ground. Light a candle, swing your incense; my point is this: We invent our strategy to solve problems we don't understand. We almost guarantee that we will miss the mark, and wallow in appropriate self-doubt, waiting for the Lord to tap us on the shoulder, to welcome us to the promised land...Ain't gonna happen".

She continued, "How can we keep the door open for increasing awareness, while acknowledging that the final answer will be hidden from those of us still alive. How sad...that we have such an appetite that can't be satisfied. We are Yings with no Yangs in sight! So bearing this bad news to heart, what's the challenge? We must stop asking questions for which no one has answers. Therefore, accept only small challenges, where some benefit may occur. A tiny step forward is better than a giant step backwards. Tomorrow, we will eat more roughage."

Pokey complained of being tired, and feverish. He took an extra dose of Nyquil and excused himself for the evening. The next morning he was absent from the breakfast table. Rita fed some grits to Mr. Pee who seemed downcast. Pokey's fever had abated and he came in the kitchen looking for morning coffee. "Last night the fevers came back, Wanda woke me up to say good bye. She said she had found new harmony in the silence that remained after she was able to turn off the constant music that been plaguing her. I knew she had found the answers she had been seeking for so long. In fact you could tell just by looking at her, that some transformation had taken place in her soul, for want of a better word. Wanda looked like a female version of Buddha, obviously full of a vast contentment and refuge. Her peace flowed into me, displacing all, and I mean all, my fears and isolation.

This time I was smart enough just to enjoy the moment without trying to understand exactly what appetite I was feeding. That horse that I had been on before was still dependable. This time, Wanda, lead me in some silent musical exercises. They were kind of dull, lifeless forms for me until I began to feel new kinds of harmony full of surprising subdominates. But I still felt that it was all about forms without content. Patterns without purpose. Structure without import. "Here." Wanda said, "All you have to do is fill in the blanks!"

"Wanda's visit didn't last very long, and when I was fully engaged melding with her, suddenly one of my hidden spirits brought me back to Lost Grove.

And I found my self involved in a strange dream. I am not sure how I got into this big mansion, I think I had some car problems and had come for help. I remember entering through the basement door, and going up to the second floor. It was a pretty ritzy place, almost like the Waldorf, with hot and cold running maids! Then it started to get weird! This older gray haired dude made a pass at me. I'm not going to tell you the details, but I declined, and he went away. But I remember thinking maybe I rushed to judgment. Maybe things were not adding up for me. The guy had the prettiest blue eyes, and a smooth manner.

But then there was a colossal bang! A larger force that seemed to hold me down, compressing and molding my body and soul. I could hardly breathe; in some ways I felt like I was being born again. Zipping joyfully down the old birth canal! So now I am the reluctant traveler returning home, tired and worn out. Not proud, but content for now. Give me a couple of days, and I might get back to normal. I still have a few blanks to fill in."

Rita observed, "I'm disappointed that Wanda seems to be avoiding coming to meet the rest of us. I guess it will have to be okay. Not much we can do but hear your take on it. For me, I would want to play some of my music for her, even though you say she said she prefers silence. Just like I can't play my music forever, without resting, you'd think Wanda might tire of the eternal silence. Form without content might be another one sided coin."

Rita and Emma finished up the dishes and took out the trash for Monday pick-up. Pokey and Tony were busy working on a new, smaller stage for the puppet theater. They were hoping to be able to take their stage indoors to school auditoriums.

Back in the school bus Rita was relaxing into another D-flat visit with the Yamaha electric keyboard, while Emma went on line to check her mail. Her brother needed her signature for a liquor license application so she was going to have to go back to Saratoga Springs sooner than she had planned.

When Rita finished her piano reveries, she turned on the BBC radio. Emma was still on the Internet. "Rita, here's something that fits into your program, I found it under doubt definitions in Google. It's a quote from someone named Saul Alinski, listen to this, Alinski says "I've never joined any organization—not even the ones I've organized myself. I prize my own independence too much. And philosophically, I could never accept any rigid dogma or ideology, whether it's Christianity or Marxism. One of the most important things in life is what Judge Learned Hand described as 'that ever-gnawing inner doubt as to whether you're right.' If you don't have that, if you think you've got an inside track to absolute truth, you become doctrinaire, humorless and intellectually constipated. The greatest crimes in history have been perpetrated by such religious and political and racial fanatics, from the persecutions of the Inquisition on down to Communist purges and Nazi genocide."

Rita laughed and sang her three fold Amens.

On Thursday Rita got a call from a Midwest veterinarian, who had found a new use for the rape preventers. The vet, a Mrs. Donna Weinbrennen, had a daughter, Julie, who had experimented with the rape preverters. She had put one on her neck, just one of the smaller style. The problem came about when Julie happened to be with her mom for a service call to the Rocking Circle R ranch. The owners, Kent and Peter had a reluctant sire, Judson, a twenty-one percent coal black Morgan horse. Even with the mares squirting him in the face, Judson seemed unmoved. That is, until he smelled Julie's rape preventer.

Judson came right up to Julie who liked horses anyway. His nostrils were wet and wide open as he inhaled the scent coming from Julie's rape preventer. He seemed to savor the moment, and then exhaled, spraying a mist over Julie's neck and the protector.

"Hey boy, I'm not what you need."

Dr. Weinbrennen was watching Julie and Judson, and put two and two together and figured that somehow the odor of the protector was affecting the stud horse's libido. Kent and Peter were over joyed. They had spent quite a bit for Judson, so it was more than a pleasure to watch Judson having his way once again with the fillies.

Dr. Weinbrennen said, "I think I'm going to do more research to see if there are any bad side effects. I expect that your poultice might not be universally effective to the same degree. If there are no adverse side effects, there might be a good market. You might look into a small ad in the Monthly Veterinarian Journal."

On Friday UPS brought a small package to the front office. It was from an eighth grader named Vernon in Montevalo, Alabama, who had a unique idea for a basic improvement to the rape protectors. Vern's sample incorporated a thin bladder of scent that was truly sickening when released. This improvement allowed the bearer to smell fresh as a daisy under normal circumstances. But If the need arose, one potential rape victim could be saved by just squeezing the little bladder. Vernon wrote, "Just look for the purple dot, and squeeze it!

Rita wasn't sure if the market was ready for this item, but Pokey felt it worth investigating with a small test market. "I think that the devices could take a different form. Instead of the running sores, we can make forms that look like jewelry. A new kind of useful fashion. We may have to provide a towel to tidy up, to feel fresh again. We can work out the details."

The board agreed to get two quotes for product liability insurance indemnifying all concerned. The new items were planned to be proprietary, as well as private label. Each package, each style, each brand had its own UPC number. Some also carried European codes for the United Kingdom and EC. Rita observed, "you know, it's duck soup to add items when we already have items in the distribution network. We still are going to need active brokers who have detail people checking our shelf placement. While we don't have much competition in our category, we still have to get eye level shelf placement."

Later, after supper, Pokey and Tony left to work on their audio tape. Emma joined Rita in the school bus for some music and a Fosters. The rains had started again with occasional thunder. Rita punched on her Yamaha keyboard to the harpsichord mode, and aimlessly flowed along sounding like Bach or Vivaldi played by a Mariachi band. Emma ended up laughing, and singing along.

They went out to the green room and returned to their sleeping bags at the back of the bus. Emma turned on the little night light, "You know, I can kind of understand Tony, he's probably gay, but I don't understand what keeps you and Albert from gettin' on with it. He seems pretty down to earth, kind of a generic guy."

"Well, Emma, I'm just as glad that he doesn't test my virtue! That's one less problem that I have to deal with. Why make a problem when none exists? We do OK Emma, actually we do better that just OK. I'm not complaining. Though, just between us, have you taken a good look at his crotch?"

Emma giggled, "Yeah, I have. Last week, I saw it. Kind of accidentally, I went to wake him up to go to town and he had been sleeping in the nude. He got up and quickly dressed. I'd say he's not too big and not to little, I would guess he's pretty average to average plus that way. Though I can tell you it did seem to be pretty hairy, I don't know if I really like that or not. I don't see any problem oneway or the other. I can adjust, if you know what I mean."

"Anyway," Rita concluded, "for now I really have to make up my mind on college. Hairy bodies can wait! I've been accepted by both Pembroke and Radcliff, but I can't decide. If I find that I need stud service, I think I will know where to go. I can start at the frat houses at Brown and Harvard. For fun maybe I should go to Radcliff because I'd be around the Berklee Music program. I used to think it was really a tough school to get into. Just Google Berklee and you'll see. You know, I've got time, there's no emergency."

Twenty Eight

In the back of the henhouse, Pokey had been exploring alternative gassing agents to stabilize the permeability of the Great Stuff®. Since they had learned to accept only the medium density foam rather than the high density standard, the lifetime of the new rigid foam became nearly infinite. Now Pokey was working toward finding a perfect final coating for the dervish.

Rita was on their computer terminal exploring the patent bases on line. Emma and Tony were watching her progress on her video monitor. Tony was not understanding some of the distinctions. "You amaze me Rita, how do you know so much about this shit?"

"Tony, my dad many years ago worked in the field with Dupont, and Union Carbide. He was eventually lead chemist at Dow chemical's Buffalo Laboratory. I still have some of his papers at home. Basically they are beyond me...just a lot of advanced polymer chemistry stuff. What did impress me was how just a little improvement here or there can be patentable. In my dad's files there's lots of legal briefs that he authored, protecting Dow from infringement suits. Dad didn't have a law degree, but he told the lawyers what Dow needed to see happen. He was well liked and very well paid. Someone told me he made Dow what it is today. I'm guessing that his estate may be in probate for some time. It's probably pretty complex. I think the estate has automatic options it can request in the stock option department at Dow. Mr. Nims, the man who brought me here, is working on it. I'm still waiting to hear from him."

"Incredible!" said Tony. "The improvements to the vacuum processing and maintenance routine might be truly space age. But then what do I know? You know I'm thinking, we may be at the gateway of a whole new technology that might have more than global implications. A lot more! Think downstream. For what ever reasons mankind wants to move into far galaxies. The problem may come in finding ways to sustain life during the voyage. A miniature ecosystem must encapsulate new space age systems that have zero wastes. Zero waste! It may be, after all, a very long trip! Of course there has to be an energy pak to manage the voyage. Fortunately that is not the current problem. We have that technology, but seem to lack a good definition of our planetary goal. In other words, where are we going and why?"

"I don't know," said Rita, that whole trip, if you will, seems a bit looney tunes if you ask me. You can build yourself a spaceship if you want. Nothing new there. And I suppose you could find folks ready for the trip. But not for me! What does intrigue me is this possible field of vacuum panel insulation. That, my friend, would be a gold mine if we could patent our improvements to the Dow prior art with the Greatstuff® medium vacuum improvement. That we should look into, no matter what. If we could prevail at court, we would have all, and I mean all, the money we could ever want. So...do I have a second?

"Sure, I'll second the motion," said Pokey, "Thinking again globally, our vacuum panels can represent the answer to two huge problems, namely we are running out of oil while heating up the atmosphere. Our panels can cut the need for space heating which lightens the demand load on the generating system."

"Okay Rita, Motion carried on a unanimous vote."

Later Tony was scratching his head, "I was thinking last night about what my next chapter should be. I started to really look inside myself. Sometimes I feel connected and at other times lost in space. I wonder is my yearning just a symptom of some sort of existential estrangement? A release from loneliness? Is yearning a special kind of desire?" Rita opened her Websters again, "here it says long, yearn, hanker, pine, hunger, and thirst all mean to have an urgent desire for something. It says yearn is an eager, restless, often passionate longing."

"That's interesting. Sounds like it might fit. So what is an urgent desire," asked Pokey. "Let me look up that one."

"Hmm...Desire...Desire, wish, want, crave, covet all mean

to long for, and desire usually stresses ardor...and crave often definitely implies the impulsion of physical or mental appetite or need."

"Well Pokey, my problem is that when I go to the world of music, I find a whole new rich environment. So rich, that I can't easily come back out of it. Its like going from a technicolor world back into a gray scale only view. Maybe useful, maybe not. There's a lot of ways to be boring or bored, but few summit experiences. Where's our instruction booklet?

So for now, my question for myself is, should I chase the windmill or not. Is it OK to stay at home so to speak?"

"Here's how I see it Pokey, Pure pleasures reinforce our sense of self. They bring all kinds of an Intoxication that according to the dictionary can be happy or sad. When I sit down first thing in the morning at the piano, I begin to improvise and find that by letting my horse go, I cruise into newly created vistas astonishingly vibrant and coherent visions. I find a sense of healthy inner value, self-approval that was there all along but unnoticed. It feels like an unconscious agent is at work drafting new responses, all in concert with my physical body that has its own identity, storing up all kinds of habits. I think this may happen even while we are asleep. What are we, but our feelings, feelings in time and place? I'm thinking for many self-approval must be hard to achieve. What are the impediments to self-discovery? Where chastity is untested, maybe doubt and insecurity can flourish!

So I'm thinking there will always be some variety in our existence, always unsubstantially present, undefined. Waiting for a spectator to come along. The science of being normal, may be colorful, maybe not."

Rita paused at her keyboard, "I wonder if anything could be more rewarding than a life in piano music. My muse, my creative side, is at home here at this keyboard; all I have to do is ask. I knock at my own door and welcome myself, asking what's new Dude? As I play, my soul breathes free, and I soar like Jonathan

Livingston Seagull! It is hard for me to want any thing more. Nay, it's impossible! It's also hard to describe, kind of an awakening, or a phase change. But common sense tells me, Rita, you know not what you know not. I am in an ongoing process, unfolding. My central being is alive and unfolding as I watch it. I know I'm on the right track, and for now, I have very very few regrets.

Sometimes I regret that I never took up the violin, after my Dad willed his instrument to me. And I start thinking about Lang Lang, and his brilliance. It both humbles me and spurs me on to get deeper into a richer sonic landscape. You know what I mean? My music is like a drug for me. And its legal," laughed Rita. "Is it too far out that I get so entirely satisfied when I am with my keyboard. Sometimes I think that I don't deserve this level of contentment. Like it should have taken me years instead of months to get where I am. My last question is always going to be, where's my next aha coming from. Maybe I'll always be a seeker and never a finder, and just maybe, I'll have to give up my piano in order to grow in ways that I know not. It is uncharted territory for me.

Then I think, Rita, just follow your passion. So what if it selfish of me, its purely selfish by definition. What's wrong with that?

Sometimes I wonder if adjusting is harder or easier as we age. Maybe we are inclined to not be surprised; to appear well adjusted and content. The image of a born leader. Sometimes I think the capacity to see clearly requires a certain existential doubt. Back to Learned Hand!

There seems to me that sometimes life can radiate quick events that are on the cutting edge of our awareness. Does this viewpoint empower a person? Does every one need a vacation in some way repeatedly?"

The UPS truck came for its pickup at four thirty, and dropped off another registered parcel from Nims, Martin and Halliday. There was a transcript of legal proceedings of the ninth district court in Manhatten. It seemed to Rita that she was free to reenter the US using her real name at any time.

The next day Nims called Rita on her cell to find out her plans.

Rita had a few questions, "Mr. Nims, I'll need to know if my current location matches the information on the stock certificates. Maybe its not important, but I know that all my dividends were to be added to the Dow patent royalties. I hope my old digital bank ID will still access the trust account balances. But for now, Mr. Nims, I have to decide on Radcliff, Pembroke, or maybe Berkeley in Boston. I have your internet address, so I will keep you informed. I gave you my address before, it won't be changed for now. For now I have a lot of loose ends to tidy up.

At suppertime Pokey put together a special cream of onion soup using bacon drippings to brown his onions plus some sautéed mushrooms. A half cup of pancake mix thickened the soup just right. During supper Tony still had some questions about foot fetishes, and functions of washing feet in church.

They googled the internet to see more about this kissing business among the disciples. "Wow! There tons and tons of stuff here about religions and kissing in bible stories. Lets see, here it says: According to Penn, the kiss helped to increase social cohesiveness in four primary ways, one, it was seen to establish and enact the church as a new family, and two, it was understood as binding souls together through pneumatological exchange. Hmmm..it goes on, it functioned as a ritual of reconciliation in situations of discord or estrangement, and, finally, as a unification of physical bodies, it tacitly symbolized and focally portrayed the social body as a unified entity."

"Well, anyway" Pokey observed, "I told you all before that I would stay through our experimental development. We've gone there, done that, and I'm feeling, the road less traveled is still ahead of me."

Pokey turned to Rita, "you know, I'm thinking we kind of tend to notice where we are, only after we leave the moment. Rita, maybe you've got to decide, or figure out, who is pulling your strings. Where is your puppeteer leading you? What is your next step? Is music going to be enough for you? Or can you add a companion relationship. And of course, you still have time to define yourself."

Rita opened a Fosters, "I don't see any puppeteer, Pokey. When I play my music, nobody else is involved. That's the bottom line. You can disagree, but I trust that I have my foot in the door of perception. It sure is not at all clear. I wish it were. Maybe we can agree that the process of loving is vague, but nonetheless a real option? Maybe we need to understand better both the seeds of our discontentment and well as its opposite, contentment, or joy. That's it! We need to find handles, to get a good grip on this joy process."

Tony added, "I love that line from Shakespeare, I think it was in Richard the third, now is the winter of our discontent, made glorious summer! I don't know why some phrases seem to mean more than others."

Pokey thought a bit, "I don't know Tony, maybe as a constant, theoretically, somewhere we might find an example of pure, unadulterated, truth...that is timeless, but I don't think its at all likely."

Rita summed it up, ""Well, in my mind, I think some parts of us are kind of pre-wired to expect a rational world, even if its exact nature is hidden from us. How else can learning take place? Duh!"

Pokey got up to adjust his underwear, "In a way that thought covers our puppet story. Our focus has kind of evolved. I started with a Billy Graham model. That would be kind of old fashioned, and not very novel or fun. I still am sold on our puppet format. You know, entertain, involve, sing, and challenge only a little. But still plant seeds! Plant expectations! A New Day is coming! Get Ready for the new age. It will be here before you know it!"

Tony laughed, "I can hear the trumpets announcing our arrival at our next gig. Indeed the Lord works in mysterious fields."

Pokey continued, "You know I was thinking the other morning, while in the green room, you know that's kind of where some of my best ideas come from. Anyway, I was thinking, maybe we should step up to the international plate and offer some of our new ideas. Look at the all the religious ugly strife, inhumanity. Some would say that the ecumenical council of churches could and should do more to force brotherhood into hot spots. Maybe, if we are on target so-to-speak, we should look at the continuing tribal wars. All we can do here is to help our corner of the world. We seek to light the spark of compassion, but just how, we're not sure. Maybe there's no single answer."

Pokey summed up. "It seems like a pilgrim fellowship meeting to me; while many evangelists profess to know the right pathways to God, it's really all a matter open to constant questioning."

"Yeah," Rita observed, "We question just about everything. Maybe that's a mistake. Maybe we have to decide if there's anything left not to question. What is the value of questioning for us, if we seem not to be finding any answers? Poor St. Theresa. Poor Christ on the cross."

Twenty Nine

Emma pulled together two tidy bags of her clothes and journals. Tony brought in two beautiful salmon with a cheese fondue sauce. He had been to the market and bought some sprigs of fresh parsley. All that was left to do was to make the lemon zest. He grated the lemon and gently dusted the salmon, reserving some of the spread for when the fish were turned toward the end of the broil.

The salmon were baked slowly at 300 degrees for twenty minutes on each side. Then Tony brought the salmon out to breathe and squeezed some fresh lemon.

Rita helped gather the Lost Grove crew, with staff from the distribution center making a total of thirty-two.

Emma had decided to take a short commuter flight to Albany rather than the ferry.

The staff had laid out buffets several times over the years, so all the program worked well. The gourmet buffet line worked well. Tony was at the end, deftly portioning the baked salmon in cheese sauce.

The occasion demanded some sort of company speech. It fell upon Rita to speak. "Hello, Folks! We are gathered to bid farewell to one of our creative crew who has to go to the halls of Ivy. We will miss her, and our door will always be open if she finds the time to come back to help us. That said, let us raise a toast for the creative talent we have enjoyed. Hip! Hip! Hooray!

Emma had no choice but to smile demurely and to sit down.

Later back home, Rita observed, "You know, sometimes I feel like a schizophrenic with a split personality. My mind eagerly seeks to understand the world out there, while inside, my body has its own view point. For some, I'm guessing the mind can use sex as a jumping off spot, while the body can fill its own needs.

I've discovered to feel really at home with yourself, must be the eternal goal for every man. So if there is a problem in your world, it can be seen not as an impediment, but rather, a gateway, a stepping-stone to a fuller understanding of our human condition.

Rita continued, "perhaps we can come up with a list of ingredients, or aspects, for an advanced intellect. What accommodations are needed? What questions require answers? How many appetites do we have? I'm guessing we all have a normal need to be understood by our peers."

"And I know that there are all kinds of physical pleasures, including shameless sex, great food, fun exercise as well as hard work. We need work outs for our bodies and our minds. Otherwise, don't we kind of rot on the vine?

Rita continued "You know, I sometimes feel like there might be a real pleasure waiting for me if I find some stud that wants to service me. You know it's all in how I am becoming a young woman. So is there some great awakening for me when I loose my virginity? Hmm. You know, for me right now, my mind is happy with its present placement. My body is also pretty happy with my music; maybe I shouldn't say my music, but rather our music. I'm feeling my music is a wonderful expression of my soul, nobody else's. It's alive in the moment, a partnership between my body and my mind. I wish I could describe the reality, but it is beyond words. Sometimes I'm kind of astonished at the intensity I feel in the experience. I don't know...should life astonish me? What are the alternatives? At the end of life, are there any alternatives?

Pokey stirred the fire in the stove, "I can relate that years ago I experimented and decided to walk a different path. Yeah. I was young and didn't know any better. I was at the New Day church camp on Lake Geneva. Some of the guys had some wine. After lights out, they invited some of the girls for a party in our tent. One of the older girls, Pepita Sanches Sales, got a chill and ended up crawling into my sleeping bag. It wasn't her first time. Pepita's dad, Reverend Sales, was our minister with our youth group and she made me promise not to say anything, or she said she would say I had raped her. I can see why some guys have sex problems.

For me, parts of sex are fine. Been there, done that. But there are other things, other pursuits that simply attract me more."

"Well, I just wasn't sure about you," said Rita. All this searching for God's purpose, well, it kind of sounds weird. I never thought of you as a priest, you know, celibate."

Pokey added some split oak to the fire, "Well, I am never sure of my final destination. But I do think that I'm on the right track. You know Jesus speaks of being devoted in Mathew 19 where he speaks of his calling to be a "eunuch" before God. That is someone who made a decision to remain single and childless so that he could dedicate 100% of his effort to serving our God. I mean, all I'm doing is also pointing to a certain direction, without really defining the goal. Does that make any sense to you? Don't ask me to justify this thing. I guess in the end I am learning to accept my life as a mortal. There's nothing more precious than our lives. No reason not to praise the Lord without even getting a glimpse of him."

"Maybe we have to learn how to see Jesus. Maybe everybody has to learn this vision, by trial and error? I only know that I am not going to complain about death. Rather I need to sing joyfully, if, albeit, a little unfocused. Ya got another Fosters?

Rita went to the fridge, "Yeah, Tony has gotten to know Pete Dailey and Walter Trepling, the drivers of the Fosters brewery truck. They come by once a week and check our cooler."

Pokey poured some warm water into the yellow plastic water basin and set it on the floor. He explained, "I remember the first time I washed someone else's feet. I just wanted to understand more about Christ, and to experience for myself what Christ may have experienced."

Pokey opened his Revised Standard, "Here it is in John 12, the Bible says, when he had finished washing their feet, he put on his clothes and returned to his place. "Do you understand what I have done for you?" he asked them. 13 "You call me 'Teacher' and 'Lord,' and rightly so, for that is what I am. 14 Now that I, your Lord and Teacher, have washed your feet, you also should wash one another's feet. 15 I have set you an example that you should do as I have done for you. 16 Very truly I tell you, no servant is greater than his master, nor is a messenger greater than the one who sent him. 17 Now that you know these things, you will be blessed if you do them.

"So folks, anybody ready for a cleansing? Tony? Rita? How about it Aunt Sarah? You're not too old to be reborn!

Sarah thought a minute, "Well, you know, I'm trying to remember the last sinful thing I've done...I'm not coming up with very much. Maybe I drink a bit too much...is that a sin? I don't always eat enough proteins and fat, so I tire out pretty quick. Years ago I guess, in retrospect, I didn't show a lot of smarts. I did some pretty outlandish stunts down in Galveston, I could have killed somebody or other. I remember the FBI talking with me about some stolen cars up in Oklahoma City. I had rented a garage from Louie Cervantes. The FBI agent wouldn't tell me much. I think Louie went back to Nogales. Drugs might have been involved."

"No Aunt Sarah, our foot washing isn't going to offer a balm for your guilts and regrets. But maybe in time you'll find an injury worthy of asking our Lord for help. Till then, procrastination maybe is the best thing for you. Just remember the Lord Jesus waits at the door, ready when you are!

"So...Tony, the water is still warm, you'll enjoy it probably more than anyone cause you're an artist and interested in growing with new experiences."

"Well, if you put it that way, what have I got to loose?"

Pokey knelt on his knees and took a few minutes of concentrated inner prayer. He began to quietly hum a slow melody as he washed Tony's right foot first, being careful to spread the toes apart, softly scrubbing the webbing between them, "Oh that feels really good, really good."

The left foot came next followed by warm moist towels and a final massage that had Tony moaning with relief. "Oh I didn't even know that knot of tension was there. I wonder where that came from. Hard to tell. I feel better, like some weight has been lifted. I wonder how the apostles felt when Jesus was finished. And what's this about Jesus putting on his clothes when he was done washing. Was he naked? Is he kind of a trend setter?"

"You know, this can be part of our new grounding therapy. Massaging feet can be a transforming routine, pleasing to all kinds of characters. Good Jews can follow Christ in their own fashion. Even agnostics can be open to new experiences, built into our species. Isn't meaning where we find it? For every individual as well our society as a whole?"

Rita explains, "You don't understand. When I get tuned into myself, I feel like I am riding a horse. When I get into my music, it becomes an addiction of sorts. I find I need the piano as a lover. It fulfills me. It answers me. It reflects me. And there doesn't seem to be any ugly danger waiting in the wings."

The puppet factory sales went on line September the twelfth. The initial offering was sold out after three weeks. After some consternation, it was decided to add a graveyard shift to the packaging line. The packers were given a two dollar bonus per hour, bringing their hourly rate to twenty eight dollars Canadian.

Now Rita was able to get new merchandise for the pipeline. Along the way Pokey decided to make a new puppet based on Emma's role out front, so that he could still use her in the show after she planned to leave. He took digital photos of her profile and frontal sides. From these he created his skull shape and inserted the colored glass eyes. He then coated the entire volume of clay with five coats of rubber latex. Once that had cured, it was easy to remove the skin from the mold, as in taking a glove off.

Emma looked at her miniature, and laughed, "you could almost use this head inside out, except for the weird looking nose. My nose isn't that bad!"

Pokey agreed, turning the latex form back to its initial shape. Upon this he applied the final colored latex, carefully adding the final eyelid skin over the glass eye globes.

Once the latex dried Rita helped add the eyelashes and hair.

Tony took still photos and some short videos of the work in progress for instructional purposes.

Rita cleaned up the work benches and the kitchen counter and sink. Out of habit from St. Theresa's she polished the chrome faucets till they shone. Along about seven Rita and Tony noticed aunt Sarah pulling away from Lost Grove motors with Alice and the spreader. Tony sat down by the cook stove, "I wonder why she doesn't ask the company driver, Toe Head, to take her places. I've told her Pokey pays him plenty just to be on hand twenty four seven."

About an hour later, Aunt Sarah returned with the spreader and came into the office for a Fosters, "I guess the Maunday Easter service will be tomorrow night. I had it written on the wrong day on my Ipad. Stupid mistake." She laughed. "Well, I guess I'll retire to my trailer for another few chapters of Michner's Hawaii.

Rita and Emma also decided to call it a day, and disappeared to the school bus. Tomorrow Rita hoped to pass the drivers test.

The next morning, Aunt Sarah's cell phone rang before sun up. It was a young intern at Channel 23, looking for directions to Lost Grove. They had gotten lost and their GPS system wasn't working.

Aunt Sarah called everyone together, "Gosh CBC is coming here this morning. Somehow our secret is out. Who knew? The news has picked up on the first lighter than air solid."

By ten o'clock the news group from CBC had three nomad units out side the station with three cameras and a sound technician with her head set. The local news reporter, Alister McBride took center stage.

"Today we are at the real headquarters of one of our most successful new businesses to start up right here. We're at a place called Lost Grove. I'm Alister McBride and this tomorrow, tonight."

The camera pulled back to reveal Aunt Sarah next to the Fixall shop sign. She had changed into a clean set of clothes and had brushed her hair that now was tied into a long pony tail. Behind the shop sign Pokey had pulled up the Astronomical puppet stage.

From inside the shop, Rita had a pretty good view of the back sides of Aunt Sarah and Allister McBride. Tony had turned on the CBC which was being carried live on Channel 23. Tony got annoyed that for some reason the sound seemed ahead of the video. He watched the sound technician closely, "hey! There's something about that woman that reminds me of somebody I've seen before, but I can't put my finger on it."

"I'm here with the owner of Lost Grove, Miss Sarah Jane Chamberlin. Good Morning Sarah."

"You can call me Miss Chamberlin, if you like. Just remember to call me in time for dinner," laughed Sarah. Allister laughed good naturely and took out his cheat sheet, "So... Sarah...what's this we hear about people flying about under their own power?"

"Well, I don't know everything about it. You know?" Aunt Sarah chuckled, "Should I look for a good broom? Like there's always change, and we either resist it, or fall in line to support the change. I know sometimes around here the talk gets pretty high "faluting." Sometimes higher in more ways than one. I hear everybody is looking for God the highest, you know what I mean? I'm kind of on the outside lookin' in, you know what I mean? You'd be better off talking with my niece, Rita Chamberlin. She should be around here somewhere."

Rita came out from the back room and went over behind Aunt Sarah to her usual stool in front of the puppet stage. Sarah turned to her, "Rita, these folks want to know something about the rumors about aliens coming from space. Can you help them out?"

Rita smiled demurely and looked down. "Well, we all have to confess that the universe is such a big world and our history started such a long time ago. You know, two thousand years ago some thought Jesus Christ was an alien. We've been taught to seek the mountain-top for the best view. Anyway, that's the goal of our Astronomical Lecture Society. We seek the top of the mountain, but for now we have to sow seeds of understanding and forgiveness for being here below, merely human. Here behind me is one of my guides here at Lost Grove, my good friends, Albert the Pokey monster. And his friend Bolt"

Pokey had taken his usual position behind the proscenium, and now came up on stage with one of his favorite puppets, good old Bolt Uptight. Nearly bald, Bolt had very bushy white eyebrows, and lots of white hair growing from his ears and nose.

"Welcome Mr. McBride. It is a pleasure to meet you in person. My name is Bolt. Bolt Uptight! Miss Chamberlin has graciously allowed us to build our new stage in this old bread truck. We will soon be leaving our home here to go on the road, preaching the gospel for the new age soon to confront us. We have seen hoards of people, hundreds looking for answers in all the wrong places. So we have a mission to point the way! You know what I mean?"

McBride stepped over opposite Rita, "Well Bolt, we're still looking for the news of some new kind of flying saucer. Our viewers of Channel 23 will be fascinated to find out just who has the lead on this."

"There have also been rumors of a flying carpet over at the Hari Krishnas," said Pokey's Bolt. Maybe you should talk to them. You probably passed by their farm on your way here. Their farm manager is a Sufi named Happy Jack, he sometimes stops by here to get some work done by Miss Chamberlin. If anyone is up in the clouds it is Happy Jack, and I don't think he is on anything."

Rita agreed, "Yes Sir, Mr. McBride, Happy Jack should be able to help you in your search for higher states. If he isn't there, he may be at the Hari Krishna temple in Quebec City serving in the food line.

Alister Mcbride thanked Aunt Sarah and Rita for their lead for the follow up evening news. The crew packed their flood lamps back in the Channel 23 van and soon were gone.

Pokey came out from behind the puppet stage, "Whew! That was a close one. Who do you suppose started that so called rumor? What prompts their fear? Isn't it fear of the unknown?" Pokey was packing up his Bolt. "We are seldom afraid of the known, it is the mystery of the unknown that bothers us. It is the Christ knocking on your door. And of course we are afraid. Afraid of failing, afraid of death. Actually it is not a black and white contrast as I see it. No right or wrong. No moral or immoral, no fully male, no fully female."

"Yes but," continued Rita, "God gave us insight and fear for a reason. Without death before us, we might just party on, wasting time, our most precious asset. Since most of us will be dead a long time, we shouldn't waste our time now."

On Channel 23 noontime news the next day Happy Jack was the special focus at the Hare Krishna temple. He was in his usual morning focusing routine, dressed in his temple orange sari, chanting the litany of all the names of Krishna. Usually Jack could complete his chanting in two hours. While softly chanting these names, Jack could break his reality and ask a question, or make a statement. And then return to his chant.

When interrupted by McBride, Happy Jack admitted that he did a lot of spiritual flying. Jack said it wasn't that hard to do, that all he did was to put his arms behind him so that he could soar.

McBride signed off, "Well folks that's our last story of tomorrow tonight. The future may be in the clouds, but for now we're down here in everyday reality. This is Alister McBride reporting from rural Quebec. We'll look forward to seeing you again tomorrow on tomorrow today."

Father Fritch came in the next morning to the fixall shop, with his hedge trimmer. He found Pokey and Rita who had turned on the tele to see the morning news. Aunt Sarah joined them with a stack of pan cakes. The news did not mention anything about Lost Grove or Happy Jack.

Pokey wondered, "I'm glad they didn't dig a little deeper, they might have discovered our Dervish. We took it for one trial test, and it worked pretty fine. Sure! We agreed that sometimes it seemed unsteady in its relative position. And we could probably refine its mechanical linkage, that is, if that's where we want to go. For me, as you know, I signed on just to prove how our theory could be put to use. So we did it. It would be easy to develop the dervish into many commercial applications. We could start with a test run at our local post office. After proving its use, we could go on. To Ottawa, to Washington, New York, London."

Rita poured herself another cup of coffee, "Nah, Pokey. The Post Office is going nowhere. They are closing offices all the time. Running huge deficits. They missed getting electrified. They lost the package war with United Parcel. My personal passion isn't with it anyway. All along you know I have been planning on exploring college. I think I know what its going to be like, but maybe I can learn new things. Here at Lost Grove, we have worked hard and built two fully functioning web sites, not to mention the Rape kit business. If we both depart, to whom shall we give our corporate reins?"

Father Fritch took his plate over to the sink and also poured himself another cup of coffee. "I think there might a possibility that the diocese could operate the rape protector operation. It could generate funds sorely needed for our legal services, and recruitment operations. Of course, I'm not the one to authorize such a change. I'd have to go to the bishop."

Aunt Sarah agreed, "The Repair shop was all that I needed, and sometimes I wish I could go back to the way it was. It was a lot simpler, and predictable. Now it seems that every day we are kind of challenged. I find myself wallowing in nostalgia, for the good old days. I'm even rereading Death in Venice!"

Rita warmed up her cup of coffee and had to ask a different question, "We seem to be having a hard time defining our goals. What we want to change, and what are we afraid of loosing. What I wonder, is,... can I love the Lord without having any firm idea if he or she cares a hoot. Well, I'm afraid it feels good to worship, its almost too pleasurable. We look for a connection, sometimes desperately. So we keep coming back to the problem of vague desire. I ask myself, am I supposed to look inward for my answer, or should I be finding God in the sunrise. Maybe we can feel God's presence in the darkness rather than in the dawn. We can seek a Buddha consciousness. I kind of go there during my musical journeys. But then my attention and appetite move on. So I end up wondering, that maybe it is Okay to act in worship of the divine, however imperfect our focus. To act without good intent would be contrary to our own good. Pretty clear don't you think? So, for now I am content with an imperfect love. Rude to complain don't you think?

Pokey agreed, "We decided some time ago that our mission is to stimulate people to seek the Lord in their own hearts. Yes! To act as if there might be a loving God who might forgive us our faults, as we forgive those who seek to hurt us. But we also can desire fun. I'm thinking fun can come to us in lots of ways. The more, the better!

I'm thinking that Christ himself clearly enjoyed having a good time. He probably had a twinkle in his eyes when he told his parables. Similarly, we can lead by example with our puppet show. But I'm thinking we should go on the road to get some more direct experience, you know...to hone our craft up a notch or two. We've got to get used to our music tracks in the background, so that everything is smooth. We might seem strange to some people, but we might be icons for the new age. And yet we will never neglect to honor our forebears, in spite of their ignorance, for they had more to learn than we do. That's because we are lucky. We've learned from their mistakes."

Rita laughed, "But I don't know if anything really has changed. The King will never know for sure if he has clothes on or not. Mother Teresa's love and devotion will go unrequited. I'm thinking we will always be on this seasonal merry-go-round. Like going from darkness into light, from warmth to cold and back again. From major to minor. We sense that we are traveling, but again we don't sense leaving home nor arriving at our destination.

What is, is. What is not, is not.

Summing up, I'm feeling each of us is on loan to this reality that we share. The world can use us for good or bad. In more ways than one or two. To me, the future is limitless, time will tell all, if you know what I mean!"

Rita continued, "Me? I can only experience who I am, right now in this moment! Maybe I can put it this way: I'm feeling life is a process locked into an ever-changing moment. Truth, like life, is revealed from moment to moment. We can debate its meaning as we experience it. But the banquet in front of us is more than words can touch. There's a difference between poetry and prose. Today we can welcome life as an invitation to dance. Or we can invite regret and remorse to color our every moment. I guess, its all a matter of our character choice."

Pokey added some walnut chunks to the fire, "So what constitutes falsities? The non-truths? Is it the absence of light? The sound of one hand clapping? Or is everything shades of gray with no absolute blacks or whites. Is outer space limited? When did time start? Who planned our genome? Is the maker revealed by his creations? My guess is that there's no harm in acting as if we understand the challenges before us. To seek to be a balm for the estrangement people feel. It is a simple goal, to do no harm!"

Aunt Sarah seemed to be dozing off, "Well boys and girls, tomorrow is another day. I'm taking Alice back to town, so I wouldn't mind some help emptying our spreader."

Emma volunteered, "I can help for sure. Tony's going to take me to the airport on Wednesday. In fact, if you want, I'll go along with you. I'm taking notes for my honors project. It's a requirement for advance placement in the English degree program. I'll be able to skip the freshman orientation grammar 101."

Emma and Rita retired to the bus and slipped into their sleeping bags. Rita, out of habit, tuned the radio to BBC London, but after only a few minutes, turned it off, and went to the keyboard. "Emma, if you don't mind, I feel a need to kind of re-ground myself. Its kind of like my shadow side is off there in the closet, kind of a polar opposite. Weird! Right? Maybe if I can synthesize my own duality, and hear it in the moment, then I can kind of discover myself. Underlined, in bold face. But then, I've learned, I gotta let go of the expectations, to see a little bit of reality, if only for a moment. It all comes together in my music, my improv."

Rita closed her eyes and felt the cool plastic keys. After a while, she let her left hand give a pulse before her right hand answered in its own cadence. One motif morphed into another. She drifted on, feeling plugged in, at home. Emma turned out the light, "Rita that's really something else, I don't know what to call it."

Rita thought a moment, "Emma, it's the weirdest thing that I am feeling as I play the keys. I look down at them, as I'm improvising, and its like there is someone else in charge, moving to kind of a foreign rhythm. I kind of feel that I'm in charge of steering my boat from mood to mood, motif to motif, dark to light. Certainly I don't care one bit if my fingers miss strike once in a while. That's life! What blows my mind is the evolving variety of the music that comes to me. My animation, sometimes feels like I'm one of Pokey's puppets. I can kind of direct its flow, but sometimes I worry that I'll loose my way. Kind of a musical schizophrenia. I'm beginning to understand where Glenn Gould goes off to when he plays Bach."

"Sounds like maybe you've got too much idle time on your hands," said Emma. "Maybe getting to college will help clarify things for you. The university clinic maybe can give you some help. When do you have to decide if its Pembroke or Radcliffe?

"You know I thought I might just rent a small apartment in Cambridge near the elevated for the first year. But then I'm thinking dorm life might be a good experience for a number of reasons. Maybe I can find something near Berkelee.

Next day, Pokey made two last minute adjustments to the lifting callipers in the Dervish. After supper he invited Aunt Sarah to take a short test ride. They were careful when they rolled the Dervish out from the hanger under the cover of darkness.

They were still not ready to explain their craft to the public. Emma and Rita finished up the dishes while Tony fed Mr. Pee.

Aunt Sarah already knew how to use the joystick that both rotated and slipped up and down. She fastened her seat belt, "I still am amazed at the silence on board. Just amazed. Lets head out for the dump."

They kept slightly above the treetops. After a few minutes the dump came into view, Sarah banked a little bit and slowed down, "Oh look! There are still people down there! We best head for home. You know, it would really be great if we could carry a bigger load. But that's going to require a lot more vacuum than we can get now." Pokey agreed, "As far as I am concerned, we can leave that problem for others to solve. Besides I signed on to prove our theory, that's all. My passion still is to bring the Lord to life with our puppets."

Silently the Dervish came down to rest at the egg farm brooder sheds, stirring up the leaves. Aunt Sarah stepped down first. Pokey purged the bladder, thus adding weight to their specific density. They locked up the hanger and returned to the office for a Fosters.

"How'd it go?" asked Tony. Aunt Sarah volunteered, "It was the best ever. We used so little fuel...at that rate we could have gone on for a couple of thousand kilometers, or fifteen hours or so."

Pokey agreed, "Yeah, it was pretty smooth sailing. We could still do some fine-tuning, but for now I need to finish our puppet stage so we can go to the Edmonton Educators Conference. We've been offered a weeks worth of work. The ladies aid group in Edmonton will give us free accommodations. I think one of ladies knew about us from some service one of them got here years ago."

There was hoar frost when morning dawned. Emma and Aunt Rita had a light breakfast and set out for town. Back on River Road, they pulled up with the spreader by the Taft mailbox. Aunt Sarah stopped to look over a floor polisher, still in its original shipping carton. "How weird! Emma, can you pick it up?"

"Sure can. It's at the right price! And look! It's got the

1original warranty papers, ready to mail in. On Ebay, who knows how much it might bring. Seventy five or better?"

They stopped for some coffee at Donna's Post house, then looked in on Sharon Rows's antique shop. They parked in the alley behind the main street shops, and had their pick from both sides of the alley. At the rear of the municipal building they found three boxes of books being discarded by the library. "Look here, Aunt Sarah, there's old National Geographics. Here's one, July 1906."

"Its your call," answered Aunt Sarah. "They're a heavy lot. We've still got room, and they look like they're in pretty good shape.

Thirty

Christmas Eve brought Father Radke back to Lost Grove Motors. It was just before lunch when the phone rang, Aunt Sarah picked up her cell phone, looked at the caller ID and wondered, "Its the church rectory...Hello...yes, hello father."

"Sara, my organist Mable Blight, has taken sick. And I'm wondering if your niece could help us out tonight."

Rita and Aunt Sarah had no trouble promising to come to the aid of the church, for after all it was Christmas. When it came time to leave for the midnight mass, Pokey decided to join the pilgrimage. They set off in the spreader behind Alice and arrived in time for Rita to run through the evening program.

The program listed the hymns but Rita had no idea what to play during the offertory. Behind the pulpit Rita saw the Steinway that was occasionally used for the Christmas pageant as well as for the Easter sunrise service. It was still an hour before the service was to begin, when Pokey asked Rita to play the introit on the grand. Rita opened the keyboard and placed the hymnal on the rack. "It's been a year since I played a real keyboard."

Aunt Sarah was sitting on the deacon's bench, next to the communion table. "Rita, you've never sounded so good! Its like you're breathing life into your music, something different, something new!"

Rita closed the hymnal and returned to the organ. "Yeah, I kind of get lost in a very special world that until recently I never knew existed. It feels like a higher state of mind, where I cruise along, like on a racing horse, like in some of my dreams. But this is different. This is real, more real than anything I've felt before. Its feels like an addiction, a habit that keeps on giving. This time I felt the music coming to me, not just through my ears, but strangely I felt the music vibrations coming from the piano keys themselves. I guess that it's one way that a real piano is different from my electric Yamaha. It's both spooky and tantalizing, like drugs I'm guessing."

Father Radke opened the vestry doors and rang the old bell in the tower. As the congregation entered and genuflected before the chancel, Rita began playing the Meditation from the Christmas Opera by Rimsky Korsakov.

Father Radke had a few prepared remarks before the offertory. He then lighted the last candle on the altar. Rita played some quiet background meditations in D flat while Father Radke dipped his communion wafer into the challis. He then served Rita at the organ who then improvised on one of her favorite hymns, number 414, Faith of our Fathers. Father Radke then served the congregation.

Pokey, Aunt Sarah, and Emma approached the rail for communion. Tony remained in his pew, because he was from an Anabaptist home that celebrated Christmas on January 6.

When communion was over, Father Radke wiped the challis clean and returned it to the sideboard. He gave Rita her signal to play his recessional.

On the way home it started to snow big clusters of snowflakes. Tony started to sing silent night. Pokey joined in and Rita sang the alto part. Back home Aunt Sarah concocted a crockpot of Christmas Punch that she called a wassailing.

Even Rita had a second mug, "I'm going to remember this evening, I hope forever! It's a new beginning in a way. When I played that grand piano tonight I tapped into something that is a new level for me at the piano. I'm just now trying to make sense of it all. My music that I have been playing on my Yamaha no longer fulfills me. I need the real thing. I'm going to ask Father Radke if I can practice at least one day a week on their Steinway. It's a new day! There's something new in my connection to the music. I'm feeling that I'm finding myself in the moment of loosing myself. My soul, or..., my essence is riding that horse under me, I feel like I'm giving up some control, handing it over to my handler that is there in the shadow of my life. The music that floods through me is like some emotional encyclopedia, sad, joyous, sometimes gated and, at other times random. Total variety. It's weird. I feel messages flowing down to my finger tips, with surprise after surprise. I can feel like I am one of Pokeys puppets, just a channel. A divine connection. Or I can step in without emotions and play mechanically. But I feel that always there has to be variety. My mind demands it. Otherwise I feel trapped, and in a way dead. I dread a life without meaning. I haven't really gone that far in this, can I say, this journey of self-discovery. Sometimes I feel like a moth flying around a candle. Then I start to wonder, is there a danger that I'll forget who I am? Can there be that much potential variety in each of us? I don't know. But for me, I'm discovering my essence at my keyboard."

Pokey agreed, "I think both Tony and I may have a similar field to work. We are both pointing the way and enjoying our trip."

Aunt Sarah laughed, "ain't that just plain old tripping? Like Krishnamurti advised years ago, you have to put your expectations on the back burner, for reality to open up to you."

"Yeah, its a weird trip to cast away expectations. To court surprise, to invoke learning without concluding. Kind of an oxymoron, don't you think? Maybe we should call our puppet show, the new moron show."

"No!" said Rita "Get real! Morons don't teach! They're too busy enjoying the simple side of life, and who's to say which reality is more accurate, anyway! I'm just going to go ahead and let my body show me the way to go, I can't ignore the music flowing from me! Gosh no! There's nothing sweeter. Sure, it can have a few flaws, but the spirit, the spark of my life is there. And all along, up to now, for me, I didn't know where to look or ask. Now that I'm seeing new options, I don't know how many new doorways to expect. I guess, just color me growing. To be defined later."

Aunt Sarah got up to go, "Yeah but, to be alive, don't you kind of have to be like the Roman god, Janus who looked both forward and backward. It's all about beginnings. I guess it all starts tomorrow! But for now, this old girl, needs to be excused."

Pokey was the last to leave with Mr. Pee. The quiet snow

sparkled over Lost Grove Motors as he stepped into his camper, got Mr. Pee fresh water and took out his journal. He thought for a while, and wrote,

"Sometimes I feel that my soul is outside of myself. And I wonder what other desires may be inbred in my soul? I think of a robin building its first nest. How does it know what makes a good nest? Does it know, or remember, what "home" used to look and feel like. What does the hen think about, just sitting there, waiting? Where does my mind go as I doze off? This morning after my breakfast I lay down in bed watching the changing color show in my darkened mind. My focus would shift right to left and back. The figure ground connection showed infinite variations. So I began to ponder what God had in mind when she invented Mankind. Was she looking for an audience? Why would she do that? That would predicate some sort of a give and take relationship. Hmm...does God want change and innovation? Maybe God is only found in our new moments. I guess we may never know for sure, one way or another."

"Yeah" Pokey said to himself. He got up, put some walnut on the fire and started mixing some pancake batter for breakfast. One by one Tony, Rita, and Aunt Sarah came together for Pokey's farewell breakfast. They had plenty of time together, reminiscing and wondering what the future was going to bring for everyone. Rita had her bank draft that would cover all of her first semester tuition. "I still haven't decided if I want some dorm life, with all the sororities and fraternities. But then a big part of me is leaning toward the Berklee music school. I hope to just spend a few days with mom's trust's lawyers and maybe a couple of days at her old flat on 93rd. They tell me I need to go over the estate inventory and mark stuff to discard or auction."

"But you know Pokey and Aunt Sarah, part of me is going to miss our trips to the dump and, you know, I'm even going to miss our rape preventer business. You know it makes for a good story anyway! When I decide where my next nest is going to be, I'll give you a call so you can send my files and clothes. OK?"

Aunt Sarah decided to go with Pokey to the airport at Murray Say. She found a clean pair of dark denim coveralls to go with her favorite plaid blouse. Tony stayed home with Emma to watch the parts counter

Sunday, August 30th

Tony and Pokey had a leisurely breakfast with Aunt Sarah. They looked over the appointments and Emailed the parts order. After lunch they packed up their clothes for their tour along with all eleven puppets. They were ready for the new day.

Made in the USA
Charleston, SC
09 November 2015